THE
WALKING
DEAD

By Robert Kirkman and Jay Bonansinga

The Walking Dead: Rise of the Governor
The Walking Dead: The Road to Woodbury

THE
WALKING
DEAD

THE ROAD TO WOODBURY

ROBERT KIRKMAN
AND JAY BONANSINGA

TOR

First published in the US 2012 by Thomas Dunne Books,
an imprint of St Martin's Press

First published in Great Britain 2012 by Tor
an imprint of Pan Macmillan, a division of Macmillan Publishers Limited
Pan Macmillan, 20 New Wharf Road, London N1 9RR
Basingstoke and Oxford
Associated companies throughout the world
www.panmacmillan.com

ISBN 978-0-330-54136-7

7 9 8 6

A CIP catalogue record for this book is available from
the British Library.

Printed and bound by CPI Group (UK) Ltd, Croydon, CR0 4YY

Visit www.panmacmillan.com to read more about all our books
and to buy them. You will also find features, author interviews and
news of any author events, and you can sign up for e-newsletters
so that you're always first to hear about our new releases.

Dedicated to Jilly (*L'amore della mia vita*)
—Jay Bonansinga

For all the people who have made me look far
more talented than I actually am over the years:
Charlie Adlard, Cory Walker, Ryan Ottley, Jason Howard,
and of course . . . mister Jay Bonansinga
—Robert Kirkman

ACKNOWLEDGMENTS

Special thanks to Robert Kirkman, David Alpert, Brendan Deneen, Nicole Sohl, Circle of Confusion, Andy Cohen, Kemper Donovan, and Tom Leavens.

—Jay Bonansinga

For my father, Carl Kirkman, who taught me the value of working for yourself and showed me what someone can accomplish if they work hard and focus on what they want to achieve. And for my father-in-law, John Hicks, who gave me the confidence to take the plunge and quit my day job and strike out on my own. I owe a lot to both of you.

—Robert Kirkman

PART 1

Red Day Rising

Life hurts a lot more than death.
—Jim Morrison·

ONE

No one in the clearing hears the biters coming through the high trees.

The metallic ringing noises of tent stakes going into the cold, stubborn Georgia clay drown the distant footsteps—the intruders still a good five hundred yards off in the shadows of neighboring pines. No one hears the twigs snapping under the north wind, or the telltale guttural moaning noises, as faint as loons behind the treetops. No one detects the trace odors of putrid meat and black mold marinating in feces. The tang of autumn wood smoke and rotting fruit on the midafternoon breeze masks the smell of the walking dead.

In fact, for quite a while, not a single one of the settlers in the burgeoning encampment registers any *imminent* danger whatsoever—most of the survivors now busily heaving up support beams hewn from found objects such as railroad ties, telephone poles, and rusty lengths of rebar.

"Pathetic . . . look at me," the slender young woman in the ponytail comments with an exasperated groan, crouching awkwardly by a square of paint-spattered tent canvas folded on the ground over by the northwest corner of the lot. She shivers in her bulky Georgia Tech sweatshirt, antique jewelry, and ripped jeans. Ruddy and freckled, with long, deep-brown hair that dangles in tendrils wound with delicate little feathers, Lilly Caul is a bundle of nervous tics, from the constant yanking of stray wisps of hair back behind her ears to the compulsive gnawing of fingernails. Now, with her small hand she clutches the hammer tighter and repeatedly whacks at the metal stake, grazing the head as if the thing is greased.

"It's okay, Lilly, just relax," the big man says, looking on from behind her.

"A two-year-old could do this."

"Stop beating yourself up."

"It's not *me* I want to beat up." She pounds some more, two-handing the hammer. The stake goes nowhere. "It's this stupid stake."

"You're choked up too high on the hammer."

"I'm what?"

"Move your hand more toward the end of the handle, let the tool do the work."

More pounding.

The stake jumps off hard ground, goes flying, and lands ten feet away.

"Damn it! *Damn it!*" Lilly hits the ground with the hammer, looks down and exhales.

"You're doing fine, babygirl, lemme show you."

The big man moves in next to her, kneels, and starts to gently take the hammer from her. Lilly recoils, refusing to hand over the implement. "Give me a second, okay? I can handle this, I *can*," she insists, her narrow shoulders tensing under the sweatshirt.

She grabs another stake and starts again, tapping the metal crown tentatively. The ground resists, as tough as cement. It's been a cold October so far, and the fallow fields south of Atlanta have hardened. Not that this is a bad thing. The tough clay is also porous and dry— for the moment at least—hence the decision to pitch camp here. Winter's coming, and this contingent has been regrouping here for over a week, settling in, recharging, rethinking their futures—if indeed they *have* any futures.

"You kinda just let the head fall on it," the burly African-American demonstrates next to her, making swinging motions with his enormous arm. His huge hands look as though they could cover her entire head. "Use gravity and the weight of the hammer."

It takes a great deal of conscious effort for Lilly not to stare at the black man's arm as it pistons up and down. Even crouching in his sleeveless denim shirt and ratty down vest, Josh Lee Hamilton cuts an imposing figure. Built like an NFL tackle, with monolithic shoulders, enormous tree-trunk thighs, and thick neck, he still manages to carry himself quite gently. His sad, long-lashed eyes and his deferential brow, which perpetually creases the front of his balding pate, give off an air of unexpected tenderness. "No big deal . . . see?" He shows her again and his tattooed bicep—as big as a pig's belly—jumps as he wields the imaginary hammer. "See what I'm sayin'?"

Lilly discreetly looks away from Josh's rippling arm. She feels a faint frisson of guilt every time she notices his muscles, his tapered back, his broad shoulders. Despite the amount of time they have been spending together in this hell-on-earth some Georgians are calling "the Turn," Lilly has scrupulously avoided crossing any intimate boundaries with Josh. Best to keep it platonic, brother-and-sister, best buds, nothing more. Best to keep it strictly business . . . especially in the midst of this plague.

But that has not stopped Lilly from giving the big man coy little sidelong grins when he calls her "girlfriend" or "babydoll" . . . or making sure he gets a glimpse of the Chinese character tattooed above Lilly's tailbone at night when she's settling into her sleeping bag. Is she leading him on? Is she manipulating him for protection? The rhetorical questions remain unanswered.

For Lilly the embers of fear constantly smoldering in her gut have cauterized all ethical issues and nuances of social behavior. In fact, fear has dogged her off and on for most her life—she developed an ulcer in high school, and had to be on antianxiety meds during her aborted tenure at Georgia Tech—but now it simmers constantly inside her. The fear poisons her sleep, clouds her thoughts, presses in on her heart. The fear makes her do things.

She seizes the hammer so tightly now it makes the veins twitch in her wrist.

"It's not rocket science *ferchrissake*!" she barks, and finally gets control of the hammer and drives a stake into the ground through sheer rage. She grabs another stake. She moves to the opposite corner of the canvas, and then wills the metal bit straight through the fabric and into the ground by pounding madly, wildly, missing as many blows as she connects. Sweat breaks out on her neck and brow. She pounds and pounds. She loses herself for a moment.

At last she pauses, exhausted, breathing hard, greasy with perspiration.

"Okay . . . that's one way to do it," Josh says softly, rising to his feet, a smirk on his chiseled brown face as he regards the half-dozen stakes pinning the canvas to the ground. Lilly says nothing.

The zombies, coming undetected through the trees to the north, are now less than five minutes away.

Not a single one of Lilly Caul's fellow survivors—numbering close to a hundred now, all grudgingly banding together to try and build a ragtag community here—realizes the one fatal drawback to this vacant rural lot in which they've erected their makeshift tents.

At first glance, the property appears to be ideal. Situated in a verdant area fifty miles south of the city—an area that normally produces millions of bushels of peaches, pears, and apples annually—the clearing sits in a natural basin of seared crabgrass and hard-packed earth. Abandoned by its onetime landlords—probably the owners of the neighboring orchards—the lot is the size of a soccer field. Gravel drives flank the property. Along these winding roads stand dense, overgrown walls of white pine and live oak that stretch up into the hills.

At the north end of the pasture stands the scorched, decimated remains of a large manor home, its blackened dormers silhouetted against the sky like petrified skeletons, its windows blown out by a recent maelstrom. Over the last couple of months, fires have taken out large chunks of the suburbs and farmhouses south of Atlanta.

Back in August, after the first human encounters with walking corpses, the panic that swept across the South played havoc with the emergency infrastructure. Hospitals got overloaded and then closed down, firehouses went dark, and Interstate 85 clogged up with wrecks. People gave up finding stations on their battery-operated radios, and then started looking for supplies to scavenge, places to loot, alliances to strike, and areas in which to hunker.

The people gathered here on this abandoned homestead found

each other on the dusty back roads weaving through the patchwork tobacco farms and deserted strip malls of Pike, Lamar, and Meriwether counties. Comprising all ages, including over a dozen families with small children, their convoy of sputtering, dying vehicles grew . . . until the need to find shelter and breathing room became paramount.

Now they sprawl across this two-square-acre parcel of vacant land like a throwback to some depression-era Hooverville, some of them living in their cars, others carving out niches on the softer grass, a few of them already ensconced in small pup tents around the periphery. They have very few firearms, and very little ammunition. Garden implements, sporting goods, kitchen equipment—all the niceties of civilized life—now serve as weapons. Dozens of these survivors are still pounding stakes into the cold, scabrous ground, working diligently, racing some unspoken, invisible clock, struggling to erect their jury-rigged sanctuaries—each one of them oblivious to the peril that approaches through the pines to the north.

One of the settlers, a lanky man in his midthirties in a John Deere cap and leather jacket, stands under the edge of a gigantic field of canvas in the center of the pasture, his chiseled features shaded by the gargantuan tent fabric. He supervises a group of sullen teenagers gathered under the canvas. "C'mon, ladies, put your backs into it!" he barks, hollering over the din of clanging metal filling the chilled air.

The teens grapple with a massive wooden beam, which serves as the center mast of what is essentially a large circus tent. They found the tent back on I-85, strewn in a ditch next to an overturned flatbed truck, a faded insignia of a giant paint-chipped clown on the vehicle's bulwark. Measuring over a hundred meters in circumference, the stained, tattered canvas big top—which smells of mildew and animal dung—struck the man in the John Deere hat as a perfect canopy for a common area, a place to keep supplies, a place to keep order, a place to keep some semblance of civilization.

"Dude . . . this ain't gonna hold the weight of it," complains one of the teens, a slacker kid in an army fatigue coat named Scott Moon. His long blond hair hangs in his face and his breath shows as he huffs and struggles with the other tattooed, pierced goth kids from his high school.

"Stop your pissin' and moanin'—it'll hold the thing," the man in the cap retorts with a grunt. Chad Bingham is his name—one of the family men of the settlement—the father of four girls: a seven-year-old, nine-year-old-twins, and a teenager. Unhappily married to a meek little gal from Valdosta, Chad fancies himself a strict disciplinarian, just like his daddy. But his daddy had boys and never had to deal with the nonsense perpetrated by females. For that matter, Chad's daddy never had to deal with rotting pus pockets of dead flesh coming after the living. So now Chad Bingham is taking charge, taking on the role of alpha male . . . because, just as his daddy used to say, *Somebody's gotta do it.* He glares at the kids. "Hold it steady!"

"That's as high as it's gonna go," one of the goth boys groans through clenched teeth.

"*You're* high," Scott Moon quips through a stifled little giggle.

"Keep it steady!" Chad orders.

"What?"

"I said, hold the dad-blamed thing *STEADY!*" Chad snaps a metal cotter pin through a slot in the timber. The outer walls of the massive canvas pavilion shudder in the autumn wind, making a rumbling noise, as other teens scurry toward the far corners with smaller support beams.

As the big top takes shape, and the panorama of the clearing becomes visible to Chad through the tent's wide opening at one end, he gazes out across the flattened brown weeds of the pasture, past the cars with their hoods up, past the clusters of mothers and children on the ground counting their meager caches of berries and vending-machine detritus, past the half-dozen or so pickups brimming with worldly possessions.

For a moment, Chad locks gazes with the big colored dude thirty yards away, near the north corner of the property, standing guard over Lilly Caul like a gigantic bouncer at some outdoor social club. Chad knows Lilly by name, but that's about it. He doesn't know much else about the girl—other than the fact that she's "some chick friend of Megan's"—and he knows less about the big man. Chad has been in proximity with the giant for weeks and can't even remember his name. Jim? John? Jack? As a matter of fact, Chad doesn't know anything about *any* of these people, other than the fact that they're all pretty goddamn desperate and scared and crying out for discipline.

But for a while now, Chad and the big black dude have been sharing loaded glances. Sizing each other up. Taking the measure of each other. Not a single word has been exchanged but Chad feels challenges being issued. The big man could probably take Chad in a hand-to-hand situation but Chad would never let it come to that. Size doesn't matter to a .38 caliber bullet, which is conveniently chambered in the steel-plated Smith & Wesson Model 52 tucked down the back of Chad's wide Sam Browne belt.

Right now, though, an unexpected current of recognition arcs across the fifty yards between the two men like a lightning bolt. Lilly continues to kneel in front of the black man, angrily beating the crap out of tent stakes, but something dark and troubling glints in the black dude's gaze suddenly as he stares at Chad. The realization comes quickly, in stages, like an electrical circuit firing.

Later, the two men will conclude, independently, that they—along with everybody else—missed two very important phenomena occurring at this moment. First, the noise of the tent construction in the clearing has been drawing walkers for the last hour. Second, and perhaps more importantly, the property is hampered by a single critical shortcoming.

In the aftermath, the two men will realize, privately, with much chagrin, that due to the natural barrier provided by the adjacent forest, which reaches up to the crest of a neighboring hill, any natural sound behind the trees is dampened, muffled, nearly deadened by the topography.

In fact, a college marching band could come over the top of that plateau, and a settler would not hear it until the cymbals crashed right in front of his face.

Lilly Caul remains blissfully unaware of the attack for several minutes—despite the fact that things begin unfolding at a rapid rate all around her—the noise of the clanging hammers and voices are replaced by the scattered screams of children. Lilly continues angrily driving stakes into the ground—mistaking the yelps of the younger ones for play—right up until the moment Josh grabs the nape of her sweatshirt.

"What—" Lilly jerks with a start, twisting around toward the big man with eyes blinking.

"Lilly, we gotta—"

Josh barely gets the first part of a sentence out when a dark figure stumbles out of the trees fifteen feet away. Josh has no time to run, no time to save Lilly, no time to do anything other than snatch the hammer out of the girl's hand and shove her out of harm's way.

Lilly tumbles and rolls almost instinctively before getting her bearings and rising back to her feet, a scream stuck in the back of her throat.

The trouble is, the first corpse that comes staggering into the clearing—a tall, pasty-colored walker in a filthy hospital smock with half his shoulder missing, the cords of his tendons pulsing like worms—is followed by two other creatures. One female and one male, each one with a gaping divot for a mouth, their bloodless lips oozing black bile, their shoe-button eyes fixed and glazed.

The three of them trundle with their trademark spasmodic gait, jaws snapping, lips peeling away from blackened teeth like piranhas.

In the twenty seconds it takes the three walkers to surround Josh, the tent city undergoes a rapid and dramatic shift. The men go for their homemade weapons, those with iron reaching down to their improvised holsters. Some of the more brazen women scramble for two-by-fours and hay hooks and pitchforks and rusty axes. Caretakers sweep their small children into cars and truck cabs. Clenched fists slam down on door locks. Rear loading gates clang upward.

Oddly, the few screams that ring out—from the children, mostly, and a couple of elderly women who may or may not be in early-stage senility—dwindle quickly, replaced by the eerie calm of a drill team or a provisional militia. Within the space of that twenty seconds, the noise of surprise quickly transitions into the business of defense, of repulsion and rage channeled into controlled violence. These people have done this before. There's a learning curve at work here. Some of the armed men spread outward toward the edges of the camp, calmly snapping hammers, pumping shells into shotgun breeches, raising the muzzles of stolen gun-show pistols or rusty family revolvers. The first shot that rings out is the dry pop of a .22 caliber Ruger—not the most powerful weapon by any means, but accurate and easy to shoot—the blast taking off the top of a dead woman's skull thirty yards away.

The female barely gets out of the trees before folding to the ground in a baptism of oily cranial fluid, which pours down over her in thick rivulets. This takedown occurs seventeen seconds into the attack. By the twentieth second, things begin happening at a faster clip.

On the north corner of the lot Lilly Caul finds herself moving, rising up on the balls of her feet, moving with the slow, coiled stiffness of a sleepwalker. Instinct takes over, and she finds herself almost *involuntarily* backing away from Josh, who is quickly surrounded by three corpses. He has one hammer. No gun. And three rotting mouths full of black teeth closing in.

He pivots toward the closest zombie while the rest of the camp scatters. Josh drives the sharp end of the hammer through Hospital Smock's temple. The cracking noise brings to mind the rending of an ice-cube tray. Brain matter fountains, the puff of pressurized decay released in an audible gasp, as the former inpatient collapses.

The hammer gets stuck, wrenched out of Josh's big hand as the walker folds.

At the same time, other survivors fan out across all corners of the clearing. On the far edge of the trees Chad gets his steel-plated Smith up and roaring, hitting the eye socket of a spindly old man missing half his jaw, the dead geriatric spinning in a mist of rancid fluids, pinwheeling into the weeds. Behind a line of cars a tent pole skewers a growling female through the mouth, pinning her to the trunk of a live oak. On the east edge of the pasture an axe shears open a rotting skull with the ease of a pomegranate being halved. Twenty yards away the blast of a shotgun vaporizes the foliage as well as the top half of a decaying former businessman.

Across the lot, Lilly Caul—still backing away from the ambush engulfing Josh—jerks and quakes at the killing racket. The fear prickles over her flesh like needles, taking her breath away and seizing up her brain. She sees the big black man on his knees now, clawing for the hammer, while the other two walkers scuttle spiderlike across the fallen tent canvas toward his legs. A second hammer lies in the grass just out of his reach.

Lilly turns and runs.

It takes her less than a minute to cover the ground between the row of outer tents and the center of the pasture, where two dozen weaker souls are huddled among the crates and provisions stashed under the partially erected circus tent. Several vehicles have fired up, and are now pulling next to the huddling throng in clouds of carbon monoxide. Armed men on the back of a flatbed guard the women and children as Lilly ducks down behind a battered steamer trunk, her lungs heaving for air, her skin crawling with terror.

She stays like that for the duration of the attack, her hands over her ears. She doesn't see Josh near the tree line, getting his hand around the hammer embedded in the fallen cadaver, wrenching it free at the last possible instant and swinging it toward the closest attacker. She doesn't see the blunt end of the hammer striking the male zombie's mandible, staving in half the rotting skull with the tremendous force of Josh's blow. And Lilly misses the last part of the struggle; she misses the female nearly getting her black incisors around Josh's ankle before a shovel comes down on the back of her head. Several men have reached Josh in time to dispatch the final zombie, and Josh rolls away, unharmed and yet trembling with the adrenaline and tremors of a near miss.

The entire attack—now vanquished and fading away in a soft drone of whimpering children, dripping fluids, and the escaping gases of decomposition—has encompassed less than one hundred and eighty seconds.

Later, dragging the remains off into a dry creek bed to the south, Chad and his fellow alpha dogs count twenty-four walkers in all—a totally manageable threat level . . . for the time being, at least.

"Jesus, Lilly, why don't you just suck it up and go apologize to the man?" The young woman named Megan sits on a blanket outside the circus tent, staring at the untouched breakfast in front of Lilly.

The sun has just come up, pale and cold in the clear sky—another day in the tent city—and Lilly sits in front of a battered Coleman stove, sipping instant coffee from a paper cup. The congealed remnants of freeze-dried eggs sit in the camp skillet, as Lilly tries to shake the guilt-ridden ruminations of a sleepless night. In this world there is no rest for the weary *or* the cowardly.

All around the great and tattered circus tent—now fully assembled—the bustle of other survivors drones on, almost as if the previous day's attack never happened. People carry folding chairs and camp tables into the great tent through the wide opening at one end (probably once the entrance for elephants and clown cars), as the tent's outer walls palpitate with the shifting breezes and changes in air pressure. In other parts of the encampment more shelters are going up. Fathers are gathering and taking inventory of firewood, bottled water, ammunition, weapons, and canned goods. Mothers are tending to children, blankets, coats, and medicine.

Upon closer scrutiny a keen observer would see a thinly veiled layer of anxiety in every activity. But what is uncertain is which danger poses the greatest threat: the undead or the encroaching winter.

"I haven't figured out what to say yet," Lilly mutters finally, sipping her lukewarm coffee. Her hands haven't stopped shaking. Eighteen hours have passed since the attack, but Lilly still stews with shame, avoiding contact with Josh, keeping to herself, convinced that he hates her for running and leaving him to die. Josh has tried to talk to her a few times but she couldn't handle it, telling him she was sick.

"What is there to say?" Megan fishes in her denim jacket for her little one-hit pipe. She tamps a tiny bud of weed into the end and sparks it with a Bic, taking a healthy toke. An olive-skinned young woman in her late twenties with loose henna-colored curls falling around her narrow, cunning face, she blows the green smoke out with a cough. "I mean look at this dude, he's huge."

"What the hell does that mean?"

Megan grins. "Dude looks like he can take care of himself, is all I'm saying."

"That has nothing to do with it."

"Are you sleeping with him?"

"What?" Lilly looks at her friend. "Are you serious?"

"It's a simple question."

Lilly shakes her head, lets out a sigh. "I'm not even going to dignify that with—"

"You're not . . . are you? Good-Little-Doobie-Lilly. Good to the last drop."

"Would you stop?"

"Why, though?" Megan's grin turns to a smirk. "Why have you not climbed on top of that? What are you waiting for? That body . . . those guns he's got—"

"Stop it!" Lilly's anger flares, a sharp splitting pain behind the bridge of her nose. Her emotions close to the surface, her trembling returning, she surprises even her*self* with the volume of her voice. "I'm not like you . . . okay. I'm not a social butterfly. Jesus, Meg. I've lost track. Which one of these guys are you with now?"

Megan stares at her for a second, coughs, then loads up another one-hit. "You know what?" Megan offers the pipe. "Why don't you take it down a little bit? Chill?"

"No, thanks."

"It's good for what ails ya. It'll kill that bug you got up your ass."

Lilly rubs her eyes, shakes her head. "You are a piece of work, Meg."

Megan gulps another hit, blows it out. "I'd rather be a piece of work than a piece of shit."

Lilly says nothing, just keeps shaking her head. The sad truth is, Lilly sometimes wonders if Megan Lafferty is not exactly that—a piece of shit. The two girls have known each other since senior year at Sprayberry High School back in Marietta. They were inseparable back then, sharing everything from homework to drugs to boyfriends. But then Lilly got designs on a career, and spent two years of purgatory at Massey College of Business in Atlanta, and then on to Georgia Tech for an MBA she would never get. She wanted to be a fashionista, maybe run a clothing design business, but she got as far as the reception area of her first interview—a highly coveted internship with Mychael Knight Fashions—before chickening out. Her old companion, fear, put the kibosh on all her plans.

Fear made her flee that lavish lobby and give up and go home to

Marietta and resume her slacker lifestyle with Megan, getting high, sitting on couches, and watching reruns of *Project Runway.*

Something had changed between the two women in recent years, however, something fundamentally chemical—Lilly felt it as strong as a language barrier. Megan had no ambition, no direction, no focus, and was okay with that. But Lilly still harbored dreams—stillborn dreams, perhaps, but dreams nonetheless. She secretly longed to go to New York or start a Web site or go back to that receptionist at Mychael Knight and say, "Oops, sorry, just had to step out for a year and a half . . ."

Lilly's dad—a retired math teacher and widower named Everett Ray Caul—always encouraged his daughter. Everett was a kind, deferential man who took it upon himself, after his wife's slow death from breast cancer back in the midnineties, to raise his only daughter with a tender touch. He knew she wanted more out of life, but he also knew she needed unconditional love, she needed a family, she needed a home. And Everett was all she had. All of which made the events of the last couple of months so hellish for Lilly.

The first outbreak of walkers hit the north side of Cobb County hard. They came from blue-collar areas, the industrial parks north of Kennesaw woods, creeping into the population like malignant cells. Everett decided to pack Lilly up and flee in their beat-up VW wagon, and they got as far as U.S. 41, before the wreckage slowed them down. They found a rogue city bus a mile south of there—careening up and down the back streets, picking survivors up—and they almost made it onboard. To this day, the image of her father pushing her through the bus's folding door as zombies closed in haunts Lilly's dreams.

The old man saved her life. He slammed that accordion door behind her at the last possible instant, and slid to the pavement, already in the grip of three cannibals. The old man's blood washed up across the glass as the bus tore out of there, Lilly screaming until her vocal cords burned out. She went into a kind of catatonic state then, curled into a fetal position on a bench seat, staring at that blood-smeared door all the way to Atlanta.

It was a minor miracle that Lilly found Megan. At that point in the outbreak, cell phones still worked, and she managed to arrange a rendezvous with her friend on the outskirts of Heartsfield Airport. The two women set out together on foot, hitchhiking south, flopping in deserted houses, just concentrating on survival. The tension between them intensified. Each seemed to be compensating for the terror and loss in different ways. Lilly went inward. Megan went the other direction, staying high most of the time, talking constantly, latching on to any other traveler who crossed their path.

They hooked up with a caravan of survivors thirty miles southwest of Atlanta—three families from Lawrenceville, traveling in two minivans. Megan convinced Lilly there was safety in numbers, and Lilly agreed to ride along for a while. She kept to herself for the next few weeks of zigzagging across the fruit belt, but Megan soon had designs on one of the husbands. His name was Chad and he had a bad-ass good-old-boy way about him, with his Copenhagen snuff under his lip and his navy tattoos on his wiry arms. Lilly was appalled to see the flirting going on amid this waking nightmare, and it wasn't long before Megan and Chad were stealing off into the shadows of rest stop buildings to "relieve themselves." The wedge between Lilly and Megan burrowed deeper.

It was right around this time that Josh Lee Hamilton came into the picture. Around sunset one evening the caravan had gotten pinned down by a pack of the dead in a Kmart parking lot, when the big African-American behemoth came to the rescue from the shadows of the loading dock. He came like some Moorish gladiator, wielding twin garden hoes with the price tags still flagging in the wind. He easily dispatched the half-dozen zombies, and the members of the caravan thanked him profusely. He showed the group a couple of brand-new shotguns in the back aisles of the store, as well as camping gear.

Josh rode a motorcycle, and after helping load the minivans with provisions, he decided to join the group, following along on his bike as the caravan made their way closer to the abandoned orchards patchworking Meriwether County.

Now Lilly had begun to regret the day she agreed to ride on the back of that big Suzuki. Was her attachment to the big man simply a projection of her grief over the loss of her dad? Was it a desperate act of manipulation in the midst of unending terror? Was it as cheap and transparent as Megan's promiscuity? Lilly wondered if her act of cowardice—deserting Josh on the battlefield yesterday—was a sick, dark, subconscious act of self-fulfilling prophecy.

"Nobody said you're a piece of shit, Megan," Lilly finally says, her voice strained and unconvincing.

"You don't have to say it." Megan angrily taps the pipe on the stove. She levers herself to her feet. "You've totally said enough."

Lilly stands. She has grown accustomed to these sudden mood swings in her friend. "What is your problem?"

"You . . . you're my problem."

"The hell are you talking about?"

"Forget it, I can't even handle this anymore," Megan says. The rueful tone of her voice is filtered by the hoarse buzz of the weed working on her. "I wish you luck, girlie-girl . . . you're gonna need it."

Megan storms off toward the row of cars on the east edge of the property.

Lilly watches her pal vanish behind a tall trailer loaded with cartons. The other survivors take very little notice of the tiff between the two girls. A few heads turn, a few whispers are exchanged, but most of the settlers continue busying themselves with the gathering and accounting of supplies, their somber expressions tight with nervous tension. The wind smells of metal and sleet. There's a cold front creeping in.

Gazing out across the clearing, Lilly finds herself momentarily transfixed by all the activity. The area looks like a flea market crowded with buyers and sellers, people trading supplies, stacking cordwood, and chatting idly. At least twenty smaller tents now line the periphery of the property, a few clotheslines haphazardly strung between trees, blood-spattered clothing taken from walkers, nothing wasted, the threat of winter a constant motivator now. Lilly sees children playing jump rope near a flatbed truck, a few boys kicking a soccer ball. She sees a fire burning in a barbecue pit, the haze of smoke wafting up over the roofs of parked cars. The air is redolent with bacon grease and hickory smoke, an odor that, in any other context, might suggest the lazy days of summer, tailgate parties, football games, backyard cookouts, family reunions.

A tide of black dread rises in Lilly as she scans the bustling little settlement. She sees the kids frolicking . . . and the parents laboring to make this place work . . . all of them zombie fodder . . . and all at once Lilly feels a twinge of insight . . . a jolt of reality.

She sees clearly now that these people are doomed. This grand plan to build a tent city in the fields of Georgia is not going to work.

TWO

The next day, under a pewter-colored sky, Lilly is playing with the Bingham girls in front of Chad and Donna Bingham's tent, when a grinding noise echoes over the trees along the adjacent dirt access road. The sound stiffens half the settlers in the area, faces snapping toward the noise of an approaching engine, which is groaning through its low gears.

It could be anyone. Word has spread across the plagued land of thugs pillaging the living, bands of heavily armed rovers stripping survivors of everything including the shoes on their feet. Several of the settlers' vehicles are currently out on scavenging reconnaissance but you never know.

Lilly looks up from the girls' hopscotch court—the squares have been etched in a little bare patch of brick-red clay with a stick—and the Bingham girls all freeze in mid-skip. The oldest girl, Sarah, shoots a glance at the road. A skinny tomboy in a faded denim jumper and down vest with big inquisitive blue eyes, fifteen-year-old Sarah, the whip-smart ringleader of the four sisters, softly utters, "Is that—"

"It's okay, sweetie," Lilly says. "Pretty sure it's one of ours."

The three younger sisters start craning their necks, looking for their mom.

Donna Bingham is presently out of view, washing clothes in a galvanized tin drum out behind the family's large camping tent, which Chad Bingham lovingly erected four days ago, equipping it with aluminum cots, racks of coolers, vent stacks, and a battery-operated DVD player with a library of children's fare such as *The Little Mermaid* and *Toy Story 2*. The sound of Donna Bingham's shuffling footsteps can be heard coming around the tent as Lilly gathers up the children.

"Sarah, get Ruthie," Lilly says calmly yet firmly as the engine noises close the distance, the vapor of burning oil rising above the tree line. Lilly rises to her feet and quickly moves over to the twins. Nine-year-old Mary and Lydia are identical cherubs in matching peacoats and flaxen pigtails. Lilly herds the little ones toward the tent flap while Sarah scoops up the seven-year-old Ruthie—an adorable little elf with Shirley Temple curls hanging over the collar of her miniature ski jacket.

Donna Bingham appears around the side of the tent just as Lilly is ushering the twins into the enclosure. "What's going on?" The mousy woman in the canvas jacket looks as though a stiff wind might blow her over. "Who is it? Is it rovers? Is it a stranger?"

"Nothing to worry about," Lilly tells her, holding the tent flap open as the four girls file into the shadows. In the five days since the contingent of settlers arrived here, Lilly has become the de facto babysitter, watching over various groups of offspring while parents go out scavenging or go on walks or just grab some alone time. She's happy for the welcome distraction, especially now that the babysitting can provide an excuse to avoid all contact with Josh Lee Hamilton. "Just stay in the tent with the girls until we know who it is."

Donna Bingham gladly shuts herself inside the enclosure with her daughters.

Lilly whirls toward the road and sees the grill of a familiar fifteen-forward-speed International Harvester truck materializing in a haze of wood smoke at the far end of the road—coming around the bend in gasps of exhaust—sending a wave of relief through Lilly. She smiles in spite of her nerves and starts toward the bare ground on the west edge of the field, which serves as a loading area. The rust-bucket truck clatters across the grass and shudders to a stop, the three teenagers riding in the back with the roped-down crates nearly tumbling forward against the pockmarked cab.

"Lilly Marlene!" the driver calls out the open cab window as Lilly comes around the front of the truck. Bob Stookey has big greasy hands—the hands of a laborer—wrapped around the wheel.

"What's on the menu today, Bob?" Lilly says with a wan smile. "More Twinkies?"

"Oh, we got a full gourmet spread with all the trimmings today, little sis." Bob cocks his deeply lined face toward the crew in back. "Found a deserted Target, only a couple of walkers to deal with . . . made out like bandits."

"Do tell."

"Let's see . . ." Bob jerks the shift lever into park and kills the rumbling engine. His skin the color of tanned cowhide, his droopy eyes rimmed red, Bob Stookey is one of the last men in the New South still using pomade to grease his dark hair back over his weathered head. "Got lumber, sleeping bags, tools, canned fruit, lanterns, cereal, weather radios, shovels, charcoal—what else? Also got a bunch of pots and pans, some tomato plants—still with a few warty little tomaters on the vines—some tanks of butane, ten gallons of milk that expired only a couple of weeks ago, some hand sanitizer, Sterno, laundry soap, candy bars, toilet paper, a Chia Pet, a book on organic farming, a singing fish for my tent, and a partridge in a pear tree."

"Bob, Bob, Bob . . . no AK-47s? No dynamite?"

"Got something better than that, smarty pants." Bob reaches over to a peach crate sitting on the passenger seat next to him. He hands it through the window to Lilly. "Be a darlin' and put this in my tent while I help these three stooges in back with the heavy stuff."

"What is it?" Lilly looks down at the crate full of plastic vials and bottles.

"Medical supplies." Bob opens his door and climbs out. "Need to keep 'em safe."

Lilly notices half a dozen pint bottles of liquor wedged in between the antihistamines and codeine. She gazes up at Bob and gives him a look. "Medical supplies?"

He grins. "I'm a very sick man."

"I'll say," Lilly comments. She knows enough about Bob's background by now to know that aside from being a sweet, genial, somewhat lost soul, as well as being a former army medic—which makes him the only inhabitant of the tent city with any medical training—he is also an inveterate drunk.

In the early stages of their friendship, back when Lilly and Megan were still on the road, and Bob had helped them out of a jam at a rest stop crawling with zombies, Bob had made feckless attempts to hide his alcoholism. But by the time the group had settled here in this deserted pastureland five days ago, Lilly had begun regularly helping Bob stagger safely back to his tent at night, making sure nobody robbed him—which was a real threat in a group this large and varied and filled with so much tension. She liked Bob, and she didn't mind babysitting *him* as well as the little ones. But it also added an additional layer of stress that Lilly needed as much as she needed a high colonic.

Right now, in fact, she can tell he needs something else from her. She can tell by the way he's wiping his mouth thoughtfully with his dirty hand.

"Lilly, there's something else I wanted to—" He stops and swallows awkwardly.

She lets out a sigh. "Spit it out, Bob."

"It's none of my business . . . all right. I just wanted to say . . . aw, hell." He takes a deep breath. "Josh Lee, he's a good man. I visit with him now and again."

"Yeah . . . and?"

"And I'm just saying."

"Go on."

"I'm just . . . look . . . he ain't doing too good right about now, all right? He thinks you're sore at him."

"He thinks I'm what?"

"He thinks you're mad at him for some reason, and he ain't sure why."

"What did he say?"

Bob gives her a shrug. "It's none of my beeswax. I ain't exactly privy to . . . I don't know, Lilly. He just wishes you wasn't ignoring him."

"I'm not."

Bob looks at her. "You sure?"

"Bob, I'm telling you—"

"All right, look." Bob waves his hand nervously. "I ain't telling you what to do. I just think two people like y'all, good folks, it's a shame something like this, you know, in these times . . ." His voice trails off.

Lilly softens. "I appreciate what you're saying, Bob, I do."

She looks down.

Bob purses his lips, thinks it over. "I saw him earlier today, over by the log pile, chopping wood like it was going outta style."

The distance between the loading area and the stack of cordwood measures less than a hundred yards, but crossing it feels like the Bataan Death March to Lilly.

She walks slowly, with her head down, and her hands thrust in the pockets of her jeans to conceal the trembling. She has to weave through a group of women sorting clothes in suitcases, circle around the end of the circus tent, sidestep a group of boys repairing a broken skateboard, and give wide berth to a cluster of men inspecting a row of weapons spread out on a blanket on the ground.

As she passes the men—Chad Bingham included in their number, holding court like a redneck despot—Lilly glances down at the tarnished pistols, eleven of them, different calibers, makes, and models, neatly arrayed like silverware in a drawer. The pair of 12-gauge shotguns from Kmart lie nearby. Only eleven pistols and the shotguns, and a limited number of rounds—the sum total of the settlers' armory—now standing as a thin tissue of defense between the campers and calamity.

Lilly's neck crawls with gooseflesh as she passes, the fear burning a hole in her guts. The trembling increases. She feels as though she's running a fever. The shaking has always been an issue for Lilly Caul. She remembers the time she had to deliver a presentation to the admission committee at Georgia Tech. She had her notes on index cards and had rehearsed for weeks. But when she got up in front of those tenured professors in that stuffy meeting room on North Avenue, she shook so much she dropped the stack of cards all over the floor and completely choked.

She feels that same kind of nervous tension right now—amplified by a factor of a thousand—as she approaches the split-rail fence along the western edge of the property. She feels the trembling in her facial features, and in her hands inside her pockets, so intense now it feels like the tremors are about to seize up her joints and freeze her in place. "Chronic anxiety disorder," the doctor back in Marietta called it.

In recent weeks, she has experienced this kind of spontaneous palsy in the immediate aftermath of a walker attack—a spell of shuddering that lasts for hours afterward—but now she feels a deeper sense of dread flooding through her that comes from some inchoate, primal place. She is turning inward, facing her own wounded soul, twisted by grief and the loss of her father.

She jumps at the crack of an axe striking timber, her attention yanked toward the fence.

A group of men stand in a cluster around a long row of dry logs. Dead leaves and cottonwood swirl on the wind above the tree line. The air smells of wet earth and matted pine needles. Shadows dance behind the foliage, tweaking Lilly's fear like a tuning fork in her brain. She remembers nearly getting bitten back in Macon three weeks ago when a zombie lurched out at her from behind a garbage Dumpster. To Lilly, right now, those shadows behind the trees look just like the passageway behind that Dumpster, rotten with menace and the smell of decay and horrible miracles—the dead coming back to life.

Another axe blow makes her start, and she turns toward the far end of the woodpile.

Josh stands with his shirtsleeves rolled up, his back to her. An oblong sweat stain runs down his chambray shirt between his massive shoulder blades. His muscles rippling, the skin folds in his brown nape pulsing, he works with a steady rhythm, swinging, striking, yanking back, bracing, swinging again with a *thwack!*

Lilly walks up to him and clears her throat. "You're doing it all wrong," she says in a shaky voice, trying to keep things light and casual.

Josh freezes with axe blade in midair. He turns and looks at her, his sculpted ebony face pearled with sweat. For a moment, he looks shell-shocked, his twinkling eyes belying his surprise. "You know, I figured somethin' wasn't working right," he says finally. "I've only been able to split about a hundred logs in fifteen minutes."

"You're choked down way too low on the handle."

Josh grins. "I knew it was somethin' like that."

"You have to let the logs do the work for ya."

"Good idea."

"You want me to demonstrate?"

Josh steps aside, hands her the axe.

"Like this," Lilly says, trying her best to appear charming and witty and brave. Her trembling is so bad the axe head quivers as she makes a feeble attempt to split a log. She swings and the blade side-swipes the wood, then sticks into the ground. She struggles to pull it free.

"Now I get it," Josh says with an amused nod. He notices her shaking, and his grin fades. He moves next to her. He puts his huge hand over hers, which is white-knuckling the axe handle as she struggles to pull it out of the clay. His touch is tender and soothing. "Everything's gonna be okay, Lilly," he says softly.

She lets go of the axe and turns to face him. Her heart races as she looks into his eyes. Her flesh goes cold, and she tries to put her feelings into words, but all she can do is look away in shame. Finally she manages to find her voice. "Is there someplace we can go and talk?"

"How do you do it?"

Lilly sits with her legs crossed Indian-style, on the ground under the massive branches of a live oak, which dapple the carpet of matted leaves around her with a skein of shadows. She reclines against the gigantic tree trunk as she speaks. Her eyes remain fixed on the swaying treetops in the middle distance.

She has a faraway look that Josh Lee Hamilton has seen now and again on the faces of war veterans and emergency room nurses—the gaze of perpetual exhaustion, the haggard look of the shell-shocked, the thousand-yard stare. Josh feels the urge to take her delicate, slender body into his arms and hold her and stroke her hair and make everything all better. But he senses somehow—he knows—now is not the time. Now is the time to listen.

"Do what?" he asks her. Josh sits across from her, also cross-legged, wiping the back of his neck with a damp bandanna. A box of cigars sits on the ground in front of him—the last of his dwindling supply. He is almost hesitant to go through the last of them—a superstitious twinge that he'll be sealing his fate.

Lilly looks up at him. "When the walkers attack . . . how do you deal with it without being . . . scared shitless?"

Josh lets out a weary chuckle. "If you figure that out, you're gonna have to teach me."

She stares at him for a moment. "Come on."

"What?"

"You're telling me you're scared shitless when they attack?"

"Damn straight."

"Oh, please." She tilts her head incredulously. "You?"

"Let me tell you something, Lilly." Josh picks up the package of cigars, shakes one loose, and sparks it with his Zippo. He takes a thoughtful puff. "Only the stupid or the crazy ain't scared these days. You ain't scared, you ain't paying attention."

She looks out beyond the rows of tents lined along the split-rail fence. She lets out a pained sigh. Her narrow face is drawn, ashen. She looks as though she's trying to articulate thoughts that just stubbornly refuse to cooperate with her vocabulary. At last she says, "I've been dealing with this for a while. I'm not . . . proud of it. I think it's messed up a lot of things for me."

Josh looks at her. "What has?"

"The wimp factor."

"Lilly—"

"No. Listen. I need to say this." She refuses to look at him, her eyes burning with shame. "Before this . . . outbreak happened . . . it was just sort of . . . inconvenient. I missed out on a few things. I screwed some things up because I'm a chickenshit . . . but now the stakes are . . . I don't know. I could get somebody killed." She finally manages to look up into the big man's eyes. "I could totally ruin things for somebody I care about."

Josh knows what she's talking about, and it puts the squeeze on his heart. From the moment he laid eyes on Lilly Caul he had felt feelings that he hadn't felt since he was a teenager back in Greenville—that kind of rapturous fascination a boy can fix upon the curve of a girl's neck, the smell of her hair, the spray of freckles along the bridge of her nose. Yes, indeed, Josh Lee Hamilton is smitten. But he is *not* going to screw this relationship up, as he had screwed up so many before Lilly, before the plague, before the world had gotten so goddamn bleak.

Back in Greenville, Josh developed crushes on girls with embarrassing frequency, but he always seemed to muck things up by rushing it. He would behave like a big old puppy licking at their heels. Not this time. This time, Josh was going to play it smart . . . smart and cautious and one step at a time. He may be a big old dumb-ass hick from South Carolina but he's not stupid. He's willing to learn from his past mistakes.

A natural loner, Josh grew up in the 1970s, when South Carolina was still clinging to the ghostly days of Jim Crow, still making futile attempts to integrate their schools and join the twentieth century. Shuffled from one ramshackle housing project to another with his single mom and four sisters, Josh put his God-given size and strength to good use on the gridiron, playing varsity ball for Mallard Creek High School with visions of scholarships in his eyes. But he lacked the one thing that sent players up the academic and socioeconomic ladders: *raw aggression.*

Josh Lee Hamilton had always been a gentle soul . . . to a fault. He let far weaker boys pick on him. He deferred to all adults with a "yessim" or "yessir." He simply had no fight in him. All of which is why his football career eventually petered out in the mid-eighties. That was right around the time his mother, Raylene, got sick. The doctors said it was called "lupus erythematosus," and it wasn't terminal, but for Raylene it was a death sentence, a life of chronic pain and skin lesions and near paralysis. Josh took it upon himself to be his mom's caretaker (while his sisters drifted away to bad marriages and dead-end jobs out of state). Josh cooked and cleaned and took good care of his mama, and within a few years he got good enough at cooking to actually get a job in a restaurant.

He had a natural flair for the culinary, especially cooking meat, and he moved up the ranks at steakhouse kitchens across South Carolina and Georgia. By the 2000s, he had become one of the most sought-after executive chefs in the Southeast, supervising large teams of sous-chefs, catering upscale social events, and getting his picture in *Atlanta Homes and Lifestyles*. And all the while he managed to run his kitchens with kindness—a rarity in the restaurant world.

Now, amid these daily horrors, beset with all this unrequited love, Josh longed to cook something special for Lilly.

Up until now, they had subsisted on things like canned peas and Spam and dry cereal and powdered milk—none of which would provide the proper backdrop for a romantic dinner or a declaration of love. All the meat and fresh produce in the area had gone the way of the maggots weeks ago. But Josh had designs on a rabbit, or a wild boar that might be roaming the neighboring woods. He would make a ragout, or a nice braise with wild onions and rosemary and some of that Pinot Noir that Bob Stookey had scavenged from that derelict liquor store, and Josh would serve the meat with some herbed polenta, and he would add extra special touches. Some of the ladies in the tent city had been making candles from the suet they found in a bird feeder. That would be nice. Candles, wine, maybe a poached pear from the orchard for dessert, and Josh would be ready. The orchards were still lousy with overripe fruit. Maybe an apple chutney with the pork. Yes. Absolutely. Then Josh would be ready to serve Lilly dinner and tell her how he feels about her, how he wants to be with her and protect her and be her man.

"I know where you're going with this, Lilly," Josh finally says to her, tamping his cigar's ash on a stone. "And I want you to know two things. Number one, there's no shame in what you did."

She looks down. "You mean running away like a whipped dog when you were under attack?"

"Listen to me. If the shoe was on the other foot, I would've done the same damn thing."

"That's bullshit, Josh, I didn't even—"

"Let me finish." He snubs out the cigar. "Number two, I *wanted* you to run. You didn't hear me. I hollered for you to get the Sam Hell outta there. Makes no sense—only one of them hammers within grasp, both of us trying to mix it up with them things. You understand what I'm saying? You don't need to feel any shame for what you done."

Lilly takes a breath. She keeps looking down. A tear forms and rolls down the bridge of her nose. "Josh, I appreciate what you're trying to—"

"We're a team, right?" He leans down so he can see her beautiful face. "Right?"

She nods.

"The dynamic duo, right?"

Another nod. "Right."

"A well-oiled machine."

"Yeah." She wipes her face with the back of her hand. "Yeah, okay."

"So let's keep it that way." He throws her his damp bandanna. "Deal?"

She looks at the do-rag in her lap, picks it up, looks at him and manages a grin. "Jesus Christ, Josh, this thing is totally gross."

Three days pass in the tent city without an attack of any note. Only a few minor incidents sully the calm. One morning, a group of kids stumble upon a quivering torso in a culvert ditch along the road. Its gray, wormy face cocked toward the treetops in perpetual, groaning agony, the thing looks as though it recently tangled with a mechanical reaper, and has ragged stumps where its arms and legs once were. Nobody can figure out how the limbless thing got there. Chad puts the creature down with a single hatchet blow through its rotting nasal bone. On another occasion, out by the communal toilets, an elderly camper realizes, with heart-skipping dismay, that during his afternoon bowel movement, he is unwittingly shitting on a zombie. Somehow the roamer got itself stuck down in the sewage trough. The thing is easily dispatched by one of the younger men with a single thrust of a post-hole digger.

These prove to be isolated encounters, though, and the middle of the week progresses uneventfully.

The respite gives the inhabitants time to organize, finish erecting the last of their shelters, stow supplies, explore the immediate area, settle into a routine, and form coalitions and cliques and hierarchies. The families—ten of them in all—seem to carry more weight in the decision-making process than do single people. Something about the gravitas of having more at risk, the imperative of protecting children, maybe even the symbolism of carrying the genetic seeds of the future—all of it adding up to a kind of unspoken seniority.

Among the patriarchs of the families, Chad Bingham emerges as the de facto leader. Each morning, he leads the communal pow-wows inside the circus tent, assigning duties with the casual authority of a Mafia capo. Each day, he struts along the edges of the camp with his snuff defiantly bulging under his cheek, his pistol in full view. With winter in the offing, and troubling noises behind the trees at night, Lilly worries about this ersatz figurehead. Chad has been keeping his eye on Megan, who has been shacking up with one of the other fathers, in plain view of everybody including the man's pregnant wife. Lilly worries that the whole semblance of order here rests on top of a tinderbox.

Lilly's tent and Josh's tent sit a mere ten yards away from each other. Each morning, Lilly awakens and sits facing the zippered end of her tent, gazing out at Josh's tent, drinking her instant Sanka and trying to sort out her feelings for the big man. Her cowardly act still gnaws at her, haunts her, festers in her dreams. She has nightmares of the bloody folding door on that rogue bus back in Atlanta, but now, instead of her father being devoured, sliding down that smeared glass, Lilly sees Josh.

His accusing eyes always wake her up with a start, the cold sweat soaked through her nightclothes.

On these dream-racked nights, lying sleepless in her moldy sleeping bag, staring at the mildewed roof of her tiny tent—she acquired the used pup tent on a raid of a deserted KOA camp, and it reeks of smoke, dried semen, and stale beer—she inevitably hears the noises. Faint, off in the distant darkness beyond the rise, behind the trees, the sounds mingle with the wind and crickets and rustling foliage: unnatural snapping noises, jerky shuffling sounds, which remind Lilly of old shoes tumbling and banging inside a dryer.

In her mind's eye, mutated by terror, the distant noises conjure images of terrible black-and-white forensic photos, mutilated bodies blackened by rigor mortis and yet still moving, dead faces turning and leering at her, silent snuff films of dancing cadavers jitterbugging like frogs on a hot skillet. Lying wide awake each night, Lilly ruminates about what the noises might actually mean, what is going on out there, and when the next attack will come.

Some of the more thoughtful campers have been developing theories.

One young man from Athens named Harlan Steagal, a nerdy grad student with thick horn-rims, begins holding nightly philosophy salons around the campfire. Jacked up on pseudoephedrine, instant coffee, and bad weed, the half a dozen or so social misfits grope for answers to the imponderable questions tormenting everybody: the origins of the plague, the future of mankind, and perhaps the timeliest issue of them all, the walkers' patterns of behavior.

The consensus among the think tank is that there are only two possibilities: *(a)* zombies have no instinct, purpose, or behavioral pattern other than involuntary feeding. They are merely sputtering nerve endings with teeth, bouncing off each other like deadly machines that simply need to be "turned off." Or *(b)* there is a complex pattern of behavior going on here that no survivor has figured out yet. The latter begs the question of how the plague is transmitted from the dead to the living—is it only through the bite of a walker?—as well as questions of horde behavior, *and* of possible Pavlovian learning curves, *and* even larger-scale genetic imperatives.

In other words—to put it in the patois of Harlan Steagal: *"Are the dead things like playing out some weird, fucked-up, trippy evolutionary thing?"*

Lilly overhears much of this rambling discourse over those three days and pays it little heed. She has no time for conjecture or analysis. The longer the tent city goes on without being assailed by the dead, the more Lilly feels vulnerable, despite the safety precautions. With most of the tents now erected and a barricade of vehicles parked around the periphery of the clearing, things have quieted down. People are settled in, keeping to themselves, and the few campfires or cooking stoves that are employed for meals are quickly extinguished for fear of errant smoke or odors attracting unwanted intruders.

Still, Lilly becomes exceedingly nervous each night. It feels as though a cold front is moving in. The night sky gets crystalline and cloudless, a new frost forming each morning on the matted ground and fencing and tent canvases. The gathering cold reflects Lilly's dark intuition. Something terrible seems imminent.

One night, before turning in, Lilly Caul pulls a small leatherbound paper calendar from her backpack. In the weeks since the advent of the plague, most personal devices have failed. The electrical grid has gone down, fancy batteries have run their course, service providers have vanished, and the world has reverted to the fundamentals: bricks, mortar, paper, fire, flesh, blood, sweat, and whenever possible, *internal combustion*. Lilly has always been an analog girl—her place back in Marietta brims with vinyl records, transistor radios, windup clocks, and first editions crammed into every corner—so she naturally starts keeping track of the plague days in her little black binder with the faded American Family Insurance logo embossed in gold on the cover.

On this night, she puts a big *X* on the square marked Thursday, November 1.

The next day is November 2—the day her fate, as well as that of many others, will irrevocably change.

Friday dawns clear and bitingly cold. Lilly stirs just after sunrise, shivering in her sleeping bag, her nose so cold it feels numb. Her joints ache as she hurriedly piles on the layers. She pushes herself out of her tent, zipping her coat and glancing at Josh's tent.

The big man is already up, standing beside his tent, stretching his massive girth. Bundled in his fisherman's sweater and tattered down vest, he whirls, sees Lilly, and says, "Cold enough for ya?"

"Next stupid question," she says, coming over to his tent, reaching for the thermos of steaming instant coffee gripped in his huge, gloved hand.

"Weather's got people panicked," he says softly, handing the thermos over. With a nod, he indicates the three trucks idling along the road across the clearing. His breath shows in puffs of vapor as he talks. "Bunch of us heading up into the woods, gathering as much firewood as we can load."

"I'll come with."

Josh shakes his head. "Talked to Chad a minute ago, I guess he needs you to watch his kids."

"Okay. Sure. Whatever."

"You keep that," Josh says, gesturing toward the thermos. He grabs the axe that sits canted against his tent and gives her a grin. "Should be back by lunchtime."

"Josh," she says, grabbing his sleeve before he can turn away. "Just be careful in the woods."

His grin widens. "Always, babydoll . . . always."

He turns and marches off toward the clouds of visible exhaust along the gravel road.

Lilly watches the contingent hopping into cabs, jumping up onto running boards, climbing into cargo bays. She doesn't realize at this point the amount of noise they're making, the commotion caused by three large trucks embarking all at once, the voices calling to each other, doors slamming, the fog bank of carbon monoxide.

In all the excitement, neither Lilly, nor anyone else for that matter, realizes how far the racket of their departure is carrying out over the treetops.

Lilly senses danger first.

The Binghams have left her inside the circus tent, in charge of the four girls, who now frolic across the floor of matted grass, scampering amid the folding tables, stacks of peach crates, and tanks of butane. The interior of the circus tent is illuminated by makeshift skylights—flaps in the ceiling pulled back to let in the daylight—and the air in there smells of must and decades of moldy hay impregnated into the canvas walls. The girls are playing musical chairs with three broken-down lawn chairs scattered across the cold earthen floor.

Lilly is supposed to be the music.

"Duh-do-do-do . . . duh-da-da-da," Lilly croons halfheartedly, murmuring an old Top 40 hit by the Police, her voice thin and weak, as the girls giggle and circle the chairs. Lilly is distracted. She keeps glancing through the loading entrance at one end of the pavilion, a large swath of the tent city visible in the gray daylight. The grounds are mostly deserted, those who are not away scavenging now hiding in their tents.

Lilly swallows her terror, the cold sun slanting down through the far trees, the wind whispering through the big-top tent. Up on the rise, shadows dance in the pale light. Lilly thinks she hears shuffling sounds up there somewhere, behind the trees maybe; she's not sure. It might be her imagination. Sounds inside the fluttering, empty tent play tricks on the ears.

She turns away from the opening and scans the pavilion for weapons. She sees a shovel leaning against a wheelbarrow filled with potting soil. She sees a few garden implements in a dirty bucket. She sees the remains of the breakfast dishes in a plastic garbage can—paper plates crusted with beans and Egg Beaters, wadded burrito wrappers, empty juice boxes—and next to it a plastic storage container with dirty silverware. The silverware came from one of the retrofitted camper/pickups, and Lilly makes note of a few sharp knives in the container but mostly she sees plastic "sporks" sticky with food gunk. She wonders how effective a spork would be against a monstrous drooling cannibal.

She silently curses the camp leaders for not leaving firearms.

Those who remain on the property include the older settlers—Mr. Rhimes, a couple of spinsters from Stockbridge, an eighty-year-old retired teacher named O'Toole, a pair of geriatric brothers from an abandoned nursing home in Macon—as well as a couple dozen adult women, a good portion of them too busy now with laundry duty and philosophical chatter along the back fence to notice anything amiss.

The only other souls currently present in the tent city are children—ten sets of them—some still huddling against the cold in their private tents, others kicking a soccer ball around in front of the derelict farmhouse. Each gaggle of kids has an adult woman in charge of them.

Lilly looks back out the exit and sees Megan Lafferty, way in the distance, sitting perched on the porch of the burned-out house, pretending to be babysitting and not smoking pot. Lilly shakes her head. Megan is supposed to be watching the Hennessey kids. Jerry Hennessey, an insurance salesman from Augusta, has been carrying on with Megan for days now in a not-too-discreet fashion. The Hennessey kids are the second-youngest kids in the encampment—at ages eight, nine, and ten respectively. The youngest children in the settlement are the Bingham twins and Ruthie, who at this moment pause in their play to stare impatiently at their nervous babysitter.

"C'mon, Lilly," Sarah Bingham calls out with her hands on her hips, catching her breath near a stack of fruit crates. The teenager wears an adorable, stylish imitation-angora sweater that breaks Lilly's heart. "Keep singing."

Lilly turns back to the children. "I'm sorry, sweetie, I just—"

Lilly stops herself. She hears a noise coming from outside the tent, from up in the trees. It sounds like the creaking bulwark of a listing ship . . . or the slow squeak of a door in a haunted house . . . or, more likely, the weight of a zombie's foot on a deadfall log.

"Girls, I'm—"

Another noise cuts off Lilly's words. She spins toward the tent's opening at a loud rustling sound, which rings out from the east, shattering the stillness a hundred yards away, coming from a thicket of wild rose and dogwood.

A flock of rock pigeons suddenly takes flight, the swarm bursting out of the foliage with the inertia of a fireworks display. Lilly stares, transfixed for a single instant, as the flock fills the sky with a virtual constellation of gray-black blots.

Like controlled explosions, along the far edge of the camp, another two flocks of pigeons erupt. Cones of fluttering specks punch up into the light, scattering and re-forming like ink clouds undulating in a clear pool.

The rock pigeons are plentiful in this area—"sky rats" they're called by the locals, who claim the pigeons are actually quite delicious if boned and grilled—but their sudden appearance in recent weeks has come to signify something darker and more troubling than a possible food source.

Something has stirred the birds from their resting place and is now making its way toward the tent city.

THREE

"Girls, listen to me." Lilly quickly shuffles over to the youngest Bingham girl and scoops her up in her arms. "I'm gonna need you to come with me."

"Why?" Sarah gives Lilly that patented teenage sulk. "What's wrong?"

"Don't argue with me, sweetie, please," Lilly says softly, and the look in Lilly's eyes straightens the teenager with the power of a cattle prod. Sarah hastily turns and takes the twins by their hands, then starts shepherding them toward the exit.

Lilly stops in her tracks in the middle of the tent's opening when she sees the first zombie burst out of the trees forty yards away—a big male with a hairless scalp the color of a bruise and eyes like milk glass—and all at once Lilly is shoving the kids back into the pavilion, clutching Ruthie in her arms and uttering under her breath, "Change in plans, girls, change in plans."

Lilly quickly urges the kids back into the dim light and moldy air of the empty circus tent. She sets the seven-year-old down on the matted weeds by a steamer trunk. "Everybody be very quiet," Lilly whispers.

Sarah stands with a twin on either side of her, the teenager's face aghast, wide-eyed with terror. "What's going on?"

"Just stay there and be quiet." Lilly hurries back to the tent opening and wrestles with the massive flap, which is cinched ten feet up with rope ties. She yanks at the ropes, until the tent flap falls across the gap.

The original plan—which flickered instantaneously across Lilly's mind—was to hide the kids in a vehicle, preferably one with its keys still in its ignition, in case Lilly had to make a quick escape. But now, all Lilly can think of doing is huddling silently in the empty pavilion and hoping that the other campers fend off the assault.

"Let's all play a different game now," Lilly says when she returns to the huddling girls. A scream rings out from somewhere across the property. Lilly tries to stanch her trembling, a voice resonating in her head, *Goddammit, you stupid bitch, you gotta grow some balls for once in your life, for these kids.*

"A different game, right, right, a different game," Sarah says, her eyes glittering with fear. She knows now what's going on. She clutches the small hands of her twin sisters and follows Lilly between two high stacks of fruit crates.

"Gonna play hide-and-seek," Lilly says to little Ruthie, who is mute with horror. Lilly gets the four girls situated in the shadows behind the crates, each child crouched down low now and breathing hard. "Have to stay very still—and very, very, very quiet. Okay?"

Lilly's voice seems to comfort them temporarily, although even the youngest knows now this is no game, this is not make-believe.

"I'll be right back," Lilly whispers to Sarah.

"No! Wait! NO, DON'T!" Sarah clutches at Lilly's down jacket, holding on to her for dear life, the teenager's eyes pleading.

"I'm just going to grab something across the tent, I'm not leaving."

Lilly extricates herself and scuttles on her hands and knees across the carpet of pressed grass to the pile of buckets near the long central table. She grabs the shovel that leans against the wheelbarrow, then crawls back to the hiding place.

All the while, terrible sounds layer and build outside the wind-blown walls of the pavilion. Another scream pierces the air, followed by frantic footsteps, and then the sound of an axe sinking into a skull. Lydia whimpers, Sarah shushes her, and Lilly crouches down in front of the girls, her vision blurring with terror.

The frigid wind tosses the skirt of the tent's walls, and for a brief moment, under the momentary gap, Lilly glimpses the onslaught in progress. At least two dozen walkers—only their shuffling, muddy feet visible like a brigade of upright stroke victims—converge on the tent-strewn field. The running feet of survivors, mostly women and elderly, are fleeing in all directions.

The spectacle of the attack temporarily distracts Lilly from the noise behind the girls.

A bloody arm lurches under the tent flap only inches away from Sarah's legs.

Sarah shrieks as a dead hand clamps down on her ankle, its blackened fingernails digging in like talons. The arm is gouged and tattered, clad in the ripped sleeve of a burial suit, and the girl convulses in shock. Moving on instinct, the teenager crawls away—the force of her movement yanking the rest of the zombie inside the tent.

A dissonant chorus of squeals and shrieks rings out from the sisters as Lilly springs to her feet with the shovel clutched tightly in sweaty palms. Instinct kicks in, Lilly spinning and cocking the shovel high. The dead man bites at the air with snapping-turtle fury, as the teenager writhes and crawls across the cold ground, crying out garbled yelps of terror, dragging the zombie with her.

Before the rotting teeth get a chance to penetrate, Lilly brings the shovel down hard on the zombie's skull, the impact making a flat clanging noise like the chime of a broken gong. The crack of the cranium vibrates up Lilly's wrists and makes her cringe.

Sarah breaks free of the cold fingers and struggles to her feet.

Lilly brings the shovel down again . . . and again . . . as the iron scoop rings its flat church-bell clang and the dead thing deflates in a rhythmic black gush of arterial blood and rotting gray matter. By the fourth blow, the skull caves in, making a wet cracking noise, the black spume bubbling across the matted grass.

By this point, Sarah has joined her sisters, each girl clinging to the other, each bug-eyed and whimpering with horror as they back toward the exit, the great canvas flap billowing noisily in the wind behind them.

Lilly turns away from the mangled corpse in the tattered pin-striped suit and starts toward the opening twenty-five feet away, when all at once she freezes in place, grabbing Sarah's sleeve. "Wait, Sarah, wait—WAIT!"

At the other end of the circus tent, the giant tarpaulin flap furls upward in the wind, revealing at least half a dozen walkers crowding in on the exit. They shuffle spastically into the tent—all adults, both male and female, clad in torn, blood-spattered street clothes, bunched together in an awkward grouping—their wormy cataract-filmed eyes fixing on the girls.

"This way!" Lilly yanks Sarah toward the opposite end of the circus tent—maybe a hundred and fifty feet away—and Sarah scoops the tike up into her arms. The twins scurry after them, slipping on the wet, matted grass. Lilly points at the bottom of the canvas wall—now a hundred feet away—and whispers breathlessly, "Gonna sneak under the tent."

They get halfway to the opposite wall when another walker appears in their path.

Apparently this slimy, mutilated corpse in faded denim dungarees—with half its face torn away on one side in a ragged starburst of red pulp and teeth—got in under the tarp and now comes straight for Sarah. Lilly steps between the zombie and the girl and swings the shovel as hard as she can, making contact with the mangled cranium and sending the thing staggering sideways.

The zombie slams into the center pillar, and the raw inertia and deadweight knocks the timber out of its mooring. Guidelines snap. There's a cracking noise like a ship breaking through ice and three of the four Bingham girls let out ululating shrieks as the massive big top collapses into itself, snapping the smaller rigging posts like matchsticks and pulling stakes out of the ground around it. The conical ceiling sinks like a vast soufflé.

The tent falls on the girls and the world goes dark and airless and full of slithering movement.

Lilly flails at the heavy fabric and struggles to get her bearings, still grasping the shovel, the tarpaulin pressing down on her with the sudden weight of an avalanche. She hears the muffled squealing of the children and she sees daylight fifty feet away. She crabs under the tent toward the light with the shovel in one hand.

At last she brushes a foot against Sarah's shoulder. Lilly cries out: "Sarah! Take my hand! Grab the girls with the other and PULL!"

At this point, for Lilly, the passage of time—as it often does in catastrophes-in-progress—begins to retard, as several things transpire almost simultaneously. Lilly reaches the end of the tent and bursts out from under the deflated canvas, and the wind and cold wake her up, and she yanks Sarah out with all her might, and two of the other girls get dragged out behind Sarah—their voices shrieking like teakettles on the boil.

Lilly springs to her feet and helps Sarah up with the other two little girls.

One girl—Lydia, the youngest of the twins by a "good half an hour," as Sarah claims—is missing. Lilly pushes the other girls away from the tent and tells them to stay back but stay close. Then Lilly whirls toward the tent and sees something that stops her heart.

Shapes are moving under the fallen circus tent. Lilly drops the shovel. She stares. Her legs and spine seize up into blocks of ice. She can't breathe. She can only stare at the small lump of fabric undulating madly twenty feet away—little Lydia struggling to escape—the sound of the child's scream dampened by the tarp.

The worst part—the part that encases Lilly Caul in ice—is the sight of the *other* lumps tunneling steadily, molelike, toward the little girl.

At that moment, the fear pops a fuse in Lilly's brain, the cleansing fire of rage traveling through her tendons and down her marrow.

She lurches into action, the burst of adrenaline driving her to the edge of the fallen tent, the rocket fuel of anger in her muscles. She yanks the canvas up and over her head, crouching down and reaching for the girl. *"LYDIA, SWEETIE, I'M RIGHT HERE!! COME TO ME, SWEETIE!!"*

Lilly sees in the pale diffuse darkness under the tarpaulin the little flaxen-haired girl, fifteen feet away, frog-kicking and scrambling to escape the clutches of the canvas. Lilly hollers again and dives under the tarp and reaches out and gets a piece of the little girl's jumper. Lilly pulls with all her might.

That's when Lilly sees the ragged arm and bloodless blue face appearing in the dark only inches behind the child, making a drunken grab for the little girl's Hello Kitty sneaker. The rotting, jagged fingernails claw the sole of the child's tennis shoe just as Lilly manages to yank the nine-year-old out from under the folds of reeking fabric.

Both Lilly and child tumble backward into the cold light of day.

They roll a few feet, and then Lilly manages to pull the little girl into a bear hug. "It's okay, baby, it's okay, I got you, you're safe."

The child sobs and gasps for breath but there's no time to comfort her. The din of voices and rustling canvas rises around them as the camp is attacked.

Lilly, still on her knees, waves the other girls over to her. "Okay, girls, listen to me, listen, we have to be quick now, quick, stay close, and do exactly as I say." Lilly huffs and puffs as she stands. She grabs the shovel, turns, and sees the chaos spreading across the tent city.

More walkers have descended upon the camp. Some of them move in clusters of three and four and five, growling and drooling with rabid, feral hunger.

Amid the screams and pandemonium—settlers fleeing in all directions, car engines firing up, axes swinging, clotheslines collapsing— some of the tents shudder with violent struggles going on *inside*, the assailants burrowing through gaps, ferreting out the paralyzed inhabitants. One of the smaller tents falls onto its side, legs scissoring out one end. Another enclosure quakes in a feeding frenzy, the translucent nylon walls displaying silhouettes of blood mist like ink blots.

Lilly sees a clear path leading to a row of parked cars fifty yards away and turns to the girls. "I need you all to follow me . . . okay? Stay very close and don't make a sound. All right?"

After a series of frantic, silent nods, Lilly yanks the girls across the lot . . . and into the fray.

The survivors of this inexplicable plague have quickly learned that the biggest advantage a human enjoys over a reanimated corpse is speed. Under the right circumstances, a human can easily outrun even the stoutest walking cadaver. But this physical superiority is overwhelmed in the face of a swarm. The danger increases exponentially with each additional zombie . . . until the victim is engulfed in a slow-moving tsunami of ragged teeth and blackened claws.

Lilly learns this harsh reality on her way to the closest parked car.

The battered, gore-streaked silver Chrysler 300 with the luggage cap on the roof sits on the gravel shoulder of the access road less than fifty yards from the circus tent, parked at an angle in the shade of a locust tree. The windows are up, but Lilly still has reason to believe they can at least gain access, if not start the car. The odds are about even that the keys are in the ignition. People have been leaving keys in cars for a while now for quick escapes.

Unfortunately, the property now teems with the dead, and Lilly and the girls barely traverse ten yards of weed-whiskered turf before several attackers move in on each flank. "Stay behind me!" Lilly cries out to her charges, and then swings the shovel.

The rusty iron bangs into the mottled cheek of a female in a blood-spattered housecoat, sending the walker careening into a pair of nearby males in greasy dungarees, who tumble like bowling pins to the ground. But the female stays upright, staggering at the blow, flailing for a moment, then coming back for more.

Lilly and the girls get another fifteen yards closer to the Chrysler when another battery of zombies blocks their path. The shovel zings through the air, smashing through the bridge of a younger walker's nose. Another blow hits the mandible of a dead woman in a filthy mink coat. Yet another blow cracks the skull of an old hunched crone with intestines showing through her hospital smock, but the old dead lady merely staggers and backpedals.

At last, the girls reach the Chrysler. Lilly tries the passenger door and finds it—blessedly—unlocked. She gently but quickly shoves Ruthie into the front seat as the pack of walkers closes in on the sedan. Lilly sees the keys dangling off the slot in the steering column—another stroke of luck. "Stay in the car, honey," Lilly says to the seven-year-old, and then slams the door.

By this point, Sarah reaches the right rear passenger door with the twins.

"SARAH, LOOK OUT!"

Lilly's keening scream rises above the primordial din of growling that fills the air, as a dozen or so dead loom behind Sarah. The teenager yanks open the rear door, but has no time to get the twins inside the car. The two smaller girls trip and sprawl to the grass.

Sarah screams a primal wail. Lilly tries to get in between the teen and the attackers with the shovel, and Lilly manages to bash in another skull—the huge cranium of a putrified black man in a hunting jacket—sending the attacker staggering back into the weeds. But there are too many walkers now, lumbering in from all directions to feed.

In the ensuing chaos, the twins manage to crawl into the car and slam the door.

Her sanity snapping, her eyes filling with white-hot rage, Sarah turns and lets out a garbled cry as she shoves a slow-moving walker out of her way. She finds an opening, pushes her way through it, and flees.

Lilly sees the teenager racing toward the circus tent. "SARAH, DON'T!!"

Sarah gets halfway across the field before an impenetrable pack of zombies closes in on her, blocking her path, latching on to her back and overpowering her. She goes down hard, eating turf, as more of the dead swarm around her. The first bite penetrates her imitation-angora sweater at the midriff, taking a chunk of her torso, sparking an earsplitting shriek. Festering teeth sink into her jugular. The dark tide of blood washes across her.

Twenty-five yards away, near the car, Lilly fights off a growing mass of gnashing teeth and dead flesh. Maybe twenty walkers in all now—most of them exhibiting the grotesque buzzing adrenaline of a feeding frenzy as they surround the Chrysler—their blackened mouths working and smacking voraciously, while behind blood-smeared windows, the faces of three little girls look on in catatonic horror.

Lilly swings the shovel again and again—her efforts futile against the growing horde—as the cogs and gears of her brain seize up, mortified by the grisly sounds of Sarah's demise on the ground across the property. The teenager's shrieking deteriorates and sputters into a watery series of caterwauls. At least a half-dozen walkers are on her now, burrowing in, chewing and tearing at her gushing abdomen. Blood fountains from her shuddering form.

Over by the row of cars, Lilly's midsection goes icy cold as she slams the shovel into another skull, her mind crackling and flickering with terror, ultimately fixing on a single course of action: *Get them away from the Chrysler.*

The silent dog-whistle urgency of that single imperative—*get them away from the children*—galvanizes Lilly and sends a jolt of energy down her spine. She turns and swings the shovel at the Chrysler's front quarter panel.

The clang rings out. The children inside the car jerk with a start. The livid blue faces of the dead turn toward the noise.

"C'MON! C'MON!!" Lilly lunges away from the Chrysler, moving toward the nearest car lined up in the haphazard row of vehicles—a beat-up Ford Taurus with one window covered in cardboard—and she strikes the edge of the roof as hard as she can, making another harsh metallic clang that gets the attention of more of the dead.

Lilly darts toward the next car in line. She bangs the scoop against the front left quarter panel, issuing another dull clang.

"C'MON!! C'MON!! C'MON!!"

Lilly's voice rises above the clamor like the bark of a sick animal, stretched thin with horror, hoarse with trauma, toneless, a touch of madness in it. She slams the shovel against car after car, not really knowing exactly what she's doing, not really in control of her actions anymore. More zombies take notice, their lazy, awkward movements drawn to the noise.

It takes Lilly mere seconds to reach the end of the row of vehicles, slamming the shovel into the last vehicle—a rust-pocked Chevy S-10 pickup—but by that point, most of the assailants have latched on to her clarion call, and now slowly, stupidly, clumsily wander toward the sound of her traumatized shouts.

The only walkers that remain are the six that continue to devour Sarah Bingham on the ground in the clearing by the great, billowing circus tent.

"C'MON!! C'MON!! C'MON!! C'MON!! C'MON!! C'MON!! C'MON!! C'MONNNNN!!!!!" Lilly vaults across the gravel road and dashes up the hill toward the tree line.

Pulse racing, vision blurred, lungs heaving for air, she drops the shovel and digs her hiking boots into the mire as she ascends the soft forest floor. She plunges into the trees. Her shoulder bangs against the trunk of an ancient birch, the pain flaring in her skull, stars shooting across her line of vision. She moves instinctively now, a horde of zombies coming up the rise behind her.

Zigzagging through the deeper woods, she loses her sense of direction. Behind her, the pack of walkers has slowed and lost her scent.

Time loses all meaning. As though in a dream, Lilly feels motion slow down, her screams refusing to come out, her legs bogging down in the invisible quicksand of nightmares. The darkness closes in as the forest thickens and deepens.

Lilly thinks of Sarah, poor Sarah, in her sweet little pink angora sweater, now bathed in her own blood, and the tragedy drags Lilly down, yanking her off her feet and throwing her down to the soft floor of matted pine needles and decaying matter and endless cycles of death and regeneration. Lilly lets out a paroxysm of pain on a breathless sob, her tears rolling down her cheeks and moistening the humus.

Her weeping—heard by no one—goes on for quite some time.

The search party finds Lilly late that afternoon. Led by Chad Bingham, the group of five men and three women—all heavily armed— see Lilly's light blue fleece jacket behind a deadfall log a thousand yards due north of the tent city, in the gelid darkness of the deep woods, in a small clearing under a canopy of loblolly branches. She appears to be unconscious, lying in a patch of brambles. "Careful!" Chad Bingham calls out to his second-in-command, a skinny mechanic from Augusta by the name of Dick Fenster. "If she's still movin', she might've turned already!"

Nervous breaths showing in the chill air, Fenster cautiously goes over to the clearing with his snub-nosed .38 drawn and ready, hammer back, trigger finger twitching. He kneels down by Lilly, takes a good long look, and then turns back to the group. "She's all right! She's alive . . . ain't bit or nothing . . . still conscious!"

"Not for long," Chad Bingham utters under his breath as he marches toward the clearing. "Chickenshit fucking whore gets my baby killed—"

"Whoa! Whoa!" Megan Lafferty steps between Chad and the deadfall. "Hold on a second, hold on."

"Get outta my way, Megan."

"You gotta take a deep breath."

"Just gonna talk to her."

An awkward pause seems to weigh down on everybody present. The other members of the search party stand back in the trees, looking down, their drawn, exhausted faces reflecting the day's horrible work. Some of the men are red-eyed, stricken with loss.

Returning from their firewood-gathering expedition, the noise of their engines and axes still ringing in their ears, they were shocked to find the tent city in ghastly disarray. Both human and zombie alike littered the blood-soaked grounds, sixteen settlers slaughtered, some of them devoured—nine of them children. Josh Lee Hamilton did the dirty work of finishing off the remaining walkers and the unfortunate humans whose remains were left intact. Nobody else had the heart to shoot their friends and loved ones in the head to ensure their eternal rest. The incubation period—strangely—seems to be more and more unpredictable lately. Some victims reanimate within minutes after a bite. Others take hours—even days—to turn. At this moment, in fact, Josh is still back at camp, supervising a disposal crew, preparing the victims for mass burial. It'll take them another twenty-four hours to get the circus tent back up.

"Dude, listen, seriously," Megan Lafferty says to Chad, her voice lowering and becoming softly urgent. "I know you're torn up and all but she saved three of your girls. . . . I told you I saw it with my own eyes. She drew the walkers away, she fucking risked her life."

"I just—" Chad looks as though he's either going to cry or scream. "I just . . . want to talk."

"You got a wife back at camp's gonna lose her mind with grief . . . she needs you."

"I just—"

Another awkward beat of silence. One of the other fathers starts to softly weep in the shadows of the trees, his handgun falling to the ground. It's nearly five o'clock and the cold is squeezing in, the puffs of vapor wafting in front of all of their tortured faces. Across the clearing, Lilly sits up and wipes her mouth, and tries to get her bearings. She looks like a sleepwalker. Fenster helps her to her feet.

Chad looks down. "Fuck it." He turns and walks away, his voice trailing after him. "Fuck it."

The next day, under a frigid overcast sky, the tent dwellers have an improvised graveside service for their fallen friends and loved ones.

Nearly seventy-five survivors gather in a large semicircle around the mass burial site on the east edge of the property. Some of the mourners hold candles flickering stubbornly against the October winds. Others clutch at each other in convulsive grief. The searing pain on some of the faces—especially those of grieving parents—reflects the agonizing randomness of this plague world. Their children were taken with the arbitrary suddenness of a lightning bolt, and now the mourners' faces sag with desolation, their parboiled eyes shimmering in the unrelenting silver sunlight.

The cairns are set into the clay, stretching up the gentle rise of bare ground beyond the split-rail fence. Small piles of stones mark each of the sixteen graves. Some markers have hanks of wildflowers carefully wedged between the rocks. Josh Lee Hamilton made sure Sarah Bingham's marker got adorned with a lovely bouquet of little white Cherokee roses, which grow in profusion along the edges of the orchards. The big man had grown fond of the feisty, whip-smart teenager . . . and her death has wrenched his heart in two.

"God, we ask that you take our lost friends and neighbors into your hands," Josh says now from the edge of the fence, the wind buffeting his olive-drab army coat stretched across his massive shoulders. His deeply etched face glistens with tears.

Josh grew up Baptist, and although he lost most of his religion over the years, he asked his fellow survivors earlier this morning if he might say a few words. Baptists don't put much stock in prayers for the dead. They believe the righteous instantly go to heaven at the time of death—or, if you're a nonbeliever, you instantly go to hell—but Josh still felt obliged to say something.

He saw Lilly earlier in the day, and he held her for a moment, whispering words of comfort to her. But he could tell something was wrong. Something was going on inside her beyond mere grief. She felt limp in his enormous arms, her slender form trembling ceaselessly like a wounded bird. She said very little. Only that she needed to be alone. She didn't show up for the burial service.

"We ask that you take them to a better place," he goes on, his deep baritone voice cracking. The work of body disposal has taken its toll on the big man. He struggles to hold it together but his emotions are strangling his vocal chords. "We ask that you—you—"

He can't go on. He turns away, and he bows his head and lets the silent tears come. He can't breathe. He can't stay here. Barely aware of what he's doing, he finds himself moving away from the crowd, away from the soft, horrible sound of weeping and praying.

Among the many things he has missed today in his daze of sadness is the fact that Lilly Caul's decision to avoid the burial service is not the only conspicuous absence. Chad Bingham is also missing.

"Are you okay?" Lilly keeps her distance for a moment, standing on the edge of the clearing, wringing her hands nervously, about fifteen feet away from Chad Bingham.

The wiry man in the John Deere cap says nothing for the longest time. He just stands on the edge of the tree line, his head bowed, his back to her, his shoulders slumped as though carrying a great weight.

Minutes before the burial service began, Chad Bingham surprised Lilly by showing up at her tent and asking her if they could talk privately. He said he wanted to set things right. He said he didn't blame her for Sarah's death, and from the heartbreaking look in his eyes, Lilly believed him.

Which is why she followed him up here to a small clearing in the dense grove of trees lining the northern edge of the property. Barely two hundred square feet of pine-needle-matted ground, bordered by mossy stones, the clearing lies under a canopy of foliage, the gray sunlight filtering down in beams of thick dust motes. The cool air smells of decay and animal droppings.

The clearing is far enough away from the tent city to provide privacy.

"Chad—" Lilly wants to say something, wants to tell him how sorry she is. For the first time since she met the man—initially appalled by his willingness to conduct a dalliance with Megan right under his wife's nose—Lilly now sees Chad Bingham as simply human . . . imperfect, scared, emotional, confused, and devastated by the loss of his little girl.

In other words, he's just some good old boy—no better or worse than any of the other survivors. And now Lilly feels a wave of sympathy washing over her. "You want to talk about it?" she asks him at last.

"Yeah, I guess . . . maybe not . . . I don't know." His back still turned, his voice comes out like a leaky faucet, in fits and starts, as faint as water dripping. The sorrow knots his shoulder blades, makes him tremble slightly in the shadows of the pines.

"I'm so sorry, Chad." Lilly ventures closer to him. She has tears in her eyes. "I loved Sarah, she was such a wonderful girl."

He says something so softly Lilly cannot hear it. She moves closer.

She puts her hand gently on the man's shoulder. "I know there's nothing anybody can say . . . a time like this." She speaks to the back of his head. The little plastic strap on the back of his cap says SPALDING. He has a small tattoo of a snake between the cords of his neck. "I know it's no consolation," Lilly adds then, "but Sarah died a hero—she saved the lives of her sisters."

"Did she?" His voice rises barely above a whisper. "She was such a good girl."

"I know she was . . . she was an amazing girl."

"You think so?" His back still turned. Head bowed. Softly shuddering shoulders.

"Yes I do, Chad, she was a hero, she was one in a million."

"Really? You think so?"

"Absolutely."

"Then why didn't you do your *FUCKING JOB*!" Chad turns around and strikes Lilly so hard with the back of his hand that she bites through her tongue. Her head whiplashes, and she sees stars.

Chad hits her again and she stumbles backward, tripping over an exposed root and tumbling to the ground. Chad looms over her, his fists clenching, his eyes blazing. "You stupid, worthless bitch! All you had to do is protect my girls! Fucking chimpanzee could do that!"

Lilly tries to roll away but Chad drives the steel toe of his work boot into her hip, tossing her sideways. Pain stabs her midsection. She gasps for air, her mouth filling with blood. "P-please duh—"

He reaches down and yanks her back to her feet. Holding her up by the front of her sweatshirt, he hisses at her, his sour breath hot on her face, "You and your little slutty friend think this is a party? You smoking dope last night? Huh? HUH?"

Chad smashes a right hook into Lilly's jaw, cracking her teeth and sending her back to the ground. She lands in a heap of agony, two of her ribs cracked, the blood choking her. She can't breathe. Icy cold spreads through her and blurs her vision.

She can barely focus on Chad Bingham's ropy, compact form hovering over her, dropping down on her with tremendous weight, straddling her, the drool of uncontrollable rage leaking out of the corner of his mouth, his spittle flying. "Answer me! You been smoking weed when you're with my kids?"

Lilly feels Chad's powerful grip closing around her throat, the back of her head banging off the ground now. "ANSWER ME, YOU FFFUHHHH—"

Without warning, a third figure materializes behind Chad Bingham—pulling him off Lilly—the identity of this rescuer barely visible.

Lilly only sees a blur of a man so enormous he blots out the rays of the sun.

Josh gets two good handfuls of Chad Bingham's denim jacket and then yanks with all his might.

Either through a sudden spike of adrenaline coursing through the big man, or simply due to Chad's relatively scrawny girth, the resulting heave-ho makes Chad Bingham look like a human cannonball. He soars across the clearing in a high arc, one of his boots flying off, his cap spinning into the trees. He slams shoulder first into an enormous ancient tree trunk. His breath flies out of him, and he flops to the ground in front of the tree. He gasps for breath, blinking with shock.

Josh kneels by Lilly and gently raises her bloody face. She tries to speak but can't get her bleeding lips around the words. Josh lets out a pained breath—a sort of gut-shot moan. Something about seeing that lovely face—with its sea-foam eyes and delicately freckled cheeks, now stippled with blood—sends him into a rage that draws a gauzy filter down over his eyes.

The big man rises, turns, and marches across the clearing to where Chad Bingham lies writhing in pain.

Josh can see only the milky-white blur of the man on the ground, the pale sunlight beaming down through the musty air. Chad makes a feeble attempt to crawl away but Josh easily catches the man's retreating legs, and with a single decisive yank, Chad's body is wrenched back in front of the tree. Josh stands the wiry man up against the trunk.

Chad stammers with blood in his mouth. "This ain't—it ain't none of your—pleeeease—m-my brother—you don't have to DDUHHH—!"

Josh slams the man's flailing body against the bark of the hundred-year-old black oak. The impact cracks the man's skull and dislocates his shoulder blades with the violent abruptness of a battering ram.

Chad lets out a garbled, mucusy cry—more primal and involuntary than conscious—his eyes rolling back in his head. If Chad Bingham were repeatedly hit from behind by a massive battering ram, the series of impacts would not rival the force with which Josh Lee Hamilton now begins slamming the sinewy man in denim against the tree.

"I'm not your brother," Josh says with eerie calm, a low velvety voice from some hidden, inaccessible place deep within him, as he bangs the rag doll of a man against the tree again and again.

Josh rarely loses control like this. Only a handful of times in his life has it happened: Once, on the gridiron when an opposing offensive tackle—a good old boy from Montgomery—called him a nigger . . . and on another occasion when a pickpocket in Atlanta grabbed his mother's purse. But now the quiet storm inside him rages harder than ever before—his actions unmoored and yet somehow controlled—as he repeatedly slams the back of Chad Bingham's cranium against the tree.

Chad's head flops with each impact, the sick thud getting more and more watery now as the back of the skull caves. Vomit roars out of Chad—again an involuntary phenomenon—the particles of cereal and yellow bile looping down, unnoticed, across Josh Lee Hamilton's ham-hock forearms. Josh notices Chad's left hand groping for the grip of his steel-plated Smith & Wesson tucked inside the back of his belt.

Josh easily tears the pistol out of Chad's pants and tosses the weapon across the clearing.

With his last scintilla of strength, his brain sputtering from multiple concussions and the hemorrhage leaking out the back of his fractured skull, Chad Bingham makes a futile attempt to drive a knee up into the big man's groin, but Josh quickly and handily blocks the knee with one forearm, and then delivers an extraordinary blow—a great winding backhand slap, a surreal echo of the slap delivered moments ago to Lilly—which sends Chad Bingham hurling sideways.

Chad sprawls to the ground fifteen feet away from the tree trunk.

Josh can't hear Lilly stumbling across the clearing. He can't hear her strangled voice, "Josh, NO! NO! JOSH, STOP, YOU'RE GOING TO KILL HIM!!"

All at once, Josh Lee Hamilton wakes up, and blinks as though discovering that he's been sleepwalking and has found himself naked and wandering down Peachtree Boulevard during rush hour. He feels Lilly's hands on his back, clawing at his coat, trying to yank him back and away from the man lying in a heap on the ground.

"You're gonna kill him!"

Josh whirls. He sees Lilly—bruised and battered, her mouth full of blood, barely able to stand or breathe or speak—directly behind him, her watery gaze locked on to his. He pulls her into an embrace, his eyes welling with tears. "Are you okay?"

"I'm fine . . . please, Josh . . . you have to stop before you kill him."

Josh starts to say something else but stops himself. He turns and looks down at the man on the ground. Over the course of that terrible, silent pause—as Josh moves his lips but is unable to make a sound or put a thought into words—he sees the deflated body on the ground, lying in a pool of its own fluids, as still and lifeless as a bundle of rags.

FOUR

"Hold still, honey." Bob Stookey gently turns Lilly's head so he can get a better angle on her fat lip. He carefully dabs a pea-sized amount of antibiotic on the split, scabbed flesh. "Almost done."

Lilly jerks at the pain. Bob kneels next to her, his first-aid kit open on the edge of the cot on which Lilly lies prone, staring up at the canvas ceiling. The tent glows with the pale rays of late-afternoon sun, which shine through the stained fabric walls. The air is cold and smells of disinfectant and stale liquor. Lilly has a blanket draped across her bare midriff and bra.

Bob needs a drink. He needs one badly. His hands are shaking again. Lately, he's been flashing back to his days in the U.S. Marine Hospital Corps. One tour in Afghanistan eleven years ago, emptying bedpans at Camp Dwyer—it seems like a million light years away—could never have prepared him for *this*. He was on the sauce back then as well, barely made it out of Medical Education and Training in San Antonio due to the drinking, and now the war has come home for Bob. The shrapnel-riddled bodies he patched in the Middle East were nothing compared to the battlefields left behind in the wake of *this* war. Bob has dreams of Afghanistan sometimes— the walking dead mingling and infecting the ranks of the Taliban in Grand Guignol fashion—the cold, dead, gray arms sprouting from the walls of mobile surgical suites.

But patching Lilly Caul is an altogether different proposition for Bob—far worse than being a battlefield medic or cleaning up the aftermath of a walker attack. Bingham did a number on her. Best Bob can tell, she has at least three busted ribs, a major contusion to her left eye—which may or may not involve a vitreous hemorrhage or even retinal detachment—as well as a nasty series of bruises and lacerations to her face. Bob feels ill-equipped—both in technique and medical supplies—to even *pretend* to treat her. But Bob is the only game in town around here, and so he has now jury-rigged a splint of bedsheets, hardback book covers, and elastic bandages around Lilly's midsection and has applied his dwindling supply of antibiotic cream to her superficial wounds. The eye worries him the most. He needs to watch it, make sure it heals properly.

"There we go," he says, applying the last daub of the cream to her lip.

"Thanks, Bob." Lilly's speech is impeded by the swelling, a slight lisp on the *s*. "You can send your bill to my insurance company."

Bob lets out a humorless chuckle and helps her pull her coat back over her bandaged midsection and bruised shoulders. "What the hell happened out there?"

Lilly sighs, sitting up on the cot, gingerly zipping the coat and cringing at the stabbing pains. "Things got a little . . . carried away."

Bob finds his dented flask of cheap hooch, sits back on his folding chair, and takes a long medicinal swig. "At the risk of stating the obvious . . . this ain't good for anybody."

Lilly swallows as though trying to digest broken glass. Tendrils of her auburn hair dangle in her face. "You're telling me."

"They're meeting right now in the big top about it."

"Who is?"

"Simmons, Hennessey, some of the older guys, Alice Burnside . . . you know . . . sons and daughters of the revolution. Josh is . . . well, I've never seen him like this. He's pretty messed up. Just sitting on the ground outside his tent like a sphinx . . . ain't saying a word . . . just staring into space. Says he'll go along with whatever they decide."

"What does that mean?"

Bob takes another healthy sip of his medicine. "Lilly, this is all new. Somebody murdered a living person. These people ain't dealt with anything like this before."

" 'Murdered'?"

"Lilly—"

"That's what they're calling it now?"

"I'm just saying—"

"I gotta go talk to them." Lilly tries to stand but the pain drives her back to the edge of the cot.

"Whoa there, Kemo sabe. Take it easy." Bob leans over and gently steadies her. "I just gave you enough codeine to calm a Clydesdale."

"Goddammit, Bob, they're not going to lynch Josh for this, I'm not gonna let that happen."

"Let's just take it one step at a time. You ain't goin' nowhere right now."

Lilly lowers her head. A single tear wells up and drips from her good eye. "It was an accident, Bob."

Bob looks at her. "Maybe let's just focus on healing right now, huh?"

Lilly looks up at him. Her busted lip is swollen to three times its normal size, her left eye shot with red, the socket already blackened and bruised. She pulls the collar of her thrift shop overcoat tighter and shivers against the cold. She wears a number of oddball accessories that catch Bob's eye: macramé bracelets and beads and tiny feathers woven into the tendrils of amber locks falling across her devastated face. It's curious to Bob Stookey how a girl can still pay attention to fashion in this world. But that is part of Lilly Caul's charm, part of the fiber of her being. From the little fleur-de-lis tattoo on the back of her neck to the meticulous rips and patches in her jeans, she is one of those girls who can make ten dollars and an afternoon at a secondhand store stretch into an entire wardrobe. "This is all my fault, Bob," she says in a hoarse, somnolent voice.

"That's a load of crap," Bob Stookey counters after taking another pull off the tarnished flask. Maybe the liquor has begun to loosen Bob's lips, because he feels a twinge of bitterness. "My guess is, knowin' that Chad character, he'd been asking for this for a while now."

"Bob, that's not—"

Lilly stops herself when she hears the crunch of footsteps outside the tent. The shadow of a leviathan falls across the canvas. The familiar silhouette pauses for a moment, lurking awkwardly outside the zippered front flap of Bob's tent. Lilly recognizes the figure but says nothing.

A huge hand gently folds back the tent flap and a large, deeply lined brown face peers in. "They said I could—they gave me three minutes," Josh Lee Hamilton says in a choked, sheepish baritone.

"What are you talking about?" Lilly sits up and stares at her friend. "Three minutes for what?"

Josh kneels in front of the tent flap, looking at the ground, struggling to tamp down his emotions. "Three minutes to say good-bye."

"*Good-bye?*"

"Yeah."

"What do you mean, *'good-bye'*? What happened?"

Josh lets out a pained sigh. "They took a vote . . . decided the best way to deal with what happened was to send me packing, kick me outta the group."

"*What!*"

"I suppose it's better than gettin' hung from the highest tree."

"You didn't—I mean—it was completely accidental."

"Yeah, sure," Josh says, staring at the ground. "Poor fella accidentally bumped into my fist a whole bunch of times."

"Under the circumstances, though, these people know what kind of man—"

"Lilly—"

"No, this is wrong. This is just . . . wrong."

"It's over, Lilly."

She looks at him. "Are they letting you take any supplies? One of the vehicles maybe?"

"I got my bike. It'll be okay, I'll be awright . . ."

"No . . . no . . . this is just . . . *ridiculous.*"

"Lilly, listen to me." The big man pushes his way partially into the tent. Bob glances away out of respect. Josh crouches down, reaches out and gently touches Lilly's wounded face. From the way Josh's lips are pressed together, the way his eyes are shimmering, the lines deepening around his mouth, it's clear he's holding in a tidal wave of emotion. "This is how it's gotta play out. It's for the best. I'll be fine. You and Bob hold the fort down."

Lilly's eyes well up. "I'll go with you, then."

"Lilly—"

"There's nothing for me here."

Josh shakes his head. "Sorry, babydoll . . . it's a single ticket."

"I'm coming with you."

"Lilly, I'm real sorry but that ain't in the cards. It's safer here. With the group."

"Yeah, it's real stable here," she says icily. "It's a regular love fest."

"Better here than out there."

Lilly looks at him through ravaged eyes, tears beginning to track down her battered face. "You can't stop me, Josh. It's my decision. I'm coming along and that's all there is to it. And if you try and stop me, I will hunt you down, I will stalk you, I will find you. I'm coming with you and there's nothing you can do about it. You can't stop me. Okay? So just . . . deal with it."

She buttons up her coat, slips her feet into her boots, and starts gathering up her things. Josh watches in dismay. Lilly's movements are tentative, interrupted by intermittent flinches of pain.

Bob exchanges a glance with Josh, something unspoken yet powerful passing between the two men, as Lilly gets all her stray items of clothing stuffed into a duffel bag and pushes her way out of the tent.

Josh lingers in the mouth of the tent for a moment, looking back in at Bob.

Bob finally shrugs and says with a weary smile: *"Women."*

Fifteen minutes later, Josh has the saddlebags of his onyx Suzuki street bike brimming with tins of Spam and tuna fish, road flares, blankets, waterproof matches, rope, a rolled-up pup tent, a flashlight, a small camp stove, a collapsible fishing rod, a small .38 caliber Saturday night special, and some paper plates and spices cribbed from the common area. The day has turned blustery, the sky casting over with ashy dark clouds.

The threatening weather adds another layer of anxiety to the proceedings as Josh secures the luggage bags and glances over his shoulder at Lilly, who stands ten feet away on the edge of the road, shrugging on an overstuffed backpack. She cringes at a sharp pain in her ribs as she tightens the straps on the pack.

From across the property, a handful of self-proclaimed community leaders look on. Three men and a middle-aged woman stand stoically watching. Josh wants to holler something sarcastic and withering to them but holds his tongue. Instead, he turns to Lilly and says, "You ready?"

Before Lilly can answer a voice rings out from the east edge of the property.

"Hold on, folks!"

Bob Stookey comes trundling along the fence with a large canvas duffel slung over his back. The clanking rattle of bottles can be heard—Bob's private stock of "medicine," no doubt—and there's a strange look on the old medic's face, a mixture of anticipation and embarrassment. He approaches cautiously. "Before y'all ride off into the sunset, I got a question for ya."

Josh gives the man a look. "What's going on, Bob?"

"Just answer me one thing," he says. "You got any medical training?"

Lilly comes over, her brow furrowed with confusion. "Bob, what do you need?"

"It's a simple question. Do either of you yahoos got any legitimate medical credentials?"

Josh and Lilly share a glance. Josh sighs. "Not that I know of, Bob."

"Then let me ask you something else. Who in the flying fuck's gonna watch that eye for infection?" He gestures toward Lilly's hemorrhaged eye. "Or keep tabs on them fractured ribs for that matter?"

Josh looks at the medic. "What are you trying to say, Bob?"

The older man shoots a thumb at the row of vehicles parked along the gravel access road behind him. "As long as y'all are gallivanting off into the wild blue yonder, wouldn't it make more sense to do it with a certified U.S. Marine Medical Corpsman?"

They put their stuff in Bob's king cab. The old Dodge Ram pickup is a monster—pocked with rust scars and dents—with a retrofitted camper top on the extended cargo bay. The camper's windows are long and narrow and as opaque as soap glass. Lilly's backpack and Josh's saddlebags go in through the rear hatch, and get wedged between piles of dirty clothes and half-empty bottles of cheap whiskey. There's a pair of rickety cots back there, a large cooler, three battered first-aid kits, a tattered suitcase, a pair of fuel tanks, an old leather doctor's bag that looks like it came from a pawnshop, and a phalanx of garden implements shoved against the firewall in front—shovels, a hoe, a few axes, and a nasty-looking pitchfork. The vaulted ceiling rises high enough to accommodate a slouching adult.

As he stows his bags, Josh sees scattered pieces of a disassembled 12-gauge shotgun, but no sign of any shells. Bob carries a .38 snubnose, which probably couldn't hit a stationary target at ten paces with no wind—and that's if and only if Bob is sober, which is rarely the case. Josh knows they will need firearms and ammunition if they want a fighting chance of survival.

Josh slams the hatch and feels somebody else watching them from across the property.

"Hey, Lil!"

The voice sounds familiar, and when Josh turns around, he sees Megan Lafferty, the girl with the ruddy brown curls and unhinged libido, standing a couple of car lengths away, next to the gravel shoulder. She holds hands with the stoner kid—what's his name?—with the stringy blond hair in his face and the ratty sweater. Steve? Shawn? Josh can't remember. All Josh remembers is putting up with the girl's bed-hopping all the way from Peachtree City.

Now the two slacker kids stand there, watching with buzzard-like intensity.

"Hey, Meg," Lilly says softly, somewhat skeptically, as she comes around the back of the truck and stands next to Josh. The sound of Bob banging around under the truck's hood can be heard in the awkward silence.

Megan and the stoner kid approach cautiously. Megan measures her words as she addresses Lilly: "Dude, I heard you were like taking off for higher ground."

Next to Megan the stoner giggles softly. "Always up for getting *higher.*"

Josh shoots the kid a look. "What can we do for you fine young people?"

Megan doesn't take her eyes off Lilly. "Lil, I just wanted to say . . . like . . . I hope you're not like pissed at me or anything."

"Why would I be pissed at *you*?"

Megan looks down. "I said some things the other day, I wasn't really thinking straight . . . I just wanted to . . . I don't know. Just wanted to say I was sorry."

Josh glances over at Lilly, and in that brief moment of silence before she responds, he sees the essence of Lilly Caul in a single instant. Her bruised face softens. Her eyes fill with forgiveness. "You don't have to be sorry for anything, Meg," Lilly tells her friend. "We're all just trying to keep our shit together."

"He really fucked you up bad," Megan says, pondering the ravages of Lilly's face.

"Lilly, we gotta get going," Josh chimes in. "Gonna be dark soon."

The stoner kid whispers to Megan, "You gonna ask them or what?"

"Ask us what, Meg?" Lilly says.

Megan licks her lips. She looks up at Josh. "It's totally fucked up, the way they're treating you."

Josh gives her a terse nod. "Appreciate it, Megan, but we really have to be taking off."

"Take us with you."

Josh looks at Lilly, and Lilly stares at her friend. Finally Lilly says, "Um, see, the thing is . . ."

"Safety in fucking numbers, man," the stoner kid enthuses with his dry little nervous pot giggle. "We're like totally in *warrior mode*—"

Megan shoots her hand up. "Scott, would you put a cork in it for *two minutes*." She looks up at Josh. "We can't stay here with these fascist assholes. Not after what happened. It's a fucking mess here, people don't trust each other anymore."

Josh crosses his big arms across his barrel chest, looking at Megan. "You've done your share to stir things up."

"Josh—" Lilly starts to intercede.

Megan suddenly looks down with a crestfallen expression. "No, it's okay. I deserve that. I guess I just . . . I just forgot what the rules are."

In the ensuing silence—the only sounds the wind in the trees and the squeaking noises of Bob futzing under the hood—Josh rolls his eyes. He can't believe what he's about to agree to. "Get your stuff," he says finally, "and be quick about it."

Megan and Scott ride in back. Bob drives, with Josh on the passenger side and Lilly in the narrow enclosure in the rear of the cab. The truck has a modified sleeping berth behind the front seat with smaller side doors and a flip-down upholstered bench that doubles as a bed. Lilly sits on the tattered bench seat and braces herself on the handrail, every bump and swerve coaxing a stabbing pain in her ribs.

She can see the tree line on either side of the road darkening as they drive down the winding access road that leads out of the orchards, the shadows of late afternoon lengthening, the temperature plummeting. The truck's noisy heater fights a losing battle against the chill. The air in the cab smells of stale liquor, smoke, and body odors. Through the vents, the scent of tobacco fields and rotting fruit—the musk of a Georgia autumn—is faintly discernible, a warning to Lilly, a harbinger of cutting loose from civilization.

She starts looking for walkers in the trees—every shadow, every dark place a potential menace. The sky is void of planes or birds of any species, the heavens as cold, dead, and silent as a vast gray glacier.

They make their way onto Spur 362—the main conduit that cuts through Meriwether County—as the sun sinks lower on the horizon. Due to the proliferation of wrecks and abandoned cars, Bob takes it nice and easy, keeping the truck down around thirty-five miles an hour. The two-lane turns blue-gray in the encroaching dusk, the twilight spreading across the rolling hills of white pine and soybeans.

"What's the plan, captain?" Bob asks Josh after they've put a mile and a half behind them.

"Plan?" Josh lights a cigar and rolls down the window. "You

must be mistaking me for one of them battlefield commanders you used to sew up in Iraq."

"I was never in Iraq," Bob says. He has a flask between his legs. He sneaks a sip. "Did a nickel's worth in Afghanistan, and to be honest with ya, that place is looking better and better to me."

"All I can tell ya is, they told me to get outta town, and that's what I'm doin'."

They pass a crossroads, a sign that says FILBURN ROAD, a dusty, desolate farm path lined with ditches, running between two tobacco fields. Josh makes note of it and starts thinking about the wisdom of being on the open road after dark. He starts to say, "I'm startin' to think, though, maybe we shouldn't stray too far from—"

"Josh!" Lilly's voice pierces the rattling drone of the cab. "Walkers—look!"

Josh realizes that she's pointing at the distant highway ahead of them, at a point maybe five hundred yards away. Bob slams on the brakes. The truck skids, throwing Lilly against the seat. Sharp pain like a jagged piece of glass slices through her ribs. The muffled thump of Megan and Scott slamming into the firewall in back penetrates the cab.

"Son of a buck!" Bob grips the steering wheel with weathered, wrinkled hands, his knuckles turning white with pressure as the truck idles noisily. "Son of a five-pointed *buck*!"

Josh sees the cluster of zombies in the distance, at least forty or fifty of them—maybe more, the twilight can play tricks—swarming around an overturned school bus. From this distance, it looks as though the bus has spilled clumps of wet clothing, through which the dead are sorting busily. But it quickly becomes clear the lumps are human remains. And the walkers are feeding.

And the victims are children.

"We could just ram our way through 'em," Bob ventures.

"No . . . no," Lilly says. "You serious?"

"We could go around 'em."

"I don't know." Josh tosses the cigar through the vent, his pulse quickening. "Them ditches on either side are steep, could roll us over."

"What do you suggest?"

"What do you have in the way of shells for that squirrel gun you got back there?"

Bob lets out a tense breath. "Got one box of pigeon shot, 25-grain, about a million years old. What about that peashooter?"

"Just what's in the cylinder, I think there's five rounds left and that's it."

Bob glances in the rearview mirror. Lilly sees his deeply lined eyes sparking with panic. Bob is looking at Lilly when he says, "Thoughts?"

Lilly says, "Okay, so even if we take out most of them, the noise is gonna draw a swarm. You ask me, I say we avoid them altogether."

Right then, a muffled thudding noise makes Lilly jump. Her ribs twinge as she twists around. In the narrow little window on the back wall of the cab, Megan's pale, anxious face hovers. She pounds her palm on the glass and mouths the words *What the fuck?*

"Hold on! It's okay! Just hold on!" Lilly yells through the glass, then turns to Josh. "Whaddaya think?"

Josh looks out his window at the long, rust-dimpled mirror. In the oblong reflection, he sees the lonely crossroads about three hundred yards back, barely visible in the dying light. "Back up," he says.

Bob looks at him. "Say what?"

"Back up . . . hurry. We're gonna take that side road back there."

Bob jacks the lever into reverse and steps on it. The truck lurches. The engine whines, the gravitational tug pulling everybody forward.

Bob bites his lower lip as he wrestles the steering wheel, using the side mirror to guide him, the truck careening backward, the front end fishtailing, the gears screaming. The rear end approaches the crossroads.

Bob locks up the brakes and Josh slams into his seat as the truck's rear end skids off the far shoulder of the two-lane, tangling with a knot of wild dogwood, cattails, and mayapple, sending up a cloud of leaves and debris. No one hears the shuffling sounds of something dead stirring behind the scrub brush.

No one hears the faint scrape of the dead thing lumbering out of the foliage and clamping its dead fingers around the king cab's rear bumper until it's too late.

Inside the rear camper compartment, each of them tumbling to the floor in the violent pitching motions of the truck, each of them giggling hysterically, Megan and Scott are oblivious to the zombie now attached to the running board in the rear. As the Dodge Ram slams into drive and blasts down the perpendicular dirt road, they each climb back onto their makeshift seats fashioned out of peach crates, each still giggling furiously.

The air inside the cramped camper is blue from the haze of an entire bowl of sativa weed, which Scott fired up ten minutes ago. He's been conserving his stash, nursing it, dreading the inevitable day he would run out and would have to figure out how to grow it in the sandy clay.

"You just farted when you fell," Scott chortles at Megan, his eyes already dreamy and blistered with a major buzz humming behind his eyes.

"I most certainly did not," she counters in her uncontrollable giggle, trying to balance herself on the crate. "That was my fucking shoe scraping the fucking floor."

"Bullshit, dude, you *so* farted."

"Did not."

"You did, you *so did*—you just ripped one, and it was such a girl fart."

Megan roars with laughter. "What the fucking hell is a girl fart?"

Scott guffaws. "It's—it's kinda like—kinda like a cute little toot. Like a little train engine. *Toot-toot.* The little fart that could . . ."

They both bend over with an uncontainable spasm of hilarity as a livid, milky-eyed face rises up like a small moon in the dark surface of the window at the rear of the camper. This one is male and middle-aged and nearly bald, its scalp mapped with deep blue veins and wisps of mildew-gray hair.

Neither Megan nor Scott sees it at first. They don't see the wind blowing its mossy strands of thinning hair, or its greasy lips peeling back to expose blackened teeth, or the fumbling of insensate, rotting fingers as they push through the gap in the partially sprung hatch.

"OH, SHIT!" Scott blurts the words out on a stutter of sputtering laughter when he sees the intruder boarding. "OH, SHIT!!"

Megan now doubles over with convulsive laughter as Scott spins and falls on his face and then scuttles madly across the narrow floor space on his hands and knees toward the garden implements. He's not laughing anymore. The zombie is already halfway inside the camper. The sound of its buzz-saw snarl and the stench of its decomposed tissues fill the air. Megan finally sees the intruder and she starts to cough and wheeze, her laughter garbling slightly.

Scott reaches for the pitchfork. The truck swerves. The zombie—all the way inside now—stumbles drunkenly sideways and slams into the wall. A stack of crates tumbles. Scott gets the pitchfork up and moving.

Megan scuttles backward, sliding along on her ass, burrowing into the far corner. The terror in her eyes seems incongruous with her high-pitched, hiccupping giggles. Like a motor that won't stop turning, her garbled, deranged laughter continues as Scott stands up on wobbling knees and lunges with the pitchfork as hard as he can in the general direction of the moving corpse in front of him.

The rusty tines strike the side of the thing's face as it's turning.

One of the spikes impales the zombie's left eye. The other points go into the mandible and jugular. Black blood ejaculates across the camper. Scott lets out a war cry and pulls the implement free. The zombie staggers backward toward the windblown hatch—which is flapping now—and for some reason, the second blow gets a huge, convulsive, crazed laugh out of Megan.

The tines sink into the thing's skull.

This is so goddamn hilarious to Megan: the funny dead man shuddering as though electrocuted, with the fork sunk in his skull, his arms reaching impotently at the air. Like a silly circus clown in whiteface, with big goofy black teeth, the thing staggers backward for a moment, until the wind pressure pulls it out of the flapping rear hatch.

The pitchfork slips free of Scott's grasp and the zombie tumbles off the truck. Scott falls on his ass, landing in a pile of clothes.

Both Megan and Scott crack up now at the absurdity of the

zombie careening to the road with the pitchfork still planted in its skull. They both scuttle on hands and knees to the rear hatch and gaze out at the human remains receding into the distance behind them—the pitchfork still sticking straight out of its head like a mile marker.

Scott pulls the hatch shut and they both crack up again in spasms of stoned laughter and frenzied coughing.

Still giggling, her eyes wet, Megan turns toward the front of the camper. Through the cab window, she can see the backs of Lilly's and Josh's heads. They look preoccupied—oblivious to what just occurred only inches away from them. They appear to be pointing at something in the distance, way up on the crest of an adjacent hill.

Megan can't believe that nobody in the cab heard the commotion in the rear camper. Was the road noise that loud? Was the struggle drowned out by the sound of giggling? Megan is about to bang on the glass when she finally sees what all the pointing is about.

Bob is turning off the road and heading up a steep dirt path toward a building that may or may not be abandoned.

FIVE

The deserted gas station sits at the top of a hill overlooking the surrounding orchards. Bordered on three sides by weed-whiskered clapboard fencing and scattered garbage Dumpsters, the place has a hand-painted sign over its twin fuel islands—one diesel and three gas pumps—which says FORTNOY'S FUEL AND BAIT. The single-story building features a flyspecked office, a retail store, and a small service garage with a single lift.

When Bob pulls in to the cracked cement lot—his lights off in order to avoid detection—night has fallen into full darkness, and the king cab's tires crunch on broken glass. Megan and Scott peer out of the rear hatch, taking in the shadows of the abandoned property, as Bob pulls the truck around behind the garage area, out of the line of vision of any nosy passersby.

He parks the truck between the carcass of a wrecked sedan and a pillar of tires. A moment later, the engine cuts off and Megan hears the squeak of the passenger door and the heavy thud of Josh Lee Hamilton stepping out and coming around the back of the camper.

"Y'all stay put for a second," Josh says softly, evenly, after opening the camper door and seeing Megan and Scott crouched near the hatch like a couple of owls. Josh doesn't notice the blood spatters on the walls. He checks the cylinder of his .38, the blue steel gleaming in the darkness. "Gonna check this place for walkers."

"I don't mean to be rude but *what the fuck*?" Megan says, her buzz completely gone now, replaced by a kind of jagged adrenaline surge.

"Didn't you guys see what happened back here? Didn't you hear what was going on?"

Josh looks at her. "All I heard was a couple of potheads partying to beat the band—smells like Mardi Gras in a whorehouse back here."

Megan tells him what happened.

Josh gives Scott a look. "Surprised you had the wherewithal . . . your brain scrambled like that." Josh's expression softens. He lets out a sigh and smiles at the kid. "Congratulations, junior."

Scott gives him a cockeyed little grin. "My first kill, boss."

"Chances are it won't be your last," Josh says, snapping the cylinder shut.

"Can I just like ask one more thing?" Megan says then. "What're we *doing* here? I thought we had enough gas."

"It's too hairy out there for night travel. Best to hunker down till morning. Gonna need you two to stay put until you get the all clear."

Josh walks off.

Megan shuts the door. In the darkness, she feels Scott's gaze on her. She turns and looks at him. He has a weird look in his eyes. She grins at him. "Dude, I gotta admit, you *are* pretty damn handy with the garden tools—pretty goddamn bad-ass with that pitchfork."

He grins back at her. Something changes in his eyes, as though he sees her for the first time—despite the darkness—and he licks his lips. He wipes a strand of dirty blond hair from his eyes. "It was nothing."

"Yeah, right." For a while now, Megan has been marveling at how much Scott Moon resembles Kurt Cobain. The resemblance seems to radiate off him with atavistic magic, his face shimmering in the darkness, his scent—patchouli oil and smoke and sweet-leaf and bubble gum—casting out and swirling in Megan's brain.

She grabs him and mashes her lips on top of his, and he pulls her hair, and grinds his mouth into hers, and soon their tongues are intertwined and their midsections are gnashing against each other.

"Fuck me," she whispers.

"Here?" he utters. "Now?"

"Maybe not," she says, looking around, breathless. Her heart races. "Let's wait until he's done inside and we'll find a place."

"Cool," he says, and he reaches out and fondles her through her torn Grateful Dead T-shirt. She jams her tongue in his mouth. Megan needs him now, this instant—she needs relief, badly.

She pulls away. In the darkness, the twosome stare at each other, breathing hard, like wild animals that would kill each other if they weren't the same species.

Megan and Scott find a place to consummate their lust only moments after Josh issues the all clear.

The two stoners don't fool anybody, in spite of their perfunctory attempts to be discreet: Megan feigns exhaustion and Scott suggests that he fix her a place to sleep on the floor of the storeroom in the rear of the retail shop. The cramped storage area—two hundred square feet of mildewed tile and exposed plumbing—reeks of dead fish and cheese bait. Josh tells them to be careful and rolls his eyes as he walks away, disgusted, and maybe, just maybe, a little jealous.

The thumping sounds start up almost immediately, even before Josh returns to the office, where Lilly and Bob are unpacking a knapsack full of supplies for the night. "What the hell is that?" Lilly asks the big man when he returns.

Josh shakes his head. The muffled thudding noises of two bodies going at it in the other room reverberate through the tight quarters of the filling station. Every few moments, a gasp or a moan swells above the rhythmic fucking sounds. "Young love," he says with exasperation.

"You gotta be kidding me." Lilly stands shivering in the dark front office as Bob Stookey nervously unpacks bottled water and blankets from a crate, pretending not to hear the carnal noises. Lilly holds herself as though she might disintegrate at any moment. "So this is what we have to look forward to?"

The power at Fortnoy's is down, the fuel reservoirs empty, and the air in the building as cold as a walk-in refrigerator. The retail shop appears to be picked clean. Even the filthy refrigerator is emptied of earthworms and minnows. The front office features a dusty rack of magazines, a single vending machine running low on stale candy bars and bags of chips, rolls of toilet paper, a few overturned plastic contour chairs, a shelf of antifreeze and car deodorizers, and a scarred wooden counter on which sits a cash register that looks like it belongs in the Smithsonian. The register's drawer is open and empty.

"Maybe they'll get it out of their systems." Josh checks his last cigar, which sits partially burned down in his jacket pocket. He glances around the office for a smoke rack. The place looks ransacked. "Looks like the Fortnoy boys left in a hurry."

Lilly touches her bruised eye. "Yeah, I guess the looters got here before we did."

"How you holdin' up?" Josh asks her.

"I'll live."

Bob glances up from his crate of supplies. "Have a seat, Lillygirl." He positions one of the contour chairs against the window. The light of the harvest moon shines in and stripes the floor in silver dusty shadows as Bob cleans his hands with a sterile wipe. "Let's check them bandages."

Josh watches as Lilly takes a seat and Bob opens a first-aid kit.

"Hold still now," Bob admonishes softly as he carefully dabs an alcohol wipe around the crusty edges of Lilly's injured eye. The skin under her brow has swollen to the size of a hardboiled egg. Lilly keeps flinching, and that bothers Josh. He bites back the urge to go to her, to hold her, to stroke her downy soft hair. The sight of those wavy mahogany tendrils dangling down across her narrow, delicate, bruised face is killing the big man.

"Ouch!" Lilly cringes. "Go easy, Bob."

"Got a nasty shiner there, but if we can keep it clean, you oughtta be good to go."

"Go where?"

"That's a damn good question." Bob carefully unhooks the Ace bandage around her ribs, gently palpates the bruised areas with his fingertips. Lilly flinches again. "Ribs ought to heal on their own, as long as you don't get into any wrestling matches or marathon races."

Bob replaces the elastic bandage around her midriff, then puts a fresh butterfly bandage on her eye. Lilly gazes up at the big man. "What are you thinking, Josh?"

Josh looks around the place. "We'll spend the night here, take turns keeping watch."

Bob tears off a piece of surgical tape. "Gonna get colder than a witch's boob in here."

Josh sighs. "Saw a generator in the garage, and we got blankets. Place is pretty secure and we're up high enough on this ridge to see any large numbers of them things forming out there before they get to us."

Bob finishes up and closes the first-aid kit. The muffled sounds of fornication dwindle in the other room, a momentary break in the action. In that brief stretch of silence, over the sound of the wind rattling the signage out front, Josh hears the distant a cappella of the dead—that faint telltale throb of dead vocal cords—like a broken pipe organ, moaning and gurgling in atonal unison. The noise stiffens the tiny hairs on the back of his neck.

Lilly listens to the distant chorus. "They're multiplying, aren't they?"

Josh shrugs. "Who knows."

Bob reaches into the pocket of his tattered down coat. He roots out his flask, thumbs off the cap, and takes a healthy swig. "You think they smell us?"

Josh goes over to the grimy front window and gazes out at the night. "I think all the activity at Camp Bingham's been drawing 'em out of the woodwork for weeks now."

"How far from base camp are we, ya think?"

"Not much more than a mile or so, as the crow flies." Josh gazes out over the pinnacles of distant pines, their swaying ocean of boughs as dense as black lace. The sky has cleared, and now the heavens are spangled with a riot of icy-cold stars.

Across the needlework of constellations rise wisps of wood smoke from the tent city.

"Been thinking about something . . ." Josh turns and looks at his companions. "This place ain't the Ritz but if we can do a little scavenging, maybe find some more ammunition for the guns . . . we might be better off staying put for a while."

The notion hangs in the silent office for a moment, sinking in.

———

The next morning, after a long, restless night sleeping on the cold cement floor of the service bay—making do with threadbare blankets and taking shifts standing guard—they have a group meeting to decide what to do. Over cups of instant coffee prepared on Bob's Coleman stove, Josh convinces them that the best thing to do is stay holed up there for the time being. Lilly can heal up, and if necessary, they can steal provisions from the nearby tent city.

By this point, nobody puts up much of a fight. Bob has discovered a stash of whiskey under a counter in the bait shop, and Megan and Scott alternate between getting high and "spending quality time" in the back room for hours on end. They work hard that first day to secure the place. Josh decides against running the generator indoors for fear of gassing them to death with the fumes, and worries about running it outdoors for fear of drawing unwanted attention. He finds a wood-burning stove in the storeroom and a pile of lumber scraps out behind one of the Dumpsters.

Their second night at Fortnoy's Fuel and Bait, they get the temperature up to tolerable levels in the service area by keeping the stove going full blast, and Megan and Scott noisily keep each other warm in the back room under layers of blankets. Bob gets drunk enough not to notice the cold, but he seems disturbed by the muffled bumping sounds coming from the storeroom. Eventually, the older man gets so loaded he can barely move. Lilly helps him into his bedroll as though putting a child down for the night. She even sings a lullaby to him—a Joni Mitchell song, "The Circle Game"—as she tucks the mildewed blanket around his aging, wattled neck. Oddly, she feels responsible for Bob Stookey, even though *he's* the one who's supposed to be nursing *her*.

Over the next few days, they reinforce the doors and windows, and they wash themselves in the big galvanized sinks in the rear of the garage. They settle into a sort of grudging routine. Bob winterizes his truck, cannibalizing parts off some of the wrecks, and Josh supervises regular reconnaissance missions to the outer edges of the tent city a mile to the west. Under the campers' noses, Josh and Scott are able to steal firewood, fresh water, a few discarded tent rolls, some canned vegetables, a box of shotgun shells, and a case of Sterno. Josh notices the fabric of civilized behavior straining at the seams in the tent city. He hears more and more arguments. He sees fistfights among some of the men, and heavy drinking going on. The stress is taking its toll on the settlers.

During the darkness of night, Josh keeps a tight lid on Fortnoy's Fuel and Bait. He and the others stay inside, keeping as quiet as possible, burning a minimum number of emergency candles and lanterns, jumping at the intermittent noises caused by the increasing winds. Lilly Caul finds herself wondering which is the deadlier menace—the zombie hordes, her fellow human beings, or the encroaching winter. The nights are getting longer and the cold is setting in. It's forming rimes of frost on the windows and getting into people's joints, and although no one talks about it much, the cold is the silent menace that could actually destroy them far easier and more efficiently than any zombie attack.

In order to fight the boredom and constant undercurrents of fear, some of the inhabitants of Fortnoy's develop hobbies. Josh begins rolling homemade cigars out of tobacco leaves that he harvests from neighboring fields. Lilly starts a diary, and Bob finds a treasure trove of old fishing lures in an unmarked trunk in the bait shop. He spends hours in the ransacked retail shop, perched at a workbench in back, compulsively winding fly-fishing lures for future use. Bob plans to bag some nice trout, redfish, or walleyes in the shallows of a nearby river. He keeps the bottle of Jack Daniel's under the bench at all times, tippling from it day and night.

The others notice the rate at which Bob is going through the hooch, but who can blame him? Who can blame anybody for drowning his nerves in this cruel purgatory? Bob is not proud of his drinking. In fact, he's downright ashamed of it. But that's why he needs the medicine—to stave off the shame, and the loneliness, and the fear, and the horrible night terrors of blood-spattered bunkers in Kandahar.

On Friday of that week, in the wee hours of the night—Bob notes in his paper calendar that the date is November 9—he finds himself back at the workbench in the rear of the shop, winding flies, getting shit-faced as usual, when he hears the shuffling noises coming from the storeroom. He hadn't noticed Megan and Scott slipping away earlier that evening, nor had he detected the telltale odors of marijuana residue cooking in a pipe, nor had he heard the muffled giggling coming through the thin walls. But now he notices something else that had eluded his attention that day.

He stops fiddling with the lures and glances across the rear corner of the room. Behind a large, battered propane tank, a gaping hole in the wall is clearly visible in the flickering light of Bob's lantern. He pushes himself away from the bench and goes over to the tank. He shoves it aside and kneels down in front of a six-inch patch of missing wallboard. The hole looks like it was formed by water damage, or perhaps the buckling of plaster during the humid Georgia summers. Bob glances over his shoulder, making sure he's alone. The others are fast asleep in the service area.

The groans and gasps of wild sex draw Bob's attention back to the damaged wall.

He peers through the six-inch gap and into the storeroom, where the dim light of a battery-operated lantern throws moving shadows up and across the low ceiling. The shadows pump and thrust in the darkness. Bob licks his lips. He leans in closer to the hole, nearly falling over in his drunken state, bracing himself against the propane tank. He can see a small portion of Scott Moon's pimpled ass rising and falling in the yellow light, Megan beneath the young man, legs spread, her toes curling with ecstasy.

Bob Stookey feels his heart pinch in his chest, his breath sticking in his craw.

The thing that mesmerizes him the most is not the naked abandon with which the two lovers are going at each other, nor is it the animalistic grunts and mewls filling the air. The thing that holds Bob Stookey rapt is the sight of Megan Lafferty's olive skin in the lamplight, her russet curls splayed across the blanket beneath her head, her hair as lustrous and shiny as honey. Bob can't stop gaping at her, the longing welling up inside him.

He can't tear his gaze from her, even when a floorboard creaks behind him.

"Oh—Bob—I'm sorry—I didn't . . ."

The voice comes from the shadows of the doorway across the retail shop, from the passageway into the front office, and when Bob jerks away from the hole in the wall, whirling around to face his inquisitor, he nearly falls over. He has to hold on to the propane tank. "I wasn't trying to—this ain't—I—I ain't—"

"It's okay—I was just—I wanted to make sure you were okay." Lilly stands in the doorway dressed in her sweatshirt, knit scarf, and sweatpants—her sleeping attire—averting her bandaged face, looking away, her eyes filled with an awkward combination of pity and disgust. The bruising around her eyes has gone down quite a bit. She's moving around a lot better, her ribs healing.

"Lilly, I wasn't—" Bob staggers toward her, holding his big hands up in a gesture of contrition, when he trips on a loose floorboard. He tumbles, sprawling to the floor and letting out a gasp. Amazingly, the carnal noises continue unabated in the adjacent room—an arrhythmic cadence of huffing and slapping flesh.

"Bob, are you okay?" Lilly rushes over to him, kneels, and tries to help him up.

"I'm fine, I'm fine." He gently pushes her away. He rises drunkenly to his feet. He can't look her in the eye. He doesn't know what to do with his hands. He glances across the room. "I thought I heard something suspicious coming from outside."

"Suspicious?" Lilly gazes at the floor, at the wall—anywhere but at Bob. "Oh . . . okay."

"Yeah, it was nothing."

"Oh . . . that's good." Lilly slowly backs away. "Just wanted to make sure you were okay."

"I'm good, I'm good. It's getting late, I'm thinking I'll turn in."

"Good, Bob. You do that."

Lilly turns and makes a hasty exit, leaving Bob Stookey alone in the lantern light. He stands there for a moment, staring at the floor. Then he moves slowly across the room to the bench. He finds the bottle of Jack, thumbs off the cap, and raises it to his lips.

He downs the remaining fingers of booze in three breathless gulps.

"I'm just wondering what's gonna happen when he runs out of booze."

Bundled in her ski jacket and knit beret, Lilly follows Josh down a narrow path winding between columns of pines. Josh makes his way through the foliage, the 12-gauge cradled in his huge arms, moving toward a dry creek bed strewn with boulders and dead-fall. He wears his ratty lumberjack coat and stocking cap, his breath showing as he talks. "He'll find some more . . . don't worry about old Bob . . . juicers always manage to find more juice. To be honest, I'm more worried about us running out of food."

The woods are as silent as a chapel as they approach the banks of the creek. The first snow of the season filters down through the high boughs above them, swirling on the wind, sticking to their faces.

They've been at Fortnoy's for almost two weeks now, and have gone through over half the supply of drinking water and nearly all the canned goods. Josh has decided it's probably best to use up their single box of shotgun shells on killing a deer or a rabbit rather than defending themselves against a zombie attack. Besides, the camp-fires, noise, and activity at the tent city have drawn most of the walker activity away from the gas station in recent days. Josh is now calling upon his childhood memories of hunting with his uncle Vernon up on Briar Mountain in order to get the scent back, get the old skills back. Once upon a time, Josh was an eagle-eyed hunter. But now, with this broken-down squirrel gun and frozen fingers . . . who knows?

"I worry about him, Josh," Lilly says. "He's a good man but he's got issues."

"Don't we all." Josh glances over his shoulder at Lilly coming down the hill, carefully stepping over a fallen log. She looks strong for the first time since the incident with Chad Bingham. Her face has healed nicely, barely showing any discoloration. The swelling has gone down around her eye, and she's no longer limping or fa-voring her right side. "He sure fixed you up nice."

"Yeah, I'm feeling a lot better."

Josh pauses on the edge of the creek and waits for her. She joins him. He sees tracks in the hard-packed mud at the bottom of the creek bed. "Looks like we got a deer crossing here. I'm thinkin' we follow the creek, ought to meet up with a critter or two."

"Can we take a quick rest first?"

"You bet," Josh says, motioning for her to have a seat on a log. She sits. He joins her, holding the shotgun across his lap. He lets out a sigh. He feels a tremendous urge to put his arm around her. What is *wrong* with him? Stricken with puppy love like some stupid teenager in the midst of all these horrors?

Josh looks down. "I like the way you take care of each other, you and old Bob."

"Yeah, and you take care of all of us."

Josh lets out a sigh. "Wish I could have taken better care of my mama."

Lilly looks at him. "You never told me what happened."

Josh takes a deep breath. "Like I told you, she was pretty sick for quite a few years . . . thought I was gonna lose her a few times . . . but she lived long enough to—" He stops, the sorrow ratcheting his insides, swelling up in him, surprising him with its suddenness.

Lilly sees the pain in his eyes. "It's okay, Josh, if you don't want to—"

He makes a feeble gesture, a wave of his big brown hand. "I don't mind telling you what happened. I was still trying to get into work each morning at that point, still trying to get a paycheck in the early days of the Turn, just a few biter sightings back then. I ever tell you what I do? My profession?"

"You told me you were a cook."

He gives her a nod. "Pretty serious one, if I do say so myself." He looks at her, his voice softening. "Always wanted to fix you a proper dinner." His eyes moisten. "My mama taught me the basics, rest her soul, taught me how to make a bread pudding that would bring tears to your eyes and joy to your belly."

Lilly smiles at him, then her smile fades. "What happened to your mom, Josh?"

He stares at the dusting of snow on the matted leaves for quite some time, marshaling the energy to tell the story. "Muhammad Ali's got nothing on my mama . . . she was a fighter, she fought that sickness like a champ, for years. But *sweet*? She was sweet as the day is long. Shaggy dogs and misfits—she would take anybody in, the raggiest-ass individuals, hardened panhandlers, homeless, it didn't matter. She would take 'em in and call 'em 'honey child' and make them corn bread and sweet tea until they stole from her or got in a fight in her front parlor."

"Sounds like she was a saint, Josh."

Another shrug. "Wasn't the best living conditions for me and my sisters, I'll be honest with ya. We moved around a lot, different schools, and every day we would come home and find our place filled with strangers, but I loved the old gal."

"I can see why."

Josh swallows hard. Here it comes. The bad part, the part that haunts his dreams to this day. He gazes at the snow on the leaves. "It happened on a Sunday. I knew my mama was failing, wasn't thinking straight. One doctor told us it was Alzheimer's comin' on. At this point, the dead was getting into the projects, but they still had the warning sirens comin' on, announcements and shit. Our street was blocked off that day. When I left for work, Mama was just sittin' at the window, staring out at them things slipping through the cordons, getting picked off by them SWAT guys. I didn't think anything of it. I figured she'd be okay."

He pauses, and Lilly doesn't say anything. It's clear to both of them that he has to share this with another human being or it will continue to eat away at him. "I tried to call her later that day. Guess the lines were down. Figured no news was good news. I think it was about five-thirty when I knocked off that day."

He swallows the lump in his throat. He can feel Lilly's gaze on him.

"I was rounding the corner at the top of my street. I flash my ID at the guys at the roadblock when I notice a lot of activity down the block. SWAT guys coming and going. Right in front of my building. I pull up. They holler at me to get the hell outta there and I tell them, hey, man, ease on back, I live here. They let me through. I see the front door to our apartment building wide open. Cops coming out and going in. Some of them carrying . . ."

Josh chokes on the words. He breathes. Braces himself. Wipes moisture from his eyes. "Some of them was carrying—*whattyacallem*—specimen containers? For human organs and such? I run up the stairs two at a time. I think I knocked over one of them cops. I get to our door on the second floor and there's these dudes in hazmat suits blocking the entrance and I shove 'em aside and go in and I see . . ."

Josh feels the sorrow creeping up his gorge, strangling him. He pauses to take a breath. His tears burn and track down his chin.

"Josh, you don't have to—"

"No, it's awright, I need to . . . what I saw in there . . . I knew right off the bat what had happened. I knew the second I saw that window open and the table set. Mama had her wedding dishes out. You would not *believe* the blood. I mean, the place was painted in it." He feels his voice cracking, and he swims against the tide of tears. "There was at least six of them things on the floor. SWAT guys must've took 'em out. There was . . . not much left of Mama." He chokes. Swallows. Flinches at the searing pain in his chest. "There was . . . pieces of her on the table. With the good china. I saw . . . I saw . . . her fingers . . . all chewed up next to the gravy boat . . . what was left of her body . . . slumped in a chair . . . her head was all lolled over to one side . . . neck opened up—"

"Okay . . . Josh, you don't need to . . . I'm sorry . . . I'm so sorry."

Josh looks at her as though seeing her face in a new light, hovering there in the diffuse, snowy radiance, her eyes far away, as though in a dream.

Through her tears, Lilly Caul meets the big man's gaze and her heart clenches. She wants to hold him, she wants to comfort this gentle colossus, stroke his massive shoulders and tell him it's all going to be all right. She has never felt this close to another human being and it's killing her. She doesn't deserve his friendship, his loyalty, his protection, his love. What does she say? Your mama's in a better place now? She refuses to diminish this terribly profound moment with stupid clichés.

She starts to say something else when Josh speaks up again in a low, drained, defeated voice, not taking his eyes off her. "She invited

them things in for corn bread and beans . . . she took them in . . .
like shaggy dogs . . . because that's what she does. Loves all God's
creatures." The big man slumps and his shoulders tremble as tears
drip off his grizzled jaw and onto the front of his Salvation Army
lumber jacket. "Probably called them 'honey-child' . . . right up until the moment they ate her."

Then the big man lowers his head and lets out an alarming
sound—half sob, half insane laughter—as the tears stream down
his enormous, sculpted brown face.

Lilly moves closer. She puts her hand on his shoulder. She says
nothing at first. She touches his gigantic hands, which are clasped
around the shotgun across his lap. He looks up at her, his expression a mask of emotional ruin. "Sorry I'm so . . ." he utters in barely
a whisper.

"It's okay, Josh. It's okay. I'm here for you always. I'm with you
now."

He cocks his head, wipes his face, and manages a broken smile.
"I guess you are."

She kisses him—quickly, but on the lips—a little more than a
friendly smack. The kiss lasts maybe a couple of seconds.

Josh drops the gun, puts his arms around her, and returns the
gesture, and the contrary emotions flow through Lilly as the big
man lets his lips linger on hers. She feels herself floating on the
windswept snow. She can't sort out the undercurrent of feelings
making her dizzy. Does she pity this man? Is she manipulating
him again? He tastes like coffee and smoke and Juicy Fruit gum.
The cold snow touches Lilly's eyelashes, the warmth of Josh's lips
melting the chill. He has done so much for her. She owes him her
life ten times over. She opens her mouth, presses her chest against
his, and then he pulls away.

"What's wrong?" She looks up at him, searches his big sad brown
eyes. Did she do something wrong? Did she step over a line?

"Nothing at all, babydoll." He smiles and leans down and kisses
her cheek. It's a warm kiss—soft, tender, a promise of more to come.
"Timing, you know," he says then. He picks up the shotgun. "Not
safe here . . . don't feel right."

For a moment, Lilly can't figure out whether he's referring to the woods not being right, or if he's talking about the two of them. "I'm sorry if I—"

He gently touches her lips. "I want it to be just right . . . when the time comes."

His smile is the most guileless, clean, sweet smile Lilly has ever seen. She returns his smile, her eyes misting over. Who would have thought, in the midst of all this horror—a perfect gentleman?

Lilly starts to say something else when a sharp noise grabs their attention.

Josh hears the faint drumming of hooves first, and gently shoves Lilly back behind him. He raises the squirrel gun's rusty single barrel. The pounding noises rise. Josh thumbs the hammer back.

At first, he thinks he's seeing things. Above them, coming down the embankment, throwing leaves and debris in their wake, a pack of animals—impossible to identify at first, just a blur of fur—charge through the foliage directly toward them. "Get down!" Josh yanks Lilly back behind a deadfall log on the edge of the creek bed.

"What is it?" Lilly crouches down behind the worm-eaten wood.

"Dinner!" Josh raises the gun's back sight to his eyes and aims at the oncoming deer—a small cluster of does with bushy ears pinned, and eyes as wide as billiard balls—but something stops Josh from firing. His heart throbs in his chest, his skin flushing with gooseflesh—the realization exploding in his brain.

"Josh, what's the matter?"

The deer roar past Josh, snapping twigs and throwing stones as he sidesteps the stampede.

Josh swings the gun up at the darker shadows coming behind the animals. "Run, Lilly!"

"What?—No!" She rises up behind the log, watching the deer vault across the riverbed. "I'm not leaving you!"

"Cross the creek, I'm right behind you!" Josh aims the shotgun up at the shapes coming down the hill, weaving through the undergrowth.

Lilly sees the horde of zombies lumbering toward them, at least twenty, sideswiping trees and bumping into each other. "Oh, shit."

"GO!"

Lilly scrambles across the gravelly trough and plunges into the shadows of the adjacent forest.

Josh backs away, aiming the front sight at the leading edge of the swarm coming toward him.

All at once, in that single instant before he fires, he sees oddly shaped bodies and garb, strange burned faces and costumes mutilated practically beyond recognition, and Josh realizes what happened to the previous owners of the lost three-ring circus tent—the unfortunate members of the Cole Brothers' Family Circus.

SIX

Josh squeezes off a shot.

The blast cracks open the sky, the pigeon grain punching a divot through the forehead of the closest midget. Twenty feet away, the little rotting corpse convulses backward, banging into three other dwarfs in bloody clown face and snarling black teeth. The little zombies—as stunted and deformed as sickly gnomes—scatter sideways.

Josh takes one last glance at the surreal intruders closing in on him.

Behind the midgets, stumbling down the embankment, comes a motley assortment of dead performers. A giant strong man with a handlebar mustache and musculature torn open in bloody gouges lumbers alongside a morbidly obese female cadaver, half nude, her fat rolls dangling over her genitals, her milky eyes buried in a face as lumpy as stale dough.

Bringing up the rear, a haphazard assortment of dead carnies, freaks, and contortionists follow stupidly. Encephalitic pinheads, their tiny mouths snapping, stumble along beside ragged trapeze artists in garish sequins and gangrenous faces, followed by multiple amputees trundling along spasmodically. The pack moves in fits and starts, as feral and hungry as a school of piranhas.

Josh lurches away, vaulting across the dry creek bed in a single leap.

He scuttles up the opposite bank and plunges into the neighboring woods with the shotgun over his shoulder. There is no time to reload another shell. He can see Lilly in the distance, sprinting toward the denser trees. He catches up with her in a matter of seconds and directs her to the east.

The two of them vanish into the shadows before what remains of the Cole Brothers' Family Circus even has a chance to stagger across the creek.

On their way back to the gas station, Josh and Lilly run into a smaller herd of deer. Josh gets lucky and bags one of the juvenile does with a single blast. The booming report echoes up across the sky—far enough from Fortnoy's to avoid drawing attention, but close enough to lug the trophy back home—and the whitetail goes down gasping and twitching.

Lilly has trouble taking her eyes off the carcass as Josh rigs his belt around its hindquarters and drags the steaming remains nearly half a mile back to Fortnoy's. In this Plague World, death in any context—human or animal—has taken on new implications.

That night, the mood lightens among the inhabitants of the gas station.

Josh dresses the deer in the back of the service area, in the same galvanized sinks in which they've been bathing, and he slaughters enough of the animal to last them weeks. He keeps the excess meat outside, in the deepening cold of the back lot, and he prepares a feast of organ meat, ribs, and belly, slow cooked in the broth of some instant chicken soup that they found in the bottom drawer of Fortnoy's office desk, along with shavings of wild meadow garlic and nettle stems. They have some canned peaches to accompany the braised deer, and they gorge themselves.

The walkers leave them alone for most of the evening—no sign of the circus dead or any other enclave. Josh notices during dinner that Bob cannot take his eyes off Megan. The older man seems taken with the girl, and for some reason this worries Josh. For days now, Bob has been very cold and brusque toward Scott (not that the kid has noticed anything in his constant state of flakiness). Nevertheless, Josh feels the volatile chemical bonds of their little tribe being tested, stressed, altered.

Later, they sit around the woodstove and smoke Josh's home-made cigars and share a few ounces of Bob's whiskey stash. For the first time since leaving the tent city—perhaps since the advent of the plague—they feel almost normal. They talk of escape. They speak of desert islands and antidotes and vaccines and finding happiness and stability again. They reminisce about the things they took for granted before the plague broke out: shopping in grocery stores and playing in parks and going out for dinner and watching TV shows and reading the newspaper on Sunday mornings and going to clubs to hear live music and sitting at Starbucks and shopping at Apple stores and using Wi-Fi and getting mail through that anachronistic thing known as the postal service.

They each have their pet pleasures. Scott bemoans the extinction of good weed, and Megan longs for the days when she could hang out at her favorite bar—Nightlies in Union City—and enjoy the free cucumber shooters and shrimp skewers. Bob pines for ten-year-old bourbon the way a mother might yearn for a lost child. Lilly remembers her guilty pleasures of haunting secondhand stores and thrift shops for the perfect scarf or sweater or blouse—the days when finding cast-off clothing wasn't a matter of survival. And Josh recalls the number of gourmet food shops he could find in the Little Five Points area of Atlanta—everything from good kimchi to rare pink truffle oil.

Either through some vagary of the wind, or perhaps the combined noise of their laughter—as well as the ticking and rattling of the woodstove—the troubling noises drifting out over the trees from the tent city go unnoticed that night for hours.

At one point—after the little dinner party breaks up and each of them finds their way back to their bedroll on the floor of the service area—Josh thinks he hears something strange echoing under the sound of the breeze tapping against the glass doors. But he simply passes it off as the wind and his imagination.

Josh offers to take the first shift, sitting watch in the front office, so he can make sure the noises are nothing. But hours go by before he hears or sees anything out of the ordinary.

The front office has a large, filthy plate-glass window across its front façade, much of the glass blocked by shelving, racks of maps and travel guides, and little pine deodorizers. The dusty merchandise blocks any sign of trouble rising up and over the distant sea of pines.

The wee hours pass, and eventually Josh dozes off in his chair.

His eyes remain shut until 4:43 A.M., at which point the first faint sound of engines coming up the hill jar him awake with a start.

Lilly stirs awake to the sound of heavy boot steps pounding through the office doorway. Sitting up against the garage wall, her ass freezing, she doesn't notice that Bob is already awake in his tangled nest of blankets across the garage.

Sitting up and looking around the service bay, Bob Stookey apparently heard the engine noises mere seconds after they had awakened Josh out in the office. "The hell is going on?" he mumbles. "Sounds like the Indy 500 out there."

"Everybody up," Josh says, storming into the garage, frantically looking around the greasy floor, searching for something.

"What's wrong?" Lilly rubs the sleep from her eyes, her heart starting to thump. "What's going on?"

Josh comes over to her. He kneels and speaks softly yet urgently. "Something's going down out there, vehicles moving fast, real reckless and shit—I don't want to get caught unawares."

She hears the roar of engines, the pinging of gravel flying. The noises are getting closer. Lilly's mouth goes dry with panic. "Josh, what are you looking for?"

"Get dressed, babydoll, quick." Josh glances across the room. "Bob—you see that box of .38 caliber slugs we brought back?"

Bob Stookey torques himself up to a standing position, awkwardly pulling his work trousers over his long underwear, a slice of moonlight coming through the skylight and striping his deeply-lined features. "I put it over on the workbench," he says. "What's the deal, captain?"

Josh hurries over and grabs the box of ammo. He reaches under his lumberjack coat, pulls the .38 snubbie from his belt, flicks open the cylinder, and loads it while he talks. "Lilly, you go get the lovebirds. Bob, I'm gonna need you to get that pigeon gun of yours and meet me out front."

"What if they're friendly, Josh?" Lilly pulls her sweater on, steps into her muddy boots.

"Then we got nothing to worry about." He whirls back toward the doorway. "Get moving, both of you." He lurches out of the room.

Heart racing, flesh prickling with terror, Lilly hurries across the garage, charges through the archway, and then down the narrow aisle of the retail store. A single hanging lantern lights her way.

"You guys! Wake up!" she says after reaching the storeroom door and pounding loudly.

Shuffling noises, bare feet on cold floorboards, then the door clicks partially ajar. Megan's drowsy, dazed face peers out on a cloud of skunk-weed smoke. "¿Qué pasa? dude—what the fuck?"

"Get up, Megan, we got trouble."

The girl's face goes instantly taut and alarmed. "Walkers?"

Lilly shakes her head emphatically. "I don't think so, unless they've learned how to drive cars."

Minutes later, Lilly joins Bob and Josh out in front of Fortnoy's—in the frigid, crystalline, predawn air—while Scott and Megan huddle behind them in the office doorway with blankets wrapped around themselves. "Oh, my God," Lilly utters, almost to herself.

A little less than a mile away, over the crest of the neighboring trees, a vast miasma of smoke rises up and blots out the stars. The horizon behind it glows a sickly pink, and it looks as though the black ocean of pines is on fire. But Lilly knows it's not the forest that's burning.

"What have they done?"

"This ain't good," Bob murmurs, the shotgun clutched in his cold hands.

"Get back," Josh says, thumbing the hammer back on the .38 police special.

The engine noises close in, maybe a few hundred yards away now, coming up the winding farm road—the sources of the noise still obscured behind a veil of night and the trees bordering the property—their headlights creating wildly arcing beams. Tires skid and careen through gravel. Rays of light shoot up into the sky, then across the tops of trees, then back across the road.

One of the headlights flares across the Fortnoy's sign and Josh mutters, "What the hell is wrong with them?"

Lilly stares at the first vehicle that comes into view—a late-model sedan—swerving up the snaking gravel road, then going into a skid. "What the fuck?"

"They ain't stoppin'! THEY AIN'T STOPPIN'!!" Bob starts backing away from the twin beams of deadly halogen light.

The car skids into the lot, roaring out of control across the fifty yards of pea gravel bordering Fortnoy's property, the rear end raising a thunderhead of dust in the indigo predawn chill.

"LOOK OUT!"

Josh springs into action, grabbing Lilly by the sleeve and pulling her out of harm's way, while Bob spins toward the office and screams at the top of his lungs at the two lovers huddling wide-eyed in the open doorway.

"GET OUTTA THERE!!"

Megan yanks her stoner boyfriend out of the door and across the apron of cracked cement flanking the fuel islands. The sedan—revealing itself, as it looms closer and closer, to be a battered Cadillac DeVille—screeches and fishtails toward the building. Bob lunges toward Megan. Scott lets out a garbled cry.

Another vehicle—a battered SUV with a broken luggage carrier—comes squealing and careening into the lot. Bob grabs Megan and gently shoves her toward the soft weeds beyond the service doors. Scott dives for cover behind a Dumpster. Josh and Lilly duck behind a wreck near the front sign.

The sedan mows down the closest fuel pump and keeps going, its engine whining furiously. The other vehicle goes into a spin. Lilly watches in shock from about fifty feet away, behind the wreck, as the sedan crashes into the front window.

The sickening crunch of glass and metal makes Lilly jerk with a start. Debris and sparks go flying as the sedan penetrates the front of the building.

The car keeps going, rear wheels keening and spinning on the floor, destroying half the building with the force of a giant wrecking ball. Lilly puts her hand to her mouth. The front half of Fortnoy's roof collapses on the sedan as it comes to rest in the retail store.

The SUV slams sideways into the diesel pump, setting the fumes alight. Fire booms upward in a sheath and licks at the rising vapors. The windows of the SUV flicker a dull yellow from something burning *inside* it. Lilly silently thanks God that the fuel reserves are empty, or she and her friends would be vaporized by now.

The SUV comes to rest at an angle under the awning, its high beams still shining brightly, illuminating the building like stage lights in a hallucinatory play.

For a moment, the silence crashes down on the property until the crackle of flames and the sizzle of fluids are all that can be heard.

Josh cautiously moves out from behind the wreck, still clutching his .38 revolver. Lilly joins him and is about to say something like, *What the hell just happened*, when she notices the headlights of the SUV are shining directly into the building, a wide pool of light falling directly on the rear of the sedan.

Inside the car's rear window—fractured by huge starbursts of broken glass—something moves. Lilly sees the back of someone's shoulders, slowly turning, pivoting awkwardly, revealing a pale, discolored face.

All at once, Lilly knows exactly what happened.

Moments later, things at Fortnoy's start unraveling at a rapid rate as Josh calls out to the others in a frantic whisper. *"Get away from the building!"*

Across the lot, Bob, Megan, and Scott still crouch in the weeds behind the Dumpster. They slowly rise and start to answer.

"SSSSSHHHHHHHHH!!" Josh points at the building, indicating the dangers inside, and whispers loud enough to get them moving. *"Hurry up! Get over here!!"*

Bob understands instantly, and he takes Megan's hand and creeps around the flickering flames of the diesel pump. Scott follows.

Lilly stands next to Josh. "What are we gonna do? All our stuff's in there."

The front of the station and half its interior are totaled, the sparks still sputtering, the water mains still flooding the cold floors.

In the glare of the SUV's headlight beams, one of the sedan's flapping rear doors suddenly creaks open wider, a decomposed leg clad in rags stepping out in fitful, spastic movements.

"The place is gone, babydoll," Josh says under his breath. "S-O-L . . . forget it."

Bob and the others join Josh and Lilly, and for a brief instant they stand there, still in shock, catching their collective breaths. Bob still clutches the shotgun in his sweaty palms. Megan looks sick. "What the fuck happened?" she mutters almost rhetorically.

"Folks must have tried to get away," Josh speculates. "Must've had a passenger that got bit, and they turned in the car."

Inside the wrecked building, a zombie emerges from the sedan like a deformed fetus being born.

"Bob, you got your keys on ya?"

Bob looks at Josh. "They're in the truck."

"In the ignition?"

"Glove box."

Josh turns to the others. "I want y'all to wait here, keep your eye on that walker, might be more in there. I'm gonna get the truck."

Josh turns away but Lilly grabs him. "Wait! Wait!! You're telling me we're just gonna leave all our stuff in there, all our supplies?"

"No choice."

He heads around the left side of the smoking pumps while the others stand there stunned and speechless. Twenty-five feet away, the SUV thumps, a half-ajar door creaking open, the firelight blooming. Lilly jerks. Megan gasps as another dead thing pushes its way out of the vehicle.

Bob fiddles a shotgun shell into the breech with shaking hands.

The others back away toward the road, Scott mumbling hysterically, "Shit, man, shit . . . shit . . . shit . . . shit . . . shit . . . shit . . ."

The thing that emerges from the SUV, burned beyond recognition, staggers toward them, its mouth gaping with black drool. The back of its collar and part of its left shoulder still crackle with tiny flames, the smoke around its skull like a halo. Apparently an adult male, half the skin of its face burned off, it barely remains upright as it shuffles slowly toward the smell of humans.

Bob can't get the shell seated properly, his shakes are so bad now.

No one sees the flare of taillights across the lot behind the row of wrecks, and no one hears the rumble of the king cab's engine firing up or the squeal of its rear tires digging in as the engine roars.

The burning zombie approaches Megan, who turns to run and trips on a patch of loose gravel. She sprawls to the pavement as Scott cries out and Lilly tries to help her up and Bob struggles with the shotgun.

The walker gets within inches of them when the blur of metal appears.

Josh backs the Ram directly into the zombie, and the impact of the protruding trailer hitch impales the thing, sending the charred corpse flying in a cloud of sparks. The thing breaks apart in the middle, the torso flinging off one way, the lower extremities spinning in the other.

One of the blackened, sizzling organs strikes Megan in the back, splattering her with hot, oily bile and fluids. She lets out a scream.

The pickup skids to a stop next to them, and they pile in, yanking a hysterical Megan in through the back hatch. Josh floors it.

The truck barrels out of the lot and down the winding access road.

All told, a mere three and a half minutes have elapsed since the onslaught . . . but in that time, the destinies of all five survivors have irrevocably changed.

They decide to head down the hill and turn north, weaving through the forest toward the tent city. They proceed cautiously, with their lights off and eyes wide open. In the rear camper, Scott and Megan peer through the firewall window, while Bob and Lilly, side by side in the cab next to Josh, scan the landscape with feverish concentration. No one says a word. They all harbor the unspoken dread of investigating the extent of the damage to the tent city—the resources of the vast encampment now paramount to their survival.

By this point, dawn has broken, the edges of the horizon—pale blue behind the trees—already beginning to drive the shadows from the gullies and culverts. The air is bitter cold and scented with the char of recent fires. Josh keeps both hands on the wheel as the pickup snakes through the cool shadows rising above the tent city.

"STOP! JOSH! STOP!"

Josh stomps on the brakes at the zenith of a hill overlooking the southern edge of the camp. The pickup scrapes to a halt.

"Oh, my God."

"Christ Almighty."

"Let's turn around." Lilly chews on her fingernail, gazing through a break in the foliage. She can see what's left of the tent city in the distance. The air reeks of burned flesh and something worse, something deathly foul, like a mass infection. "There's nothing we can do here."

"Hold on a second."

"Josh—"

"What in God's name happened down there?" Bob murmurs to nobody in particular, staring through the gap in the trees that opens like a proscenium above the meadow fifty yards below. Early-morning sunbeams shoot down through scrims of smoke, making the devastation look almost unreal, like footage from a silent movie. "Looks like Godzilla attacked the place."

"You think somebody went crazy?" Lilly keeps staring at the smoking ruins.

"I don't think so," Josh says.

"You think walkers caused this?"

"I don't know, maybe there was a big old swarm of 'em and a fire started."

Down in the meadow, along the edges of the encampment, flaming cars sit in disarray. Scores of smaller tents still burn, sending up black gouts of smoke into the acrid sky. In the center of the field, the circus tent has been reduced to a smoldering endoskeleton of metal poles and guide wires. Even the hard-packed ground burns in places, as though someone spooned out dollops of liquid flames. Smoking bodies litter the grounds. For a brief, surreal moment, Josh is reminded of the *Hindenburg* disaster, the flaming debris of the airship in its catastrophic death throes.

"Josh . . ."

The big man turns and looks at Lilly, whose face is turned away now, scanning the edges of the forest on either side of the king cab. Her voice lowers several registers until she sounds almost groggy with terror. "Josh . . . um . . . we have to get out of here."

"What is it?"

"Holy fuckin' Jesus." Bob sees what Lilly sees, and the air in the cab crackles with tension. "Get us outta here, captain."

"What are you—"

Then Josh sees the problem: the countless shadowy figures emerging from the trees—almost in synchronous marching order— like a vast school of fish stirred from the depths. Some of them still smolder with thin wisps of smoke leaching off their tattered rags. Others trundle along with robotic hunger, their curled claws outstretched. Hundreds and hundreds of cataract-white eyes reflect the pale light of dawn as they lock on to the lone vehicle in their midst. The hairs on Josh's thick neck stiffen.

"JOSH, GO!"

He yanks the steering wheel and slams the pedal down, and the three hundred and sixty cubic inches roar. The truck lurches into a one-eighty, plowing through a dozen zombies and taking down a small pine in the process. The noise is incredible, the wet wrenching of dead limbs and snapping of timbers as the debris and blood kick up across the front quarter panel. The rear end wags violently, smashing into a cluster of walkers and tossing Megan and Scott around the camper. Josh pulls back onto the road and floors it, booming back down the hill in the direction from which they just came.

They barely make it to the adjacent road at the bottom of the hill before they realize at least three zombies have attached themselves, barnaclelike, to the pickup.

"Shit!" Josh sees one in his side mirror, clinging to the vehicle on the driver's side, near the rear quarter panel, feet on the running board, tangled in strapping ropes, its tattered clothing caught in the camper's metal trim. "Stay cool, everybody—we got some hangers-on!"

"*What!*" Lilly turns toward the passenger window and sees a dead face pop up across the glass like a jack-in-the-box. The face twitches and snarls at her, its inky drool flagging in the wind. Lilly lets out a startled gasp.

Josh concentrates on the road, making a wild turn, then heading north at a steady forty-five miles an hour, moving toward the main two-lane, purposely swerving in an attempt to fling the zombies off the pickup.

Two of the walkers have clamped on to the driver's side, one on the passenger side—and they hold fast—either caught on the truck, or strong enough in their spastic hunger to hold on. "Bob! You got any more of them shells in the cab?"

"They're in the back!"

"Shit!"

Bob shoots a glance at Lilly. "Darlin,' I believe there's a crowbar on the floor behind the passenger seat—"

The truck swerves. One of the walkers tears free, tumbling to the road and pinwheeling down an embankment. Muffled screams come from the back. The sound of glass breaking comes through the wall. Lilly finds the greasy three-foot length of iron with the hooked end on the rear floor. "Found it!"

"Give it to me, honey!"

Josh looks out at the side mirror and sees a second zombie slip free of its mooring and fall to the rushing pavement beneath the wheels. The truck bumps over the corpse and keeps barreling.

Bob hollers in his gravelly wheeze, twisting around toward the sleeper window, raising the crowbar. "Get back, Lilly, cover your face!"

Lilly cowers, shielding herself, as Bob strikes out at the zombie in the window.

The curved end of the crowbar slams against the window but merely chips a divot out of the reinforced safety glass. The zombie snarls, tangled in bungee cords—its toneless growl a Doppler echo on the wind.

Bob lets out a cry and then slams the crowbar into the window again and again, as hard as he can, until the curved tip breaks through the safety glass and plunges into the dead face. Lilly turns away.

The crowbar impales the cadaver through the roof of its mouth and gets stuck. Bob gapes in horror. Behind the mosaic of fractured glass the skewered head hangs suspended in the wind for a moment, the dull glow behind its sharklike button eyes still animated, the mouth still pulsing around the iron as if trying to eat the crowbar.

Lilly can't look. She presses back against the corner, shaking convulsively.

Josh swerves again, and the zombie finally tears loose in the wind, falling to the pavement and vanishing under the wheels. The rest of the window blows away, a tissue of shattered glass imploding and swirling into the cab. Bob flinches, awash in adrenaline, and Josh keeps barreling forward as Lilly curls into a fetal position in back.

They finally reach the main access road and Josh heads south, picking up speed, calling out loud enough for the folks in the back to hear: "Everybody hold on!"

Without another word, Josh accelerates, hands welded to the steering wheel, weaving and lurching around pockets of wrecked, abandoned vehicles for another couple of miles, keeping an eye on the side mirror, making sure they are clear and safely out of range of the swarm.

They put five miles between them and the cataclysm before Josh applies the brakes and stops on the gravel shoulder of a deserted stretch of rural wasteland. The silence that descends on the truck is unreal. Only the sound of their heartbeats in their ears and the high, lonesome whistle of the wind can be heard.

Josh glances over his shoulder at Lilly. The look on her faintly bruised face, the way she's curled up in the corner of the floor, hugging her bended knees against her chest, shivering as though suffering from hypothermia—all of it worries him. "You okay, babydoll?"

Lilly manages to swallow the lump of terror in her throat and gives him a look. "Just peachy."

Josh gives her a nod, then hollers loud enough to be heard back in the camper. "Everybody okay back there?"

Megan's face in the window says it all. Her ruddy features screwed up with nervous tension, she grudgingly gives them a noncommittal thumbs-up.

Josh turns and gazes through the windshield. He breathes hard, as though recovering from a sprint. "Damn things are definitely multiplying."

Bob rubs his face, breathing hard, fighting the shakes. "Getting more brazen, too, you ask me."

After a pause Josh says, "Must've happened fast."

"Yeah."

"Poor bastards didn't know what hit 'em."

"Yeah." Bob wipes his mouth. "Maybe we oughtta go back, try and draw them things away from the camp."

"What for?"

Bob chews the inside of his cheek. "I don't know . . . could be survivors."

Another long pause hangs in the cab, until Lilly finally says, "Not likely, Bob."

"Could be supplies left over we could use."

"Too risky," Josh says, scanning the landscape. "Where the hell are we, anyway?"

Bob roots a map out of a cluttered door pocket. He unfolds it with shaking hands and traces his nail across the tiny capillaries of unmarked farm roads. He still labors to catch his breath. "Best I can tell, we're somewhere south of Oakland—tobacco country." He tries to hold the map steady in his shaking hands. "Road we're on ain't on the map—at least it ain't on *this* map."

Josh stares into the distance. The morning sun hammers down on the narrow two-lane. The unmarked road, which is fringed in weeds and littered with an abandoned wreck every twenty yards or so, snakes along a plateau between two tobacco farms. On either side of the unmarked two-lane, the fields have overgrown with neglect, the weeds and kudzu twining up the slats of weather-beaten guardrails. The shaggy, ramshackle nature of the fields reflects the months that have transpired since the plague broke out.

Bob folds up the map. "What now?"

Josh shrugs. "Ain't seen a farmhouse for miles, seems like we're far enough out in the boonies to avoid another swarm of them things."

Lilly climbs back onto the bench. "What are you thinking, Josh?"

He puts the truck into drive. "I'm thinking we keep heading south."

"Why south?"

"For one, we'll be moving away from the population centers."

"And . . . ?"

"And maybe, if we keep movin' . . . we can keep the cold weather in our rearview."

He gives it some gas and starts to pull back onto the road when Bob grabs his arm.

"Not so fast, captain."

Josh stops the truck. "What is it now?"

"Don't mean to be the bearer of bad news." Bob points at the gas gauge. "But I just put the last drops of my reserves in her last night."

The needle is riding just below *E*.

SEVEN

They search the area for tanks to siphon or gas stations to plunder, and they come up empty. Most of the wrecks along this desolate stretch of farm road are burned to crisps or abandoned with bone-dry tanks. They notice only scattered dead roaming the distant farmlands—lone cadavers wandering aimlessly, far enough away to easily elude.

They decide to sleep in the Ram that night, taking shifts sitting watch and rationing their canned goods and fresh water. Being this far out in the boonies proves to be a blessing as well as a curse. The worrisome lack of fuel and provisions is offset by the lack of walker activity.

Josh admonishes everybody to keep their voices down and make as little noise as possible during their exile in this barren hinterland.

As darkness closes in that first night, and the temperature nose-dives, Josh runs the engine as long as possible, then resorts to running the heater off the battery. He knows he can't keep this up for long. They cover the broken sleeper window with cardboard and duct tape.

They each sleep fitfully that night in the cramped quarters of the truck—Megan, Scott, and Bob in the camper, Lilly in the rear of the cab, and Josh in the front, barely able to stretch his massive body out across the two large bucket seats.

The next day, Josh and Bob get lucky and find an overturned panel van a mile to the west, its rear axle broken but the rest of it intact, its gas tank almost full. They siphon eighteen gallons into three separate containers, and make it back to the Ram before noon. They take off and make their way southeast—crossing another twenty miles of fallow farmland—before stopping for the night under a desolate train trestle, where the wind sings its constant mournful aria through the high-tension wires.

In the darkness of the reeking truck, they argue about whether they should keep moving or find a place to light. They bicker about petty things—sleeping arrangements, rationing, snoring, and stinky feet—and they generally get on each other's nerves. The floor space inside the camper is less than a hundred square feet, much of it covered with Bob's cast-off detritus. Scott and Megan sleep like sardines against the back hatch while Bob tosses and turns in his semisober delirium.

They live like this for almost a week, zigzagging in a southwesterly direction, following the tracks of the West Central Georgia Railway, scavenging fuel when they can. Tempers strain to the breaking point. The camper walls close in.

In the dark, the troubling noises behind the trees get closer every night.

One morning, while Scott and Megan slumber in back, Josh and Lilly sit on the Ram's front bumper, sharing a thermos of instant coffee in the early-morning light. The wind feels colder, the sky lower—the smell of winter in the air. "Feels like more snow's coming," Josh softly observes.

"Where's Bob gone off to?"

"Says he saw a creek off to the west, not far, took his fishing rod."

"Did he take the shotgun?"

"Hatchet."

"I'm worried about him, Josh. He's shaking all the time now."

"He'll be okay."

"Last night I saw him sucking down a bottle of mouthwash."

Josh looks at her. Lilly's injuries have almost completely healed, her eyes clear now for the first time since the beating. Her bruises have all but faded, and she removed the bandages around her ribs the previous afternoon to find that she could walk almost normally without them. But the pain of losing Sarah Bingham still gnaws at her—Josh can see sorrow etched on her sleeping face, late at night. From the front seat, Josh has been watching her sleep. It's the most beautiful thing he has ever seen. He longs to kiss her again but the situation hasn't warranted such luxuries. "We'll all be doing a lot better when we find some real food," Josh says then. "I'm getting mighty tired of cold Chef Boyardee."

"Water's getting low, too. And there's something else I've been thinking about that's not exactly giving me a warm, cozy feeling."

Josh looks at her. "Which is?"

"What if we run into another swarm? They could push the damn truck over, Josh. You know it as well as I do."

"All the more reason to keep moving, keep heading south, below the radar."

"I know, but—"

"More likely to find supplies, we keep moving."

"I understand that but—"

Lilly stops when she sees the silhouette of a figure way off in the distance, maybe three hundred yards away, up on the train trestle, moving this way, following the tracks. The figure's long, narrow shadow, outlined in the dust motes of morning sunlight, flickers down through the slatted ties and crossbeams—moving too fast to be a zombie.

"Speak of the devil," Josh says when he finally recognizes the figure.

The older man approaches, carrying an empty bucket and collapsible fishing rod. He trundles along quickly between the rails, urgency burning on his face. "Hey, y'all!" he calls down breathlessly to them as he reaches the stepladder near the overpass.

"Keep it down, Bob," Josh cautions him, walking over to the base of the trestle, Lilly at his side.

"Wait'll you see what I found," Bob says, descending the ladder.

"Catch a big one, did ya?"

He hops to the ground. He catches his breath, his eyes shimmering with excitement. "No, sir, didn't even find the goddamn crick." He manages a gap-toothed grin. "But I did find something better."

The Walmart sits at the intersection of two rural highways, a mile north of the train tracks, its tall interstate sign with its trademark blue letters and yellow starburst visible from the elevated trestles along the woods. The closest town is miles away, but these isolated big box stores have proven to be lucrative retail outlets for farming communities, especially ones this close to a major interstate like U.S. 85—the Hogansville exit only seven miles to the west.

"All right . . . here's what I'm thinking," Josh says to the others, after pulling up to the lot entrance, which is partially blocked by an abandoned flatbed truck, its front end wrapped around a sign pole. The cargo—mostly lumber—lies strewn across the wide lanes leading into the vast parking lot, which is littered with wrecks and abandoned vehicles. The massive low-slung superstore in the distance looks deserted but looks can be deceiving. "We check out the lots first, make a few circles, just get the lay of the land."

"Looks pretty empty, Josh," Lilly comments as she chews on her thumbnail in the rear berth. For the entire fifteen-minute journey across dusty back roads, Lilly has chewed every available fingernail down to the quick. Now she gnaws on a cuticle.

"Hard to tell just by looking," Bob pipes in.

"Keep your eyes peeled for walkers or any other movement," Josh says, putting the truck into gear and slowly bumping over the spilled lumber.

They circle the property twice, paying closest attention to the shadows of loading docks and entranceways. The cars in the lot are all empty, some burned to blackened husks. Most of the store's glass doors are blown out. A carpet of broken shards glistens in the cold afternoon sun across the front entrance. The store inside is as dark as a coal mine. Nothing moves. Inside the vestibule, a few bodies litter the floor. Whatever happened here happened a while ago.

After his second sweep, Josh pulls up to the front of the store, puts the truck in park, leaves the engine idling, and checks the last three rounds nestled in the cylinder of his .38 police special. "Okay, I don't want to leave the truck untended," he says and turns to Bob. "You got how many shells left?"

Bob snaps open the squirrel gun with trembling hands. "One in the breech, one in my pocket."

"Okay, here's what I'm thinking—"

"I'm going with you," Lilly says.

"Not without a weapon you aren't, not until we know it's safe in there."

"I'll grab a shovel from the back," she says. She glances over her shoulder and sees Megan's face in the window, owlish and expectant as she cranes her neck to see through the windshield. Lilly looks back at Josh. "You're gonna need another pair of eyes in there."

"Never argue with a woman," Bob mumbles, jacking open the passenger door and stepping out into the windy, raw air of the late-autumn afternoon.

They go around back, open the camper's rear hatch, and tell Megan and Scott to stay in the cab with the truck idling until the all-clear signal comes; and if they see any trouble, they should blast the horn like crazy. Neither Megan nor Scott puts up much of an argument.

Lilly grabs one of the shovels, and then follows Josh and Bob across the cement threshold of the store's front façade, the sounds of their footsteps crackling over broken glass drowned by the wind.

Josh forces one of the automatic doors open and they enter the vestibule.

They see the old man without a head lying on the stained parquet near the entrance in a dried pool of blood—now as black as obsidian—the ragged threads of his viscera blossoming out of his neck. Pinned to the little blue greeter's vest, the name tag, which is askew and partially visible, says WALMART on the top, and ELMER K on the bottom. The big yellow happy face insignia is stippled with blood. Lilly stares at poor headless Elmer K for quite some time as they make their way deeper into the empty store.

The air is almost as cold as outside and smells of coppery mold and decay and rancid proteins like those of a giant compost pile. Constellations of bullet holes crown the lintel above the hair care center to the left, while garish Rorschach patterns of arterial spray mark the doorway of the vision center on the right. Shelves either stand empty—already plundered—or overturned on the floor.

Josh raises one of his huge hands and orders his cohorts to stop for a moment as he listens to the silence. He scans the acres of retail space, much of which is littered with headless bodies, unidentifiable streaks of carnage, overturned shopping carts, and trash. The rows of checkout conveyors on the right stand silent and stained with blood. The pharmacy center, cosmetics counter, and health and beauty on the left are also riddled with bullet holes.

Signaling to the others, Josh cautiously continues on, his gun at the ready, his heavy boot steps crunching over debris as he moves deeper into the reeking shadows.

The farther they get from the entrance doors, the darker the aisles become. The pale daylight barely penetrates the far grocery aisles on the right, with its spills and broken glass mingling with human remains, or the home and office and fashion sections on the left, with their scattered clothing and dismembered mannequins. The departments in the rear of the store—toys, electronics, sporting goods, and shoes—lie in utter darkness.

Only the dry silver beams of battery-powered emergency lights illuminate the shadowy depths of the far aisles.

They find flashlights in the hardware department, and shine the beams into the far reaches of the store, making note of all the useful provisions and tools. The more they investigate, the more excited they become. By the time they've circled the entire fifteen thousand square feet of retail space—finding only a few scattered human remains in the early stages of decomposition, innumerable overturned shelves, and rats scurrying from the sounds of their footsteps—they are convinced that the store is safe—picked over, certainly, but *safe*.

At least for the moment.

"Pretty sure we got the place to ourselves," Josh says at last as the threesome returns to the diffuse light of the front vestibule.

They lower their weapons and flashlights. "Looks like some shit went down in here," Bob says.

"I ain't no detective." Josh gazes around the walls and floors awash in bloodstains that could pass for Jackson Pollock paintings. "But I'd say some folks turned in here a while back, and then you got layers of people comin' in and helpin' themselves to what was left."

Lilly looks at Josh, her expression still tight with nervous tension. She glances at the headless greeter. "You think we could clean the place up, maybe stay here a while?"

Josh shakes his head. "We'd be sitting ducks, place is way too tempting."

"It's also a gold mine," Bob pipes in. "Plenty of stuff on the high shelves, maybe stockrooms in back with merchandise, could be damn useful to us." His eyes twinkle, and Josh can tell the older man has taken careful accounting of the top shelves of the liquor department, still brimming with unopened bottles of hooch.

"I saw some wheelbarrows and hand dollies in the garden department," Josh says. He looks at Bob, then he looks at Lilly and grins. "I think our luck just changed for the better."

They load up three wheelbarrows with down coats, winter boots, thermal underwear, stocking caps, and gloves from the fashion department. They throw in a pair of walkie-talkies, tire chains, towlines, a socket-wrench kit, road flares, motor oil, and antifreeze. They get Scott to help them, leaving Megan in the truck to watch for intruders.

From the grocery department—where most of the meats, produce, and dairy products are either missing or have long since spoiled— they procure boxes of instant oatmeal, raisins, protein bars, ramen noodles, jars of peanut butter, beef jerky, cans of soup, spaghetti sauce, juice boxes, cartons of dry pasta, canned meats, sardines, coffee, and tea.

Bob raids what is left of the pharmacy. Most of the barbiturates, painkillers, and antianxiety meds are long gone, but he finds enough leftovers to open a private practice. He takes some Lanacane for first aid, amoxicillin for infections, epinephrine for kicking a heart back to life, Adderall for keeping alert, lorazepam for calming the nerves,

Celox for stanching blood loss, naproxen for pain, loratadine for opening air passages, and a good assortment of vitamins.

From other departments, they acquire irresistible luxury items—items that aren't exactly paramount to their survival but might nonetheless bring momentary relief from the grim business of staying alive. Lilly chooses an armful of hardcover books—novels mostly—from the newsstand area. Josh finds a collection of hand-rolled Costa Rican cigars behind the courtesy desk. Scott discovers a battery-operated DVD player and selects a dozen movies. They take a few board games, some playing cards, a telescope, and a small digital voice recorder.

They make a trip out to the truck, stuffing the camper to the gills with the goodies, before returning and starting in on the treasure trove of useful items in the darkness at the rear of the store.

"Shine it over to the left, babydoll," Josh asks Lilly from the aisle outside the sporting goods department. Josh holds two large heavy-duty duffel bags appropriated from the luggage department.

Scott and Bob stand nearby, watching expectantly, as Lilly sweeps the narrow beam of her flashlight across the disaster area that once trafficked in soccer balls and Little League bats.

The yellow shaft of light crosses mangled displays of tennis rackets and hockey sticks, cannibalized bicycles and heaps of workout clothes and baseball gloves strewn across the blood-spattered floor. "Whoa . . . right there, Lilly," Josh says. "Hold it steady."

"Shit," Bob says from behind Lilly. "Looks like we're too late."

"Somebody beat us to 'em," Josh grumbles as the flashlight plays across the shattered glass display case to the left of the fishing poles and tackle. The case is empty, but from the look of the indentations and hooks left behind, it's obvious the enclosure housed a wide variety of hunting rifles, target pistols, and street-legal handguns. The racks on the wall behind the display are also empty. "Shine it on the floor for a second, honey."

In the dull cone of light, a few stray shells and bullets are visibly scattered across the floor.

They walk over to the gun counter and Josh drops the duffel

bags, then squeezes his massive form behind the case. He takes the flashlight and shines it down along the floor. He sees a few stray boxes of ammunition, a bottle of gun oil, a receipt pad, and a blunt silver object peeking out from under the case. "Hold on a second . . . *hold the phone*."

Josh kneels. He reaches under the counter and pulls the blunt steel end of a muzzle out from under the bottom of the case.

"Now we're talking," he says, holding the gun up in the light for all to see.

"Is that a Desert Eagle?" Bob steps in closer. "Is that a .44?"

Josh grips the gun like a boy on Christmas morning. "Whatever the hell it is, it's heavy as shit. Thing must weigh ten pounds."

"May I?" Bob takes the gun. "Holy Christ . . . this is the goddamn howitzer of handguns."

"Now all we need are bullets."

Bob checks the clip. "Manufactured by bad-ass Hebrews, gas-operated . . . the only semiauto of its kind." Bob looks up at the high shelves. "Shine that light up yonder . . . see if they got any .50 caliber express up there."

A moment later, Josh finds a stack of cartons marked "50-C-R" on the top shelf. He boosts himself up and grabs half a dozen cartons.

Meanwhile, Bob thumbs the release and the magazine falls into his greasy hand. His voice goes soft and low, as though he's speaking to a lover. "Nobody designs firearms like the Israelis . . . not even the Germans. This bad boy can penetrate tank armor."

"Dude," Scott says finally, standing behind Bob with a flashlight. "You planning on shooting that thing or fucking it?"

After an awkward moment, they all burst out laughing—even Josh can't resist chuckling—and despite the fact that their laughter is brittle and fraught with nerves, it serves to break the tension in that silent warehouse of blood and looted shelves. They have had a good day. They've hit the jackpot here in this temple of discount consumerism. More importantly, they've acquired something here far more valuable than mere provisions: They have found a glimmer of hope that they'll make it through the winter . . . that they just may come out the other side of this nightmare.

Lilly hears the noise first. Her laughter instantly dies and she looks around as though waking with a start from a dream. "What was that?"

Josh stops laughing. "What's the matter?"

"Did you hear that?"

Bob looks at her. "What's wrong, darlin'?"

"I heard something." Her voice is low and taut with panic.

Josh turns his flashlight off and looks at Scott. "Turn the flashlight off, Scott."

Scott extinguishes the light and the rear of the store is plunged into darkness.

Lilly's heart thumps as they stand there in the shadows for a moment, listening. The store is silent. Then another creaking noise penetrates the stillness.

It comes from the front of the store. A wrenching sound, like rusty metal squeaking, but faint, so faint it's impossible to identify.

Josh whispers, "Bob, where's the shotgun?"

"Left it up front, with the wheelbarrows."

"Great."

"What if it's Megan?"

Josh thinks about it. He gazes out at the stillness of the store. "Megan! That you?"

No answer.

Lilly swallows air. Dizziness courses over her. "You think walkers could push the door open?"

"A stiff breeze could blow it open," Josh says, reaching behind his belt for the .38. "Bob, how handy are you with that bad-ass pistol?"

Bob already has one of the ammo boxes open. He fishes for bullets with trembling, filthy fingers. "Way ahead of you, captain."

"All right, listen—"

Josh starts to whisper instructions when another noise fills the air—muffled but distinct—clearly the sound of frozen hinges rasping somewhere near the entrance. Someone or some *thing* is pushing itself into the store.

Bob fiddles bullets into an empty magazine, his hands shaking. He drops the magazine, the clip hitting the floor and spilling rounds.

"Dude," Scott comments under his breath, nervously watching Bob on his hands and knees retrieving the stray bullets like a little boy madly gathering marbles.

"Listen up," Josh hisses at them. "Scott, you and Bob take the left flank, head toward the front of the store through the grocery department. Babydoll, you follow me. We'll grab an axe from home and garden on the way."

Bob, on the floor, finally manages to get the bullets into the clip, then slams the magazine into the pistol and levers himself back to his feet. "Gotcha. C'mon, junior. Let's do it."

They split off and move through the darkness toward the pale light.

Lilly follows Josh through the shadows of the auto care center, past ransacked shelves, past heaps of litter strewn across the tile flooring, past home and office, past crafts. They move as quietly as possible, staying low and close together, Josh communicating with hand gestures. He has the .38 in one hand, the other hand coming up suddenly and signaling for Lilly to stop.

From the front of the store, the sound of shuffling footsteps can now clearly be heard.

Josh points at a fallen display in the do-it-yourself department. Lilly creeps around behind a display of lightbulbs and finds the floor littered with rakes and pruning shears and three-foot-long axes. She grabs one of the axes and comes back around the lightbulbs, her heart hammering, her flesh crawling with terror.

They approach the front entrance. Lilly can see an occasional flash of movement on the other side of the store as Scott and Bob close in along the west wall of the grocery department. By this point, whatever it is that's slithering into the Walmart seems to have fallen silent and still. Lilly can't hear a thing other than her chugging heart.

Josh pauses behind the pharmacy counter, crouching down. Lilly joins him. Josh whispers to her, "You stay behind me, and if one of them things gets past me, give it a good whack in the center of the head with that thing."

"Josh, I know how to kill a zombie," Lilly retorts in a harsh whisper.

"I know, honey, all I'm saying . . . just make sure you whack it hard enough the first time."

Lilly nods.

"On three," Josh whispers. "You ready?"

"Ready."

"One, two—"

Josh stops cold. Lilly hears something that doesn't compute.

Josh grabs her and holds her steady against the bottom of the pharmacy counter. Paralyzed with indecision, they crouch there for a moment, a single incongruous thought screaming in Lilly's brain.

Zombies don't talk.

"Hello?" The voice echoes across the empty store. "Anybody home?"

Josh hesitates behind the counter for another brief moment, weighing his options, his brain swimming with panic. The voice sounds friendly . . . sort of . . . definitely male, deep, maybe a little bit of an accent.

Josh glances over his shoulder at Lilly. She's holding the axe like a baseball bat, poised to strike, her lips quivering with terror. Josh holds his huge hand up—making a "give me a second" gesture—and he's about to make his move, letting up on the pistol's hammer, when another voice rings out, instantly changing the dynamic.

"LET HER GO, YOU SONS OF BITCHES!"

Josh lunges out from behind the counter with his .38 raised and ready to fire.

Lilly follows with the axe.

A group of six men—all heavily armed—stand in the vestibule.

"Easy . . . easy, easy, easy . . . *whoa*!" The leader, the guy standing out in front of the pack—a high-powered assault rifle in his arms, the muzzle raised menacingly—looks to be in his late twenties, early thirties at the most. Tall, rangy, dark complexioned, he wears a do-rag on his head. The sleeves of his flannel shirt are scissored off. His arms are heavily muscled.

At first, things are happening almost too quickly for Josh to track as he stands his ground with the barrel of his .38 pinned on Bandanna Man.

From behind the checkout lanes, Bob Stookey charges toward the intruders with his Desert Eagle gripped in both hands, commando-style, his red-rimmed eyes wide with drunken heroism. "LET HER GO!" The object of his pique stands behind the bandanna dude, held captive by a younger member of the raiding party. Megan Lafferty squirms angrily in the grip of a wild-eyed black kid, a greasy hand across her mouth, keeping her quiet.

"BOB—DON'T!" Josh bellows at the top of his lungs, and the booming authority of his voice seems to slam the brakes on Bob's gallantry. The older man falters at the end of the checkout lanes, stuttering to a stop a mere twenty feet from the guy holding Megan prisoner. Breathing hard, the old juicer stares helplessly at Megan. Josh can see the emotions all stirred up in the older man.

"Everybody chill!" Josh orders his people.

Scott Moon appears behind Bob with the old squirrel gun raised.

"Scott, cool it with the shotgun!"

The man in the bandanna doesn't lower his AK-47. "Let's dial it down, folks, come on—we're not looking to get into any O.K. Corral–type situation here."

Behind the dark-skinned dude stand five other men with heavy-duty weaponry. Mostly in their thirties, some black, some white, some in hip-hop street attire, others in ragged army fatigues and down vests, they look rested and well fed and maybe even a little high. Most importantly to Josh, they look as though they would just as soon start blasting as engage in any kind of diplomacy.

"We're cool," Josh says, but he's fairly certain that the tone of his voice, the set of his jaw, and the fact that he too has refrained from lowering his gun—all of this probably sends a countervailing message to Bandanna Man. "Aren't we, Bob? Aren't we cool?"

Bob mumbles something inaudible. The Desert Eagle remains in its upright, locked position, and for a brief and awkward moment, the two groups stand each other off with guns pointed at key pieces of anatomy. Josh doesn't like the odds—the intruders are packing enough firepower to take down a small garrison—but on the other hand, Josh's side has three working firearms all pointed, at the moment, directly at the raiding party's leader, whose loss might put a serious kink in this little posse's group dynamic.

"Let the girl go, Haynes," Bandanna Man orders his underling.

"But what about—"

"I said let her go!"

The wild-eyed black kid shoves Megan toward her comrades, and Megan stumbles for a moment, nearly falling, but then manages to stay upright and stagger over to Bob. "What a bunch of fucking dicks!" she grumbles.

"You okay, sweetie?" Bob asks, putting his free arm around her, but not taking his eyes (or the barrel of the magnum) off the intruders.

"Assholes snuck up on me," she says, rubbing her wrists, glowering back at them.

Bandanna Man lowers his gun and addresses Josh. "Look, we can't take any chances these days, we didn't know you from Adam . . . we're just looking after our own."

Unconvinced, Josh keeps the .38 beaded directly on Bandanna Man's chest. "What does that have to do with snatching that girl outta the truck?"

"Like I said . . . we didn't know how many of you we were dealing with . . . who she was gonna warn . . . we didn't know anything."

"You own this place?"

"No . . . whaddaya mean? No."

Josh gives him a cold smile. "Then lemme make a suggestion . . . as to where we go from here."

"Go ahead."

"There's plenty of stuff left in here . . . why don't y'all let us pass and you can have the rest."

Bandanna Man turns to his gang. "Guns down, guys. Come on. Step it on back. Come on."

Almost reluctantly the rest of the intruders comply and lower their weapons.

Bandanna Man turns back to Josh. "Name's Martinez . . . I'm sorry we got off on the wrong foot."

"Name's Hamilton and it's nice to meet you and I'd appreciate it if you'd let us pass."

"No problema, mi amigo . . . but can I just make a suggestion to *you* before we conclude our business together?"

"I'm listening."

"First off, is there any way you could stop pointing those guns at us?"

Josh keeps his eyes on Martinez as he lowers his gun. "Scott, Bob . . . go ahead . . . it's okay."

Scott puts the shotgun on his shoulder and leans against a check-out belt to listen. Bob reluctantly lowers the muzzle of the Desert Eagle, shoves it behind his belt, and keeps his arm around Megan.

Lilly sets her axe—head down—on the floor, leaning it against the pharmacy counter.

"Thanks, I appreciate it." Martinez takes a deep breath and lets out a sigh. "What I'm wondering is this. You seem like you got your head screwed on straight. You got the right to take all that merchandise outta here . . . but can I ask where you're taking it?"

"Truth is, we ain't taking it anywhere," Josh says. "We're getting it to go."

"You folks living on the road?"

"What difference does it make?"

Martinez shrugs. "Look, I know you got no reason to trust me, but the way things are, folks like us . . . we can be mutually beneficial to each other. You know what I'm saying?"

"To be honest, no . . . I don't have a fuckin' clue as to what you're saying."

Martinez sighs. "Let me lay my cards on the table. We could part ways right here and now, no harm no foul, wish each other the best . . ."

"Sounds good to me," Josh says.

"We got a better option, though," the man says.

"Which is?"

"A walled-in place, just up the road, people just like you and me, trying to make a place to live."

"Go on."

"No more running, is what I'm saying. We secured part of a town. It ain't much . . . yet. We got some walls up. Place to grow food. Generators. Heat. We definitely got room for five more."

Josh doesn't say anything. He looks at Lilly. He can't read her face. She looks exhausted, scared, confused. He looks at the others. He sees Bob's wheels turning. Scott looks at the floor. Megan stares balefully out at the intruders through tendrils of curly hair.

"Think about it, man," Martinez goes on. "We could split up what's left in this place and call it a day or we could join forces. We need good strong backs. If I wanted to rob you, fuck with you, mess you up . . . wouldn't I have done it already? I got no reason to make trouble. Come with us, Hamilton. Whaddaya say? There's nothing out there on the road but more shit and winter rolling in. Whaddaya say, man?"

Josh looks at Martinez for a long moment, until finally Josh says, "Give us a second."

They gather over by the checkout counters.

"Dude, you gotta be fucking kidding me," Megan says to Josh in a low, tense whisper. The others huddle around the big man in a semi-circle. "You're thinking about going somewhere with these scumbags?"

Josh licks his lips. "I don't know . . . the more I look at these dudes, the more they look just as scared and freaked out as we are."

Lilly chimes in. "Maybe we could just check the place out, see what it's like."

Bob looks at Josh. "Compared with livin' in tents on the ground with a bunch of hotheads? How bad could it be?"

Megan groans. "Is it just me, or have you people lost your fucking minds?"

"Megan, I don't know," Scott says. "I'm like thinking what do we have to lose?"

"Shut up, Scott."

"Okay, look," Josh says, holding up a huge hand and cutting off the debate. "I don't see any harm in following them, checking the place out. We'll keep our guns, keep our eyes open, and we'll decide when we see the place." He looks at Bob, then looks at Lilly. "Cool?"

Lilly takes a deep breath. Then gives him a nod. "Yeah . . . cool."

"Terrific," Megan grumbles, following the others back toward the entrance.

It takes another hour and the combined efforts of the two groups to go through the rest of the store for heavy items required by the town. They raid the lawn and garden center and home repair for lumber, fertilizer, potting soil, seeds, hammers, and nails. Lilly senses an edgy quality to the uneasy truce between the two contingents. She keeps tabs on Martinez out of the corner of her eye, and she notices an unspoken hierarchy to the ragtag raiding party. Martinez is definitely the honcho, ruling the others with simple gestures and nods.

By the time they get Bob's Ram and the two vehicles from the walled-in town—a panel van and flatbed truck—loaded to the gills, twilight is closing in. Martinez gets behind the wheel of the van, and tells Bob to follow along behind the flatbed . . . and the convoy starts out for the town.

As they wend their way out of the dusty Walmart lot and start up the access road toward the highway, Lilly sits in the back sleeper compartment, gazing through the bug-streaked windshield, as Bob concentrates on keeping up with the exhaust-belching flatbed. They pass tangles of wreckage and dense forests on either side of the farm road, behind which shadows are deepening. A fine mist of sleet rolls in on the north wind.

In the steel-gray twilight, Lilly can barely see the lead vehicle—several car lengths ahead of them—a glimpse of Martinez in the side mirror, his tattooed arm resting on the outer edge of the open window as he drives.

It could be Lilly's imagination, but she is almost positive she sees the bandanna-clad head of Martinez turning toward his passengers, saying something, sharing some intimate tidbit, and then getting a huge reaction from his comrades.

The men are laughing hysterically.

PART 2

This Is How the World Ends

The evil that men do lives after them; the good is often
interred with their bones.

—William Shakespeare

EIGHT

The convoy makes two stops on their way to the walled-in town—
the first at the junction of Highways 18 and 109, where an armed
sentry consults with Martinez for a moment before waving the vehicles on. A heap of human remains lies in a nearby ditch, still
smoldering from a makeshift funeral pyre. They make the second
stop at a roadblock near the town sign. By this point the sleet has
turned to a wet snow, spitting across the macadam on angular
gusts, a very rare phenomenon for Georgia this early in December.

"Looks like they got some serious firepower," Josh comments
from the driver's seat, as he waits for the two men in olive-drab camo
suits and M1 rifles to finish chatting with Martinez three car lengths
ahead of the Ram. Shadows thrown by the headlights obscure the
distant faces as they talk, the snow swirling, the Ram's windshield
wipers beating out a sullen rhythm. Lilly and Bob remain silent and
fidgety as they watch the exchange.

Full darkness has fallen, and the lack of a power grid and the bad
weather give the outer rings of the town a medieval quality. Flames
burn here and there in oil drums, and the signs of a recent skirmish
mar the wooded vales and pine groves circling the town. In the distance the scorched rooftops, bullet-riddled trailers, and torn power
lines reflect a series of past upheavals.

Josh notices Lilly studying the rust-pocked green sign up ahead,
visible in the wash of headlamp beams, the signpost planted in the
white, sandy earth.

WELCOME TO
WOODBURY
POPULATION 1,102

Lilly turns to Josh and says, "How are you feeling about all this?"

"Jury's still out. But it looks like we're about to get further orders."

Up ahead, in luminous motes of snow passing through the headlight beams, Martinez turns away from the confab, lifts his collar, and starts trudging back toward the Ram. He walks with a purpose, but still has that congenial smile plastered over his dark features. He lifts his collar against the cold as he approaches Josh's window.

Josh rolls down the window. "What's the deal?"

Martinez smiles. "Gonna need you to hand over your firearms for the time being."

Josh stares at him. "Sorry, brother, but that ain't gonna happen."

The convivial smile lingers. "Town rules . . . you know how it is."

Josh slowly shakes his head. "Ain't gonna happen."

Martinez purses his lips thoughtfully, then smiles some more. "Can't say I blame you, walking into something like this. Tell you what. Can you leave the rabbit gun in the truck for now?"

Josh lets out a sigh. "I guess we could do that."

"And you mind keeping the sidearms tucked away? Out of sight?"

"We could do that."

"Okay . . . if you want the nickel tour I could ride along with you folks. You got room for one more?"

Josh turns and gives Bob a nod. With a shrug the older man unsnaps his safety belt and gets out, then turns and squeezes into the rear enclosure next to Lilly.

Martinez comes around the passenger side and climbs into the cab. He smells of smoke and machine oil. "Take it nice and slow, cousin," he says, wiping the moisture from his face, gesturing toward the panel van ahead of them. "Just follow the dude in the van."

Josh gives the Ram some gas and they follow the van through the roadblock.

They bump over a series of railroad tracks and enter the town from the southeast. Lilly and Bob remain silent in the rear enclosure, as Josh scans the immediate area. To his right a busted sign reading PIGGLY IGGLY stands over a parking lot littered with dead bodies and broken glass. The grocery store is caved in on one side as though blasted by dynamite. Tall cyclone fencing, gouged and punched out in places, runs along the road known alternately as Woodbury Highway or Main Street. Grisly lumps of human carnage and twisted, scorched metal litter patches of exposed ground—the white, sandy earth practically glowing in the snowy darkness—an eerie sight reminiscent of a desert war zone smack-dab in the middle of Georgia.

"Had a pretty big dustup a few weeks ago with a flock of biters." Martinez lights a Viceroy and opens his window a few inches. The smoke curls out into the wind-lashed snow, vanishing like ghosts. "Things got outta hand for a while, but luckily cooler heads prevailed. Gonna be taking a hard left up here in a second."

Josh follows the van around a hairpin and down a narrower section of road.

In the dark middle distance, behind a veil of windswept sleet, the heart of Woodbury comes into view. Four square blocks of turn-of-the-century brick buildings and power lines crowd a central intersection of merchants, wood-frame homes, and apartment buildings. Much of it is laced with cyclone fences and idle construction sites that appear to be recent additions. Josh remembers when they used to call these places "wide spots in the road."

Woodbury's width seems to extend about half a dozen blocks in all directions, with larger public areas carved out of the wooded wetlands to the west and north. Some of the rooftop chimneys and vent stacks sprout columns of thick black smoke, either from generator exhaust or woodstoves and fireplaces. Most of the street lamps are dark, but some glow in the darkness, apparently running on emergency juice.

As the convoy approaches the center of town, Josh notices the van pulling up to the edge of a construction site. "Been working on the wall for months," Martinez explains. "Pretty near got two square blocks completely protected, and we plan on expanding it—moving the wall back farther and farther as we go."

"Not a bad idea," Josh mutters, almost under his breath, as he ponders the massive high wall of wooden timbers and planks, cannibalized pieces of cabin logs, siding, and two-by-fours, at least fifteen feet tall, extending along the edge of Jones Mill Road. Portions of the barricade still bare the scars of the recent walker attacks, and even in the snow-swept dark the claw marks and patched areas and ricochet holes and bloodstains, as black as tar, call out to Josh.

The place vibrates with latent violence, like some throwback to the Wild West.

Josh brings the truck to a stop, as the van's rear doors jack open and one of the Young Turks hops out the back and then goes over to a seam in the fortification. He pulls open a hinged section, swinging the gate wide enough for the two vehicles to pass through. The van rumbles through the gap, and Josh follows.

"Got about fifty people and change," Martinez continues, taking a deep drag off the Viceroy and blowing it out the window. "Place over there, on the right, that's kind of a food center. Got all our supplies, bottled water, medicine stashed in that place."

As they pass, Josh sees the faded old sign—DEFOREST'S FEED AND SEED—its storefront fortified and reinforced with burglar bars and planking, two armed guards standing out front smoking cigarettes. The gate closes behind them as they roll slowly along, venturing deeper into the secure zone. Other denizens stand around, watching them pass—people bundled up on boardwalks, standing in vestibules—shell-shocked expressions behind scarves and mufflers. Nobody looks particularly friendly or happy to see them.

"Got a doctor on board, working medical center and whatnot." Martinez tosses his cigarette butt out the window. "Hope to expand the walls at least another block by the end of the week."

"Not a bad setup," Bob comments from the backseat, his watery eyes taking it all in. "If ya don't mind my asking, what the hell is that?"

Josh sees the top of the massive edifice a few blocks beyond the walled-in area, toward which Bob is now pointing a greasy finger.

In the hazy darkness it looks like a flying saucer has landed in the middle of a field beyond the town square. Dirt roads circle the thing, and dim lights twinkle in the snow above its circular rim.

"Used to be a dirt racetrack." Martinez grins. In the green glow of the dashboard lights the smirk looks almost lupine, devilish. "Hillbillies love their races."

"'Used' to be?" Josh asks.

"Boss laid down the law last week, no more races, too much noise. Racket was drawing biters."

"There's a boss here?"

The smirk on Martinez's face curdles into something unreadable. "Don't worry, cousin. You'll be meeting him soon enough."

Josh sneaks a glance at Lilly, who is busily gnawing on her fingernails. "Not sure we're gonna be sticking around very long."

"It's up to you." Martinez gives a noncommittal shrug. He slips on a pair of fingerless, leather Carnaby gloves. "Keep in mind, though, those mutual benefits I was talking about."

"I'll do that."

"Our apartments are all filled up but we still got places you can stay in the center of town."

"Good to know."

"I'm telling you, once we get that wall expanded, you'll have your pick of places to live."

Josh says nothing.

Martinez stops smirking and all at once, in the dim green light, he looks as though he's remembering better days, maybe a family, maybe something painful. "I'm talking about places with soft beds, privacy . . . picket fences and trees."

A long pause of awkward silence.

"Lemme ask you something, Martinez."

"Shoot."

"How did *you* end up here?"

Martinez lets out a sigh. "God's honest truth, I don't really remember."

"How's that?"

He gives another shrug. "I was alone, ex-wife got bit, my kid up and disappeared. I guess I didn't give a shit about much of anything anymore but killing biters. Went on kind of a rampage. Put down a whole slew of those ugly motherfuckers. Some locals found me passed out in a ditch. Took me here. Swear to God that's about all I remember." He cocks his head as though reconsidering. "I'm glad they did, though, especially now."

"What do you mean?"

Martinez looks at him. "This place ain't perfect but it's safe, and it's only gonna get safer. Thanks in no small part to the guy we got in charge now."

Josh looks at him. "This is the 'boss' guy I assume you're talking about?"

"That's right."

"And you say we're gonna get a chance to meet this guy?"

Martinez holds up a gloved hand as if to say, *Just wait*. He pulls a small two-way radio from the breast pocket of his flannel shirt. He thumbs the switch and speaks into the mouthpiece. "Haynes, take us to the courthouse . . . they're waiting for us over there."

Another loaded glance passes between Josh and Lilly as the lead vehicle pulls off the main road and heads across the town square, a statue of Robert E. Lee guarding a kudzu-covered gazebo. They approach a flagstone government building on the far edge of the park, its stone steps and portico ghostly pale in the snow-veiled darkness.

The community room lies at the rear of the courthouse building, at the end of a long, narrow corridor lined with glass doors leading into private offices.

Josh and company gather in the cluttered meeting room, their boots dripping on the parquet floor. They are exhausted and in no mood to meet the Woodbury Welcome Wagon but Martinez tells them to be patient.

Snow ticks against the high windows as they wait. The room, warmed by space heaters and dimly lit with Coleman lanterns, looks as though it has seen its share of heated exchanges. The crumbling plaster walls bare the scars of violence. The floor is strewn with overturned folding chairs and littered with wadded documents. Josh notices blood streaks on the front wall, near a tattered

Georgia state flag. Generators thrum in the bowels of the edifice, vibrating the floor.

They wait a little over five minutes—Josh pacing, Lilly and the others sitting on folding chairs—before the sound of heavy boots echo out in the corridor. Someone is whistling as the footsteps approach.

"Welcome, folks, welcome to Woodbury." The voice that emanates from the doorway is low and nasally, and filled with faux conviviality.

All heads turn.

Three men stand in the doorway with smiles on their faces that don't match their cold, lidded stares. The man in the middle radiates a weird kind of energy that makes Lilly think of peacocks and fighting fish. "We can always use more good people around here," he says, and steps into the room.

Lean and rawboned in his ratty fisherman's sweater, his cinder-black hair shapeless and shaggy, he sports a five o'clock shadow of whiskers on his face that he's already trimming and styling into the beginnings of a Fu Manchu mustache. He has a strange nervous tic that is hardly noticeable—he blinks a lot.

"Name's Philip Blake," he says, "and this is Bruce over here, and that's Gabe."

The other two men—both older—follow on the younger man's heels like guard dogs. Not much of a greeting from these two—other than a few grunts and nods—as they stand slightly behind the man named Philip.

Gabe, on the left, the Caucasian, is a fireplug of a man with a thick neck and jarhead crew cut. Bruce, on the right, is a dour black man with an onyx shaved head. Each of these men holds an impressive automatic assault rifle across his chest, fingers on the trigger pads. For a moment Lilly cannot take her eyes off the guns.

"Sorry about the heavy artillery," Philip says, indicating the weaponry behind him. "We had a little dustup in town last month, got kinda hairy for a while. Can't take any chances now. Too much at stake. Your names are . . . ?"

Josh introduces the group, going around the room and ending on Megan.

"You look like somebody I knew once," Philip informs Megan, the man's eyes all over her now. Lilly does not like the way this guy is looking at her friend. It's very subtle but it bothers her.

"I get that a lot," Megan says.

"Or maybe it's somebody famous. Doesn't she look like somebody famous, guys?"

The "guys" behind him have no opinion. Philip snaps his fingers. "That chick from *Titanic!*"

"Carrie Winslet?" the one named Gabe speculates.

"You stupid fucking idiot, it's not Carrie, it's *Kate . . . Kate . . .* Fucking *Kate* Winslet."

Megan gives Philip a cockeyed smile. "I've been told Bonnie Raitt."

"I *love* Bonnie Raitt," Philip enthuses. " 'Let's Give 'Em Something to Talk About.' "

Josh speaks up. "So you're 'the boss' we've been hearing about?"

Philip turns to the big man. "Guilty as charged." Philip smiles and goes over to Josh and extends a hand. " 'Josh' was it?"

Josh shakes the man's hand. The expression on Josh's face remains noncommittal, polite, deferential. "That's right. We appreciate you taking us in for a while. Not sure how long we'll be staying."

Philip smiles at him. "You just got here, friend. Relax. Check the place out. You won't find a safer place to live. Believe me."

Josh gives a nod. "Looks like you got the walker problem under control."

"We get our share, I won't lie to you. Pack of 'em comes through every few weeks. Had a bad situation a couple of weeks ago but we're getting the town squared away."

"Looks like it."

"Basically we run on the barter system." Philip Blake looks around the room, regarding each of these newcomers as a coach might size up a new team. "I understand you folks scored big at a Walmart today."

"We did all right."

"You're all welcome to take what you need in trade."

Josh looks at him. "Trade?"

"Goods, services . . . whatever you got to contribute. As long as you respect your fellow citizens, keep your noses clean, abide by the rules, pitch in . . . you can stay as long as you like." He looks at Josh. "Gentleman of your . . . *physical endowment* . . . we can use around here."

Josh thinks it over. "So you're some kind of 'elected official'?"

Philip glances at his guards, and the other men grin, and Philip bursts out laughing. He wipes his mirthless eyes and shakes his head. "I'm more like—what's the phrase?—'pro tem'? President pro tem?"

"I'm sorry?"

Philip waves off the question. "Put it this way, not long ago this place was under the thumb of some power-hungry assholes, got too big for their britches. I saw the need for leadership and I volunteered."

"Volunteered?"

Philip's smile fades. "I stepped up, friend. Times like these. Strong leadership is a necessity. We got families here. Women and children. Old people. You got to have somebody watching the door, somebody . . . decisive. You understand what I'm saying?"

Josh nods. "Sure."

Behind Philip, Gabe, still smirking, mumbles, "President Pro Tem . . . I like that."

From across the room, Scott, perched on a windowsill, chimes in: "Dude, you sure *look* like a president . . . with those two Secret Service dudes."

An awkward moment of silence presses down on the group as Scott's breathy little weed-giggle fades and Philip turns to glance at the stoner across the room. "What's your name again, sport?"

"Scott Moon."

"Well, Scott Moon, I don't know about president. Never saw myself as the chief executive type." Another cold smile. "I'd be governor at best."

They spend that night in the gymnasium of the local high school. The aging brick building, situated outside the walled-in zone, sits on the edge of a vast athletic field riddled with shallow graves.

Cyclone fences bear the damage of a recent walker attack. Inside the gym, makeshift cots crowd the varnished basketball court. The air smells of urine and body odors and disinfectant.

The night drags for Lilly. The fetid corridors and breezeways connecting the dark schoolrooms creak and moan in the wind all night, while strangers toss and turn across the dark gymnasium, coughing, wheezing, murmuring feverish ruminations. Every few moments a child cries out.

At one point Lilly glances at the cot next to her, on which Josh slumbers fitfully, and she sees the big man jerking awake from a nightmare.

Lilly reaches over and offers her hand, and the big man takes it.

The next morning, the five newcomers sit in a huddle around Josh's cot, as the ashen sunlight slants down through dust motes and stripes the sick and wounded as they hunch on their meager, stained bedsheets. Lilly is reminded of Civil War encampments and jury-rigged morgues. "Is it just me," she says softly, under her breath to her fellow travelers, "or does this place have a weird vibe?"

"That's putting it lightly," Josh says.

Megan yawns and stretches. "It sure beats sleeping in Bob's little dungeon-on-wheels."

"You got that right," Scott concurs. "I'll take a shitty cot in a stinky gym any day of the week."

Bob looks at Josh. "Gotta admit, captain . . . you could make an argument for staying here for a while."

Josh laces his boots, pulls on his lumberjack coat. "Not sure about this place."

"What's on your mind?"

"I don't know. I'm thinking we take this one day at a time."

"I agree with Josh," Lilly says. "Something about this place bothers me."

"What's not to like?" Megan combs fingers through her hair, scrunching her curls. "It's safe, they got supplies, they got guns."

Josh wipes his mouth thoughtfully. "Look. I can't tell any of you folks what to do. Just be careful. Watch each other's backs."

"Duly noted," Bob says.

"Bob, for the time being, I'm thinking we ought to keep the truck locked up."

"Copy that."

"Keep your .44 handy."

"Gotcha."

"And we ought to all remember where the truck is at all times, you know, just in case."

They all agree, and then they agree to split up that morning and investigate the rest of the town—get a feel for the place in the light of day. They will meet back up that afternoon at the high school and they will reassess at that point whether to go or stay.

The harsh light of day shines down on Lilly and Josh as they exit the high school, turning up their collars against the wind. The snow has blown over, and the weather has turned blustery. Lilly's stomach growls. "You feel like getting some breakfast?" she proffers to Josh.

"Got some of that stuff from Walmart in the truck, if you can stand beef jerky and Chef Boyardee again."

Lilly shudders. "I don't think I can look at another can of SpaghettiOs."

"I got an idea." Josh feels the breast pocket of his flannel jacket. "Come on . . . I'm buying."

They turn west and make their way down the main drag. In the bitter gray daylight the seams of the town reveal themselves. Most of the storefronts sit empty, boarded or barred, the pavement scarred with skid marks and oil spills. Some of the windows and signs show the marks of bullet holes. Passersby keep to themselves. Here and there, bare patches of ground reveal dirty white sand. It seems the whole village is built on sand.

No one offers a greeting as Lilly and Josh pass through the walled area. Most of those who are out at this hour carry building materials or bundles of supplies, and seem to be in a hurry to get where they're going. There's a sullen, prisonlike atmosphere in the air. Quadrants of the town are sectioned off with huge, temporary cyclone fences. The growl of bulldozers drifts on the breeze. On the eastern horizon, a man with a high-powered rifle paces along the top edge of the racetrack arena.

"Morning, gentlemen," Josh says to three old codgers sitting on barrels outside the feed and seed store, watching Lilly and Josh like buzzards.

One of the old men—a wizened, bearded troll in a tattered overcoat and slouch hat—shows a smile full of rotten teeth. "Mornin', big fella. Y'all are the newbies, ain't ya?"

"Just got in last night," Josh tells him.

"Lucky you."

The three coots share a garbled chuckle as if enjoying a private joke.

Josh smiles and lets the joke pass. "Understand this is the food center?"

"You could call it that." More mucusy chuckling. "Keep an eye on your woman."

"I'll do that," Josh says, taking Lilly's hand. They climb the steps and go inside.

In the dim light a long, narrow retail store stretches before them, smelling of turpentine and must, gutted of its shelves, packed with crates up to the ceiling: dry goods, toilet paper, gallon jugs of water, bed linen, and unidentified cartons of merchandise. The single customer present—an older woman bundled in down and scarves—sees Josh and brushes past him, hurrying out the door, averting her eyes. The cool air vibrates with the artificial warmth of space heaters and the crackle of human tension.

In the rear corner of the store, among sacks of seed stacked to the rafters, sits a makeshift counter. A man in a wheelchair is positioned behind the counter, flanked by two armed guards.

Josh walks up to the counter. "How y'all doin' this morning?"

The man in the wheelchair looks up through lidded eyes. "Holy shit, you're a big one," he comments, his long, straggly beard twitching. He wears faded army dungarees, and a headband cinches his greasy, iron-gray ponytail. His face is a map of degradation, from his rheumy red-rimmed eyes to his ulcerated beak of a nose.

Josh ignores the comment. "Just wondering if y'all have any fresh produce? Or maybe some eggs we might take off your hands in trade?"

The man in the wheelchair stares. Josh can feel the suspicious gazes of the armed guards. The gunmen are both young, black, dressed in quasi-gang colors. "Whaddaya have in mind?"

"The thing is, we just brought in a whole slew of items from Walmart with Martinez . . . so I'm wondering if we can work something out."

"That's between you and Martinez. What else you got for me?"

Josh starts to answer when he notices all three men are staring at Lilly, and the way they're staring at her puts Josh's hackles up.

"What'll this buy me?" Josh says finally, shooting his cuff, fiddling with the buckle of his watchband. He snaps it off and lays the sports watch on the counter. It's not a Rolex but it's no Timex, either. The chronograph set him back three hundred bucks ten years ago when his catering job was bringing in decent money.

Wheelchair Man looks down his blemished nose at the shiny thing on the counter. " 'The tarnation is that?"

"It's a Movado, worth five hundred easy."

"Not around here it ain't."

"Give us a break, will ya? Been eating outta cans for weeks."

The man picks up the watch and inspects it with a sour expression as though it's covered in feces. "I'll give ya fifty dollars' worth of rice and beans, slab bacon, and them Egg Beaters."

"C'mon, man. Fifty dollars?"

"Got some white peaches in back, too, just came in from the road, I'll throw those in. That's all I can do."

"I don't know." Josh looks at Lilly, who stares back at him with a shrug. Josh looks at Wheelchair Man. "I don't know, man."

"That'll keep the two of you going for a week."

Josh sighs. "That's a Movado, man. That's a fine piece of craftsmanship."

"Lookit, I ain't gonna argue with—"

A baritone voice from behind the guards rings out, interrupting the man in the wheelchair. "What the fuck's the problem?"

All heads turn toward a figure coming around the corner of

the stockroom, wiping his bloody hands in a towel. The tall, gaunt, weathered man wears a horribly stained butcher's apron, the fabric mottled with blood and marrow. His chiseled, sunburned face, set off by ice-chip blue eyes, glowers at Josh. "There a problem here, Davy?"

"Everything's hunky-dory, Sam," the man in the wheelchair says, not taking his eyes off Lilly. "These folks were somewhat dissatisfied with my offer, and they were just leaving."

"Hold on a second." Josh raises his hands in a contrite gesture. "I'm sorry if I offended you but I didn't say I was—"

"All offers are final," Sam the Butcher announces, throwing his grisly-looking towel on the counter and glaring at Josh. "Unless . . ." He seems to change his mind. "Forget it, never mind."

Josh looks at the man. "Unless what?"

The man in the apron looks at the others, then purses his lips thoughtfully. "See . . . what most folks do around here is work off their debts, pitching in on the wall, patching fences, stacking sandbags and such. You'll definitely get more bang for your buck offering up them big muscles of yours in trade." He gives Lilly a look. " 'Course there's all kinds of services a person could provide, all kinds of ways to get more *bang*." He grins. "Especially a person of the female persuasion."

Lilly realizes the men behind the counter are all looking at *her* now, each of them grinning lasciviously. At first she's taken by surprise, and she just stands there blinking. Then she feels all the blood rushing out of her face. She gets dizzy. She wants to kick over the table, or storm out of that musty-smelling chamber, knocking over the shelves and suggesting that they all fuck themselves. But the fear, the throat-closing fear—her old nemesis—holds her paralyzed, her feet nailed to the floor. She wonders what the hell is wrong with her. How did she survive this long without getting devoured? All she's been through and she can't even deal with a few sexist pigs?

Josh speaks up. "Okay, you know what . . . this is not necessary."

Lilly looks at the big black man and sees his huge, square jaw tensing. She wonders whether Josh is talking about the concept of Lilly trading sexual services not being necessary or these thugs making crude, chauvinist comments not being necessary. The store gets very quiet. Sam the Butcher levels his gaze at Josh.

"Don't be so quick to judge, Big Hoss." An ember of contempt smolders in the butcher's humorless blue eyes. He wipes his slimy hands on the apron. "Little lady with a body like that on her, you could be swimming in steak and eggs for a month."

The smirks on the other men turn to laughter. But the butcher barely smiles. His impassive stare seems to be locked on to Josh with the intensity of an arc welder. Lilly feels her heart racing.

She puts a hand on Josh's arm, which is pulsing under his lumberjack coat, tendons as coiled as telephone cable. "C'mon, Josh," she says, almost under her breath. "It's okay. Get your watch and let's go."

Josh smiles respectfully at the laughing men. "Steak and eggs. That's a good one. Listen. Keep the watch. We'll take you up on them beans and Egg Beaters and the rest."

"Go get 'em their food," the butcher says, still with those pale blue eyes fixed on Josh.

The two guards disappear in the back for a moment, gathering up the items. They return with a crate filled with oil-spotted brown paper sacks. "Appreciate it," Josh says softly, taking the food. "We'll let you fellas get back to your business. Have a good day."

Josh ushers Lilly toward the door, Lilly hyperaware now of the gazes of the men on her backside the whole way out.

That afternoon, a commotion in one of the vacant lots on the northern edge of the village draws the attention of the townspeople.

Outside one of the cyclone fences, behind a wooded grove, a series of nauseating shrieks echoes on the wind. Josh and Lilly hear the screaming, and they race along the edge of the construction zone to see what's going on.

By the time they reach a high mound of gravel and climb to the top to see into the distance, three gunshots have rung out over the treetops a hundred and fifty yards away.

Josh and Lilly crouch down in the dying sun, the wind in their faces, as they peer around a pile of debris and notice five men in the distance, near a hole in the fence. One of the men—Blake, the self-proclaimed Governor—wears a long coat and holds what appears to be an automatic pistol in his hand. The scene crackles with tension.

On the ground in front of Blake, tangled in the jagged, torn chain-link fence, a teenage boy, bleeding from bite wounds, claws at the dirt, trying frantically to extricate himself from the fence and return home.

In the shadows of the forest, directly behind the boy, three dead walkers lie in heaps, their skulls breached by gunfire, and the narrative of what has just happened coalesces in Lilly's mind.

The boy apparently lit out by himself to explore the woods, and he was attacked. Now, badly wounded and infected, the boy, trying to return to safety, writhes in pain and terror on the ground, as Blake stands emotionlessly over him, gazing down with the impassive stare of an undertaker.

Lilly jumps when the boom of the 9-millimeter in Philip Blake's hand echoes. The boy's head erupts, and the body sags immediately.

"I don't like this place, Josh, not even a little." Lilly sits on the Ram's rear bumper, sipping tepid coffee from a paper cup.

Darkness has fallen on their second evening in Woodbury and already the town has absorbed Megan, Scott, and Bob into its folds like a multicelled organism living off fear and suspicion, acquiring new life-forms on a daily basis. The town leaders have offered the newcomers a place to live—a studio apartment above a boarded-up drugstore at the end of Main Street—well outside the walled-in area but high enough above street level to be safe. Megan and Scott have already moved much of their stuff up there and have even bartered their sleeping bags for a nickel's worth of locally grown weed.

Bob has stumbled upon a working tavern inside the safe zone, and already has traded half his rations of Walmart products for a few drink tickets and a little drunken camaraderie.

"I'm not crazy about this place myself, babydoll," Josh concurs as he paces behind Bob's camper, his breath showing in the cold. His huge hands are oily with bacon grease from the dinner he just prepared on the camper's Coleman stove, and he wipes them on his lumberjack coat. He and Lilly have been sticking close to the Ram all day, trying to decide what to do. "But we ain't looking at a lot of options right now. This place is better than the open road."

"Really?" Lilly shivers in the cold and clutches at the collar of her down coat. "You sure about that?"

"At least it's safe."

"Safe from what? It's not the walls and the fences keeping things out I'm worried about . . ."

"I know, I know." Josh lights a stogie and puffs a few swirls of smoke. "It's wound pretty tight around here. But it's pretty much like this everywhere you go nowadays."

"Jesus." Lilly shivers some more and sips her coffee. "Where's Bob, anyway?"

"Hanging out with them geezers at the taproom."

"Jesus Christ."

Josh goes over to her, puts a hand on her shoulder. "Don't worry about it, Lil. We'll rest up, we'll stockpile some stuff . . . I'll do some work in trade . . . and we'll get outta here by the end of the week." He tosses his stogie and sits next to her. "I won't let anything happen."

She looks at him. "Promise?"

"Promise." He kisses her cheek. "I'll protect you, girlie-girl. Always. Always . . ."

She kisses him back.

He puts his arms around her and kisses her on the lips. She wraps her arms around his thick neck and things begin to happen. His enormous tender hands find the small of her back, and their kiss turns to something hotter, more desperate. They intertwine, and he urges her back inside the camper, into the private darkness.

They leave the rear hatch open, oblivious to everything but each other, as they begin to make love.

It's better than either one of them dreamed it would be. Lilly loses herself in the murky dark, the light of an icy harvest moon shining in through the gap, as Josh lets all his lonely desire pour out in a series of heaving gasps. He sheds his coat, gets his undershirt off—his skin looks almost indigo in the moonlight. Lilly peels her bra up and over herself, the soft weight of her breasts splaying across her rib cage. Gooseflesh spreads down her tummy as Josh gently enters her and builds steam.

They make feverish love. Lilly forgets everything, even the savage environment outside the camper.

A minute, an hour—time is meaningless now—all of it passes in a blur.

Later, they lie among the detritus of Bob's camper, legs intertwined, Lilly's head against the massive curve of Josh's bicep, a blanket covering them, staving off the chill. Josh presses his lips against the soft convolutions of Lilly's ear and whispers, "Gonna be okay."

"Yeah," she murmurs.

"We're gonna make it."

"Absolutely."

"Together."

"You got that right." She lays her right arm across Josh's massive chest, and she looks into his sad eyes. She feels strange. Buoyant, woozy. "Been thinking about this moment for a long time."

"Me, too."

They let the silence engulf them, carrying them away, and they lie there like that for some time, unaware of the dangers lying in wait . . . unaware of the brutal outside world tightening its grasp.

Most important, they are unaware of the fact that they are being watched.

NINE

On their third day in town, the winter rains roll in, drawing a dark gray pall of misery down over Woodbury. It's already early December and Thanksgiving has come and gone without so much as a wishbone being snapped, and now the dampness as well as the cold starts getting into people's joints. The sandy lots along Main Street turn to wet plaster and the sewers swell and overflow with tainted runoff. A human hand bubbles out of one of the gratings.

That day Josh decides to trade his best chef's knife—a Japanese Shun—for bed linens and towels and soap, and he convinces Lilly to move her things into the apartment over the dry cleaner, where they can take sponge baths and find temporary refuge from the cramped quarters of the camper. Lilly stays indoors most of the day, fervently writing diary entries on a roll of wrapping paper and planning her escape. Josh keeps a close eye on her. Something feels wrong—more wrong than he can articulate.

Scott and Megan are nowhere to be found. Lilly suspects that Megan, already growing bored with Scott, is prostituting herself for dope.

That afternoon Bob Stookey finds a couple of kindred spirits in the bowels of the racetrack, where a labyrinth of cinder-block storage facilities and service areas has been turned into a makeshift infirmary. While the cold-steel rain pummels the metal beams and stanchions of the arena above them—sending a dull, hissing, incessant drone down through the bones of the building—a middle-aged man and a young woman give Bob the grand tour.

"Alice here has been a quick study as a neophyte nurse, I have to say," the man in the wire-frame reading glasses and stained lab coat comments, as he leads Bob and the young lady through an open doorway and into a cluttered examination room. The man's name is Stevens, and he's a trim, intelligent, wry sort who seems out of place to Bob in this feral town. The ersatz nurse, also in a hand-me-down lab coat, looks younger than her years. Her dishwater-blond hair is braided and pulled back from her girlish face.

"I'm still working at it," the girl says, following the men into the dimly lit room, the floor humming with the vibrations of a central generator. "I'm stuck somewhere in the middle of second-year nursing school."

"Both y'all know a lot more than I do," Bob admits. "I'm just an old battle tech."

"She had her baptism of fire last month, God knows," the doctor says, pausing next to a battered X-ray machine. "Business was brisk down here for a while."

Bob looks around the room, sees the bloodstains and the signs of chaotic triage, and he asks what happened.

The doctor and the nurse share an uneasy glance. "Changeover in power."

"Excuse me?"

The doctor sighs. "Place like this, you see a kind of natural selection going on. Only the pure sociopaths survive. It's not pretty." He takes a breath, and then smiles at Bob. "Still, it's good to have a medic around."

Bob wipes his mouth. "Not sure how much help I'd be, but I gotta admit, it sure would be nice to lean on the skills of a real doctor for once." Bob motions at one of the old, battered machines. "I see y'all got an old Siemens machine there, used to truck one of those around Afghanistan."

"Yeah, well, we're not exactly Bellevue but we've got the basics, scavenged them from area clinics . . . got infusion pumps, IV drips, a couple monitors, ECG, EEG . . . we're light on the pharmacy, though."

Bob tells them about the medicine he scavenged from Walmart. "You're welcome to any or all of it," he says. "I got a couple of spare doctor's bags full of the usual. Got extra dressings, you name it. It's yours, you need it."

"That's great, Bob. Where you from?"

"Vicksburg originally, was living in Smyrna when the Turn came. How about you folks?"

"Atlanta," Stevens replies. "Had a small practice in Brookhaven before everything went to hell."

"Also from Atlanta," the girl chimes in. "Was going to school at Georgia State."

Stevens has a pleasant look on his face. "You been drinking, Bob?"

"Huh?"

Stevens gestures toward the silver flask partially visible in Bob's hip pocket. "You been drinking today?"

Bob lowers his head, crestfallen, ashamed. "Yessir, I have."

"You drink every day, Bob?"

"Yes, sir."

"Hard liquor?"

"Yes, sir."

"Bob, I don't mean to put you on the spot." The doctor pats Bob's shoulder. "It's none of my business. I'm not judging you. But can I ask how much you're putting away every day?"

Bob's chest tightens with humiliation. Alice gazes elsewhere for a moment, out of respect. Bob swallows his shame. "I have no earthly idea. Sometimes a couple of pints, sometimes a whole fifth when I can get it." Bob looks up at the slender, bespectacled doctor. "I'll understand if you don't want me getting near your—"

"Bob, relax. You don't understand. I think it's fantastic."

"Huh?"

"Keep drinking. Drink as much as possible."

"I'm sorry?"

"You mind sharing a sip?"

Bob slowly pulls the flask, not taking his eyes off the doctor.

"Appreciate it." Stevens takes the flask, nods a thank-you, and takes a pull. He wipes his mouth and offers it to Alice.

The girl waves it off. "No, thanks, it's a little early in the day for me."

Stevens takes another sip and hands the flask back. "You stay here for any length of time you're gonna need to drink heavily."

Bob puts the flask back in his pocket. He doesn't say anything.

Stevens smiles again, and there's something heartbreaking behind the smile. "That's my prescription, Bob. Stay as drunk as possible."

On the other side of the racetrack complex, beneath the north end of the arena, a wiry, tightly coiled individual emerges from an unmarked metal door and gazes up at the sky. The rain has ceased for the moment, leaving behind a low ceiling of sooty clouds. The wiry gentleman carries a small bundle wrapped in a threadbare woolen blanket the color of dead grass, gathered at the top with rawhide.

The wiry man crosses the street and starts down the sidewalk, his raven-black hair slick with moisture and pulled back in a ponytail today.

As he walks, his preternaturally alert gaze is everywhere, practically all at once, taking in everything that goes on around him. In recent weeks the emotions that have plagued him have subsided, the voice in his head silent now. He feels strong. This town is his raison d'être, the fuel that keeps him keen and sharp.

He is about to turn the corner at the intersection of Canyon and Main when he notices a figure in his peripheral vision. The older guy—the drunk who came in a few days ago with the nigger and the girls—is emerging from the warehouse at the south end of the racetrack. The weathered old dude pauses for a moment to take a gulp from his flask, and the look on his face after swallowing and cringing at the burn is apparent to the wiry man even a block away.

In the distance, the older dude grimaces as the alcohol streams down his gullet, and the grimace is weirdly familiar to the wiry man. The grimace—full of shame and desolation—makes the wiry man feel strange and sentimental, almost tender. The older man puts the flask away and starts trundling toward Main Street with that trademark gait—half limp, half drunken amble—which many homeless people get after years of struggling on the street. The wiry man follows.

Minutes later, the wiry man cannot resist calling out to the juicer. "Hey, sport!"

Bob Stookey hears the voice—gravelly, lightly accented with a trace of Southern small town, echoing on the breeze—but he cannot locate the source.

Bob pauses at the edge of Main Street and looks around. The town is mostly deserted today, the rains driving denizens indoors.

"'Bob' is it?" the voice says, closer now, and Bob finally sees a figure approaching from behind.

"Oh, hi . . . how ya doin'?"

The man saunters up to Bob with a forced smile. "I'm doing great, Bob, thanks." Wisps of coal-black hair dangling in front of the man's chiseled face, he carries a bundle that seems to be leaking moisture, dripping on the pavement. People around town have started to call this man "the Governor"—the name has stuck—which is fine and dandy with this guy. "How you settling in to our little hamlet?"

"Real good."

"You meet Doc Stevens?"

"Yes, sir. Good man."

"Call me 'the Governor.'" The smile softens a bit. "Everybody else seems to be calling me that. What the hell? Kinda like the ring of it."

"The Governor it is," Bob says, and glances down at the bundle in the man's grip. The blanket leaks blood. Bob glances away quickly, alarmed by it, but feigning ignorance. "Looks like the rains have blown over."

The man's smile remains stamped on his face. "Walk with me, Bob."

"Sure."

They start down the cracked sidewalk, moving toward the temporary wall that stands between merchant's row and the outer streets. The sound of nail guns snapping can be heard above the wind. The wall continues expanding along the southern edge of the business district. "You remind me of somebody," the Governor says after a long pause.

"It ain't Kate Winslet, I'm betting." Bob has had enough alcohol to loosen his tongue. He chuckles to himself as he trundles along. "Or Bonnie Raitt, neither."

"Touché, Bob." The Governor glances down at his package, notices the droplets of blood leaving little coin-sized marks on the sidewalk. "What a mess I'm making."

Bob looks away, scrambles to change the subject. "Ain't y'all worried about all that pounding racket over there drawing walkers?"

"We got it under control, Bob, don't you worry about that. Got men posted out on the edge of the woods, and we try and keep the pounding down to a minimum."

"That's good to hear . . . got things figured out pretty good around here."

"We try, Bob."

"I told Doc Stevens, he's welcome to any medical supplies I got in my stash."

"You a doctor, too?"

Bob tells the man about Afghanistan, patching marines, getting an honorable discharge.

"You got kids, Bob?"

"No, sir . . . for the longest time it was just me and Brenda, my old lady. Had a little trailer outside of Smyrna, not a bad life."

"You're looking at my little bundle, aren't ya, Bob?"

"No, sir . . . whatever it is, it's none of my beeswax. Doesn't concern me."

"Where's your wife?"

Bob slows down a bit, as though the mere subject of Brenda Stookey weighs him down. "Lost her to a walker attack shortly after the Turn."

"Sorry to hear that." They approach a gated section of the wall. The Governor pauses, knocks a few times, and the seam opens. Litter swirls as a workman pulls the gate back and nods at the Governor, letting the twosome pass. "My place is just up the road a piece," the Governor says with a tilt of his head toward the east side of town. "Little two-story apartment building . . . come on over, I'll fix you a drink."

"The Governor's mansion?" Bob jokes. He can't help it. The nerves and the booze are working on him. "Ain't you got laws to pass?"

The Governor pauses, turns and smiles at Bob. "I just figured out who you remind me of."

In that brief instant, standing in that gray overcast daylight, the wiry man—who from this point on shall think of himself as "the Governor"—experiences a seismic shift within his brain. He stands there staring at a coarse, deeply lined, alcoholic good old boy from Smyrna who is the spitting image of Ed Blake, the Governor's old man. Ed Blake had that same pug nose, prominent brow, and crow's-feet around red-rimmed eyes. Ed Blake was a big drinker, too, like this guy, with the same sense of humor. Ed Blake would toss off sarcastic one-liners with the same drunken relish, cutting to the quick with his words when he wasn't slapping his family around with the back of his big, callused hands.

All at once, another part of the Governor bubbles up to the surface—a deeply buried part of him—on a wave of sentimental longing, which almost makes him dizzy as he remembers big Ed Blake in happier times, a simple hillbilly laborer who tried to fight his demons long enough to be a loving father. "You remind me of somebody I used to know a long time ago," the Governor says finally, his tone softening as he looks Bob Stookey in the eyes. "C'mon, let's go get a drink."

For the rest of their journey across the safe zone, the two men talk quietly, openly, like old friends.

At one point the Governor asks Bob what happened to his wife.

"Place we lived, this mobile home park . . ." Bob says slowly, heavily, as he hobbles along, remembering dark days. "We got overrun one day with walkers. I was out trying to scrounge up some supplies when it happened . . . by the time I got back they had gotten into our place."

He pauses and the Governor says nothing, just walks in silence, waiting.

"They were tearing into her, and I fought 'em off best I could . . . and . . . I guess they only ate enough of her that she came back."

Another agonizing pause. Bob licks his dry lips. The Governor can see that the man needs a drink badly, needs his medicine to stanch the memories.

"I couldn't bring myself to finish her off." This comes out of Bob on a choked wheeze. His rheumy eyes well up. "I ain't proud of the fact that I left her. Pretty sure she got some folks after that. Her arm and her lower body was pretty mangled but she could still get around. Them people she got, their deaths are my fault."

A pause.

"It's hard to let go sometimes," the Governor ventures at last, glancing down at his ghastly little bundle. The dripping has diminished somewhat, the blood thickening to the consistency of blackstrap molasses. Right then the Governor notices Bob pondering the blood droplets, his brow furrowed in thought. He looks almost sober.

Bob gestures at the gruesome bundle. "You got somebody turned on ya, don't ya?"

"You're not so dumb . . . are ya, Bob?"

Bob wipes his mouth pensively. "Never thought about feeding Brenda."

"C'mon, Bob, I want to show you something."

They reach the two-story brick edifice at the end of the block, and Bob follows the Governor inside.

"Stand behind me for a second, Bob." The Governor fiddles a key into a dead bolt, the door at the end of a second-floor hallway. The door clicks, and the sound of a low growl seeps out. "I would appreciate it, Bob, if you kept what you're about to see to yourself."

"No problem . . . lips are sealed."

Bob follows the Governor into a two-bedroom unit with spartan furnishings that reeks of spoiled meat and disinfectant, the windows painted over with black Rust-Oleum. A floor-length mirror near the front vestibule is covered with newspaper and masking tape. The mirror in the bathroom—visible through an open doorway—is missing, its absence evident in the pale oval outline above the sink. All the mirrors in this place have been removed.

"She's everything to me," the Governor says. Bob follows the man across the living room, down a short hallway, and through a doorway into a cramped laundry room, where the upright corpse of a little girl is chained to a U-bolt drilled into the wall.

"Oh, Lord." Bob keeps his distance. The dead girl—still in pigtails and pinafore dress, as if dressed for church—snarls and spits and flails, her chain straining at its mooring. Bob takes a step back. "Oh, Lord."

"Calm down, Bob."

The Governor kneels in front of the pint-sized zombie and lays the bundle on the floor. The girl bites at the air, blackened teeth clacking. The Governor unwraps a human head, its cranial cavity gaping on one side from a close-range gunshot.

"Oh, my." Bob notices that the human head—its pulpy concavity on one side already hectic with maggots—sports a bristly, jarhead haircut, as if it once belonged to a soldier or marine.

"This here's Penny . . . she's an only child," the Governor explains as he shoves the dripping severed head within range of the chained cadaver. "We came from a small town called Waynesboro. Penny's mother—my sweet wife, Sarah—was killed in a car crash before the Turn."

The child feeds.

Bob watches from the doorway, at once appalled and riveted, as the diminutive zombie slurps and chews the soft matter of the cranial passage as though ferreting out the meat of a lobster.

The Governor watches the feeding. The slurping noises fill the air. "My brother Brian and I—along with a few friends of mine—we set out to find greener pastures with Penny here. Made our way west, crashed in Atlanta for a spell, hooked up with some people, lost some people. Kept moving west."

The little corpse settles down, leaning against the wall with tiny, greasy, scarlet-stained fingers burrowing deep into the hollowed-out skull for morsels.

The Governor's voice drops an octave. "Had a run-in with some dirtbags at an orchard not far from here." His words falter for a moment. No tears but his voice crumbles a little. "Put my brother in charge of Penny while I fended 'em off . . . and one thing led to another."

Bob cannot move. He cannot speak in this airless chamber of stained tiles, exposed plumbing, and mold-darkened grout. He watches the tiny abomination, her ghastly face content now, stringers of brain matter hanging from her little tulip lips, her fish-belly eyes rolling back in her head as she leans back.

"My brother fucked up big-time, got my baby killed," the Governor explains now, his head down, his chin on his chest. His voice gets thick with emotion. "Brian was weak and that's all there is to it. I could not let it go, though." He looks at Bob through raw, wet eyes. "I know you can relate, Bob. I could not let go of my baby girl."

Bob can relate. His chest seizes up with sorrow for Brenda.

"I blame myself for Penny getting killed and comin' back." The Governor stares at the floor. "I kept her going with scraps and we kept headin' west. By the time we got to Woodbury my brother Brian was ape-shit crazy with guilt."

The thing that was once a little girl drops the skull as though discarding an oyster shell. She gazes around the room through her milky eyes as if awakening from a dream.

"I had to put Brian down like a sick dog," the Governor utters, almost to himself. He takes a step closer to the little thing that used to be a child. His voice becomes almost toneless. "I still see my Penny in there sometimes . . . when she's calm like this."

Bob swallows hard. Contrary emotions swirl and eddy inside him—repulsion, sadness, fear, bone-deep longing, even sympathy for this deranged individual—and he hangs his head. "You been through a lot."

"Look at that, Bob." The Governor nods toward the little zombie. The child-thing cocks its head, staring at the Governor with a vexed expression. The thing blinks its eyes. A faint trace of Penny Blake glimmers behind its eyes. "My baby's still in there. Aren't ya, honey?"

The Governor goes over to the chained creature, kneels and strokes its livid cheek.

Bob stiffens, starts to say, "Be careful, you don't want to be—"

"Here's my beautiful baby girl." The Governor strokes the thing's matted hair. The tiny zombie blinks. The pallid face changes, eyes narrowing, blackened lips peeling away from rotten baby teeth.

Bob steps forward. "Look out—"

The Penny-thing snaps its jaws at the exposed flesh of the Governor's wrist, but the Governor pulls away just in time. "Whoopsy!"

The little zombie strains at its chain, scuttling to its feet and reaching at the air . . . as the Governor backs away. He speaks in baby talk. "Wascally Wabbit . . . almost got Daddy that time!"

Bob gets woozy. He can feel his gorge rising, the bile threatening to come up.

"Bob, do me a favor and reach into that loose bundle the head came out of."

"Huh?"

"Do me a favor and grab that last little goodie in that bag over there."

Bob holds his vomit in and turns and finds the bundle on the floor and looks inside. A pale human finger, apparently male, lies at the bottom of the bag in a clot of drying blood. Hair sprouts from the knuckles, and from the ragged end protrudes a small nodule of white bone.

Something loosens inside Bob—as sudden as a rubber band snapping—as he pulls a handkerchief from his pocket, bends down, and retrieves the finger.

"Why don't *you* do the honors, my friend," the Governor suggests, standing proudly over the snapping zombie-child, his hands on his hips.

Bob feels as though his body has begun to move on its own, with a *mind* of its own. "Yeah . . . sure."

"Go ahead."

Bob stands within inches of the chain's limit, as the Penny-thing snarls and sputters noisily at him, clanging against the U-bolt. "Yeah . . . why not?"

Holding the finger out at arm's length, Bob feeds it to the creature.

The little corpse gobbles the thing, falling to its knees, two-handing the finger into her ravenous little pit of a mouth. The nauseating wet noises fill the laundry room.

The two men stand side by side, watching now. The Governor puts his arm around his new friend.

By the end of that week the men on the wall have reached the edge of the third block, along Jones Mill Road, where the U.S. Post Office sits boarded and defaced with graffiti. Along the brick wall adjacent to the parking lot some joker with a few years of college lit classes has spray-painted the words *THIS IS HOW THE WORLD ENDS NOT WITH A BANG BUT WITH A WALKER,* a constant reminder of the end of society and government services as we know them.

On Saturday Josh Lee Hamilton ends up on a work crew, hauling dollies loaded with scrap lumber from one end of the sidewalk to the other, bartering his muscles for food so that he and Lilly can continue to eat. He has run out of valuables to trade, and for the last couple of days Josh has been doing menial tasks such as emptying latrines and cleaning animal carcasses in the smokehouse. But he gladly does the work for Lilly.

Josh has fallen so deeply for the woman that he secretly lets the tears come at night, in the desolate darkness of the walk-up apartment, after Lilly has drifted off in his arms. Josh finds himself beset with the ironies of finding love among the wreckage of this plague. Filled with a kind of reckless hope, as well as the dreamy side effects of the first true intimate relationship of his life, Josh barely notices the absence of the other members of his group.

The little clique seems to have scattered to the winds. Occasionally Josh will get a glimpse of Megan at night, creeping along the balustrades of residential buildings, scantily clad and stoned. Josh has no idea whether she is still with Scott. In fact, Scott has vanished. No one seems to know where he is, and the sad truth is, nobody seems to care. Business seems to be brisk for Megan. Out of the fifty or so residents of Woodbury, less than a dozen are women, and out of those only about four are premenopausal.

Far more troubling is Bob's apparent ascendancy to town mascot. Evidently the Governor—Josh trusts this sociopath as a leader about as much as he trusts one of the walkers to coach a Little League team—has taken an interest in old Bob, and has been plying the man with good whiskey, barbiturates, and social status.

On Saturday afternoon, however, Josh puts all this out of his mind as he unloads a pallet of siding at the end of the temporary wall. Other workmen move along the flanks of the barricade, nailing planks into place. Some use hammers, others nail guns connected to gas-powered generators. The noise is troublesome if not unmanageable.

"Just stack it over there by the sandbags, cousin," Martinez says with a neighborly nod, an M1 assault rifle on his hip.

Clad in his trademark do-rag and sleeveless camo shirt, Martinez continues to be the hail-fellow-well-met. Josh cannot quite figure the man out. He seems to be the most even-tempered of the Woodbury bunch, but the bar here is not that high. Charged with supervising the ever-changing shift of guards on the walls, Martinez rarely fraternizes with the Governor, although the two of them seem to be joined at the hip. "Just try and keep the noise down to a minimum, bro," he adds with a wink, "if at all possible."

"Gotcha," Josh says with a nod and starts off-loading the four-by-six sheets of particleboard onto the ground. He sheds his lumberjack coat—the sweat has broken out on his neck and back, the winter sun high in the sky today—and he finishes the stacking in mere minutes.

Martinez comes over. "Why don't you go ahead and grab one more load before lunch."

"Roger that," Josh says, and pulls the empty dolly free of the stack, then turns and heads back down the walk, leaving his jacket—as well as his snub-nosed .38 police special—hanging on a fence post.

Josh sometimes forgets that the gun is tucked into his jacket pocket. He has yet to use the thing since coming to Woodbury; the guards have the place pretty much covered.

Over the last week, in fact, only a few attacks have occurred along the edges of the woods, or on the side roads, which have been easily and promptly quelled by the well-armed band of weekend warriors. According to Martinez, the powers that be in Woodbury have discovered a cache of weapons at a National Guard station within walking distance of the town—an entire arsenal of military-grade weaponry—which the Governor has put to good use.

The truth is, walker attacks are the least of the Governor's problems. The human population of Woodbury seems to be curdling under the pressure of postplague life. Tempers are stretched thin. People are starting to lash out at each other.

Josh crosses the two-block distance between the construction site and the warehouse in less than five minutes, thinking about Lilly and his future with her. Lost in his thoughts, he does not notice the odor wafting around him as he approaches the wood-frame building on the edge of the railroad tracks.

The warehouse once stood as a storage shed for the southern terminus of the Chattooga and Chickamauga Railway. Throughout the twentieth century tobacco farmers would ship their bundles of raw leaves up north on this line to Fayetteville for processing.

Josh trudges up to the long narrow building and parks the dolly outside the door. The edifice rises up at least thirty-five feet at the highest pitch of its weathered, gabled roof. The siding is ancient, chipped, and scarred with neglect. The single tall window by the door is broken out and boarded. The place looks like a ruined museum, a relic of the old South. Workmen have been using the building to keep the lumber dry and stash building materials.

"Josh!"

Josh pauses at the entrance when he hears the familiar voice drifting on the breeze behind him. He turns just in time to see Lilly scurrying up in her trademark funky attire—floppy hat, multicolored scarves, and a coyote coat she acquired in trade from an older woman in town—a weary smile on her slender face.

"Babygirl, you are a sight for sore eyes," Josh says, grabbing her and gently pulling her into a bear hug. She hugs him back—not exactly with unbridled abandon, more of a platonic hug—and once again Josh wonders if he has come on too strong with her. Or perhaps their lovemaking has changed some complex dynamic between them. Or maybe he has not lived up to her expectations. She seems to be holding back her affection slightly. Just slightly. But Josh puts it out of his mind. Maybe it's just the stress.

"Can we talk?" she says, looking up into his eyes with a heavy, somber gaze.

"Sure . . . you want to give me a hand?"

"After you," she says, gesturing toward the entrance. Josh turns and pries the door open.

The smell of dead flesh—mingling with the moldy, airless dark inside the storage shed—does not register at first. Nor do they notice the gap between two petrified sections of drywall in the rear of the shed, or the fact that the backside of the building is perilously exposed to a wild section of forest. The building stretches at least a hundred feet back in the darkness, draped in cobwebs and cast-off rail sections so rusted and corroded they are the color of the earth.

"What's on your mind, babydoll?" Josh crosses the cinder floor to a pile of wooden siding. The four-by-six panels look as though they came from a barn, their grooves of deep red paint chipped and scabrous with mud.

"We gotta move on, Josh, we gotta get outta this town . . . before something terrible happens."

"Soon, Lilly."

"No, Josh. Seriously. Listen to me." She tugs his arm and pulls him around so they are face-to-face. "I don't care if Megan and Scott and Bob stay . . . we gotta ditch this place. It looks all cozy and Mayberry RFD on the surface but it's rotting underneath."

"I know . . . I just have to—"

He stops when a shadow blurs outside the slats of the boarded window in his peripheral vision.

"Oh, my God, Josh, did you—"

"Get behind me," he says, realizing several things all at once. He smells the odor permeating the musk of the moldy shed, he hears the low guttural vibrations of growls coming from the rear of the building, and he sees a slice of daylight blooming through a gap in the corner.

Worst of all, Josh realizes he left his pistol in his jacket.

TEN

Right then, a burst of automatic gunfire echoes outside the storage shed.

Lilly jerks in the darkness of the shed, and Josh whirls toward the pile of lumber, when the boarded window near the front door bursts inward.

Three snarling zombies—the pressure of their collective weight forcing the ancient lumber to give way—start climbing into the shed. Two males and a female, each with deep wounds in their faces, their cheeks torn away from exposed gums and teeth like rows of dull ivory, tumble into the darkness. A chorus of snarls fills the building.

Josh barely has time to register this fact when he hears shuffling coming toward him from the rear of the dark shed. He spins and sees the enormous walker in dungarees, most likely a former farmer, his lower intestines hanging out like slimy prayer beads, shambling toward him through the shafts of dust motes, bumping drunkenly into stacks of crates and piles of old railroad ties.

"LILLY, GET BEHIND ME!"

Josh lurches toward the stack of lumber and lifts a huge panel of wood up and in front of them like a shield. Lilly presses against his back, her lungs heaving now, hyperventilating with terror. Josh raises the panel and starts toward the big walker with the inertia of a middle linebacker going into the backfield to sack a quarterback.

The walker lets out a drooling groan as Josh slams the panel into it.

The force of the blow drives the huge corpse backward and to the cinder floor. Josh slams the lumber down on top of the thing. Lilly tumbles onto the pileup. The weight of their bodies pins the giant to the cinders, its dead limbs squirming beneath the panel, its blackened fingers sticking out the sides of the wood, clawing at the air.

Outside, in the wind, the sound of an emergency bell clangs.

"MOTHERFUCK!"

Josh loses control for a moment and starts slamming the panel down on top of the enormous dead farmer. Lilly is thrown off Josh's back, as Josh rises up and starts stomping his work boot down on the panel, which is crushing the zombie's skull. Josh starts jumping up and down on the panel, letting out a series of garbled, bellowing cries, the rage contorting his face.

Brain matter gushes and spurts out from under the top of the panel, as the sick crunch of dead cranial bones gives way, the farmer going still. Huge rivulets of black fluid spread from under the wood.

All this transpires within a matter of seconds, as Lilly is backing away in horror. All at once the sound of a voice rings out from the street in front of the shed, a familiar voice, calm and collected, despite its volume—"GET DOWN, FOLKS!! GET DOWN ON THE FLOOR"—and somewhere in the back of Josh's brain he recognizes the voice of Martinez, and Josh also remembers, simultaneously, that the other three walkers are closing in from the front of the shed.

Josh jumps off the panel, spins around, and sees the three walkers approaching Lilly, reaching out for her with spastic lifeless arms. Lilly screams. Josh lurches toward her, scrambling for a weapon. Only scrap metal and sawdust litter the floor.

Lilly backs away screaming, and the din of her shriek blends with a booming, authoritative voice coming from outside the entrance: "GET DOWN ON THE FLOOR, FOLKS! DOWN ON THE FLOOR NOW!!"

Josh instantly gets it, and he grabs Lilly and yanks her to the cinders.

The three dead things loom over them, mouths gaping and

drooling, so close now Josh can smell the hideous stench of their fetid breath.

The front wall lights up—a fusillade of automatic gunfire punching a pearl necklace of holes along the drywall, each hole blooming a pinpoint of daylight. The volley strafes the midsections of the three upright cadavers, making them dance a macabre Watusi in the darkness.

The noise is tremendous. Wood shards and plaster shrapnel and bits of rotting flesh rain down on Josh and Lilly, who cover their heads.

Josh catches glimpses of the macabre dancing out of the corner of his eye, the walkers jerking and spasming to some arrhythmic drumbeat, as threads of brilliant light crisscross the darkness.

Skulls erupt. Particles fly. The dead figures deflate and collapse one at a time. The barrage continues. Thin shafts of daylight fill the shed with a cat's cradle of deadly luminous sunlight.

Silence descends. Outside the shed, the muffled noise of spent shells ringing off the pavement reaches Josh's ears. He hears the faint clanging of bolts reloading, breeches refilling, collective breaths of exertion drowned by the wind.

A moment passes

He turns to Lilly, who lies next to him, clinging to him, clutching handfuls of his shirt. She looks almost catatonic for a moment, her face pressed against the cinders. Josh hugs her close, strokes her back.

"You okay?"

"Fabulous . . . just peachy." She seems to awaken from the terror, looking down at the spreading puddle of cranial fluid. The bodies lie riddled and eviscerated only inches away. Lilly sits up.

Josh rises and helps her to her feet and starts to say something else when the creak of old wood draws his attention to the entrance. What remains of the door, its top half perforated with bullet holes, squeaks open.

Martinez peers in. He speaks hurriedly, purposefully: "You two good?"

"We're good," Josh tells him, and then hears a noise in the

distance. Voices rising in anger, echoing on the wind. A muffled crash.

"We got another fire to put out," Martinez says, "if you folks are okay."

"We're okay."

With a terse nod, Martinez wheels away from the door and vanishes into the overcast daylight.

Two blocks east of the railroad tracks, near the barricade, a fight has ensued. Fights are commonplace in the new Woodbury. Two weeks ago a couple of the butcher's guards came to blows over the rightful ownership of a well-thumbed issue of *Barely Legal* magazine. Doc Stevens had to set one fighter's dislocated jaw and patch the other boy's hemorrhaging left eye socket before that day was out.

Most of the time these brawls occur in semiprivate—either indoors or late at night—and break out over the most trivial matters imaginable: somebody looks at somebody else the wrong way, somebody tells a joke that offends somebody else, somebody just irritates somebody else. For weeks now, the Governor has been concerned about the growing frequency of serious brawls.

But until today, most of these little rumbles have been private affairs.

Today, the latest melee breaks out in broad daylight, right outside the food center, in front of at least twenty onlookers . . . and the crowd seems to fuel the intensity of the fight. At first the onlookers watch with revulsion as the two young combatants pummel each other with bare fists in the freezing wind, their inelegant blows full of spit and fury, their eyes ablaze with unfocused rage.

But soon something changes in the crowd. Angry shouts turn to whoops and hollers. Bloodlust sparks behind the eyes of the gallery. The stress of the plague comes out in angry hyena yells, psychotic cheers, and vicarious fist pumping from some of the younger men.

Martinez and his guards arrive right at the height of the fight.

Dean Gorman, a redneck farm kid from Augusta dressed in torn denim and heavy-metal tattoos, kicks the legs out from under Johnny

Pruitt, a fat, doughy pothead from Jonesboro. Pruitt—who had the temerity to criticize the Augusta State Jaguars football team—now tumbles to the sandy ground with a gasp.

"Hey! Dial it down!" Martinez approaches from the north side of the street, his M1 on his hip, still warm from the fracas at the railroad shed. Three guards follow on his heels, their guns also braced against their midsections. As he crosses the street it's hard for Martinez to see the fighters behind the semicircle of cheering onlookers.

All that's visible is a cloud of dust, flailing fists, and milling onlookers.

"HEY!!"

Inside the circle of spectators Dean Gorman slams a steel-toed work boot into Johnny Pruitt's ribs, and the fat man keens with agony, rolling away. The crowd jeers. Gorman jumps on the kid but Pruitt counters by slamming a knee up into Gorman's groin. The witnesses howl. Gorman tumbles to his side holding his privates and Pruitt lashes out with a series of sidelong blows to Gorman's face. Blood flings across the sand in dark stringers from Gorman's nose.

Martinez starts pushing bystanders aside, forcing his way into the fray.

"Martinez! Hold up!"

Martinez feels a vise grip tighten on his arm and he whirls around to see the Governor.

"Hold up a second," the wiry man says under his breath with a spark of interest glittering in his deep-set eyes. His handlebar mustache has come in dark and thick, giving his face a predatory cast. He wears a long, black duster over his chambray shirt, jeans, and stovepipe engineer boots, the tails flapping majestically in the wind. He looks like a degenerate paladin from the nineteenth century, a self-styled gunslinger-pimp. "I want to see something."

Martinez lowers his weapon, tilts his head toward the action. "Just worried somebody's gonna go and get his ass killed."

By this point Big Johnny Pruitt has his pudgy fingers around Dean Gorman's throat, and Gorman begins to gasp and blanch. The fight goes from savage to deadly in a matter of seconds. Pruitt will not let go. The crowd erupts in ugly, garbled cheers. Gorman flails and convulses. He runs out of air, his face turning the color of eggplant. His eyes bulge, bloody saliva spraying.

"Stop worrying, grandma," the Governor murmurs, watching intently with those hollowed-out eyes.

Right then Martinez realizes the Governor is not watching the fight per se. Eyes shifting all around the semicircle of shouting spectators, the Governor is *watching the watchers.* He seems to be absorbing every face, every jackal-like howl, every hoot and holler.

Meantime, Dean Gorman starts to fade on the ground, in the stranglehold of Johnny Pruitt's sausage fingers. Gorman's face turns the color of dry cement. His eyes roll back in his head and he stops struggling.

"Okay, that's enough . . . pull him off," the Governor tells Martinez.

"EVERYBODY BACK OFF!"

Martinez forces his way into the huddle with his gun in both hands.

Big fat Johnny Pruitt finally lets go at the urging of the M1's muzzle, and Gorman lies there convulsing. "Go get Stevens," Martinez orders one of his guards.

The crowd, still agitated by all the excitement, lets out a collective groan. Some of them grumble, and some launch a few boos, frustrated by the anticlimax.

Standing off to the side, the Governor takes it all in. When the onlookers begin to disperse—wandering away, shaking their heads—the Governor goes over to Martinez, who still stands over the writhing Gorman.

Martinez looks up at the Governor. "He'll live."

"Good." The Governor glances down at the young man on the ground. "I think I know what to do with the guardsmen."

At that same moment, under the sublevels of the racetrack complex, in the darkness of a makeshift holding cell, four men whisper to each other.

"It'll never work," the first man utters skeptically, sitting in the corner in his piss-sodden boxer shorts, gazing at the shadows of his fellow prisoners gathered around him on the floor.

"Shut the fuck up, Manning," hisses the second man, Barker, a rail-thin twenty-five-year-old, who glowers at his fellow detainees through long strands of greasy hair. Barker had once been Major Gene Gavin's star pupil at Camp Ellenwood, Georgia, bound for special ops duty with the 221st Military Intelligence Battalion. Now, thanks to that psycho Philip Blake, Gavin is gone and Barker has been reduced to a ragged, seminude, groveling lump in the basement of some godforsaken catacomb, left to subsist on cold oatmeal and wormy bread.

The four guardsmen have been under "house arrest" down here for over three weeks, ever since Philip Blake had shot and killed their commanding officer, Gavin, in cold blood, right in front of dozens of townspeople. Now the only things they have going for them are hunger, pure rage, and the fact that Barker is chained to the cinder-block wall to the immediate left of the locked entrance door, a spot from which one could conceivably get a jump on somebody entering the cell . . . like Blake, for example, who has been regularly coming down here to drag prisoners out, one by one, to meet some hellish fate.

"He's not stupid, Barker," a third man named Stinson wheezes from the opposite corner. This man is older, more heavyset, a good old boy with bad teeth who once ran a requisition desk at the National Guard station.

"I agree with Stinson," Tommy Zorn says from the back wall where he slumps in his underwear, his malnourished body covered with a significant skin rash. Zorn once worked as a delivery clerk at the Guard station. "He's gonna see right through this stunt."

"Not if we're careful," Barker counters.

"Who the hell is gonna be the one plays dead?"

"Doesn't matter, I'll be the one kicks his ass when he opens the door."

"Barker, I think this place has put a zap on your head. Seriously. You want to end up like Gavin? Like Greely and Johnson and—"

"YOU COCK-SUCKING COWARD!! WE'RE ALL GONNA END UP LIKE THEM YOU DON'T DO SOMETHING ABOUT IT!!"

The volume of Barker's voice—stretched as thin as high-tension wire—cuts off the conversation like a switch. For a long stretch, the four guardsmen sit in the dark without saying a word.

At last Barker says, "All we need is one of you faggots to play dead. That's all I'm asking. I'll coldcock him when he comes in."

"Making it convincing is the trouble," Manning says.

"Rub shit on yourself."

"Hardy-har-har."

"Cut yourself and rub blood on your face, and then let it dry, I don't know. Rub your eyes until they bleed. You want to get out of here?"

Long silence now.

"You're fucking guardsmen, for Chrissake. You want to rot in here like maggots?"

Another long silence, and then Stinson's voice in the darkness says, "Okay, I'll do it."

Bob follows the Governor through a secure door at one end of the racetrack, then down a narrow flight of iron stairs, and then across a narrow cinder-block corridor, their footsteps ringing and echoing in the dim light. Emergency cage lights—powered by generators—burn overhead.

"Finally it hit me, Bob," the Governor is saying, fiddling with a ring of skeleton keys clipped to his belt on a long chain. "Thing this place needs . . . is entertainment."

"Entertainment?"

"The Greeks had their theater, Bob . . . Romans had their circuses."

Bob has no idea what the man is talking about but he follows along obediently, wiping his dry mouth. He needs a drink badly. He unbuttons his olive-drab jacket, pearls of sweat breaking out on his weathered brow due to the airless, fusty dampness of the cavernous cement underground beneath the racetrack.

They pass a locked door, and Bob can swear he hears the muffled, telltale noises of reanimated dead. The trace odors of rotting flesh mingle with the mildewy stench of the corridor. Bob's stomach lurches.

The Governor leads him over to a metal door with a narrow window at the end of the corridor. A shade is pulled down over the meshed safety glass.

"Gotta keep the citizens happy," the Governor mutters as he pauses by the door, searching for the proper key. "Keep folks docile, manageable . . . pliable."

Bob waits as the Governor inserts a thick metal key into the door's bolt. But just as he is about to jack open the lock, the Governor turns and looks at Bob. "Had some trouble a while back with the National Guard in town, thought they could lord it over the people, push people around . . . thought they could carve out a little kingdom for themselves."

Confused, dizzy, nauseous, Bob gives a nod and doesn't say anything.

"Been keeping a bunch of them on ice down here." The Governor winks as though discussing the location of a cookie jar with a child. "Used to be seven of them." The Governor sighs. "Only four of them left now . . . been going through them like Grant went through Richmond."

"Going through them?"

The Governor sniffs, suddenly looking guiltily at the floor. "They've been serving a higher purpose, Bob. For my baby . . . for Penny."

Bob realizes with a sudden rush of queasiness what the Governor is talking about.

"Anyway . . ." The Governor turns to the door. "I knew they would come in handy for all sorts of things . . . but now I realize their true destiny." The Governor smiles. "Gladiators, Bob. For the common good."

Right then several things happen at once: The Governor turns and snaps up the shade, while simultaneously flipping a light switch . . . and through the safety glass a row of overhead fluorescent tubes suddenly flicker on, illuminating the inside of a three-hundred-square-foot cinder-block cell. A huge man clad only in tattered skiv-vies lies on the floor, twitching, covered with blood, his mouth black and peeled away from his teeth in a hideous grimace.

"That's a shame." The Governor frowns. "Looks like one of 'em turned."

Inside the cell—the noises muffled by the sealed door—the other prisoners are screaming, yanking at their chains, begging to be res-cued from this freshly turned biter. The Governor reaches inside the folds of his duster and draws his pearl-handled .45 caliber Colt. He checks the clip and mumbles, "Stay out here, Bob. This'll just take a second."

He snaps the lock open, and he steps inside the cell, when the man behind the door pounces.

Barker lets out a garbled cry as he tackles the Governor from be-hind, the chain attached to Barker's ankle giving slightly, reaching its limit, tearing its anchor bolt from the wall. Taken by surprise, the Governor stumbles, drops the .45, topples to the deck, gasping, the gun clattering to the floor, spinning several feet.

Bob fills the doorway, yelling, as Barker crabs toward the Gover-nor's ankles, latching on to them, digging his filthy untrimmed fin-gernails into the Governor's flesh. Barker tries to snag the skeleton keys, but the ring is wedged under the Governor's legs.

The Governor bellows as he madly crawls toward the fallen pistol.

The other men cry out as Barker loses what is left of his sanity and goes for the Governor's ankles and growls with feral white-hot killing rage and opens his mouth and bites down on the tender area around the Governor's Achilles' heel, and the Governor howls.

Bob stands paralyzed behind the half-ajar door, watching, thun-derstruck.

Barker draws blood. The Governor kicks at the prisoner and claws for the pistol. The other men try to tear themselves free, hollering inarticulate warnings, while Barker rips into the Governor's legs. The Governor reaches for the gun, which lies only centimeters out of his reach . . . until finally the Governor's long, sinewy fingers get themselves around the Colt's grip.

In one quick continuous motion the Governor spins and aims the single-action semiautomatic pistol at Barker's face and empties the clip.

A series of dry, hot booms flash in the cell. Barker flings backward like a puppet yanked by a cable, the slugs perforating his face, exiting out the back of his skull in a plume of blood mist. The dark crimson matter sprays the cinder-block wall beside the door, some of it getting on Bob, who jerks back with a start.

Across the cell the other men call out—a garble of nonsense words, a frenzy of begging—as the Governor rises to his feet.

"Please, please, I ain't turned—I AIN'T TURNED!" Across the room, Stinson, the big man, sits up, shielding his bloodstained face as he cries out. His quivering lips have been made up with mildew from the wall and grease from the door hinges. "It was a trick! A trick!"

The Governor thumbs the empty clip out of the Colt, the magazine dropping to the floor. Breathing hard and fast, he pulls another clip from his back pocket and palms it into the hilt. He cocks the slide and calmly aims the muzzle at Stinson, while informing the big man, "You look like a fucking biter to me."

Stinson shields his face. "It was Barker's idea, it was stupid, please, I didn't want to go along with it, Barker was nuts, please . . . PLEASE!"

The Governor squeezes off half a dozen successive shots, the blasts making everybody jump.

The far wall erupts in a fireworks display just above Stinson's head, the puffs of cinder-block plaster exploding in sequence, the noise a tremendous, earsplitting barrage, the sparks blossoming and some of the bullets ricocheting up into the ceiling.

The single cage light explodes in a torrent of glass particles that drives everybody to the floor.

At last the Governor lets up and stands there, catching his breath, blinking, and addressing Bob in the doorway. "What we got here, Bob, is a learning opportunity."

Across the room, on the floor, Stinson has pissed himself, mortified and yet unharmed. He buries his face in his hands and weeps softly.

The Governor limps toward the big man, leaving a thin trail of blood droplets. "You see, Bob . . . the very thing that burns inside these boys—makes 'em try stupid shit like this—is gonna make them superstars in the arena."

Stinson looks up with snot on his face now as the Governor looms over him.

"They don't realize it, Bob." The Governor aims the muzzle at Stinson's face. "But they just passed the first test of gladiatorial school." The Governor gives Stinson a hard look. "Open your mouth."

Stinson hiccups with sobs and terror, squeezing out a breathless, "C'mon, *pleeease* . . ."

"Open your mouth."

Stinson manages to open his mouth. Across the room, in the doorway, Bob Stookey looks away.

"See, Bob," the Governor says, slowly penetrating the big man's mouth with the barrel. The room falls stone silent as the other men watch, horrified and rapt. "Obedience . . . courage . . . stupidity. Isn't that the Boy Scout motto?"

Without warning the Governor lets up on the trigger, pulls the muzzle free of the weeping man's mouth, whirls around, and limps toward the exit. "What did Ed Sullivan used to say . . . ? Gonna be a really big sssshooooow!"

The tension goes out of the room like a bladder deflating, replaced by a ringing silence.

"Bob, do me a favor . . . will ya?" the Governor mutters as he passes the bullet-riddled body of Master Gunnery Sergeant Trey Barker on his way out. "Clean this place up . . . but don't take this cocksucker's remains over to the crematorium. Bring him over to the infirmary." He winks at Bob. "I'll take care of him from there."

The next day, early in the morning, before dawn, Megan Lafferty lies nude and cold and supine on a broken-down cot in the darkness of a squalid studio apartment—the private quarters of some guard whose name she can't remember. Denny? Daniel? Megan was too stoned last night to file the name away. Now the skinny young man with the cobra tattoo between his shoulder blades thrusts himself into her with rhythmic abandon, making the cot groan and squeak.

Megan places her thoughts elsewhere, staring at the ceiling, focusing on the dead flies collected in the bowl of an overhead light fixture, trying to withstand the horrible, painful, sticky friction of the man's erection pumping in and out of her.

The room consists of the cot, a ramshackle dresser, flea-bitten curtains drawn over the open window—through which a December wind whistles sporadically—and piles and piles of crates filled with supplies. Some of these supplies have been promised to Megan in return for sex. She notices a stringer of ragged fleshy objects hanging off a hook on the door, which she first misidentifies as dried flowers.

Upon closer scrutiny, though, the flowers reveal themselves in the darkness to be human ears, most likely trophies severed off walkers.

Megan tries to block out thoughts of Lilly's last words to her, spoken just last night around the flaming light of a burning oil drum. *"It's my body, girlfriend, these are fucking desperate times,"* Megan had rationalized, trying to justify her behavior. Lilly had responded with disgust. *"I'd rather starve than do tricks for food."* And then Lilly had officially ended their friendship right then, once and for all. *"I don't care anymore, Megan, I'm done, it's over, I don't want anything to do with you."*

Now the words echo in the huge, empty chasm in Megan's soul. The hole inside her has been there for years, a gigantic vacuum of sorrow, a bottomless pit of self-loathing carved out when she was young. She has never been able to fill this well of pain, and now the Plague World has opened it up like a festering, sucking wound.

She closes her eyes and thinks about drowning in a deep, dark ocean, when she hears a noise.

Her eyes pop open. The sound is unmistakable, coming from just outside the window. Faint and yet clearly audible in the windy hush of the predawn December air, it echoes up over the rooftops: *two pairs of furtive footsteps, a couple of citizens sneaking through the darkness.*

By this point, Cobra Boy has grown weary of his druggy copulation and has slipped off Megan's body. He smells of dried semen and bad breath and urine-impregnated sheets, and he starts snoring the moment the back of his head hits the pillow. Megan levers herself out of bed, careful not to awaken the catatonic customer.

She pads silently across the cool floor to the window and looks out.

The town slumbers in the gray darkness. The vent stacks and chimneys on top of buildings stand silhouetted against the dull light. Two figures are barely visible in the gloom, creeping toward the far corner of the west fence, their breaths puffing vapor in the cold wee-hour light. One of the figures towers over the other.

Megan recognizes Josh Lee Hamilton first, and then Lilly, as the two ghostly figures pause near the corner of the barricade a hundred and fifty yards away. Waves of melancholy course through Megan.

As the twosome disappears over the fence, the sense of loss drives Megan to her knees, and she silently cries in the reeking darkness for what seems like an eternity.

"Toss it down, babydoll," Josh whispers, gazing up at Lilly, as she balances on the crest of the fence, one foot over, one foot on the ledge behind her. Josh is hyperaware of the dozing night guard a hundred yards to the east, slumped on the seat of a bulldozer, his sight line blocked by the massive girth of a live oak.

"Here comes." Lilly awkwardly shrugs the knapsack off one shoulder and then tosses it over the fence to Josh. He catches it. The pack weighs at least ten pounds. It contains Josh's .38 caliber police special, a pick hammer with a collapsible handle, a screwdriver, a couple of candy bars, and two plastic bottles of tap water.

"Be careful now."

Lilly climbs down and hops onto the hard earth outside the fence.

They waste no time hanging around the periphery of town. The sun is coming up, and they want to be well out of sight of the night guard before Martinez and his men get up and return to their posts. Josh has a bad feeling about the way things are going in Woodbury. It seems as though his services are becoming less and less valuable in terms of trade. Yesterday he must have hauled three tons of fencing panels and still Sam the Butcher claims that Josh is behind in his debt, that he's taking advantage of the barter system, and that he's not working off all the slab bacon and fruit he's been going through.

All the more reason for Josh and Lilly to sneak out of town and see if they can't find their own supplies.

"Stick close, babygirl," Josh says, and leads Lilly along the edge of the woods.

They keep to the shadows as the sun comes up, skirting the edge of a vast cemetery on their left. Ancient willows hang down over Civil War–era markers, the spectral predawn light giving the place a haunted, desolate feel. Many of the headstones lie on their sides, some of the graves gaping open. The boneyard makes the flesh on the back of Josh's neck prickle, and he hurries Lilly along toward the intersection of Main and Canyon Drive.

They turn north and head into the pecan groves outside of town.

"Keep your eyes peeled for reflectors along the side of the road," Josh says as they begin to ascend a gentle slope rising into the wooded hills. "Or mailboxes. Or any kind of private drive."

"What if we don't find anything but more trees?"

"Gotta be a farmhouse . . . something." Josh keeps scanning the trees on either side of the narrow blacktop road. Dawn has broken, but the woods on either side of Canyon Drive are still dark and hectic with swaying shadows. Noises blend into each other, and skittering leaves in the wind start to sound like shuffling footsteps behind the trees. Josh pauses, digs in the knapsack, pulls his gun out, and checks the chamber.

"Something wrong?" Lilly's eyes take in the gun, then shift to the woods. "You hear something?"

"Everything's fine, babydoll." He shoves the pistol behind his belt and continues climbing the hill. "As long as we keep quiet, keep moving . . . we'll be fine."

They walk another quarter mile in silence, staying single file, hyperalert, their gazes returning every few moments to the swaying boughs of the deeper woods, and the shadows behind the shadows. The walkers have left Woodbury alone since the incident at the train shed, but Josh has a feeling they are due. He starts to get nervous about straying this far from town, when he sees the first sign of residential property.

The enormous tin mailbox, shaped like a little log cabin, stands at the end of an unmarked private drive. Only the letters L. HUNT reveal the identity of its owner, the numbers 20034 stamped into the rust-pocked metal.

About fifty yards beyond that first mailbox they find more mailboxes. They find over a dozen of them—a cluster of six at the foot of one drive—and Josh begins to sense they have hit the jackpot. He pulls the pick hammer from the knapsack and hands it to Lilly. "Keep this handy, baby. We'll follow this drive, the one with all the mailboxes."

"I'm right behind you," she says, and then follows the big man up the winding gravel path.

The first monstrosity becomes visible like a mirage in the early-morning light, behind the trees, planted in a clearing as though it landed from outer space. If the home were nestled in some tree-lined boulevard in Connecticut or Beverly Hills it would not seem so out of place, but here in the ramshackle rural nether-region the place practically takes Josh's breath away. Rising over three stories above the weed-whiskered lawn, the deserted mansion is a modern architectural wonder, all cantilevers and jutting balustrades and chockablock with roof pitches. It looks like one of Frank Lloyd Wright's lost masterpieces. An infinity pool is partially visible in the backyard, lousy with leaves. Neglect shows on the massive balconies, where icicles hang down and patches of filthy snow cling to the decks. "Must be some tycoon's summer home," Josh surmises.

They follow the road higher into the trees and find more abandoned homes.

One of them looks like a Victorian museum, with gigantic turrets that rise out of the pecan trees like some Moorish palace. Another one is practically all glass, with a veranda that thrusts out over a breathtaking hill. Each stately home features its own private pool, coach house, six-car garage, and sprawling lawn. Each is dark, closed down, boarded, as dead as a mausoleum.

Lilly pauses in front of the dark glass-encased wonder and gazes up at the galleries. "You think we can get inside?"

Josh grins. "Hand me that clawhammer, babydoll . . . and stand back."

They find a treasure trove of supplies—despite all the spoiled food, as well as signs of past break-ins, probably courtesy of the Governor and his goons. In some of the homes they find partially stocked pantries, wet bars, and linen closets brimming with fresh bedding. They find workrooms with more tools than small hardware stores. They find guns and liquor and fuel and medicine. They marvel that the Governor and his men have not yet scoured these places clean. The best part is the complete absence of walkers.

Later, Lilly stands in the foyer of an immaculate Cape Cod, gazing around at the elaborate Tiffany-style light fixtures. "You thinking what I'm thinking?"

"I don't know, girlfriend, what are you thinking?"

She looks at him. "We could *live* in one of these places, Josh."

"I don't know."

She looks around. "Keep to ourselves, stay under the radar."

Josh thinks about it. "Maybe we ought to take this one step at a time. Play dumb for a while, see if anybody else is wise to it."

"That's the best part, Josh, they've been here already . . . they'll leave it alone."

He lets out a sigh. "Let me think about it, babygirl. Maybe talk to Bob."

After searching the garages, they find a few luxury vehicles under tarps, and they begin making plans for the future, discussing the possibility of hitting the road. As soon as they get a chance to talk to Bob, they will make a decision.

They return to town that evening, slipping into the walled area unnoticed through the construction zone along the southern edge of the barricade.

They keep their discovery to themselves.

Unfortunately, neither Josh nor Lilly has noticed the one critical drawback to the luxury enclave. Most of the backyards extend about thirty yards to the edge of a steep precipice, beyond which a rocky slope plunges down into a deep canyon. Down in the winter-seared valley of that canyon, along a dry riverbed, shrouded in tangled dead vines and limbs, a pack of zombies at least a hundred strong wander aimlessly back and forth, bumping into each other.

It will take the creatures less than forty-eight hours—once the noise and smell of humans draw them out—to crawl, inch by inch, up that slope.

ELEVEN

"I still don't see why we can't just live here for a while," Lilly persists that next afternoon, flopping down on a buttery leather sofa positioned against a massive picture window inside one of the glass-encased mansions. The window wraps around the rear of the home's first floor, and overlooks the kidney-shaped pool in the backyard, covered now with a snow-crusted tarp. Winter winds rattle the windows, a fine icy sleet hissing against the glass.

"I'm not saying it's not a possibility," Josh says from across the room, where he is selecting utensils from a drawer of fine silver and putting them into a duffel bag. Evening is closing in on their second day of exploring the enclave, and they have gathered enough supplies to stock a home of their own. They have hidden some of the provisions outside Woodbury's wall, in sheds and barns. They have stashed firearms and tools and canned goods in Bob's camper, and have made plans to get one of the vehicles in working order.

Now Josh lets out a sigh and goes over to the sofa and sits down next to Lilly. "Still not convinced these places are safe," he says.

"C'mon . . . dude . . . these houses are like fortresses, the owners locked them up tight as drums before taking off in their private jets. I can't take one more night in that creepy town."

Josh gives her a sorrowful look. "Baby, I promise you . . . one day all this shit will be over."

"Really? You think?"

"I'm sure of it, babygirl. Somebody's gonna figure out what went wrong . . . some egghead at the CDC's gonna come up with an antidote, keep folks in their graves."

Lilly rubs her eyes. "I wish I had that kind of confidence."

Josh touches her hand. "'This too shall pass,' baby. It's like my mama always used to say, 'Only thing you can depend on in this world is that you can't depend on nothin' to stay the same, everything changes.'" He looks at her and smiles. "Only thing ain't never gonna change, baby, is how I feel about *you*."

They sit there for a moment, listening to the silent house tick and settle, the wind strafing the home with bursts of sleet, when something moves outside, across the backyard. The tops of several dozen heads slowly rise up behind the edge of the distant precipice, a row of rotting faces, unseen by Lilly and Josh—their backs turned to the window now—as the pack of zombies emerge from the shadows of the ravine.

Oblivious to the imminent threat, lost in her thoughts, Lilly puts her head on Josh's massive shoulder. She feels a twinge of guilt. Each day she senses Josh falling deeper and deeper for her, the way he touches her, the way his eyes light up each morning when they awaken on the cold pallet of that second-floor apartment.

Part of Lilly hungers for such affection and intimacy . . . but a part of her still feels removed, detached, guilty that she's allowed this relationship to blossom out of fear, out of convenience. She feels a sense of duty to Josh. But that's no basis for a relationship. What she's doing is wrong. She owes him the truth.

"Josh . . ." She looks up at him. "I have to tell you . . . you're one of the most wonderful men I have ever met."

He grins, not quite registering the sadness in her voice. "And you're pretty damn fine yourself."

Outside, plainly visible now through the rear window, at least fifty creatures scrabble up and over the ledge, crabbing onto the lawn, their clawlike fingers digging into the turf, tugging their dead weight along in fits and starts. Some of them struggle to their feet and begin lumbering toward the glass-enclosed edifice with mouths gaping hungrily. A dead geriatric dressed in a hospital smock, his long gray hair flagging like milkweed, leads the pack.

Inside the lavish home, behind panes of safety glass, unaware of the encroaching menace, Lilly measures her words. "You've been so good to me, Josh Lee . . . I don't know how long I could have survived on my own . . . and for that I will always be grateful."

Now Josh cocks his head at her, his grin fading. "Why do I all of a sudden get the feeling there's a 'but' in here somewhere?"

Lilly licks her lips thoughtfully. "This plague, this epidemic, whatever it is . . . it does things to people . . . makes them do things they wouldn't dream of doing any other time."

Josh's big brown face falls. "What are you sayin,' babydoll? Something's bothering you."

"I'm just saying . . . maybe . . . I don't know . . . maybe I've let this thing between us go a little too far."

Josh looks at her, and for a long moment he seems to grope for words. He clears his throat. "Ain't sure I'm following you."

By this point the walkers have overrun the backyard. Unheard through the thick glass, their atonal chorus of snarling, moaning vocalizations drowned under the drumming of sleet, the enormous regiment closes in on the house. Some of them—the old long-haired hospital patient, a limping woman without a jaw, a couple of burn victims—have closed the distance to within twenty yards. Some of the monsters stupidly stumble over the lip of the swimming pool, falling through the snow-matted tarp, while others follow the leaders with bloodlust radiating from their cue-ball eyes.

"Don't get me wrong," Lilly is saying inside the hermetically sealed environment of the stately glass house. "I will always love you, Josh . . . always. You are amazing. It's just . . . this world we're in, it twists things. I never want to hurt you."

His eyes moisten. "Wait. Hold up. You're saying being with me is something you would never dream of doing at any other time?"

"No . . . God, no. I love being with you. I just don't want to give the wrong impression."

"The wrong impression about what?"

"That our feelings for each other . . . that they're—I don't know—coming from a healthy place."

"What's unhealthy about our feelings?"

"I'm just saying . . . the fear fucks you up. I haven't been in my right mind since all this shit went down. I don't ever want you to think I'm just using you for protection . . . for survival, is what I mean."

The tears well up in Josh's eyes. He swallows hard and tries to think of something to say.

Ordinarily he would notice the telltale stench seeping into the circulatory systems of the house, the odors of rancid meat braised in shit. Or he would hear the muffled basso profundo drone outside the walls of the house—coming from outside the front and sides of the building now, not just the backyard—so resonant and low it seems to be vibrating the very foundation. Or he would see the teeming movement out of the corner of his eye, through the lozenge windows across the front foyer, behind the drawn drapes in the living room, coming at them from all directions. But he doesn't notice a thing beyond the assault on his heart.

He clenches his fists. "Why the hell would I ever think something like that, Lil?"

"Because I'm a coward!" She burns her gaze into him. "Because I fucking left you to die. Nothing will ever change that."

"Lilly, please don't—"

"Okay . . . listen to me." She gets her emotions under control. "All I'm saying is, I think we should take it down a notch and give each other—"

"OH, NO—OH, SHIT—SHIT *SHIT*!!"

In a single instant, the sudden alarm on Josh's face drives all other thoughts from Lilly's mind.

The intruders first make themselves known to Josh in a reflection on the surface of a framed family photograph across the room—a stiffly smiling assemblage of the previous owners, including a standard poodle with ribbons in its hair, the framed portrait mounted above a spinet piano—the ghostly silhouettes moving across the picture like spirit images. The faint double image reveals the house's panoramic rear window, the one behind the sofa, through which a battalion of zombies is now visible pushing toward the house.

Josh springs to his feet and whirls around just in time to see the rear window cracking.

The closest zombies—their dead faces mashed up against the glass, squashed by the slow-motion stampede behind them—trail black bile and drool across the window. It all happens very quickly. The hairline fissures spreads like time-lapse spiderwebs spinning toward each corner, as dozens of additional reanimated corpses press against the throng, exerting tremendous pressure on the window.

The glass collapses just as Josh grabs Lilly and yanks her off the sofa.

A terrific crack, like a lightning bolt striking the room, accompanies the birthing of hundreds and hundreds of arms, thrusting forward, jaws snapping, bodies tumbling over the back of the sofa on a wave of broken glass, the wet wind rushing into the gracious family room.

Josh moves without thinking, dragging Lilly with one hand across the arched hall toward the front of the house, as the hell choir of dead vocal cords chirr and grind behind them, filling the stately home with zoo noises and the stench of death. Insensate, twitching in their hunger, the zombies take very little time regaining their legs, rising back up from where they had fallen and quickly trundling forward, flailing and growling, lumbering toward their fleeing prey.

Crossing the front vestibule in a flash, Josh rips open the front door.

A wall of the undead greets him.

He flinches and Lilly shrieks, jerking back with a start, as the battery of dead arms and pincerlike fingers reach for them. Behind the arms, a mosaic of dead faces snarl and sputter, some of them drooling blood as black as motor oil, others flayed open and glistening with the pink sinew and musculature of their damaged facial tissue. One of the curled hands hooks a gob of Lilly's jacket, and Josh tears it away while letting out a booming howl—"FUCKERS!!"—and then on a jolt of adrenaline Josh gets his free hand around the edge of the door.

He slams the door on half a dozen flailing arms, and the impact—

combined with Josh's strength, as well as the deluxe quality of the heavy-duty door—severs each of the six appendages.

Flopping limbs of varying lengths splatter and quiver across the rich Italian tile.

Josh grabs Lilly and starts back toward the center of the house, but pauses at the foot of the spiral staircase when he sees the place is flooding with moving corpses. They have entered through the screen door in the mudroom on the east side of the house, and they've climbed in through the dog door on the west side, and they've wriggled in through cracks in the solarium on the north side of the kitchen. Now they surround Josh and Lilly at the base of the stairs.

Grabbing Lilly by the nape of her jacket, Josh pulls her up the steps.

On their way up the circular staircase, Josh draws his .38 and starts shooting. The first shot flashes and misses its mark entirely, chipping a divot out of the lintel along the archway. Josh's aim is off because he is dragging Lilly up the stairs one riser at a time, as the growling, gnashing, flailing horde awkwardly follows.

Some of the walkers cannot negotiate the stairs and slide back down, while others topple to their hands and knees and manage to keep crawling. Halfway up the spiral, Josh fires again and hits a dead skull, sending wet matter across the newel posts and chandelier. Some of the zombies tumble back down the steps like bowling pins. But now, so many of them are on the risers that they begin to clamber *over each other*, inching up the stairs with the frenzied hunger of salmon spawning. Josh fires again and again. Black fluids bloom in the thunder cracks, but it's futile, there are too many, far too many to fight off, and Josh knows it, and Lilly knows it.

"THIS WAY!"

Josh hollers at her the moment they reach the landing on the second floor.

The idea occurs to Josh fully formed, all at once, as he drags Lilly down the hallway toward the last door at the end of the corridor. Josh remembers checking the master bedroom the previous day, finding some useful pharmaceuticals in the medicine cabinet, and admiring the view from the second-floor bay window. He also remembers the enormous live oak standing sentry next to the window.

"IN HERE!"

The walkers reach the top of the stairs. One of them bumps the banister and stumbles backward, bowling over half a dozen other zombies, sending three of them toppling. The threesome skids down the curvature of the stairs, leaving slime trails of oily blood.

Meanwhile, at the far end of the hall, Josh reaches the bedroom door, throws it open, and pulls Lilly inside the spacious room. The door slams behind them. The silence and calm of the bedroom— with its Louis XIV furnishings, immense four-poster bed, luxurious Laura Ashley duvet, and mountain of frilly, ruffled pillows—provide surreal contrasts to the reeking, noisy menace coming down the hall outside the door. The shuffling footsteps loom. The stench grips the air.

"Get over by the window, babydoll! Be right back!!" Josh whirls and makes a beeline for the bathroom, while Lilly goes over by the huge bay window with its velveteen window treatments. She crouches down, breathlessly waiting.

Josh tears the bathroom door open and lurches into the deluxe, soapy-smelling chamber of Italian tile, chrome, and glass. There amid the Swedish sauna and enormous Jacuzzi tub he throws open the vanity cabinet under the sink. He finds the economy-sized brown bottle of rubbing alcohol.

Within seconds he has the bottle open and is back in the main room, dousing everything, flinging the clear liquid on the curtains and bedding and antique mahogany furniture. The pressure of dead weight making wooden seams creak—the noise of moving corpses piling up against the bedroom door—spurs Josh on.

He tosses the empty bottle and lunges toward the window in a single leap.

Outside the beautifully etched and leaded-glass panorama, framed in delicate ruffled curtains, a gigantic old oak stands over the roof pitches, its twisting limbs, bare in the winter light, reaching up past the weather vane at the crest of the roof. One of the gnarled limbs reaches across the second-floor window, coming within inches of the bedroom.

Josh muscles open the center window on wrought-iron hinges. "C'mon, girlfriend, time to abandon ship!" He kicks out the screen, reaches for Lilly, pulls her up and over the sill, shoves her through the gap, and out into the freezing winds. "Climb across the limb!"

Lilly awkwardly reaches out for the spiraling limb, which is the width of a ham hock, with bark as rough as cement stucco, and she holds on with a desperate vise grip. She starts shimmying her way out across the limb. The wind whistles. The twenty-foot drop seems to stretch away as though glimpsed through a backward telescope. The coach house roof wavers in and out of focus below—barely within jumping distance—as Lilly inches toward the center of the tree.

Behind her, Josh ducks back into the bedroom just as the door collapses.

Zombies pour into the room. Many of them tumble over each other, drunkenly reaching and snarling. One of them—a male missing an arm, with one eye socket cratered out as black and empty as cancer—trundles quickly toward the big black man, who stands by the window, digging frantically in his pocket. The air fills with a groaning cacophony. Josh finds his Zippo cigar lighter.

Just as the eyeless walker pounces, Josh sparks the butane and flings the lighter at the alcohol-dampened skirt around the bed. Flames blossom immediately, as Josh kicks out at the attacking zombie, sending the cadaver stumbling back across the floor.

The walker bounces across the burning bed and sprawls to the alcohol-sodden carpet as the fire licks up the pilasters. More corpses move in, agitated by the flaring light and heat and noise.

Josh wastes no time spinning around and vaulting back toward the window.

It takes less than fifteen minutes for the second floor of the glass house to go up, another five minutes for the infrastructure to collapse into itself on a tidal wave of sparks and smoke, the second floor plunging down onto the first, catching the staircase and gobbling through the warren of antiques and expensive floor coverings. The throngs of walkers inside the home are immolated by geysers of flames, the conflagration fueled by the methane of decay oozing off all the reanimated corpses. Within twenty minutes, more than eighty percent of the swarm from the ravine is vanquished in the firestorm, reduced to charred crisps inside the smoking ruins of the stately home.

Oddly, over the course of those twenty minutes, the nature of the house—with its spectacular enclosure of wraparound windows—acts as a chimney, accelerating the blaze but also burning it out quickly. The hottest part of the fire goes straight up, singeing the tops of the trees but containing the damage. The other homes in the area are spared. No sparks are carried on the winds, and the telltale cloud of smoke remains obscured behind the wooded hills, unseen by the citizens of Woodbury.

In the time it takes for the house to burn itself out, Lilly finds enough nerve to vault from the lowest limb of the oak to the roof of the coach house and then climb down the back wall to the rear door of the garage. Josh follows. By that point only a few walkers remain outside the home, and Josh easily dispatches them with the remaining three slugs in the .38's cylinder.

They get into the garage and find the duffel bag, in which they had stashed some of their previous day's take for safekeeping. The heavy canvas carryall contains a five-gallon jug of gasoline, a sleeping bag, a drip coffee machine, two pounds of French Roast, winter scarves, a box of pancake mix, writing tablets, two bottles of kosher wine, batteries, ballpoint pens, expensive red current jam, a box of matzo, and a coil of mountain-climbing rope.

Josh reloads the police special with the last six slugs in his speed loader. Then they sneak out the back door with the duffel bag over Josh's shoulder, and they creep along the outer wall. Crouching in the weeds near the corner of the garage, they wait until the last moving corpse has drifted toward the light and noise of the fire before darting across the property and into the adjacent woods.

They weave their way through the trees without exchanging a word.

The access road to the south lies deserted in the waning daylight. Josh and Lilly keep to the shadows of a dry creek bed running parallel to the winding blacktop. They head east, down the long sloping landscape, back toward town.

They cover a little more than a mile without speaking, acting like an old married couple in the aftermath of a quarrel. By this point, the fear and adrenaline have finally drained out of them, replaced by a shaky kind of exhaustion.

The near miss of the home attack and ensuing fire has left Lilly in a state of panic. She jumps at noises on either side of the path, and she cannot seem to get enough air into her lungs. She keeps smelling walker stink on the wind, and she thinks she hears shuffling sounds behind the trees, which may or may not be mere echoes of their own weary footsteps.

At last, as they turn the corner at the bottom of Canyon Road, Josh says, "Just let me get one thing straight: Are you saying you're just using me?"

"Josh, I didn't—"

"For protection? And that's it? That's as far as your feelings go?"

"Josh—"

"Or . . . are you saying you just don't want me to *feel* like you're doing that?"

"I didn't say that."

"Yeah, baby, I'm afraid you did, that's exactly what you said."

"This is ridiculous." Lilly puts her hands in the pockets of her corduroy jacket as she walks. A layer of grime and ash has turned the fabric of the coat soot gray in the late-afternoon light. "Let's just drop it. I shouldn't have said anything."

"No!" Josh is slowly shaking his head as he walks. "You don't get to do that."

"What are you talking about?"

He shoots a glance at her. "You think this is like a passing thing?"

"What do you mean?"

"Like this is summer camp? Like we're all gonna go home at the end of the season after losing our virginity and getting poison ivy." His voice has an edge. Lilly has never heard this tone before in Josh

Lee Hamilton's voice. His deep baritone skirts the fringes of rage, his jutting chin belying the hurt slicing through him. "You don't get to plant this little bomb and walk away."

Lilly lets out an exasperated sigh and cannot think of what to say, and they walk in silence for a while. The Woodbury wall materializes in the distance, the far western edge of the construction site coming into view, where the bulldozer and small crane sit idle in the waning light. The construction crew has learned the hard way that zombies—like game fish—bite more in the twilight hours.

At last Lilly says, "What the hell do you want me to say, Josh?"

He stares at the ground as he walks and ruminates. The duffel bag rattles, banging on his hip as he trudges along. "How about you're sorry? How about you've been thinking it over, and maybe you're just scared of gettin' close to somebody because you don't want to get hurt, because you've been hurt yourself, and you take it all back, what you said, you take it back and you really love me as much as I love you? How about that, huh?"

She looks at him, her throat burning from the smoke and terror. She is so thirsty. Tired and thirsty and confused and scared. "What makes you think I've been hurt?"

"Just a lucky guess."

She looks at him. Anger tightens in her belly like a fist. "You don't even know me."

He looks down at her, his eyes wide and stung. "Are you shittin' me?"

"We hooked up—what?—barely two months ago. Bunch of people scared out of their wits. Nobody knows *anybody*. We're all just . . . making do."

"You gotta be kidding me. All we been through? And I don't even *know* you?"

"Josh, that's not what I—"

"You're putting me on the same level as Bob and the stoner? Megan and them folks at the camp? Bingham?"

"Josh—"

"All them things you said to me this week—what are you saying?—you been lying? You said them things just to make me feel better?"

"I meant what I said," she murmurs softly. The guilt twists in her. For a brief instant she thinks back to that terrible moment she lost little Sarah Bingham, the undead swarming all over the little girl on those godforsaken grounds outside the circus tent. The helplessness. The paralytic terror that seized Lilly that day. The loss and the grief and the sorrow as deep as a well. The fact is, Josh is correct. Lilly has said things to him in the throes of late-night lovemaking that aren't exactly true. On some level she loves him, cares for him, has strong feelings . . . but she's projecting something sick deep within her, something that has to do with fear.

"That's just fine and dandy," Josh Lee Hamilton says finally, shaking his head.

They are approaching the gap in the wall outside town. The entranceway—a wide spot between two uncompleted sections of barricade—has a wooden gate secured at one end with cable. About fifty yards away, a single guard sits on the roof of a semitrailer, gazing in the opposite direction with an M1 carbine on his hip.

Josh marches up to the gate and angrily loosens the cable, throwing it open. The rattling noise echoes. Lilly's flesh crawls with panic. She whispers, "Josh, be careful, they're gonna hear us."

"I don't give a rat's ass," he says, swinging the gate open for her. "Ain't a prison. They can't keep us from comin' and goin'."

She follows him through the gate and down a side road toward Main Street.

Few stragglers walk the streets at this hour. Most of the denizens of Woodbury are tucked away indoors, having dinner or drinking themselves into oblivion. The generators provide an eerie thrum behind the walls of the racetrack, some of the overhead stadium lights flickering. The wind trumpets through the bare trees of the square, and dead leaves skitter down the sidewalks.

"You have it your way," Josh says as they turn right and head east down Main Street, trudging toward their apartment building. "We'll just be fuck buddies. Quick pop every now and then to relieve the tension. No muss, no fuss . . ."

"Josh, that's not—"

"You could get the same thing from a bottle of rotgut and a vibrator . . . but hey. Warm body's nice every now and then, right?"

"Josh, c'mon. Why does it have to be this way? I'm just trying to—"

"I don't want to talk about it anymore." He bites down on his words as they approach the food center.

A cluster of men gather around the front of the store, warming their hands over a flaming brazier of trash burning in an oil drum. Sam the Butcher is there, a ratty overcoat covering his blood-spackled apron. His gaunt face puckers with distaste, his diamond-chip blue eyes narrowing as he sees the two figures approaching from the west.

"Fine, Josh, whatever." Lilly thrusts her hands deeper into her pockets as she strides alongside the big man, slowly shaking her head. "Whatever you say."

They pass the food center.

"Hey! Green Mile!" Sam the Butcher's voice calls out, flinty, terse, a knife scraping a whetstone. "C'mere a minute, big fella."

Lilly pauses, her hackles up.

Josh walks over to the men. "I got a name," he says flatly.

"Well, excuse the hell outta me," the butcher says. "What was it— Hamilburg? Hammington?"

"Hamilton."

The butcher offers a vacuous smile. "Well, well. Mr. Hamilton. Esquire. Might I have a moment of your valuable time, if you aren't too busy?"

"What do you want?"

The butcher's cold smile remains. "Just outta curiosity, what's in the bag?"

Josh stares at him. "Nothing much . . . just some odds and ends."

"Odds and ends, huh? What kind of odds and ends?"

"Things we found along the way. Nothin' that would interest anybody."

"You do realize you ain't covered your debt on them *other* odds and ends I gave y'all couple days ago."

"What are you talking about?" Josh keeps staring. "I've been on the crew every day this week."

"You ain't covered it yet, son. That heating oil don't grow on trees."

"You said forty hours would cover it."

The butcher shrugs. "You misunderstood me, hoss. It happens."

"How so?"

"I said forty hours on *top* of what you logged already. Got that?"

The staring match goes on for an awkward moment. All conversation around the flaming trash barrel ceases. All eyes are on the two men. Something about the way Josh's beefy shoulder blades are tensing under his lumberjack coat makes Lilly's flesh crawl.

Josh finally gives the man a shrug. "I'll keep on workin', then."

Sam the Butcher tilts his lean, chiseled face toward the duffel bag. "And I'll thank you to hand over whatever you got tucked away in that bag for the cause."

The butcher makes a move toward the duffel bag, reaching out for it.

Josh snaps it back and away from his grasp.

The mood changes with the speed of a circuit firing. The other men—mostly older loafers with hound-dog eyes and stringy gray hair in their faces—begin to instinctively back away. The tension ratchets up. The silence only adds to the latent violence brewing— the soft snapping of the fire the only sound beneath the wind.

"Josh, it's okay." Lilly steps forward and attempts to intercede. "We don't need any—"

"No!" Josh jerks the duffel away from her, his gaze never leaving the dark, bloodshot eyes of the butcher. "Nobody's taking this bag!"

The butcher's voice drops an octave, going all slippery and dark. "You better think long and hard about fucking with me, big boy."

"The thing is, I'm not fucking with you," Josh says to the man in the bloody apron. "Just stating a fact. The stuff in this bag is ours fair and square. And nobody's taking it from us."

"Finders keepers?"

"That's right."

The old men back away farther until it feels to Lilly like she's standing in some flickering, ice-cold fighting ring with two cornered animals. She gropes for some way to ease back the tension but her words get stuck in her throat. She reaches for Josh's shoulder but he pulls away from her as though shocked. The butcher flicks his gaze at Lilly. "You better tell your beau here he's making the mistake of his life."

"Leave her out of this," Josh tells him. "This is between you and me."

The butcher sucks the inside of his cheek thoughtfully. "Tell you what . . . I'm a fair man . . . I'll give you one more chance. Hand over the goodies and I'll wipe the debt clean. We'll pretend this little tiff never happened." Something approximating a smile creases the lines around the butcher's weathered face. "Life's too short. Know what I mean? Especially around here."

"C'mon, Lilly," Josh says without moving his gaze from the butcher's lifeless eyes. "We got better things to do, stand around here flapping our jaws."

Josh turns away from the storefront and starts down the street.

The butcher goes after the duffel. "GIVE ME THAT GODDAMN BAG!"

Lilly jerks forward as the two men come together in the middle of the street.

"JOSH, NO!"

The big man spins and drives the brunt of his shoulder into the butcher's chest. The move is sudden and violent, and harkens back to Josh's gridiron years when he would clear the field for a running back. The man in the blood-stippled apron flings backward, his breath gasping out of him. He trips over his own feet and goes down hard on his ass, blinking with shock and outrage.

Josh turns and continues on down the street, calling over his shoulder. "Lilly, I said c'mon, let's go!"

Lilly doesn't see the butcher suddenly contorting his body against the ground, struggling to dig something out of the back of his belt under his apron. Lilly doesn't see the glint of blue steel filling the butcher's hand, nor does she hear the telltale snap of a safety being thumbed off a semiautomatic, nor does she see the madness in the butcher's eyes, until it's too late.

"Josh, wait!"

Lilly gets halfway down the sidewalk—coming to within ten feet of Josh—when the blast cracks open the sky, the roar of the 9-millimeter so tremendous it seems to rattle the windows half a block down the street. Lilly instinctively dives for cover, hitting the macadam hard, the impact knocking the breath out of her.

She finds her voice then, and she shrieks as a flock of pigeons erupts off the roof of the food center—the swarm of carrion birds spreading across the darkening sky like black needlepoint.

TWELVE

Lilly Caul would remember things about that day for the rest of her life. She would remember seeing the red rosette of blood and tissue—like a tuft in upholstery—blooming from the back of Josh Lee Hamilton's head, the wound appearing a nanosecond before the booming report of the 9-millimeter Glock fully registered in Lilly's ears. She would remember tripping and falling to the pavement six feet behind Josh, one of her molars cracking, another incisor biting through her tongue. She would remember her ears ringing then, a fine spangle of blood droplets on the backs of her hands and lower arms.

But most of all, Lilly would remember the sight of Josh Lee Hamilton folding to the street as though he were swooning, his enormous legs going soft and wobbly like those of a rag doll. That was perhaps the strangest part: The way the giant man seemed to instantly lose his substance. One would expect such a person to not easily give up the ghost, to fall like a great redwood or old landmark building under the wrecking ball, literally shaking the earth on impact. But the fact is, that day, in the waning blue winter light, Josh Lee Hamilton would fade out without even a whimper.

He would simply keel over and land in a silent heap on the cold pavement.

In the immediate aftermath Lilly feels her entire body seize up with chills, gooseflesh pouring down over her flesh, everything going blurry and also crystal clear at the same time, as though her spirit were separating from her earthbound self. She loses control of her actions. She finds herself rising to her feet without even being aware of it.

She finds herself moving toward the fallen man with numb, involuntary steps, the strides of an automaton. "No, wait . . . no, no, wait, wait, wait," she gibbers as she approaches the dying giant. Her knees hit the ground. Her tears run across the front of her as she reaches down and cradles his huge head and babbles, "Somebody . . . get a doctor . . . no . . . get . . . *somebody* . . . get a . . . GET A FUCKING DOCTOR, SOMEBODY!!"

Nestled in Lilly's hands, the blood getting on her sleeves, Josh's face twitches in its death throes, seeming to undulate and pass from one expression to another. His eyes rolling back, he blinks his last blinks, somehow finding Lilly's face and locking on to it with his final spark of life. "Alicia . . . close the window."

A synapse fires, a memory of an older sister fading away in his traumatized brain like a dying ember.

"Alicia, close the . . ."

His face grows still, eyes freezing and hardening in their sockets like marbles.

"Josh, Josh . . ." Lilly shakes him as though trying to kick-start an engine back to life. He's gone. She cannot see through her tears, everything going milky. She feels the wetness on her wrists from his breached skull, and she feels something tightening around the nape of her neck.

"Leave him be," a gravelly voice intones from behind her, thick with rage.

Lilly realizes someone is pulling her away from the body, a large male hand, fingers clutching a hank of her collar, tugging her back.

Something deep within her snaps.

The passage of time seems to elongate and corrupt, like that of a dream, as the butcher yanks the girl away from the body. He drags her back against the curb and she flops against the barrier, banging the back of her head, lying still now, staring up at the lanky man in the apron. The butcher stands over her, breathing hard, shaking with adrenaline. Behind him, the old geezers stand back against the storefront, shrinking into their baggy, ragged clothes, their rheumy eyes pinned wide.

Down the block, others materialize in the twilight, peering out of doorways and around corners.

"Look what you two have gone and done now!" the butcher accuses Lilly, shoving the pistol in her face. "I tried to be reasonable!"

"Get it over with." She closes her eyes. "Get it over with . . . go ahead."

"You stupid bitch, I ain't gonna kill ya!" He slaps her with his free hand. "Are you listening? Do I have your attention?"

Footsteps echo in the distance—someone running this way—which goes unheard at first. Lilly opens her eyes. "You're a murderer." She utters this over bloody teeth. Her nose is bleeding. "You're worse than a fucking walker."

"That's your opinion." He slaps her again. "Now I want you to listen to me."

The sting is bracing to Lilly. It wakes her up. "What do you want?"

Voices call out a block away, the charging footsteps closing in, but the butcher doesn't hear anything but his own voice. "Gonna take the rest of Green Mile's debt from you, little sister."

"Fuck you."

The butcher leans down and grabs her by the scruff of her jacket collar. "You're gonna work that skinny little ass until you're—"

Lilly's knee comes up hard enough to drive the man's testicles up into his pelvic bone. The butcher staggers and lets out a startled gasp that sounds like steam escaping from a broken vent.

Lilly springs to her feet, and she claws at the butcher's face. Her nails are chewed to the quicks, so they don't do much damage, but it drives the man back farther. He swings at her. She flinches away from the blow, which grazes her shoulder. She kicks him in the balls again.

The butcher staggers, reaching for his pistol.

By this point, Martinez is half a block away, running toward the scene, followed by two of his guards. He calls out, "WHAT THE FUCK?"

The butcher has gotten his Glock out of his belt and spins toward the oncoming men.

The burly, coiled Martinez pounces immediately, slamming the butt end of his M1 down on the butcher's right wrist, the sound of delicate bones crunching audible above the wind. The Glock flies out of the butcher's hand and the butcher lets out a mucusy howl.

One of the other guards—a black kid in an oversized hoodie—arrives in time to grab Lilly, pulling her away from the action. She writhes and squirms in the young man's arms as the guard holds her at bay.

"Stand down, asshole!" Martinez booms, pointing the assault rifle at the staggering butcher, but almost instantly, before Martinez can react, the butcher gets his hands around the shaft of the carbine.

The two men grapple for the gun, their inertia driving them back into the flaming barrel. The barrel spills its contents, a swirl of sparks going up, as the twosome careens toward the storefront. The butcher slams Martinez into the glass door, glass cracking in hairline fractures as Martinez slams the gun up into the butcher's face.

The butcher rears back in pain, clawing the M1 out of Martinez's grip. The assault rifle flies off across the sidewalk. The old men scatter in terror, while other townspeople arrive from all directions, some of them already sending up a frenzy of angry shouts. The second guard—an older man in aviator glasses and ratty down vest—holds the crowd back.

Martinez delivers a hard right to the butcher's jaw and sends the man in the apron crashing through the broken glass pane of the door.

The butcher lands inside the store's vestibule, sprawling to the tile floor, which is littered with glass shards now. Martinez climbs in after him.

A barrage of punishing blows from Martinez keeps the butcher pinned to the floor, his spittle and blood flinging off in pink threads. Frantically shielding his face, flailing impotently, the butcher tries to fight back but Martinez overpowers the man.

The final blow—a roundhouse punch to the butcher's jaw—knocks the man unconscious.

An awkward moment of silence follows, as Martinez catches

his breath. He stands over the man in the apron, rubbing his knuckles, trying to get his bearings. The noise of the crowd outside the food center has grown to a dull roar—most of them cheering for Martinez—like a demented pep rally.

Martinez cannot figure out what just happened. He never much cared for Sam the Butcher, but on the other hand he cannot imagine what would have gotten into this prick to make him draw on Hamilton.

"What the fuck got into you?" Martinez asks the man on the floor, speaking somewhat rhetorically, not really expecting an answer.

"The man obviously wants to be a star."

The voice comes from the gaping, jagged entrance behind Martinez.

Martinez whirls and sees the Governor standing in the doorway. Sinewy arms crossed against his chest, the long tails of his duster flapping in the breeze, the man has an enigmatic expression on his face, a mixture of bemusement and contempt and baleful curiosity. Gabe and Bruce stand behind the man like sullen totems.

Martinez is more confused than ever. "He wants to be a what?"

The Governor's expression transforms—his dark eyes glittering with inspiration, his handlebar mustache fully grown in now and twitching around the corners of a frown—which tells Martinez to step lightly. "First," the Governor says in a flat, impassive tone, "tell me exactly what happened."

"He didn't suffer, Lilly . . . remember that . . . no pain . . . he just went out like a light." Bob crouches near the curb next to Lilly, who is slumped with her head down, the tears dripping onto her lap. Bob has his first-aid kit open on the sidewalk next to her, and he is dabbing a swab of iodine on her cut face. "That's more than most of us can hope for in this shithole of a world."

"I should have stopped it," Lilly utters in a bloodless, sapped voice that sounds like a pull-string doll on its last legs. She has burned out her tear ducts. "I could have, Bob, I could have stopped it."

The silence stretches, the wind rattling in the eaves and high-tension wires. Practically the entire population of Woodbury has gathered along Main Street to gawk at the aftermath.

Josh lies supine under a sheet next to Lilly. Someone covered the body with the makeshift shroud only minutes earlier, the folds of which now soak with red blotches of blood from Josh's head wounds. Lilly tenderly strokes his leg, compulsively squeezing and massaging as though she might wake him up. Tendrils of hair are knocked loose from Lilly's ponytail, blowing across her scarred, crestfallen features.

"Hush now, honey," Bob says, placing the bottle of Betadine back into the kit. "There was nothing y'all could do, nothing at all." Bob shoots a worried glance up at the jagged, broken glass of the food center entrance. He can barely see the Governor and his men inside the vestibule, talking with Martinez. The butcher's unconscious body lies in the shadows. The Governor gestures expansively toward the body, explaining something to Martinez. "Goddamn shame is what it is," Bob says, looking away. "Goddamn crying shame."

"He didn't have a mean bone in his body," Lilly says softly, looking at the bloodstain soaking the head end of the sheet. "I wouldn't be alive, wasn't for him . . . he saved my life, Bob, all he wanted was—"

"Miss . . . ?"

Lilly looks up at the sound of an unfamiliar voice, and sees an older man in eyeglasses and white lab coat standing behind Bob. A fourth person, a twenty-something girl with blond braids, stands behind the man. She also wears a tattered lab coat and has a stethoscope and blood pressure cuff dangling around her neck.

"Lilly, this is Doc Stevens," Bob says with a nod toward the man. "And that there is Alice, his nurse."

The girl gives Lilly a respectful nod while unwinding the cuff.

"Lilly, you mind if I take a quick peek at those facial bruises?" the doctor says, kneeling next to her, putting the earbuds of his stethoscope in his ears. Lilly says nothing, just turns her gaze back to the ground. The doctor gently touches the scope to her neck, her sternum, her pulse points. He inspects her wounds, softly palpates her ribs. "Very sorry for your loss, Lilly," the doctor murmurs.

Lilly says nothing.

"Some of them wounds are old," Bob comments, rising to his feet, backing away.

"Looks like hairline fractures to number eight and nine, also to the clavicle," he says, gently nudging his fingers through her fleece jacket. "All of them pretty much healed up. Lungs sound clear." He takes the scope out of his ears, winds it around his neck. "Lilly, if you need anything you let us know."

She manages a nod.

The doctor measures his words. "Lilly, I just want you to know . . ." He pauses for a moment, groping for the right words. "Not everybody in this town is . . . like this. I know it's not much in the way of consolation right now." He looks up at Bob, then gazes at the ruined food center window, than back at Lilly. "I guess what I'm saying is, if you ever need somebody to talk to, if something is bothering you, if you need anything whatsoever . . . don't hesitate to come down to the clinic."

Seeing no reaction from Lilly, the doctor lets out a sigh and rises to his feet. He exchanges nervous glances with Bob and Alice.

Bob moves back to Lilly's side, kneels down, and says very softly, "Lilly, honey, we're gonna have to go ahead and move the body now."

At first she barely hears him, in fact doesn't even register what he's saying.

She simply continues staring at the pavement and stroking the dead man's leg and feeling empty. In anthropology class at Georgia Tech she learned about the Algonquin Indians and their belief that the spirit of the dead must be appeased. After a hunt they would literally breathe in the last breaths of a dying bear in order to honor it and accept it into their own bodies and pay homage to it. But Lilly feels only desolation and loss coming into her now from the cooling corpse of Josh Lee Hamilton.

"Lilly?" Bob's voice sounds as though it's coming from a distant solar system. "Is it okay, honey, if we go ahead and move the body?"

Lilly is silent.

Bob nods at Stevens. The doctor nods at Alice, and Alice turns and signals to two men standing their distance with a collapsible stretcher. The two men—both middle-aged cronies of Bob's from the tavern crowd—move in. Unfolding the stretcher, they come within inches of Lilly and kneel down by the body. The first man starts to gently lever the massive body onto the stretcher, when Lilly snaps her gaze up at them, blinking back tears.

"Leave him alone," she mutters, the words coming out in barely a whisper.

Bob puts a hand on her shoulder. "Lilly, honey—"

"I SAID LEAVE HIM ALONE! DON'T TOUCH HIM!! GET THE FUCK AWAY FROM HIM!!!"

Her anguished cry pierces the windswept stillness of the street, getting everyone's attention. Onlookers halfway down the block pause in their conversations and look up. People in doorways peer around corners to see what's going on. Bob waves off the two cronies, and Stevens and Alice back away in awkward silence.

The commotion has drawn several figures out of the food center. They now stand in the jagged opening of the entrance, staring at the sad state of affairs.

Bob gazes up and sees the Governor standing there, arms crossed against his chest on the glass-littered threshold, assessing the situation with his cunning, dark eyes. Bob walks sheepishly over to the entrance.

"She'll be okay," Bob says confidentially to the Governor. "She's just a little torn up right now."

"Who can blame her?" the Governor muses. "Lose your meal ticket like that." He chews the inside of his cheek for a moment, thinking. "Leave her alone for a while. We'll clean up the mess later." He thinks some more, not taking his gaze off the dead body lying next to the curb. At last he calls over his shoulder, "Gabe—c'mere!"

The stocky man in the turtleneck and flattop haircut comes over.

The Governor speaks softly. "I want you to wake up that piece-of-shit butcher, take him down to the holding cells, and throw him in with the Guard."

Gabe gives a nod, whirls, and slips back inside the food center.

"Bruce!" the Governor calls to his second in command. The black man with the shaved head and Kevlar vest comes over with an AK-47 on his hip.

"Yeah, boss."

"I want you to round everybody up, take them over to the square."

The black man cocks his head incredulously. "Everybody?"

"You heard me—everybody." The Governor gives him a wink. "Gonna have a little town hall meeting."

"We live in violent times. We're all under tremendous pressure. Every day of our lives."

The Governor barks into a megaphone that Martinez found in the defunct firehouse, the gravelly, smoky voice carrying up over the bare trees and torches. The sun has set on the town, and now the entire population mills about the darkness on the edge of the gazebo in the center of the square. The Governor stands on the stone steps of the structure, addressing his subjects with the stentorian authority of a politician crossed with a wild-eyed motivational speaker.

"I understand the pressures," he goes on, pacing across the steps, milking the moment for all it's worth. His voice echoes across the square, slapping back against the boarded-up storefronts across the street. "We've all dealt with the grief, last few months . . . losing somebody close to us."

He pauses for effect, and he sees many of the faces turning downward, eyes shimmering in the light of torches. He senses the weight of pain pressing down. He smiles inwardly, waiting patiently for the moment to pass.

"What happened at the store today didn't have to happen. You live by the sword . . . I get that. But it didn't have to happen. It was a symptom of a greater sickness. And we're gonna treat that sickness."

For a brief instant he glances back to the east, and he sees the slumped figures gathered over the shrouded body of the black man. Bob kneels behind the girl named Lilly, stroking her back, as he stares trancelike at the fallen giant under the bloody sheet.

The Governor turns back to his audience. "Starting tonight we're gonna inoculate ourselves. From now on, things are gonna be different around here. I promise you . . . things are gonna be different. Gonna be some new rules."

He paces some more, burning his gaze into each and every onlooker.

"The thing that separates us from these monsters out there is *civilization*!" He punches the word "civilization" so hard it bounces off the rooftops. "Order! Laws! The ancient Greeks had this shit down. They knew about tough love. 'Catharsis' they used to call it."

Some of the faces gaze up at him with jittery, expectant expressions.

"You see that racetrack up yonder?" he says into the bullhorn. "Take a good look!"

He turns and gives a signal to Martinez, who stands in the shadows at the base of the gazebo. Martinez thumbs a button on a two-way, and he whispers something to somebody on the other end. This is the part that the Governor insisted be carefully timed.

"Starting tonight," the Governor goes on, watching many of the heads turn toward the big, dark flying saucer planted in the clay west of town, its huge bowl-like rim rising in silhouette against the stars. "Starting right now! That's gonna be our new Greek theater!"

With the pomp and circumstance of a fireworks display, the great xenon spots above the track suddenly flare to life in sequence—making audible metallic snapping noises—sending giant blooms of silver light down on the arena. The gag gets an audible, collective sigh from many of those gathered around the gazebo, some spontaneously applauding.

"Admission is free!" The Governor feels the energy rising, crackling like static electricity, and he bears down on them. "Auditions are ongoing, folks. You want to fight in the ring? All you gotta do is break the rules. That's all you gotta do. Break the law."

He looks at them as he paces, daring them to respond. Some of them look at each other, some of them nod, while others look as though they're about to give him a "Hallelujah."

"Anyone breaks the law is gonna fight! That simple. You don't know what the laws are, all you gotta do is ask. Read the fucking Constitution. Check the Bible. Do unto others. Golden rule. All that. But hear what I'm saying. You do *unto* somebody a little too much . . . you're gonna fight."

A few voices holler out their consent, and the Governor feeds off the energy, stoking the flames. "From now on, you fuck with somebody—you break the law—you're gonna fight!"

A few more voices add to the din, the noise carrying up into the sky.

"You steal from somebody, you're gonna fight!"

Now the crowd hollers its approval, a chorus of righteous howls.

"You bang somebody's old lady, you're gonna fight!"

More voices join in, all the fear and frustration boiling over now.

"You kill somebody, you're gonna fight!"

The cheering starts to corrupt into a cacophony of angry shouts.

"You mess with somebody in any way—especially, you get some-body killed—you're gonna fight. In the arena. In front of God. To the death."

The clamor deteriorates into a mishmash of applause and whoop-ing and hollering. The Governor waits for it to subside like a wave rolling away.

"It starts tonight," he says in barely a whisper, the megaphone crackling. "It starts with this nutcase, guy that runs the general store—Sam the Butcher. Thinks he's judge, jury, and executioner."

All at once the Governor points at the arena and calls out suddenly in a voice that would not be out of place at a charismatic church ser-vice: "Who's ready for some payback? *WHO'S READY FOR SOME LAW AND ORDER?*"

The voices erupt.

Lilly gazes up and sees the abrupt exodus of nearly forty people half a block away. The crowd disperses in a noisy mass, moving al-most as one—a giant human amoeba of excited fist pumping and inarticulate, angry cheering—charging across the street toward the racetrack arena, which sits in a vast penumbra of silver light two hundred yards to the west. The sight of it turns Lilly's stomach.

She looks away and mutters, "You can take the body away now, Bob."

Standing over her, Bob leans down and tenderly strokes her shoul-der. "We'll take good care of him, honey."

She gazes into the distance. "Tell Stevens I want to make the ar-rangements."

"You got it."

"We'll bury him tomorrow."

"That sounds fine, honey."

Lilly watches the mob of citizens in the distance filing into the arena. For one terrible instant she recalls scenes from old horror movies, angry throngs of townspeople with torches and primitive weapons, closing in on Frankenstein's castle, lusting for the monster's blood.

She shudders. She realizes they are all monsters now—all of them—Lilly and Bob included. Woodbury is the monster now.

THIRTEEN

Curiosity gets the better of Bob Stookey. After escorting Lilly back to her apartment above the dry cleaner, and giving her ten milli-grams of alprazolam for sleep, he checks in with Stevens. Arrange-ments are made to move Josh's body to its temporary resting place in the makeshift morgue under the racetrack. Afterward Bob makes his way back to his camper and grabs a fresh bottle of whiskey from the back. Then he returns to the arena.

By the time he arrives at the south entrance, the crowd noises are swelling and ringing inside the structure like waves crashing against a shore, magnified by the metallic baffles of the arena. Bob creeps through the dark, fetid tunnel toward the light. He pauses just in-side the south gate and takes a healthy pull off the bottle of hooch, girding himself, buffering his nerves. The whiskey burns and makes his eyes water.

He steps into the light.

At first all he sees are blurry, indistinct shapes down on the in-field, obscured behind massive cyclone fences rising up in front of the spectators. The bleachers on either side of him are mostly empty. The citizens sit above him, scattered across the upper decks, clapping and whooping and craning their necks to see the action. The harsh brilliance of the arc light shining down makes Bob blink. The air smells of old burned rubber and gasoline, and Bob has to squint to identify what's going on down on the track.

He takes a step closer, leans toward the fence, and peers through the chain link.

Two large men grapple with each other in the center of the muddy infield. Sam the Butcher, seminude in his blood-spattered athletic trunks, his bare chest sagging, and his belly hanging over his belt, swings a jury-rigged wooden club at Stinson, the big, lumpy middle-aged guardsman. Stinson, his camo pants dark with bodily fluids, staggers and jerks back, trying to dodge the onslaught, an eighteen-inch machete in his greasy hand. The end of the butcher's club—sprouting rusty nails on one side—catches the side of Stinson's doughy face, gouging flesh.

Stinson rears backward, throwing spittle and strands of thick blood.

The crowd issues a salvo of yelps and angry cheers as Stinson topples over his own feet. Dust rises up into the sodium light as the portly guardsman hits the ground, the machete flying out of his grip and landing in the dirt. The butcher pounces with the club. Nails puncture Stinson's jugular and left pectoral before the man has a chance to roll away. The audience yowls.

Bob turns away for a moment, feeling nauseous and dizzy. He takes another huge gulp of whiskey and lets the burn soothe his terror. He takes another, and another, and finally works up enough nerve to gaze back at the action. The butcher is pummeling Stinson, sending gouts of blood—as black as tar in the sodium lights—spraying across the matted brown turf of the infield.

The wide dirt track circling the infield has armed guards at each gate, intently watching the fracas, their assault rifles cradled at the ready. Bob swallows more whiskey and averts his gaze from the grisly slaughter, focusing on the upper regions of the racetrack. The diamond-vision screen is blank, powerless, probably inoperable. The glass enclosures of VIP boxes lining one side of the arena are mostly deserted and dark . . . all except for one.

The Governor and Martinez stand behind the window of the center box, looking down on the spectacle with unreadable expressions on their faces.

Bob chugs another few fingers of whiskey—he's already halfway through the bottle—and finds himself avoiding eye contact with the crowd. In his peripheral vision he can see the faces of young and old, male and female, all riveted to the bloody skirmish. Many faces contort with a kind of manic delight. Some of the onlookers rise to their feet, hands waving as though they are finding Jesus.

Down on the field the butcher delivers one last savage blow to Stinson's kidney, the nails sinking into the guardsman's fleshy lower back. Blood bubbles and gushes, and then Stinson sags in the dirt, convulsing, twitching in his death throes. Breathing hard, drooling with psychotic glee, the butcher raises the club and faces the crowd. The spectators respond with a surge of howls.

Repulsed, woozy, going numb with horror, Bob Stookey chugs more whiskey and looks down.

"I THINK WE HAVE A WINNER!"

The amplified voice coming through the public address system echoes and feeds back with harsh, electronic squealing noises. Bob gazes up and sees the Governor behind the center box window casually speaking into a microphone. Even from this great distance, Bob can see the weird pleasure glimmering behind the Governor's eyes like two pinpoints of starlight. Bob looks back down.

"HOLD ON! HOLD ON!! LADIES AND GENTLEMEN, I THINK WE HAVE A COMEBACK!!"

Bob looks up.

On the infield, the big lump on the ground has come back to life. Lurching toward the machete, Stinson gets his blood-slick hand around the hilt and twists back toward the butcher, who has his back turned. Stinson pounces with every last ounce of strength. The butcher turns and tries to shield his face as the machete slashes.

The blade sinks into the butcher's neck deep enough to get stuck.

The butcher staggers and falls backward with the machete still planted in his jugular. Stinson moves in with drunken rage, the blood loss making him lumber and weave with eerie resemblance to a zombie. The crowd jeers and roars. Stinson pulls the machete loose and delivers another devastating blow to the butcher's neck, severing the gaunt man's head between the fifth and sixth cervical vertebrae.

The spectators cheer as the butcher's neck floods the ground with its lifeblood.

Bob looks away. He falls to his knees, one hand still clutching the chain link. His stomach lurches and he vomits on the cement floor of the mezzanine. The bottle falls but does not break. Bob pukes out the entire contents of his stomach in heaving gasps—the noise of the crowd going all watery, everything getting blurry and indistinct in his watery vision. He vomits and vomits until there is nothing left but thin strands of bile hanging off his lips. He falls back against the first row of empty bleachers. He retrieves the bottle and sucks down the rest of its contents.

The amplified voice echoes: "AND THAT, FOLKS, IS WHAT WE CALL JUSTICE!"

Outside the arena, at that moment, the streets of Woodbury could be confused with any other deserted ghost ship of a village in the Georgia countryside—abandoned and scoured clean in the advent of the plague.

At first glance, every last inhabitant appears to be missing in action—the entire population still gathered in the stadium, riveted to the final moments of the battle royale. Even the sidewalk in front of the food center has been cleared, any lingering evidence of murder mopped away by Stevens and his men, Josh's body carted off to the morgue.

Now, in the darkness, as the muffled echoes of the crowd swirl on the wind, Lilly Caul wanders the sidewalk in her fleece, torn jeans, and tattered high-tops. She cannot sleep, cannot think, cannot stop crying. The noise from the arena feels like insects crawling on her. The Xanax Bob gave her has done nothing but dull the pain, like a layer of gauze over her racing thoughts. She shivers in the cold and pauses in a dark vestibule in front of a boarded drugstore.

"It's none of my business," a voice says from the shadows. "But a young lady like yourself shouldn't be out alone on these streets."

Lilly turns and sees the glint of metal-rimmed glasses on a dark face. She sighs, wipes her eyes, and looks down. "What difference does it make?"

Dr. Stevens steps into the flickering light of torches. He stands with his hands in his pockets, his lab coat buttoned to the collar, a scarf around his neck. "How are you holding up, Lilly?"

She looks at him through her tears. "Holding up? I'm just grand."

She tries to breathe but her lungs feel as though they're full of sand. "Next stupid question."

"You might think about resting." He comes over to her and inspects her bruises. "You're still in shock, Lilly. You need sleep."

She manages a pallid smile. "I'll sleep when I'm dead." She cringes and looks down, the tears burning her eyes. "Funny thing is, I hardly knew him."

"He seemed like a good man."

She looks up, focusing on the doctor. "Is that even possible anymore?"

"Is what possible?"

"Being a good person."

The doctor lets out a sigh. "Probably not."

Lilly swallows and looks down. "I have to get out of this place." She winces at another sob building in her. "I can't deal with it anymore."

Stevens looks at her. "Join the club."

A moment of awkward silence passes.

Lilly rubs her eyes. "How do you do it?"

"Do what?"

"Stay here . . . put up with this shit. You seem like a semisane person to me."

The doctor shrugs. "Looks can be deceiving. Anyway . . . I stay for the same reason they all stay."

"And that is . . . ?"

"Fear."

Lilly looks at the paving stones. She doesn't say anything. What is there to say? The torchlight across the street dwindles, the wicks burning down, the shadows deepening in the nooks and crannies between the buildings. Lilly fights the dizziness washing over her. She doesn't want to sleep ever again.

"They're going to be coming out of there pretty soon," the doctor says with a nod toward the racetrack in the distance. "Once they've had their fill of the little horror show Blake has concocted for them."

Lilly shakes her head. "Place is a fucking madhouse, and that dude is the craziest one of all."

"Tell you what." The doctor gestures toward the opposite end of town. "Why don't we take a little walk, Lilly . . . avoid the crowds."

She exhales a pained breath, then shrugs and mutters, "Whatever . . ."

That night, Dr. Stevens and Lilly walk for over an hour in the cold, bracing air, meandering back and forth along the far fence on the east side of town, and then down along the abandoned railroad tracks inside the security fence. While they walk and talk, the crowd slowly files out of the arena, wandering back to their dwellings, bloodlust satiated. The doctor does most of the talking that night, speaking softly, ever mindful of the listening ears of guards, who are positioned at strategic corners along the barricade, equipped with guns, binoculars, and walkie-talkies.

The guards are in constant contact with Martinez, who has cautioned his men to pay close attention to the weak areas along the ramparts, and especially the wooded hills to the south and west. Martinez worries that the noise of the gladiatorial matches will very likely draw walkers.

Strolling along the outskirts, Stevens gives Lilly a lecture about the perils of conspiring against the Governor. Stevens warns her to watch her tongue, and he speaks in analogies that make Lilly's head spin. He talks of Caesar Augustus and he speaks of Bedouin dictators through history and how the hardships of desert communities spurred brutal regimes and coups and violent insurrection.

Eventually Stevens brings the conversation full circle to the unfortunate realities of the zombie plague, and suggests that bloodthirsty leaders are very likely a necessary evil now, a side effect of survival.

"I don't want to live like that," Lilly says at last, walking slowly alongside the doctor through a palisade of bare trees. The wind spits a light sleet in their faces, which stings their flesh and coats the forest with a delicate rime of ice. Christmas is only twelve days off, not that anybody would notice.

"No choice in the matter, Lilly," the doctor mutters, head down, scarf across his chin. He stares at the ground as he walks.

"You always have a choice."

"You think? I don't know, Lilly." They walk in silence for a moment. The doctor slowly shakes his head as he walks. "I don't know."

She looks at him. "Josh Hamilton never went bad. My dad sacrificed his life for me." Lilly takes a breath and struggles with her tears. "It's just an excuse. A person is *born* bad. The shit we're dealing with now . . . it's just a fucking trigger. Brings out the real person."

"Then God help us," the doctor murmurs, almost more to himself than to Lilly.

The next day, under a low, steel-gray sky, a small contingent buries Josh Lee Hamilton in a makeshift casket. Lilly, Bob, Stevens, Alice, and Megan are joined by Calvin Deets, one of the workmen, who had grown fond of Josh over the last couple of weeks.

Deets is an older man, an emaciated chain-smoker—probably in the late stages of emphysema—who has a face like an old saddlebag left out in the sun. He stands respectfully back behind the front row of friends, his Caterpillar cap in his gnarled hands, as Lilly says a few words.

"Josh grew up in a religious family," Lilly says in a choked voice, her face turned down as though addressing the frozen ground on the edge of a playground. "He believed we all go to a better place."

Other recent graves spread across the small park, some with homemade crosses or carefully stacked cairns of polished stones. The mound of dirt over Josh's grave rises up at least four feet above ground level. They had to enclose his remains in a piano case that Deets found in a warehouse—the only container big enough to accommodate the fallen giant—and it took Bob and Deets several hours to carve out a suitable hole in the icebound earth.

"Here's hoping Josh is right, because we all . . ." Lilly's voice falters, crumbles. She closes her eyes and the tears seep through her eyelids. Bob takes a step closer, puts an arm around her. Lilly lets out a sob that shudders through her. She cannot continue.

Bob says softly, "Father . . . Son and . . . Holy Spirit. Amen." The others murmur likewise. Nobody moves. The wind kicks up and blows a sheet of powdery-dry snow across the playground, nipping their faces.

Bob gently urges Lilly away from the grave. "C'mon, darlin' . . . let's get you inside."

Lilly puts up little resistance, shuffling alongside Bob as the others turn away silently, heads down, faces crestfallen. For a moment, it looks as though Megan—dressed in a worn leather jacket, which some anonymous benefactor gave her in a druggy post-coitus afterglow—is about to hurry after Lilly, maybe say something to her. But the corkscrew-haired woman with the dishwater-green eyes just lets out an anguished sigh and keeps her distance.

Stevens gives Alice a nod, and the two of them turn and head back down the side road toward the racetrack complex, turning up the collars of their lab coats against the wind. They get halfway to the main drag—safely out of earshot of the others—when Alice says to the doctor, "Did you smell it?"

He nods. "Yep . . . it's on the wind . . . it's coming from the north."

Alice sighs, shaking her head. "I knew these idiots would draw a crowd with all that noise. Should we tell somebody?"

"Martinez already knows." The doctor indicates the guard tower behind them. "Lots of saber rattling going on, God help us."

Alice lets out another sigh. "Gonna be busy next few days, aren't we?"

"That guardsman used up half our whole blood supply, gonna need some more donors."

"I'll do it," Alice says.

"Appreciate the thought, sweetheart, but we got enough A positive to last us until Easter. Besides, I take any more out of you I'll have to plant you next to the big guy."

"Should we keep searching for an O positive?"

The doctor shrugs. "Like looking for a very small needle in a very small haystack."

"I haven't checked Lilly or that other new kid, what's his name."

"Scott? The stoner?"

"Yeah."

The doctor shakes his head. "Nobody's seen hide nor hair of him in days."

"You never know."

The doctor keeps shaking his head, hands deep in his pockets, as he hastens toward the shadows of concrete archways in the distance. "Yeah . . . you never know."

That night, back in her squatter's flat above the boarded-up dry cleaner, Lilly feels numb. She's thankful that Bob has chosen to stay with her for a while. He makes her dinner—his special beef jerky Stroganoff courtesy of Hamburger Helper—and they share enough of Bob's single-malt Scotch and generic Ambien to ease Lilly's racing thoughts.

The noises outside the second-story window grow fainter and farther away—although they seem to be making Bob nervous as he tucks Lilly in. Something is going on down on the streets. Maybe trouble. But Lilly cannot focus on the distant commotion of voices and running footsteps.

She feels as though she's floating, and the moment she lays her head on the pillow she sinks into semiconsciousness. The bare floors and sheet-covered windows of the apartment blur away into a white oblivion. But right before she sinks into the void of dreamless sleep, she sees Bob's weathered face looming over her.

"Why won't you leave with me, Bob?"

The question hangs there for a moment. Bob shrugs. "Haven't really thought about it."

"There's nothing for us here anymore."

He looks away. "Governor says things are gonna get better soon."

"What's the deal with you and him?"

"Whattya talkin' about?"

"He's got a hold on you, Bob."

"That ain't true."

"I just don't get it." Lilly fades. She can barely see the weathered man sitting on the side of her bed. "He's trouble, Bob."

"He's just trying to—"

Lilly barely hears the knock on the door. She tries to keep her eyes open. Bob goes to the door, and Lilly tries to stay awake long enough to identify the visitor. "Bob . . . ? Who is it . . . ?

Footsteps. Two figures come into view over her bed like ghosts. Lilly struggles to see through the shade descending over her eyes.

Bob stands next to a gaunt, lean, dark-eyed man with a carefully trimmed Fu Manchu mustache and coal-black hair. The man smiles as Lilly sinks into unconsciousness.

"Sleep tight, girlfriend," the Governor says. "You've had a long day."

The behavior patterns of the walkers continue to baffle and enthrall the deeper thinkers among Woodbury's inhabitants. Some believe the undead move as bees in a hive, driven by something far more complex than mere hunger. Some theories involve invisible pheromonelike signals passing among zombies, producing behaviors that depend upon the chemical makeup of their prey. Others believe in dog-whistle sensory responses above and beyond mere attraction to sound or smell or movement. No single hypothesis has stuck, but most of Woodbury's residents feel certain about one aspect of zombie behavior: The advent of a herd of any size is to be dreaded and feared and treated with respect. Herds tend to grow spontaneously and take on troubling ramifications. A herd—even a small one, like the cluster of dead forming at this very moment north of town, drawn by the noise of the gladiatorial match the previous night— can overturn a truck, snap fence posts like kindling, or topple even the highest wall.

For the last twenty-four hours Martinez has been marshaling forces in order to suppress the imminent attack. Guards posted on crow's nests at the northwest and northeast corners of the wall have been keeping tabs on the progress of the flock, which first began to morph into a herd about a mile away. The guards have been sending word down the chain of command that the size of the herd has grown from a dozen or so to nearly fifty, and the pack has been moving in a lumbering zigzag through the trees along Jones Mill Road, covering the distance between the deep woods and the outskirts of town at a speed of about two hundred yards an hour, growing in number as they come. Apparently the herds move even slower, collectively, than individual walkers. It has taken this herd fifteen hours to close the distance to four hundred yards.

Now some of them begin to emerge from the leading edge of the forest, shambling out into the open fields bordering the woods and the town. They look like broken toys in the hazy, distant twilight, like windup soldiers bumping into each other, running on the fumes of malfunctioning engines, their blackened mouths contracting and expanding like irises. Even at this distance the rising moon reflects off their milky eyes in shimmering coins of light.

Martinez has three Browning .50 caliber machine guns—courtesy of the ransacked National Guard depot—placed at key junctures along the wall. One sits on the bonnet of a backhoe at the west corner of the wall. Another one is situated on top of a cherry picker at the east corner. The third is positioned on the roof of a semitrailer on the edge of the construction site. Each of the three machine guns already has an operator in place, each man equipped with a headset.

Long gleaming bandoliers of incendiary armor-piercing tracer bullets dangle from the stock of each weapon, with extras in steel boxes sitting nearby.

Other guards take positions along the wall—on ladders and bull-dozer scoops—armed with semiautomatics and long-range sniper rifles loaded with 7.62-millimeter slugs that will penetrate drywall or sheet metal. These men do not wear headsets, but each know to watch for hand signals from Martinez, who positions himself at the top of a crane gantry in the center of the post office parking lot with a two-way. Two enormous klieg lights—scavenged from the town theater—are wired up to the generator chugging in the shadows of the post office loading dock.

A voice crackles on Martinez's radio: "Martinez, you there?"

Martinez thumbs the talk button. "Copy that, chief, go ahead."

"Bob and I are on our way up there, gonna need to harvest some fresh meat."

Martinez frowns, his brow furrowing under his bandanna. "Fresh meat?"

The voice sizzles through the tiny speaker: "How much time we got before all the fun and games start?"

Martinez gazes out at the darkening horizon, the closest zombies still about three hundred and fifty yards away. He thumbs the switch. "Probably won't be within head-shot range for another hour, maybe a little less than that."

"Good," says the voice. "We'll be there in five minutes."

Bob follows the Governor down Main Street toward a wagon train of semi trucks parked in a semicircle outside the looted Menards home and garden center. The Governor walks briskly through the wintry evening air, a bounce to his step, his boot heels clicking on the paving stones. "Times like these," the Governor comments to Bob as they march along, "must feel like you're back in the shit in Afghanistan."

"Yes, sir, I have to admit it does sometimes. I remember one time I got a call to drive down to the front, pick up some marines coming off their watch. It was nighttime, cold as a well digger's ass, just like this. Air raid sirens screaming, everybody hopped up for a firefight. Drove the APC down to this godforsaken trench in the sand, and what do I find? Bunch of whores from the local village giving out blow jobs to the grunts."

"No shit."

"I shit you not." Bob shakes his head in dismay as he walks alongside the Governor. "Right in the middle of an air raid. So I tell them to can it and get in before I leave them there. One of the whores gets in the APC with the men, and I'm like, what the hell. Whatever. Just get me out of this fucking place."

"Understandable."

"So I take off with the gal still going at it in the back of the APC. But you'll never guess what happened then."

"Don't keep me in suspense, Bob," the Governor says with a grin.

"All of a sudden I hear a crash in the back, and I realize that bitch is an insurgent, and she brought an IED in with her, set it off in the cargo bay." Bob shakes his head again. "Firewall protected me, but it was a mess. Took off one of the boys' legs."

"Un-fucking-believable," the Governor marvels as he approaches the circle of eighteen-wheelers. Full darkness has fallen, and light from a torch illuminates the side of a Piggly Wiggly truck on which a grinning pig leers down at them in the dim light. "Hold that thought a second, Bob." The Governor pounds his fist on the trailer. "Travis! You in there? Hey! Anybody home?"

In a cloud of cigar smoke, the rear door springs up on rusty hinges. A heavyset black man sticks his head out of the cargo hold. "Hey, boss . . . what can I do you for?"

"Take one of the empty trailers down to the north wall, on the double. We'll meet you there with further instructions. Got that?"

"Got it, boss."

The black man hops off the rear rail and vanishes around the side of the truck. The Governor takes a deep breath and then leads Bob around the circle of trucks, and then north along a side road toward the barricade. "Pretty goddamn amazing what a man will do for nookie," the Governor muses as they stride along the dirt road.

"Ain't it?"

"These girls you came in with, Bob, Lilly and . . . what's-her-name?"

"Megan?"

"That's the one. That little thing's a firecracker. Am I right?"

Bob wipes his mouth. "Yeah, she's a cute little gal."

"Kinda flirty . . . but hey. Who am I to judge?" Another lascivious grin. "We do what we do to get by. Am I right, Bob?"

"Right as rain." Bob walks along for a moment. "Just between you and me . . . I'm kinda sweet on her."

The Governor looks at the older man with an odd mixture of surprise and pity. "This Megan gal? Well, that's great, Bob. No shame in that."

Bob looks down as he walks. "Love to spend the night with her just once." Bob's voice goes soft. "Just once." He looks up at the Governor. "But, hell . . . I know that's just a pipe dream."

Philip cocks his head at the older man. "Maybe not, Bob . . . maybe not."

Before Bob can muster a response a series of explosive clanging noises go off ahead of them. Brilliant sunbursts from the klieg lights suddenly tear open seams in the distant darkness from opposite corners of the wall, the silver beams sweeping out across the adjacent fields and tree lines, illuminating the oncoming horde of walking corpses.

The Governor leads Bob across the post office lot to the crane gantry, on which Martinez now prepares to give the order to open fire.

"Hold your fire, Martinez!" The Governor's booming voice gets everybody's attention.

Martinez gazes nervously down at the two men. "You sure about this, chief?"

The rumble of a Kenworth cab rises up behind the Governor, accompanied by the telltale beeping noises of a semi moving in reverse. Bob glances over his shoulder and sees an eighteen-wheeler backing into position by the north gate. Exhaust vapors pulse from the truck's vertical stack, and Travis leans out the driver's side window, chewing a cigar and wrestling the steering wheel.

"Gimme your walkie!" The Governor gestures at Martinez, who is already descending the metal ladder affixed to the side of the crane. Bob watches all this from a respectable distance behind the Governor. Something about all this mysterious business makes the older man uneasy.

Outside the wall the meandering mass of zombies closes the distance to two hundred yards.

Martinez reaches the bottom of the ladder and hands over the two-way. The Governor thumbs the switch and barks into the mouthpiece. "Stevens! Can you hear me? You got your radio on?"

After a beat of crackling static the doctor's voice replies, "Yes, I hear you and I don't appreciate—"

"Shut up for a second. I want you to bring that tub-of-lard guardsman, Stinson, to the north wall."

The voice crackles: "Stinson is still recovering, the man has lost a lot of blood in your little—"

"Don't fucking argue with me, Stevens . . . *JUST FUCKING DO IT NOW!*"

The Governor clicks the radio off and throws it back to Martinez.

"Open the gate!" the Governor shouts at two workmen, who stand nearby with pickaxes and anxious expressions, awaiting orders.

The two workmen look at each other.

"You heard me!" the Governor bellows. "Open the goddamn gate!"

The workmen follow orders, throwing the bolt at one end of the gate. The gate swings open, letting in a gust of cold, rancid wind.

"You ask me, we're pushing our luck with this routine," Martinez mutters under his breath, slamming an ammo magazine into his assault rifle.

The Governor ignores the comment and hollers, "Travis! Back it into position!"

The truck shudders and beeps and rattles backward into the opening.

"Now put the ramp down!"

Bob watches, completely vexed by the proceedings, as Eugene hops out of his cab with a grunt and marches around behind the truck. He throws open the vertical door and lowers the ramp to the pavement.

In the glare of spotlights the zombie contingent approaches to within a hundred yards.

Shuffling footsteps draw Bob's attention back over his shoulder.

From the shadowy center of town, in the flicker of burning trash barrels, Dr. Stevens emerges with his arm around the wounded guardsman, who hobbles along with the lethargic gait of a stroke victim.

"Watch this, Bob," the Governor says, throwing a glance over his shoulder at the older man, and then, with a wink, adds, "Beats the hell outta the Middle East."

FOURTEEN

The screams inside the empty trailer, amplified by the corrugated metal floor and steel walls, build and build, an aria of agony, which compels Bob, standing behind the crane, to look away, as the moving cadavers shamble toward the opening, drawn to the noise and smell of fear. Bob needs a drink more than ever now. He needs a lot of drinks. He needs to soak in the booze until he's blind.

At least ninety percent of the herd—all shapes and sizes, in varying degrees of disintegration, faces contorted with scowling bloodlust—press toward the rear of the trailer. The first one trips on the foot of the ramp, falling face-first with a wet splat on the tread. Others follow closely, pushing their way up the incline, as Stinson shrieks inside the enclosure, his sanity torn to shreds.

The portly guardsman, bound to the front wall of the trailer with packing straps and chains, pisses himself, as the first walkers shuffle in for the feeding.

Outside the trailer, Martinez and his men keep an eye on the stragglers along the barricade, most of them milling about aimlessly in the glare of tungsten spotlights, cocking their gray faces and glazed eyes up at the night sky as though the screaming noises might be coming from the heavens. Only about a dozen of the dead miss this opportunity to feed. The men on the 50-calibers take aim, awaiting orders to blow the stragglers away.

The trailer fills up with specimens—the Governor's growing collection of lab rats—until nearly three dozen walkers have swarmed Stinson. The unseen feeding frenzy ensues, and the screaming corrupts into watery, gagging death cries, as the last zombie staggers up the ramp and vanishes inside the mobile abattoir. The noises issuing out the back of the trailer now become almost feral, Stinson reduced to a mewling, squealing head of stock in a slaughterhouse, rendered by the ragged teeth and nails of the dead.

Out in the cold darkness Bob feels his soul contracting inward like an iris closing down. He needs a drink so badly his skull throbs. He barely hears the booming voice of the Governor.

"All right, Travis! Go ahead and pull trap now! Go ahead and close it down!"

The truck driver cautiously creeps around behind the vibrating death trailer and grabs for the rope hanging down from the lip of the door. He yanks it hard and fast, and the vertical gate slams down with a rusty squeak. Travis quickly latches the lock, and then backs away from the trailer as if from a time bomb.

"Take it back to the track, Travis! I'll meet you there in a minute!"

The Governor turns and walks over to Martinez, who stands waiting on the lower rails of the crane. "All right, you can have your fun now," the Governor says.

Martinez thumbs the radio send button. "Okay, guys—take the rest of them out."

Bob jumps at the sudden roar of heavy artillery, the noise and sparks from the .50-calibers lighting up the night. Tracer bullets streak hot pink in the dark, crisscrossing the beams of magnesium-bright klieg lights, engaging their targets in plumes of black, oily blood mist. Bob turns away once again, not interested in seeing the walkers taken apart. The Governor, however, feels differently.

He climbs halfway up the crane ladder so he can see the festivities.

In short order the armor-piercing tracers eviscerate the stragglers. Skulls blossom, florets of brain matter spitting up into the night air, teeth and hair and cartilage and bone chips shattering. Some of the zombies remain upright for many moments, as the rounds spin them in macabre death jigs, arms flailing in the stage light. Bellies burst. Glistening tissue ejaculates in the glare.

The salvo ceases as abruptly as it had begun, the silence slamming hard in Bob's ears.

For a moment the Governor savors the aftermath, the dripping sounds fading on the distant echoes of gunfire dying in the trees. The last few walkers still standing sink to the earth in heaps of bloody pulp and dead flesh, some of them now unrecognizable masses of vaguely human meat. Some of these mounds exude vapors in the chill air, mostly from the friction of the bullets and not from any kind of body heat. The Governor climbs down from his perch.

As the Piggly Wiggly truck pulls away with its load of moving cadavers, Bob swallows the urge to vomit. The ghastly noises from inside the trailer have diminished somewhat, Stinson reduced to a hollowed-out trough of flesh and bone. Now only the muffled smacking sounds of zombies feeding inside the enclosure fade away as the truck rattles toward the racetrack lot.

The Governor comes over to Bob. "Looks like you could use a drink."

Bob cannot muster a reply.

"C'mon, let's go have a cool one," the Governor suggests, slapping the man on the back. "I'm buying."

By the next morning, the north lots have been cleaned up and all evidence of the massacre has been erased. People go about their business as though nothing ever happened, and the rest of that week passes uneventfully.

Over the next five days a few walkers drift into the range of the .50-calibers—drawn by the commotion of the hordes—but mostly things remain quiet. Christmas comes and goes with very little ceremony. Most of the inhabitants of Woodbury have given up on following the calendar.

A few feeble attempts at holiday cheer seem to exacerbate the grim proceedings. Martinez and his men decorate a tree in the courthouse lobby, and they put some tinsel on the gazebo in the square, but that's about it. The Governor pipes Christmas music through the racetrack PA system, but it's more of an annoyance than anything else. The weather stays fairly mild—no snow to speak of, with temperatures remaining in the upper forties.

On Christmas Eve, Lilly goes to the infirmary to have some of her injuries checked out by Dr. Stevens, and after the examination,

the doctor invites Lilly to stick around for a little impromptu holiday party. Alice joins them, and they open cans of ham and sweet
potatoes—and they even break out a case of Cabernet, which Stevens
has been hiding in the storage closet—and they toast things like the
old days, better times, and Josh Lee Hamilton.

Lilly senses that the doctor is watching her closely for signs of
post-traumatic stress, maybe depression or some other kind of men-
tal disturbance. But ironically, Lilly has never felt more focused and
grounded in her life. She knows what she has to do. She knows that
she cannot live like this much longer, and she is biding her time until
an opportunity to escape presents itself. But maybe on some deeper
level it is *Lilly* who is doing the observing.

Maybe she is subconsciously looking for allies, accomplices, col-
laborators.

Halfway through the evening, Martinez shows up—Stevens invited the young man earlier that day to stop by for a drink—and
Lilly learns that she is not the only one here who wants out. After a
few cocktails, Martinez gets talkative, and reveals that he fears the
Governor will eventually lead them off a cliff. They argue about
which is the lesser of two evils—tolerating the Governor's madness
or drifting out in the world without a safety net—and they come to
zero conclusions. They drink some more.

At length, the evening deteriorates into a drunken bacchanal of
off-key caroling and reminiscences of holidays past—all of which
depresses everyone even further. The more they drink, the worse
they feel. But amid all the lubricating Lilly learns new things—both
trivial and important—about these three lost souls. She notices that
Dr. Stevens has the worst singing voice she has ever heard, and that
Alice has a major crush on Martinez, and that Martinez pines for an
ex-wife in Arkansas.

Most importantly, though, Lilly gets a sense that the four of them
are bonding in their collective misery, and that bond might serve
them well.

The next day, at first light—after spending the night passed out on a
gurney in the infirmary—Lilly Caul drags herself outside, blinking

at the harsh winter sunshine hammering down on the deserted town. It's Christmas morning, and the pale blue sky seems to punctuate Lilly's sense of being trapped in purgatory. Lilly's skull throbs painfully as she buttons her fleece jacket up to her chin and then makes her way eastward down the sidewalk.

Very few residents are up at this hour, the advent of Christmas morning keeping everybody hunkered inside. Lilly feels compelled to visit the playground on the east edge of the town. The desolate patch of bare ground lies behind a grove of denuded crab apples.

Lilly finds Josh's grave, the sandy dirt still freshly packed in a large mound next to his cairn. She kneels on the edge of the grave and lowers her head. "Merry Christmas, Josh," she utters into the wind, her voice hungover, thick and rusty with sleep.

Only the rustle of branches serves as a response. She takes a deep breath. "Some of the things I've done . . . the way I treated you . . . I'm not proud of." She swallows the urge to cry, the sorrow rising up in her. She bites off her tears. "I just wanted you to know . . . you didn't die in vain, Josh. . . . You taught me something important . . . you made a difference in my life."

Lilly looks down at the dirty white sand beneath her knees and she refuses to cry. "You taught me not to be scared anymore." She mutters this to herself, to the ground, to the cold wind. "We don't have that luxury these days . . . so from now on . . . I'm ready."

Her voice trails off, and she kneels there for the longest time, unaware that her right hand has been digging into the side of her leg through her jeans, hard enough to break the skin and draw blood.

"I'm ready . . ."

The turning of the New Year closes in.

Late one night, beset with the melancholy mood of the season, the man known as the Governor locks himself into the back room of his second-floor apartment with a bottle of expensive French champagne and a galvanized pail brimming with an assortment of human bodily organs.

The tiny zombie chained to the wall across the laundry room sputters and snarls at the sight of him. Her once cherubic face now chiseled with rigor mortis, her flesh as yellow as rotten Stilton, she peels her lips back away from rows of blackened baby teeth. The laundry room with its bare bulbs hanging down and exposed fiberglass insulation—impregnated now with her stench—reeks of foul, infected oils and molds.

"Calm down, sweetheart," the man with several names murmurs softly as he sits down on the floor in front of her, setting the bottle down on one side of him and the bucket on the other. He pulls a latex surgical glove from his pocket and works his right hand into it. "Daddy's got some more goodies for you, keep your tummy full."

He fishes a slimy, purplish-brown lobe from the bucket of entrails and tosses it to her.

Little Penny Blake pounces on the human kidney that has landed with a wet splat on the floor in front of her, her chain stretching to its limit with a clank. She clutches the organ with both of her little hands and gobbles the human tissue with feral abandon until the bloody bile runs between her tiny fingers and paints her face with a stain the consistency of chocolate sauce.

"Happy New Year, sweetheart," the Governor says and pries at the champagne cork. The cork resists. He worries at it with his thumbs until the thing pops, and a stream of golden bubbly percolates over the rim and onto the worn tiles. The Governor has no idea if it is actually New Year's Eve. He knows it's imminent . . . might as well be tonight.

He stares at the puddle of champagne spreading on the floor, the tiny foam of carbonation vanishing into the seams of grout. He finds himself casting his thoughts back to New Year's celebrations of his childhood.

In the old days he looked forward to New Year's Eve for months. Back in Waynesboro he and his buddies would get a whole pig delivered on the thirtieth and start it slow-roasting in the ground behind his parents' place, lining the hole with bricks—Hawaiian luau style—and they would have a two-day feast. The local bluegrass band, the Clinch Mountain Boys, would play all night long, and Philip would get really good weed, and they would party through the first and Philip would get laid and have a grand old time with—

The Governor blinks. He cannot remember if *Philip* Blake used to do this on New Year's Eve or if it was *Brian* Blake who did this. He cannot remember where one brother ends and the other begins. He stares at the floor, blinking, the champagne reflecting a dull, milky, distorted reflection of his own face, the handlebar mustache as dark as lampblack now, the eyes deep set and glinting with cinders of something like madness. He looks at himself and sees Philip Blake staring back. But something is wrong. Philip can also see a ghostly overlay superimposed across his face, an ashen, frightened simulacrum called "Brian."

Penny's watery, garbled feeding noises fade in his ears, drifting far away, and Philip takes his first hit of champagne. The gulp burns his throat as it goes down cold and astringent. The taste of it reminds him of better times. It reminds him of holiday celebrations, family reunions, loved ones coming together after a long estrangement. It tears him apart inside. He knows who he is: He's *the Governor*, he's Philip Blake, *the man who gets things done*.

But.

But . . .

Brian starts to cry. He drops the bottle, and more champagne spills across the tiles, seeping under Penny, who is oblivious to the invisible war going on at the moment within the mind of her caretaker. Brian shuts his eyes, the tears seeping out the corners of his eyelids and tracking down his face in snotty runnels.

He cries for those New Year's Eves gone by, those happy moments between friends . . . and brothers. He cries for Penny, and he cries for her woeful condition, for which he blames himself. He cannot block out the flash-frame image burned into the retina of his mind's eye: *Philip Blake lying in a cold, bloody heap next to a girl on the edge of the woods north of Woodbury.*

While Penny feeds, slurping and smacking her dead lips, and Brian softly sobs, an unexpected noise comes from across the room.

Somebody is knocking on the Governor's door.

It takes a while for the noise to register, the sound of knocking coming in a series of small bursts—hesitant, tentative—and it goes on for quite a while before Philip Blake realizes somebody is out there in the hallway banging on his door.

The identity crisis ceases immediately, the curtain in the Governor's brain sweeping back in place with the abruptness of a power blackout.

It is, in fact, *Philip* who stands, removes his surgical gloves, brushes himself off, wipes his mucusy chin with the sleeve of his sweater, pulls on his stovepipe boots, brushes his long obsidian locks from his eyes, sniffs back his emotion, and exits the laundry room, locking the door behind him.

It is Philip who crosses the living room with his trademark strut. Heart rate slowing, lungs filling with oxygen, his consciousness fully transformed back into the Governor—his eyes clear and sharp—he answers the door on the fifth series of knocks. "What the hell is so goddamn important at this hour that you can't—"

Not fully recognizing the woman standing outside the door, he stops himself. He had expected one of his men—Gabe or Bruce or Martinez—coming to bother him with some minor fire to be put out or some horseshit drama to be settled among the restless townspeople.

"Is this a bad time?" Megan Lafferty purrs with a dreamy tilt of her head, leaning against the doorjamb, the blouse under her denim jacket unbuttoned and showing generous amounts of cleavage.

The Governor pins her with his unwavering gaze. "Honey, I don't know what game you're running down right now but I'm in the middle of something."

"Just thought you might need a little company," she says with faux innocence. She looks like a caricature of a tart, her wine-colored curls mussed and hanging down in suggestive tendrils across her drugged features. She wears too much makeup and appears almost clownlike. "But I totally understand if you're busy."

The Governor lets out a sigh. A smile tugs at the corner of his mouth. "Something tells me you ain't here to borrow a cup of sugar."

Megan throws a glance over her shoulder. The jitters show on her face, in the way her gaze shifts back and forth from the shadows of the empty corridor to the doorway, in the way she holds one of her arms against her side, compulsively stroking the Chinese character tattooed on her elbow. Nobody ever comes up here. The Governor's private quarters are off-limits to even Gabe and Bruce.

"I just—I thought—I—" she stutters.

"No reason to be afraid, darlin'," the Governor says at last.

"I didn't mean to—"

"Might as well c'mon inside," he says and takes her by the arm. "Before you catch your death."

He pulls her inside and secures the door with a click. The sound of the bolt clanking home makes her jump. Her breathing quickens, and the Governor cannot help but notice the rise and fall of her surprisingly fulsome breasts underneath her décolletage, her hourglass figure, her generous hips. This little gal is ripe for breeding. The Governor searches the back of his mind for the last time he used a condom. Did he stock up? Did he have any left in his medicine cabinet? "Get you a drink?"

"Sure." Megan gazes around the spartan furnishings of the living room—the carpet remnants, the mismatched chairs and sofa pulled off the back of a Salvation Army truck. For the briefest instant she frowns, turning up her nose, probably registering the odors permeating the place from the laundry room. "Y'all got any vodka?"

The Governor gives her a grin. "I think we might be able to come up with some." He goes over to the cabinet next to the shuttered front window. He digs out a bottle, pours a few fingers in a couple of paper cups. "Got some orange juice around here somewhere," he murmurs, finding a half-empty can of juice.

He comes back over to her with the drinks. She slugs hers down in one frantic gulp. She looks as though she's been lost in the desert for days and this is her first taste of liquid. She wipes her mouth and lets loose a little belch. "Excuse me . . . sorry."

"You are just the cutest little thing," the Governor says to her with a grin. "You know something, Bonnie Raitt ain't got nothing on you."

She looks at the floor. "Reason I dropped by, I was just wondering . . ."

"Yeah?"

"Guy at the food center told me you might have some weed, Demerol maybe?"

"Duane?"

She nods. "Said you might have some good shit."

The Governor sips his drink. "Now I wonder how Duane would know such a thing."

Megan shrugs. "Anyway, the thing is—"

"Why come to me?" The Governor fixes her with that dark stare. "Why not go to your buddy Bob? He's got a whole medicine chest in that truck of his."

Another shrug. "I don't know, I was just thinking, you and me, we could like . . . make a trade."

Now she looks up at him and bites her lower lip, and the Governor feels the blood rushing to his loins.

Megan rides him in the moonlight darkness of an adjacent room. Completely nude, filmed in a cold sweat, her hair matted to her face, she pistons up and down on his erection with the empty fury of a hobbyhorse on a carousel. She feels nothing other than the painful thrusting. She feels no fear, no emotion, no regret, no shame. Nothing. Just the mechanical gymnastics of sex.

All the lights are off in the room, the only illumination coming from the transom above the drapes, through which the silver light of a wintry moon shines down across the dust motes and dapples the bare wall behind the Governor's secondhand La-Z-Boy recliner.

The man sits sprawled on the armchair, his naked, lanky body writhing beneath Megan, his head tossing backward, the veins in his neck pulsing. But he makes very little sound, shows very little pleasure in the act. Megan can only hear the regular thrumming of his breath, as he thrusts angrily into her again and again.

The La-Z-Boy chair is positioned in a way that draws Megan's peripheral attention to the wall behind her, even as she feels the man's orgasm building, the climax imminent. No pictures hang in the room, no coffee tables, no shaded lamps—only the faint shimmer of rectangular objects lining the wall. At first Megan misidentifies these objects as TV sets, a configuration reminiscent of an electronics-store display. But what would this guy be doing with two dozen TV sets? Soon Megan realizes she's hearing a low burble of white noise issuing from the objects.

"What the hell's the matter?" the Governor grunts beneath her.

Megan has twisted around, her eyes adjusting to the moon shadows. She sees things moving inside the rectangular enclosures. The ghostly movement makes her stiffen, tightening up on his genitals. "Nothing . . . nothing . . . sorry . . . I just . . . I couldn't help but—"

"Goddammit, woman!" He reaches over and flips on a battery-operated camp lantern, which sits on a crate next to the chair.

The light reveals rows of aquariums filled with severed human heads.

Megan lets out a gasp and slips off his cock, tumbling to the floor. She struggles to breathe. Lying prone on the damp carpet, her body rashing with gooseflesh, she gapes at the glass enclosures. In neatly stacked containers of fluid the zombified faces twitch and tic on ragged stumps, mouths palpitating like oxygen-starved fish, their milky eyes rolling around sightlessly in the watery capsules.

"I haven't finished!" The Governor pounces on her, rolls her over, yanks her legs open. He's still hard and enters her violently, the painful friction sending bolts of agony up her spine. "Hold still, goddammit!"

Megan sees a familiar face within the confines of the last tank on the left, and the sight of it turns her to stone. She lies supine on the floor, thunderstruck, her head turned sideways as she gapes in horror at that narrow face engulfed in bubbles in that last aquarium, as the Governor mercilessly plunges into her. She recognizes the peroxide-blond hair suspended in the fluid, forming a seaweedlike corona around the boyish features, the slack mouth, the long lashes, and the pointy button nose.

The recognition of Scott Moon's severed head coincides with the hot gush inside her as the Governor finally finishes his business.

Something deep inside Megan Lafferty crumbles apart as permanently and irreparably as a sand castle collapsing under the weight of a wave.

A moment later the Governor says, "You can get up now, honey . . . clean yourself up."

He says this to the woman without any rancor or contempt, as a proctor might inform a classroom at the end of a test that it's time to put down the pencils.

Then he sees her gaping at the aquarium containing Scott Moon's head, and he realizes this is a moment of truth, an opportunity, a critical juncture in the evening's festivities. A decisive man like Philip Blake always knows when to look for opportunities. He knows when to take advantage of a superior position. He never hesitates, never backs off, never shies away from dirty work.

The Governor reaches down and finds the elastic waistband of his underwear—which is bunched around his ankles—and pulls his briefs back up and over himself. He stands and gazes down at the woman curled into a fetal position on his floor. "C'mon, honey . . . let's go get you cleaned up and have a little talk, you and me."

Megan buries her face in the floor and mutters, "Please don't hurt me."

The Governor leans down and applies a pinch grip to the nape of her neck—nothing intense, just an attention grabber—and says, "I'm not going to ask you again . . . get your ass in the bathroom."

She struggles to her feet, holding herself as though she might burst apart at any moment.

"This way, honey." He roughly clutches her bare arm as he ushers her across the room, out the doorway, and into an adjacent bathroom.

Standing in the doorway, watching her, the Governor feels bad about manhandling her but he also knows Philip Blake would not let up at a time like this. Philip would do what has to be done, he would be strong and resolute; and the part of the Governor that used to be called "Brian" has to follow through with this.

Megan hunches over the sink and picks up the washcloth with trembling hands. She runs water and tentatively wipes herself and trembles. "I swear to God I won't tell anybody," she mutters through her tears. "I just want to go home . . . just want to be alone."

"That's what I want to talk to you about," the Governor says to her from the doorway.

"I won't tell—"

"Look at me, honey."

"I won't—"

"Calm down. Take a deep breath. And look at me. Megan, I said look at me."

She looks up at him, her chin quivering, tears tracking down her cheeks.

He looks at her. "You're with Bob now."

"I'm sorry . . . what?" She wipes her eyes. "I'm what?"

"You're with Bob," he says. "You remember Bob Stookey, guy you came here with?"

She nods.

"You're with him now. You understand? From now on you're with him."

Again she slowly nods.

"Oh and one more thing," the Governor adds softly, almost as an afterthought. "Tell anyone about *any* of this . . . and your pretty little head goes in the tank next to the stoner."

Minutes after Megan Lafferty makes her exit, vanishing into the shadows of the corridor, shivering and hyperventilating as she pulls on her coat, the Governor retires to the side room. He flops down on his La-Z-Boy and sits facing the matrix of fish tanks.

He sits there for quite a while, staring at the tanks, feeling empty. Muffled groans drift through the empty rooms behind him. The thing that was once a little girl is hungry again. Nausea begins to creep up the Governor's gorge, clenching his insides and making his eyes water. He begins to shake. A current of terror over what he's done crackles through him, turning his tendons to ice.

A moment later he lurches forward, slipping off the chair, falling on his knees, and roaring vomit. What is left of his dinner sluices across the filthy carpet. On his hands and knees he upchucks the remaining contents of his stomach, then sits back against the foot of the chair, gasping for breath.

A part of him—that deeply buried part known as "Brian"—feels the tide of revulsion drowning him. He can't breathe. He can't think. And yet he forces himself to keep gazing at the bloated, waterlogged faces staring back at him, bobbing and spewing bubbles in the tanks.

He wants to look away. He wants to flee the room and get away from these twitching, gurgling, dismembered heads. But he knows he must keep staring until his senses are numbed. He needs to be strong.

He needs to be prepared for what is to come.

FIFTEEN

On the west side of town, within the walled area, inside a second-story apartment near the post office, Bob Stookey hears a knock. Sitting up against the headboard of a brass bed, he puts down his dog-eared paperback book—a Louis L'Amour western called *The Outlaws of Mesquite*—and steps into his scuffed loafers. He pulls on his pants. He has some trouble with the zipper, his hands fumbling.

After drinking himself insensate earlier that evening, he still feels wonky and disconnected. The dizziness tugs at his focus and his stomach lurches, as he staggers out of the room and crosses the apartment to the side door, which opens out onto the darkness of a wooden landing at the top of a staircase. Bob belches and swallows bile as he pushes the door open.

"Bob . . . something horrible has . . . *Oh, God, Bob,*" Megan Lafferty sobs from the shadows of the staircase. Her face wet and drawn, her eyes sunken and red, she looks as though she's about to shatter apart like a glass figurine. She trembles in the cold, holding the collar of her denim jacket tight against the bitter winds.

"Come in, darlin', c'mon in," Bob says, pushing the door wider, his heart beating a little faster. "What in God's name happened?"

Megan staggers into the kitchen. Bob takes her by the arms and helps her over to a hard chair canted next to the cluttered dining table. She flops down in her chair and tries to speak but the sobs won't let her. Bob kneels by her chair, stroking her shoulder as she cries. She buries her face in his chest and cries.

Bob holds her. "It's okay, darlin' . . . whatever it is . . . we'll figure it out."

She moans—gut shot with anguish and horror—her tears soaking his sleeveless undershirt. He cradles her head, stroking her damp curls. After an agonizing moment, she looks up at him. "Scott's dead."

"What!"

"I saw him, Bob." She speaks in hitching gasps, her sobs shuddering through her. "He's . . . he's dead and . . . he's turned into one of those things."

"Easy, darlin', take a breath and try to tell me what happened."

"I don't *know* what happened!"

"Where did you see him?"

She sniffs back the gasps and then tells Bob in broken, half-formed sentences about the severed heads bobbing in the darkness.

"Where did you see this?"

She hyperventilates. "In the . . . over in . . . in the Governor's place."

"The Governor's place? You saw Scott at the Governor's place?"

She nods and nods. She tries to explain but the words are caught in her throat.

Bob strokes her arm. "Darlin,' what were you doing in the Governor's place?"

She tries to speak. The sobs return. She buries her face in her hands.

"Let me get you some water," Bob says at last. He hurries over to the sink and runs water into a plastic cup. Half the homes in Woodbury have no utilities, no heat or power or running water. The lucky few who still have these amenities are members of the Governor's inner circle—those to whom the makeshift power structure has bestowed perks. Bob has become a sort of sentimental favorite, and his private quarters reflect this status. Littered with empty bottles and food wrappers, tins of pipe tobacco and girlie magazines, warm blankets and electronic gadgets, the apartment has taken on the look of a shabby man-cave.

Bob brings the water over to Megan, and she gulps it from the plastic cup, some of it seeping out the sides of her mouth and soaking her jacket. Bob gently helps her remove her coat as she finishes the water. He looks away when he sees the front of her blouse buttoned haphazardly, open at the navel, a series of red blotches and deep scratches running down the length of her sternum between her pale breasts. Her bra is askew and one of her nipples shows prominently.

"Here, darlin'," he says, turning toward the linen closet in the front hall. He retrieves a blanket, comes back and tenderly wraps it around her. She gets her crying under control until the sobs have subsided into a series of jerky, shuddering breaths. She stares downward. Her tiny hands lie limp and upturned in her lap, as though she has forgotten how to use them.

"I never should have . . ." she starts to explain and then chokes back the words. Her nose runs and she wipes it. Her eyes close. "What have I done . . . Bob . . . what the fuck is wrong with me?"

"There's nothing wrong with you," he says softly and puts his arm around her. "I'm with you now, honey. I'll take care of you."

She settles down in his arms. Soon she is leaning her head on his shoulder and breathing more regularly. Soon her breaths are coming in low, thick wheezes, as though she might be falling asleep. Bob recognizes the symptoms of shock. Her flesh feels ice-cold in his arms. He wraps the blanket tighter. She nuzzles his neck.

Bob takes deep breaths, waves of emotion slamming through him.

Holding the woman tightly, he gropes for words. His mind races with contrary feelings. He is repulsed by Megan's story of severed heads and Scott Moon's dismembered corpse, as well as the fact that she paid the Governor such a questionable visit in the first place. But Bob is also overcome with unrequited desire. The nearness of her lips, the soft whisper of her breath on his collarbone, and the luster of her wild-strawberry roan curls brushing his chin—all of it intoxicates Bob faster and more profusely than a case of twelve-year-old bourbon. He fights the urge to kiss the top of her head.

"It's gonna be okay," he murmurs softly in her ear. "We'll figure it out."

"Oh, Bob . . ." Her voice sounds fuzzy, maybe still slightly high. "Bob . . ."

"Gonna be okay," he says in her ear, stroking her hair with his greasy, gnarled hand.

She cranes her head up and plants a kiss on his grizzled jawline.

Bob closes his eyes and lets the wave pour over him.

They sleep together that night, and at first Bob panics at the prospect of being in such close and intimate proximity with Megan for such a long period of time. Bob has not had sex with a woman in eleven years, not since he and his late wife, Brenda, stopped having relations. Decades of drink have put the kibosh on Bob's virility. But desire still glows within him like a smoldering ember—and he wants Megan so badly tonight he can taste it like Everclear in the back of his throat, like a finger prodding the base of his spine.

The two of them sleep restlessly in each other's arms, tangled in sweaty blankets on the double bed in the back room. Much to Bob's relief, they do not even remotely come close to having sex.

Throughout the night, Bob's feverish thoughts vacillate between half-formed dreams of making love to Megan Lafferty on a desert island, surrounded by zombie-infested waters, and sudden moments of bleary wakefulness in the shadows of that second-floor bedroom. Bob marvels at the miracle of hearing Megan's arrhythmic breathing next to him, the warmth of her hip nested against his belly, the wonder of her hair in his face, her musky-sweet scent filling his senses. In a strange way he feels whole for the first time since the plague broke out. He feels an oddly invigorating sense of hope. The troubling undercurrents of suspicion and mixed emotions about the Governor melt away in the dark limbo of that bedroom, and the momentary peace that washes over Bob Stookey eventually lulls him into a deep sleep.

Just after dawn he comes awake with a start to a piercing shriek.

At first he thinks he's still dreaming. The scream comes from somewhere outside, and it registers in Bob's ears as a ghostly echo, as if the tail end of a nightmare has just brushed across his waking state. In his half-conscious daze he reaches over for Megan and finds her side of the bed empty. The blankets are bunched at his feet. Megan is gone. He sits up with a jolt.

"Megan, honey?"

He gets out of bed and starts toward the door, the floor like ice on his bare feet, when another shriek pierces the winter winds outside his apartment. He does not notice the overturned chair in the kitchen, the drawers open, the cabinet doors agape, the signs of someone rifling through his belongings.

"Megan?"

He races toward the side door, which is partially ajar and banging in the wind.

"Megan!"

He pushes through the doorway and stumbles out onto the second-floor landing, blinking at the harsh, overcast light and the cold wind in his face.

"MEGAN!!"

At first he cannot take in all the movement and commotion around the building. He sees people gathered down below the stairs, across the street, and along the edge of the post office parking lot—maybe a dozen or so—and they're all pointing at Bob or perhaps at something on the roof. It's hard to tell. Heart hammering, Bob starts down the stairs. He does not notice the coil of towrope wound around the pilasters of the landing until he reaches the bottom of the stairs.

Bob turns and goes as cold and still as granite. "Oh, Lord, no," he utters, gazing up at the body dangling from the landing, swaying in the wind, turning lazily. "Oh, no, no, no, no, no, no, no . . ."

Megan hangs by a makeshift noose around her neck, her face as discolored and livid as antique porcelain.

Lilly Caul hears the commotion outside her window above the dry cleaner, and drags herself out of bed. She throws open the shade and sees townspeople gathered outside their doorways, some of them pointing off toward the post office with anxious expressions, speaking under their breaths. Lilly senses that something terrible has happened, and when she sees the Governor striding quickly along the sidewalk in his long coat with his goons, Gabe and Bruce, at his side, snapping ammo magazines into assault weapons, she dresses quickly.

It takes her less than three minutes to throw on her clothes, hustle down the back stairs, make her way down an alley between two buildings, and cross the two and a half blocks to the post office.

The sky churns with menacing clouds, the wind spitting sleet, and by the time Lilly sees the crowd milling about the base of Bob's stairs, she knows she's seeing the aftermath of something awful. She can tell by the expressions on the faces of the onlookers, and she can tell by the way the Governor is talking to Bob off to the side, each man gazing at the ground as they talk softly to each other, their faces screwed up with anxiety and grim resolve.

Within the circle of onlookers, Gabe and Bruce kneel on the pavement next to a sheet-covered lump, and the sight of that shrouded heap stops Lilly cold. She stands on the periphery, staring, a trickle of icy dread running down her spine. The sight of another pall-covered body on a street corner strums a terrible chord deep within her.

"Lilly?"

She turns and sees Martinez standing next to her, his leather jacket crisscrossed with a bandolier of bullets. He puts a hand on her shoulder. "She was a friend of yours, wasn't she?"

"Who is it?"

"Nobody told you?"

"Is it Megan?" Lilly pushes her way past Martinez, shoving aside several onlookers. "What happened?"

Bob Stookey steps into her path, blocking her progress, gently taking her by the shoulders. "Lil, wait, there's nothing you can do."

"What happened, Bob?" Lilly blinks at the sting in her eyes, the heavy fist in her chest. "Did a walker get her? Let me go!"

Bob holds fast on her shoulders. "No, ma'am. That's not what happened." Lilly notices Bob's eyes, raw and red rimmed, cratered out with grief. His face trembles with anguish. "These fellas will take care of her."

"Is she—"

"She's gone, Lil." Bob looks down and softly shakes his head. "Took her own life."

"What— What happened?"

Still looking down, Bob mumbles something about not being sure.

"Let me go, Bob!" Lilly pushes her way through the row of on-lookers.

"Whoa! Whoa—*slow down there, sister*!" Gabe stands up and blocks Lilly's path. The heavyset man with the bullish neck and flat-top haircut holds on to Lilly's arm. "I know she was a friend of yours—"

"Let me see her!" Lilly yanks her arm free but Gabe grabs her from behind and puts her in a firm shoulder lock. Lilly wriggles furiously. "LET GO OF ME, GODDAMMIT!"

Ten feet away, on the seared brown grass of the parkway, Bruce, the tall black man with the shaved head, kneels by the sheet-draped body, loading a .45 caliber semiautomatic with a fresh magazine. His face grim and set, he breathes deeply, preparing to complete some distasteful task. He ignores the commotion behind him.

"LET GO!" Lilly keeps writhing in the portly man's grip, her gaze locked on the body.

"Calm down," Gabe hisses. "You're making this harder than it has to—"

"Let her go!"

The deep, cigarette-cured voice comes from behind Gabe, and both Lilly and the heavyset man freeze as though startled by an ul-trasonic whistle.

They glance over their shoulders and see the Governor standing inside the circle of onlookers with his hands on his hips, his twin pearl-handled army .45s thrust into either side of his belt, gunslinger-style, his long rock-star hair—as black as India ink—bound in a ponytail and tossing in the wind. The crow's-feet around his eyes, and the lines chiseling his sunken jowls, deepen and crease and grow more prominent as his expression darkens. "It's okay, Gabe . . . let the lady say good-bye to her friend."

Lilly rushes over to the corpse on the ground, kneels, and stares at the shrouded heap, putting her hand to her mouth as though hold-ing in the tide of emotions rising in her. Bruce thumbs the safety down on his semiauto, and awkwardly backs away, standing, gazing down at Lilly as the crowd around them quiets down.

The Governor comes over and stands a respectful five feet away.

Lilly peels back the sheet and clenches her teeth, as she looks at the purplish-gray face of the woman that used to be Megan Lafferty. Eyes swollen shut, jaw set with rigor mortis, the bloodless china-doll face looks as though it has shattered into a million hairline fractures, the dark capillaries apparent now in the early stages of decomposition. The face is ghastly but also excruciatingly poignant to Lilly, wrenching her memories back to those crazy days at Sprayberry High School when the two girls would get high in the restroom and climb up on the school's roof and throw pebbles at the jocks running drills behind the basketball courts. Megan had been Lilly's best gal-pal for years, and despite the girl's faults—and there had been many—Lilly still thinks of her as a best friend. Now Lilly cannot stop staring at this unrecognizable vestige of her feisty friend.

Lilly gasps as Megan's swollen, purple-lidded eyes suddenly pop open, revealing milk-glass pupils.

Lilly does not move as the black man with the shaved head crowds in, the .45 poised to fire a direct blast into the cadaver's head. But before the hammer has a chance to fall, the sound of the Governor's voice calls out: "Hold your fire, Bruce!"

Bruce glances over his shoulder, as the Governor takes a step closer, and then says very softly, "Let her do it."

Lilly looks up at the man in the long coat, blinks, and says nothing. Her heart feels like ash, her blood running cold in her veins. Way off in the distance the sky rumbles with thunder.

The Governor steps closer. "Go ahead, Bruce. Give her the gun."

An endless moment passes, and somehow the gun ends up in Lilly's hand. Beneath her, the thing that was once Megan Lafferty convulses and tenses on the ground, its nervous system dieseling, its mouth peeling away from moldering gray teeth. Lilly can barely see through her tears.

"Put your friend down, Lilly," the Governor urges softly from behind her.

Lilly raises the gun. Megan's neck cranes upward toward her like a fetus emerging from its embryonic fluid, teeth clacking hungrily. Lilly puts the muzzle against the monster's brow.

"Do it, Lilly. Put her out of her misery."

Lilly closes her eyes. The trigger pad burns her finger like an icicle.

When she opens her eyes again the thing on the ground lunges at her, the rancid teeth going for Lilly's jugular.

It happens so quickly it almost fails to register in Lilly's brain.

The blast rings out.

Lilly topples backward, falling on her ass, the .45 slipping out of her hand as the top of Megan's cranium erupts in dark red mist, painting the sidewalk adjacent to the parkway in a spray of brain matter. The reanimated corpse sags and lies still on the tangled shroud—its sharklike eyes fixed on the dark sky.

For a moment Lilly lies supine on the ground, staring at the clouds, gripped in a state of confusion. Who fired the kill shot? Lilly never pulled the trigger. Who did the deed? Lilly blinks away her tears and manages to focus on the Governor standing over her, his grave expression fixed on something to his right.

Bob Stookey stands over the corpse of Megan Lafferty with a .38 police special still clutched in his hand, his shooting arm dangling at his side, a thin wisp of gun smoke still curling out of the barrel.

The desolation on Bob's weathered, deeply lined face is heartbreaking.

Those next few days, nobody pays much attention to the changing weather.

Bob is too busy drinking himself to death to notice anything as trivial as weather fronts, and Lilly occupies herself arranging a proper burial for Megan in a plot next to Josh. The Governor spends most of his time preparing for the next big battle in the racetrack arena. He has big plans for the next round of shows, integrating zombies into the gladiatorial matches.

Gabe and Bruce busy themselves with the nasty job of hacking up the dead guardsmen in an auxiliary warehouse beneath the track. The Governor needs body parts to feed the growing menagerie of zombies being housed in a secret room deep in the cinder-block catacombs. Gabe and Bruce enlist some of the younger men from Martinez's crew to work the chain saws in the festering, cavernous abattoir next to the morgue, rendering human remains into meat.

Meanwhile, the January rains move into the area with slow, insidious menace.

At first, the outer bands of the storm system cause very little alarm—a few scattered showers swelling the storm sewers and icing the streets—with temperatures hovering above freezing. But the distant lightning and roiling black skies on the western horizon begin to worry people. Nobody knows with any degree of certainty—nor will they ever know—why *this* winter turns out to be anomalous for Georgia. The state's relatively mild winters can be occasionally shattered by torrential rains, a nasty snowfall or two, or an ice storm here and there, but no one is prepared for what is about to sweep down across the fruit belt on a low-pressure cell slamming in from Canada.

The National Weather Service out of Peachtree City—still limping along on generators and shortwave radios—issues an early warning that week on as many frequencies as they can spark. But very few listeners benefit from the news. Only a handful of souls hear the frantic voice of the harried meteorologist, Barry Gooden, ranting about the blizzard of '93 and the floods of 2009.

According to Gooden, the bitter cold front that will smash down upon the American South over the next twenty-four hours will collide with the moist, mild, warm surface temperatures of central Georgia and very likely make these other winter storms seem like passing sprinkles. With seventy-mile-an-hour winds in the forecast, as well as dangerous lightning and a mixture of rain and sleet, the storm promises to play unprecedented havoc with the plague-ridden state. Not only will the volatile swings in temperature threaten to turn the gulley washers into blizzards, but—as the state learned only a couple of years earlier, and now with the advent of the plague—Georgians are woefully unprepared for the ravages of flooding.

A few years back, a major storm pushed the Chattahoochee River over its banks and into the highly populated areas around Roswell, Sandy Springs, and Marietta. Mudslides tore homes from their foundations. Highways lay underwater and the catastrophe resulted in dozens of deaths and hundreds of millions of dollars of damage. But *this* year—this monster forming over the Mississippi, unfurling at an alarming rate of speed—promises to be off the charts.

The first signs of extraordinary weather roar into town that Friday afternoon.

By nightfall the rain is coming down at a forty-five-degree angle on fifty-mile-an-hour gusts, falling in sheets against Woodbury's barricade, making defunct high-tension wires across the center of town sing and snap like bullwhips. Volleys of lightning turn the dark alleys to silver flickering photographic negatives, and the gutters spill over across Main Street. Most of Woodbury's inhabitants hunker down inside for the duration . . . leaving the sidewalks and boarded storefronts deserted . . .

. . . mostly deserted, that is, except for a group of four residents, who brave the rains in order to gather surreptitiously in an office beneath the racetrack.

"Leave the light off, Alice, if you don't mind," a voice says from the shadows behind a desk. The dull glimmer of wire-framed spectacles floating in the darkness is the only thing that identifies Dr. Stevens. The muffled drumming of the storm punctuates the silence.

Alice nods and stands near the light switch, nervously rubbing her cold hands against each other. Her lab coat looks ghostly in the gloomy, windowless office that Stevens has been using for a storage room.

"You called this meeting, Lilly," murmurs Martinez from the opposite corner of the room, where he sits on a stool, smoking a cheroot—the slender cigar's glowing tip like a firefly in the darkness. "What are you thinking?"

Lilly paces in the shadows near a row of metal filing cabinets. She wears one of Josh's army surplus raincoats, which is so big on her she looks like a child playing dress-up. "What am I thinking? I'm thinking I'm not going to live like this anymore."

"Meaning what?"

"Meaning this place is rotten to the core, it's sick, and this Governor dude is the sickest one of all, and I don't see things getting any better in the foreseeable future."

"And . . . ?"

She shrugs. "I'm looking at my options."

"Which are?"

She paces some more, choosing her words carefully. "Packing up and taking off by myself seems suicidal . . . but I'd be willing to take my chances out there if it was the only way to get away from this shit."

Martinez looks at Stevens, who is across the room, wiping his eyeglasses with a cloth and listening intently. The two men share an uneasy glance. Finally Stevens speaks up: "You mentioned options."

Lilly stops pacing. She looks at Martinez. "These guys you work with on the fence . . . you trust them?"

Martinez takes a drag off the cheroot, and smoke forms a wreath around his face. "More or less."

"Some more and some less?"

He shrugs. "You could say that, yeah."

"But these guys you trust more than the others, would they back you up in a pinch?"

Martinez stares at her. "What are we talking about here, Lilly?"

Lilly takes a deep breath. She has no idea if she can trust these people, but they also seem like the only sane individuals in Woodbury. She decides to play her hand. After a long pause, she says very softly, "I'm talking about regime change."

Another series of apprehensive glances pass between Martinez, Stevens, and Alice. The edgy silence throbs with the muffled noise of the storm. The winds have kicked up even higher, and thunder rattles the foundation with increasing frequency.

At last the doctor says, "Lilly, I don't think you know what you're—"

"No!" she interrupts him, looking at the floor, speaking in a cold, flat monotone. "No more history lessons, Doc. We're past that now. Past playing it safe. This dude Philip Blake has to go . . . and you know it as well as I do."

Over their heads a volley of thunder reverberates. Stevens lets out an anguished sigh. "You're going to buy yourself a gig in the gladiator ring, you keep talking like that."

Unfazed, Lilly looks up at Martinez. "I don't know you very well, Martinez, but you seem like a fairly even-tempered kind of guy . . . kind of guy who could lead a revolt, get things back on track."

Martinez stares at her. "Slow down, kiddo . . . you're gonna hurt yourself."

"Whatever . . . you don't have to listen to me . . . I don't care anymore." She makes eye contact with each of them, one at a time. "But you all know I'm right. Things are going to get a lot worse around here, we don't do something about this. You want to turn me in for treason, fine, go ahead. Whatever. But we may never get another chance to take this freak down. And I for one am not going to sit on my hands and do nothing while this place goes down in flames and more and more innocent people die. You know I'm right about this." She looks back down at the floor. "The Governor has to go."

Another barrage of thunder rattles the ribs of the building, as the silence in the storage room stretches. Finally Alice speaks up.

"She's right, you know."

SIXTEEN

The next day, the storm—now a constant bombardment of driving rain and freezing sleet—lashes southeastern Georgia with massive force. Telephone poles buckle under the weight of the onslaught, crashing down on highways choked with abandoned cars. Culverts swell and gush, flooding deserted farms, while the higher elevations are coated with treacherous layers of ice. Eleven miles southeast of Woodbury, in a wooded hollow adjacent to Highway 36, the storm hits the largest public cemetery in the southern United States.

The Edward Nightingale Memorial Gardens and Columbarium lines a mile-long bluff just south of Sprewell State Park, and features tens of thousands of historic markers. The Gothic chapel and visitor center stand at the eastern end of the property, within a stone's throw of the Woodland Medical Center—one of the state's largest hospitals. Filled with freshly-turned zombies, abandoned by the staff since the early weeks of the plague, the complex of buildings—including the morgue at Woodland, as well as the enormous labyrinth of funeral parlors underneath the sublevels of Nightingale—teems with reanimated dead, some of them fresh corpses marked for autopsies and burials, others recent DOAs tucked into drawers, all of them trapped, up to this point, in their sealed chambers.

At 4:37 P.M. Eastern Standard Time that Saturday, the nearby Flint River reaches flood levels. In photo-strobe flashes of lightning, the violent currents crash over the banks, razing farms, toppling billboards, and tossing abandoned vehicles across the farm roads like toys scattered by an angry child.

The mudslides start within an hour. The entire northern slope along the borders of the cemetery gives way, sliding toward the Flint on a slimy, brown, mealy wave—ripping graves from the ground, flinging antique caskets across the hill. Coffins break open and spill their ghastly contents into the ocean of mud and sleet and wind. Most of the ragged skeletons break apart like kindling. But many of the non-interred corpses—especially the ones who are still fresh and intact and able to crawl or scrabble—begin slithering toward high, dry land.

Ornate windows along the base of the Nightingale visitor center crack under the pressure of the floodtide, imploding, the gale-force winds doing the rest of the work, tearing sections off Gothic spires and shaving the tops of steeples and decapitating gabled rooftops. A quarter mile to the east, the rushing floodwaters hit the medical center hard, driving debris through weakened entryways and windows.

The zombies trapped inside the morgue pour out of jagged openings, many of them sucked into the currents by the violent wind and air pressure.

By five o'clock that day, a multitude of dead large enough to fill a necropolis—like a vast school of sea creatures washed onto a beach—gets deposited across the neighboring orchards and tobacco fields. They tumble, one over another, on the flood currents, some of them getting caught in trees, others tangling in floating farm implements. Some drift for miles underwater, flailing in the flickering dark with involuntary instinct and inchoate hunger. Thousands of them collect in the moraines and valleys and sheltered areas north of the highway, struggling to climb out of the mud in grotesque pantomimes of primordial man emerging from the Paleolithic soup.

Before the torrential rainstorm has passed—the brunt of it moving on toward the Eastern Seaboard that night—the population of dead now littering the countryside outnumbers the population of living residents, preplague, in the nearby city of Harrington, Georgia— which, according to the sign on Highway 36, totals 4,011 souls.

In the aftermath of this epochal storm, almost a thousand of these wayward corpses begin to coalesce into the largest herd yet witnessed since the advent of the plague. In the rain-swept darkness, the zombies slowly, awkwardly cluster and horde, until a massive throng has formed in the rolling fields between Crest Highway and Roland Road. The herd is so densely packed that from a distance the tops of their putrid heads might be mistaken for a dark, brackish, slow-moving flood tide unfurling across the land.

For no particular reason other than the inexplicable behavior of the dead—be it instinct, scent, pheromones, or random chance—the horde starts churning through the mud in a northwesterly direction, directly toward the closest population center in their path—the town called Woodbury—which lies a little over eight miles away.

The tail end of the storm leaves the farms and fields of southeastern Georgia inundated with vast, black pools of filthy standing water, the shallow sections turning to black ice, the higher areas seizing up in mud.

The weakening band of freezing rain moves through the area, icing the forests and hills around Woodbury in a glassine wonderland of glittering branches, icicle-festooned power lines, and crystalline paths—all of which would be beautiful in another time and place, another context void of plagues and desperate men.

That next day, the residents of Woodbury struggle to get the town back in working order. The Governor orders his work crews to raid a nearby dairy farm for salt blocks, which are brought back on flatbeds and broken into manageable crumbs with chain saws, then spread across roads and sidewalks. Sandbags are positioned on the south side of town, against the flooded railroad tracks, in an effort to keep the standing waters at bay. All day, under a sky the color of soot, the inhabitants mop and salt and shovel and scrape and shore up flooded nooks and crannies.

"The show must go on, Bob," the Governor says late that afternoon, standing on the warning apron of the dirt racetrack, the calcium light blazing down through the mists overhead, the thrumming of generators like a dissonant drone of a bassoon orchestra. The air smells of gas fumes, alkali, and burning garbage.

The surface of the track ripples in the wind, a sea of mud as thick as porridge. The rains hit the arena hard, and now the infield shimmers in the stadium lights with two feet of murky standing water. The ice-filmed bleachers are mostly deserted, except for a small crew of workmen who toil with squeegees and shovels.

"Huh?" Bob Stookey sits slumped on a bleacher twenty feet behind the Governor.

Belching absently, his head lolled in a drunken stupor, Bob looks like a lost little boy. An empty bottle of Jim Beam lies on the ice-rimed steel bench next to him, another one—half full—loosely gripped in his greasy, numb hand. He has been drinking steadily for the past five days, ever since he ushered Megan Lafferty out of this world.

An incorrigible drunk can maintain intoxication better than the average person. Most casual drinkers reach their optimum level of drunkenness—that painless, numbed, convivial buzz that gives shy people the strength to socialize—for only fleeting moments before edging over into complete inebriation. Bob, on the other hand, can reach oblivion after about a quart of whiskey and maintain it for days.

But now, this moment, Bob Stookey has reached the twilight of his binge. After drinking a gallon a day, he has begun to regularly nod off, to lose his grip on reality, to hallucinate and black out for hours.

"I said the show must go on," the Governor says a little louder, coming over to the chain-link fence separating himself and Bob. "These people are getting cabin fever, Bob. They need catharsis."

"Damn straight," Bob slurs in a spittle-clogged grunt. He can barely hold his head up. He gazes down through steel waffling at the Governor, who now stands only a couple of feet away, looking balefully up at Bob through the links of the cyclone fence.

In Bob's feverish gaze, the Governor looks demonic in the cold Lucolux stadium lights, a silver halo appearing around the man's slicked-back hair with its raven-feather ponytail. His breath comes out in puffs of white vapor, his Fu Manchu mustache twitching at the edges as he expounds, "Little winter storm's not gonna keep us down, Bob. I got something in mind, gonna blow these people away. You just wait. You ain't seen nothing yet."

"Sounds . . . good," Bob utters, his head lolling forward, a dark shade drawing down over his vision.

"Tomorrow night, Bob." The Governor's face floats in Bob's faltering vision, a ghostly spirit. "This is a teaching moment. From now on, things are gonna be different around here. Law and order, Bob. This'll be the greatest learning opportunity ever. And a great show to boot. Gonna rock their fucking world. It's all gonna come together in here, in this mud and shit. Bob? You with me? Bob, you okay? Stay with me, old fella."

As Bob slips off the bleacher, crumbling to the ground in another blackout, the last image burned into his mind's eye is the Governor's face, fractured by the rusty geometric diamonds of the chain-link fence.

"Where the hell is Martinez, anyway?" The Governor glances over his shoulder. "Haven't seen a trace of that asshole in hours."

"Listen to me," Martinez says, welding his gaze into the eyes of each conspirator, one by one, in the dim light of the railroad shed. The five men crouch down in a loose semicircle around Martinez, huddling in the back corner, the cobweb-draped shed as dark as a tomb. Martinez lights a cigarillo and smoke engulfs his handsome, cunning face. "You don't ease a trap over a fucking cobra—you strike as fast as possible, as hard as possible."

"When?" utters the youngest one, the one named Stevie. Crouched next to Martinez, the tall, lanky kid of mixed race wears a black silk roadie jacket and has a peach-fuzz mustache, and nervously blinks his long-lashed earnest eyes. Stevie's outward innocence is belied by his ferocious aptitude at destroying zombies.

"Soon." Martinez puffs his stogie. "I'll let you know tonight."

"Where?" asks another conspirator, an older man in a peacoat and scarf, who goes by the name of the Swede. His wild mop of blond hair, leathery face, and barrel chest, which is perpetually crossed with ammo bandoliers, give him the air of a French Resistance fighter in World War II.

Martinez looks at him. "I'll let you know."

The Swede lets out an exasperated sigh. "We're putting our asses on the line here, Martinez. Seems like you could give us a few details, what we're getting into."

Another one speaks up, a black man in a down vest named Broyles. "There's a reason he's not giving us the details, Swede."

"Yeah? Why is that?"

The black man levels his gaze on the Swede. "Margin of error."

"Come again?"

The black man looks at Martinez. "Too much to lose, somebody gets nabbed before the thing goes down, gets tortured and shit."

Martinez nods, smoking his cheroot. "Something like that . . . yeah."

A fourth man, a former mechanic from Macon named Taggert, chimes in: "What about the bookends?"

"Bruce and Gabe?" Martinez says.

"Yeah . . . you think we'll be able to flip them?"

Martinez takes another drag off the stogie. "What do *you* think?"

Taggert shrugs. "I don't think they'll ever go along with anything like this. Blake's got them so far up his ass they gargle for him at night."

"Exactly." Martinez takes a deep breath. "That's why we gotta take them out first."

"You ask me," Stevie mumbles, "most of the folks in this town got no complaints about the Governor."

"He's right," the Swede concurs with a nervous nod. "I'd say ninety percent of these people actually *like* the son of a bitch, and they're just fine with the way things are run around here. Just so the pantry stays full, the wall stays up, the show goes on . . . it's like the Germans in the 1930s when fucking Adolf Hitler—"

"Okay, put a sock in it!" Martinez tosses his cigar to the cinderstrewn floor and snubs it out with the toe of his jackboot. "Listen to me . . . everybody." He meets each man's gaze as he speaks in a low monotone shot through with nervous tension. "This thing's gonna happen, and it's gonna happen quickly and decisively . . . otherwise we're gonna end up in that slaughterhouse room getting chopped up for zombie food. He's gonna have an accident. That's all you need to know at this point. You want out, there's the door. No hard feelings. Now's your chance." He softens a little. "You guys have been good workers, honest men . . . and trust don't come easy around this place. You want to shake hands and pass on this thing, I got no problem with you. But do it now. Because once this thing goes down it ain't gonna have no reboot button on it."

Martinez waits.

Nobody says anything, nobody leaves.

That night, the temperature plummets, the winds kicking up out of the north. Chimneys spume with wood smoke across Woodbury's main drag, the generators working overtime. To the west, the great arc lights over the racetrack remain burning, the final preparations being made for the big world premiere the next evening.

Alone in her place above the dry cleaner, Lilly Caul lays a pair of handguns and extra ammunition across her bedspread—two .22 caliber Ruger Lite semiautomatics, along with an extra magazine and a carton of 32-grain Stingers. Martinez gave her the weapons, along with a quick lesson on how to reload the clips.

She stands back and stares at the gold-plated pistols with a narrowing of her eyes. Her heart quickens, her throat drying with those old familiar feelings of panic and self-doubt. She pauses. She closes her eyes and wills the fear back down her throat. She opens her eyes and holds her right hand up and ponders it as though it belongs to someone else. Her hand does not shake. It is rock steady.

She will not get a minute of sleep this night or perhaps the next.

Pulling a large knapsack from beneath the bed, she packs the weapons, the ammunition, a machete, a flashlight, nylon cord, sleeping pills, duct tape, a can of Red Bull, a cigarette lighter, a roll of plastic tarp, fingerless gloves, binoculars, and an extra down vest. She zips the knapsack shut and shoves it back under the bed.

Less than twenty-four hours remain until the mission that will change the course of her life.

Lilly bundles up in a down coat, insulated boots, and a stocking cap. She checks her windup clock on her bedside table.

Five minutes later, at 11:45 p.m., she locks up her apartment and heads outside.

The town lies deserted in the late-night chill, the air acrid with the odors of sulfur and frozen salt. Lilly has to step gingerly over the iced sidewalks, her boot steps crunching loudly. She glances over her shoulder. The streets are empty. She makes her way around the post office building to Bob's condo.

The wooden staircase from which Megan hung herself, ice-bound since the storm has passed, cracks and snaps as Lilly carefully climbs the risers.

She knocks on Bob's door. No answer. She knocks again. Nothing. She whispers Bob's name but gets no reply, no sound issuing from within. She tries the door and finds it unlocked. She lets herself in.

The dark kitchen sits in silence, the floor littered with broken dishes and crockery, puddles of spilled liquids. For a moment Lilly wonders if she should have brought a firearm. She scans the living room to her right, sees the overturned furniture and mounds of dirty laundry.

She finds a battery-operated lantern on a counter, grabs it, and flips it on. She walks deeper into the apartment and calls out, "Bob?"

The lantern light glistens off broken glass on the hallway floor. One of Bob's medical satchels lies on the carpet, overturned, its contents spilled across the floor. The wall shimmers with something sticky. Lilly gulps down the fear and moves on.

"Anybody home?"

She peers into the bedroom at the end of the hall and finds Bob on the floor, in a sitting position, leaning against the unmade bed, his head lolled forward. Clad in a stained wifebeater and boxer shorts, his skinny legs as white as alabaster, he sits stone-still and for the briefest instant Lilly mistakes him for dead.

But then she sees his chest slowly rising and falling, and she notices the half-empty bottle of Jim Beam loosely clutched in his limp right hand.

"Bob!"

She rushes over to him and gently raises his head, leaning it against the bed. His greasy, thinning hair askew, his heavy-lidded eyes bloodshot and glassy, he mumbles something like, "Too many of 'em . . . they're gonna—"

"Bob, it's Lilly. Can you hear me? Bob? It's me, it's Lilly."

His head lolls. "They're gonna die . . . we don't triage the worst of 'em . . ."

"Bob, wake up. You're having a nightmare. It's okay, I'm here."

"Crawlin' with maggots . . . too many . . . horrible . . ."

She rises to her feet, turns, and hurries out of the room. Across the hall, in the filthy bathroom, she runs some water in a dirty cup, and returns with the water. She gently takes the booze from Bob's hand and throws it across the room, the bottle shattering against the wall, splattering the cabbage-rose wallpaper. Bob jerks at the noise.

"Here, drink this," she says, and gives him a little. He coughs it down. His hands flail impotently as he coughs. He tries to focus on her but his eyes won't cooperate. She strokes his feverish brow. "I know you're hurting, Bob. It's going to be okay. I'm here now. C'mon."

She lifts him by the armpits, heaving the deadweight of his body up and onto the bed. She lays his head on the pillow. She positions his legs under the covers, then pulls the blanket up to his chin, speaking softly to him. "I know how hard it was on you, losing Megan and all, but you just have to hang in there."

His brow furrows, a look of agony contorting his pale, deeply lined, drawn face. His eyes search the ceiling. He looks like a person who has been buried alive and is trying to breathe. He slurs his words. "I never wanted to . . . never . . . it wasn't my idea to—"

"It's okay, Bob. You don't have to say anything." She strokes his brow and speaks in a low, soft tone. "You did the right thing. It's all gonna be okay. Things are gonna change around here, things are gonna get better." She strokes his cheek, the grizzled flesh cold beneath her fingertips. She begins to softly sing. She sings Joni Mitchell's "The Circle Game" to him, just like old times.

Bob's head settles back into the sweat-damp pillow, his breathing beginning to calm. His eyelids droop. Just like old times. He begins to snore. Lilly keeps singing long after he has drifted off.

"We're taking him down," Lilly says very softly to the sleeping man.

She knows he cannot hear a thing she is saying anymore, if he ever could. Lilly is speaking to herself now. Speaking to some deeply buried part of her psyche.

"It's too late to turn back now . . . we're gonna take him down . . ."

Lilly's voice trails off, and she decides to find herself a blanket and spend the rest of that night at Bob's bedside, waiting for the fateful day to dawn.

SEVENTEEN

The next morning, the Governor gets an early start on the last-minute preparations for the big show. He's up before dawn, quickly getting dressed, making coffee, and feeding Penny the last of his supply of human entrails. By seven o'clock he is out on the street, on his way to Gabe's apartment. The salt crew is already up and working on the sidewalks, the weather surprisingly mild considering the events of the last week. The mercury has risen into the lower fifties, and the sky has lightened, perhaps even stabilized, now overcast with a pale gray ceiling of clouds the color of cement. Very little wind disturbs the morning air, and the burgeoning day strikes the Governor as picture-perfect for an evening of new and improved gladiator matches.

Gabe and Bruce supervise the transfer of zombies held captive in the holding rooms beneath the track. It takes several hours to move the things into the staging areas up above, not only because the walkers are unruly beasts but also because the Governor wants to do it in secret. The unveiling of the Ring of Death has gotten the Governor's show biz juices flowing and he wants the evening's revelations to dazzle the crowd. He spends the bulk of that afternoon inside the arena, checking and double-checking the curtain drops, the public address system, the music cues, the lights, the gates, the locks, the security, and last but certainly not least, the competitors.

The two surviving guardsmen, Zorn and Manning, still wasting away in their underground holding cell, have lost most of their body fat and muscle tissue. Subsisting on scraps, stale crackers, and water for months, chained to the wall 24–7, they look like living skeletons and have very little of their sanity left intact. The only saving grace is their military training—as well as their rage—which, over the weeks of their torturous captivity, has festered and deepened and turned them into wild-eyed revenants hungry for vengeance.

In other words, if they can't rip into the throats of their captors, then they'll happily do the next best thing and rip into each other.

The guardsmen are the final piece to the puzzle, and the Governor waits until the last minute to move them. Gabe and Bruce enlist three of their beefiest workmen to go into the holding cell and inject the soldiers with sodium thiopenthol in order to soften them up for travel. They don't have far to go. Dragged along with leather restraints around their necks, mouths, wrists, and ankles, the two guardsmen are led up a series of iron stairs to the concourse level.

Once upon a time, race fans wandered these cement corridors buying T-shirts and corn dogs and beers and cotton candy. Now these tunnels lie in perpetual darkness, boarded up, padlocked, and used as temporary warehouse space for everything from fuel tanks to sealed cartons of valuables pilfered off the dead.

By six-thirty that night everything is ready. The Governor orders Gabe and Bruce to station themselves at opposite ends of the arena, inside the exit tunnels, in order to guard against any wayward contestants—or errant zombies, for that matter—attempting to flee. Satisfied with all his preparations, the Governor heads back home to change into his show garb. He dresses all in black—black leather vest, leather pants, leather motorcycle boots—and puts a leather stay in his ponytail. He feels like a rock star. He finishes off his ensemble with his trademark duster.

Shortly after seven the forty-plus residents of Woodbury begin filing into the stadium. All the posters tacked up on telephone poles and taped across store windows earlier in the week advertise the start time as seven-thirty, but everybody wants to get a good seat down in the center-front of the bleachers, get settled in, get something to drink, get their blankets and cushions situated.

The mild weather has everybody buzzing excitedly as the start time looms.

At 7:28 P.M. a hush falls over the spectators crowded around the front of the bleachers, some of them standing on the warning track, their faces pressed up against the chain-link barrier. The youngest of the men are down front, while the women and couples and older residents sit scattered across the higher rows, blankets wrapped around themselves to ward off the chill. Each and every face reflects the desperate dope hunger of a junkie in withdrawal—gaunt, wrung out, jittery. They sense something extraordinary about to occur. They smell blood on the wind.

The Governor will not disappoint.

At 7:30 on the nose—according to the Governor's self-winding Fossil wristwatch—the music in the stadium begins to sneak under the ceaseless moaning of the wind. It starts out soft and faint through the PA horns—a low chord as deep as a subterranean tremor—the overture familiar to many, even though few would be able to name the actual symphonic poem: *Also sprach Zarathustra* by Richard Strauss. Most know the piece as the theme from *2001: A Space Odyssey*, the booming horn notes coming one at a time, building on a dramatic fanfare.

A light veil of snow becomes visible up in the arc lights, a brilliant beam hitting the center of the muddy infield, a magnesium-bright pool the size of a moon crater. The crowd lets out a collective holler as the Governor strides out into the cone of light.

He raises a hand—a regal, melodramatic gesture, as the music builds to its big climactic finale—the wind tossing the tails of his duster. His boots sink six inches into the muck, the infield a mire of rain-sodden earth. He believes the mud will only add to the drama.

"Friends! Fellow residents of Woodbury!" he booms into a microphone hardwired to a PA stack behind him. His baritone rises up into the night sky, the echo slapping back across the empty stands at either end of the arena. "You've worked hard to keep this town up and running! You are about to be rewarded!"

Three and a half dozen voices—their vocal cords, as well as their sanity, stretched thin—can make a hell of a racket. The caterwauls swirl on the wind.

"Are you ready for some hard-hitting action tonight?"

The gallery lets out a cacophony of hyena yelps and wild cheers.

"Bring on the contestants!"

On cue, huge follow spots flare on across the upper decks, the noise like giant match tips striking—the beams sweeping down across the arena. One by one, the silver pools of light land on enormous black canvas curtains, each of which drapes one of the five gangways around the concourse.

At the far end of the stadium, a garage-style door rolls up and Zorn, the younger of the two guardsmen, appears in the shadows of the gangway. Clad in makeshift shoulder pads and shin guards, he holds a large machete and trembles with latent madness. He starts across the track toward the center of the infield with a feral expression on his face, moving stiffly, jerkily, a prisoner of war off the leash for the first time in many weeks.

Almost simultaneously, like a mirror image of Zorn's entrance, the garage door at the opposite end of the stadium jerks upward, and from the shadows comes Manning, the older soldier, the one with the wild gray hair and bloodshot eyes. Manning carries an enormous battle-axe and trudges through the mud not unlike a zombie himself.

As the two combatants approach each other in the center of the ring, the Governor bellows into the mike, "Ladies and gentlemen, it is with great pride that I give you the Ring of Death!"

The crowd lets out a collective gasp as the curtains around the periphery—once again, on cue—suddenly drop away, revealing clusters of snarling, decomposing, hungry zombies. Some of the spectators in the stands spring to their feet, instinctively wanting to flee, as the biters start lumbering out of their archways, arms reaching for human meat.

The biters get halfway across the infield, their awkward, shuffling steps mired in the mud, before reaching the end of their chains. Some of them—surprised by the limit of their freedom—are yanked off their feet, landing in comic fashion in the mud. Others growl angrily, flailing dead arms at the crowd and the overall injustice of their leashed captivity. The crowd jeers.

"LET THE BATTLE BEGIN!"

At the center of the infield Zorn pounces on Manning before Manning is ready—in fact, before the Governor has even had a chance to make a safe exit—and the older soldier barely has time to block the slashing blow with his weapon.

The machete comes down and grazes the axe head in a gout of sparks.

The crowd cheers as Manning careens backward into the mud, sliding through the muck, coming to within inches of the closest zombie. The walker, wild-eyed with bloodlust, snaps its jaws at Manning's ankles, the chain barely holding the creature. Manning scrambles to get back on his feet, his face ablaze with terror and madness.

The Governor smiles to himself as he walks off the infield, exiting through one of the gates.

The crowd noises echo through the dark tunnel all around him as he walks through the cement-encased shadows, chuckling to himself, thinking about how amazing it would be if one of the guardsmen got bit before the crowd's eyes and actually turned during the course of the battle. Now *that* would be entertainment.

He turns a corner and sees one of his men loading a clip into an AK-47 near a deserted food stand. The young man—an overgrown farm kid from Macon dressed in a ratty down coat and stocking cap—looks up from his weapon. "Hey, Gov . . . how's it going out there?"

"Thrills and chills, Johnny, thrills and chills," the Governor says with a wink as he passes. "Gonna go check on Gabe and Bruce at the exits . . . you make sure those walkers stay inside the infield and don't wander back toward the gates."

"Will do, boss."

The Governor moves on, turning another corner and striding down a deserted tunnel.

The muffled noise of the crowd echoes in waves down the dark passageway as he makes his way toward the east exit. He starts whistling, feeling on top of the world, when all at once he stops whistling and slows down, instinctively reaching for the .38 snubbie in his belt. Something feels wrong all of a sudden.

He comes to an abrupt halt in the middle of the tunnel. The east exit, just visible around a corner twenty feet ahead of him, sits there completely deserted. No sign of Gabe anywhere. The outer gate—a vertical door made of wooden slats, pulled down across the opening—leaks thin strands of bright light from the headlamps of an idling vehicle.

At that point the Governor notices the muzzle of an M1 assault rifle on the floor, poking around the corner—Gabe's gun—lying unattended.

"Son of a bitch!" the Governor blurts, drawing his gun and spinning around.

The blue spark of a Taser crackles in his face, knocking him backward.

Martinez moves in quickly, the Taser in one hand, a heavy leather sap in the other—as the fifty-kilovolt punch sends the Governor reeling backward, slamming into the wall, his .38 flying out of his hand.

Martinez brings the sap down hard on the Governor's temple, the dull slapping noise like a tuneless bell ringing. The Governor convulses against the wall, swinging wildly, refusing to go down. He cries out with the garbled rage of a stroke victim, the veins in his neck and temples bulging, as he kicks out at Martinez.

The Swede and Broyles stand behind Martinez on each flank, ready to move in with the rope and tape. Martinez hits the Governor again with the sap, and this time the blunt object does its work.

The Governor stiffens and slides to the floor, his eyes rolling back in his head. The Swede and Broyles close in on the quivering, twitching body curled into a fetal position on the cement.

They get the Governor tied, bound, and gagged with duct tape in less than sixty seconds. Martinez signals the men outside the gate with a quick whistle, and the slatted door suddenly jumps up.

"On three," Martinez mutters, holstering his Taser, shoving the sap behind his belt. He grabs the man's rope-bound ankles. "One, two . . . *three!*"

Broyles takes the Governor by the shoulders, Martinez lifting the legs, and the Swede leads them out through the gate into the cold wind and around the back of the idling panel van.

The rear hatch is already gaping open. They slide the body in.

Within seconds, the men have climbed into the windowless van, and all the doors have slammed, and the vehicle is lurching backward, away from the gate.

The panel van slams to a stop, then the transmission wrenches down into drive and it roars away.

Within seconds all that's left outside the entrance to the racetrack is a fading cloud of carbon monoxide.

"Wake up, you sick fuck!" Lilly slaps the Governor, the man's eyes fluttering open on the floor of the crowded van as it rumbles out of town.

Gabe and Bruce are bound and gagged near the front of the cluttered payload bay, their mouths covered with duct tape. The Swede holds a .45 Smith & Wesson on the men, their eyes wide and searching. Cartons of military ordnance line the sides of the cargo bay, everything from armor-piercing shells to incendiary bombs.

"Take it easy, Lilly," Martinez cautions, crouching near the front, a walkie-talkie clutched in his gloved hand. His face tight with nervous tension, a heretic rebelling against the church, Martinez turns away and thumbs the switch and says in a low voice, "Just follow the Jeep, and keep the lights off, and let me know when you see a roamer."

The Governor regains consciousness in stages, blinking and scanning his surroundings, testing the strength of his bonds—the elastic shackles, nylon rope, and duct tape tight around his mouth.

"You need to hear this, Blake," Lilly says to the man on the corrugated floor. "'Governor' . . . 'President' . . . 'King Shit' . . . whatever you call yourself. You think you're some kind of benevolent dictator?"

The Governor's eyes still shift around the confines of the van, not focusing on any one thing—an animal boxed in on the killing floor.

"My friends did not have to *die*," Lilly goes on, looming over the

Governor. Her eyes mist over for a moment and she hates herself for it. "You could have built this place into something great . . . a place where people could live in safety and harmony . . . instead of this twisted, sick freak show that it's become."

Near the front, Martinez thumbs the switch. "Stevie, you see anything yet?"

Through the speaker crackles the younger man's voice. "Negative . . . nothing yet . . . wait!" The sound of static, then rustling noises. Stevie's voice is heard off mike: "What the fuck is that?"

Martinez thumbs the switch. "Stevie, say again, I didn't copy that."

Static . . . rustling noises.

"Stevie! You copy? I don't want to get too far from town!"

Through the static Stevie's voice intermittently sizzles through the noise: "Stop, Taggert. . . . Stop! . . . What the fuck! WHAT THE FUCK!"

In back, Lilly wipes her eyes and latches her gaze on the eyes of the Governor. "Sex for food? Really? Seriously? That's your great society—"

"Lilly!" Martinez barks at her. "Stop it! We got a situation!" He thumbs the send button. "Broyles, stop the van!"

By this point the Governor's eyes have found Lilly's, and the man is fully awake, staring at her with a silent fury that burns holes in her soul, and she doesn't care, she doesn't even notice it.

"All the fighting and the suicides and the fear driving everyone into catatonic stupors . . . ?" She feels like spitting at him. "This is your idea of a fucking COMMUNITY—"

"Lily! Goddammit!" Martinez turns and faces her. "Would you please—"

The truck screeches to a stop, throwing Martinez backward against the firewall and tossing Lilly forward across the Governor and into a stack of ammo boxes. The cartons topple as Lilly sprawls across the floor. The walkie-talkie spins against a duffel bag. The Governor rolls from one side to the other, the duct tape coming loose from his mouth.

The crackle of Broyles's voice squawks out of the speaker. "Got a visual on a walker!"

Martinez crawls toward the two-way, snatching it up and thumbing the button. "What the hell's going on, Broyles? What's the idea of slamming on the—"

"Got another one!" the voice squawks out of the tiny speaker. "Got a couple, coming out of the . . . Oh, fuck . . . oh, fuck . . . OH, FUCK!"

Martinez thumbs the switch. "Broyles, what the hell is going on?"

Through the radio: "There's more than we—"

Static washes over the voice for a moment, and then Stevie's voice cuts through the noise: "Jesus Christ, there's a whole bunch of them coming out of the—" Static crackles for a moment. "They're coming out of the woods, man, they keep coming—"

Martinez yells into the mike, "Stevie, talk to me! Should we dump them and come back?"

More static.

Martinez screams, "Stevie! Do you copy? Should we turn around?"

Broyles's voice now: "Too many, boss! Never seen this many in one—"

A burst of static and the sound of a gunshot and glass breaking— echoing outside the walls of the van—all of it gets Lilly to her feet. She realizes what's happening, and she reaches behind her belt for the Ruger. She pulls it out and cocks the slide, glancing over her shoulder. "Martinez, call your men back, get 'em outta here!"

Martinez thumbs the button: "Stevie! Can you hear me?! Get outta here, pull back! Turn around! We'll find another place! Can you hear me? STEVIE!"

The sound of Stevie's anguished cry spurts out of the speaker, right before another barrage of automatic gunfire rattles the air . . . followed by a terrific wrenching of metal . . . and then an enormous crash.

Broyles's voice: "Hold on! They turned it over! There's too goddamn many! Hold on! We're fucked, y'all! WE ARE TOTALLY FUCKED!!"

The van shudders as the engine revs into reverse, rocketing backward, the centripetal force throwing everybody forward against the firewall. Lilly slams her shoulder against the gun rack, knocking half a dozen carbines to the floor like kindling. Gabe and Bruce roll, slamming into each other. Unbeknownst to the others, Gabe has his fingers under Bruce's shackle now and he starts wrenching at it. Bruce's gag has come loose and he booms a garbled cry: "YOU MOTHERFUCKERS, NOW WE'RE ALL GONNA DIE!"

The van bumps over an object, and then another, and another—the wet, muffled thumps rocking the chassis—and Lilly holds on to the side brace with her free hand, scanning the cargo hold.

Martinez scrambles on hands and knees toward the fallen walkie-talkie while the black man spits and curses, and Swede aims the muzzle of his .45 at the bald black man. "SHUT THE FUCK UP!"

"YOU MOTHERFUCKERS DON'T EVEN—"

The rear of the van slams into an unknown object and bogs down, the rear wheels spinning on something slick and gooey on the road, the g-forces flinging everybody into the corner. Guns fly off across the hold, and the Governor rolls against a stack of cartons that fall on him. He lets out an angry cry—the duct tape hanging from his chin now—and then he gets quiet.

Everybody gets quiet as the van sits there for a moment, very still.

Then the entire vehicle shudders. The sideways jerk gets everybody's attention. Broyles's voice crackles from the fallen two-way, something about *"too many"* or *"getting out,"* when all at once the roar of Broyles's AK-47 from the cab pierces the silence, followed by an eruption of broken glass and a human shriek.

Then things get quiet again. And still. Except for the low, droning, mucusy moans of hundreds of dead voices, which, coming through the walls of the windowless van, sound like a giant turbine engine rumbling outside the van. Something bumps the vehicle again, jerking it sideways with a violent convulsion.

Martinez grabs an assault rifle off the wall, jacks the lever back, lurches toward the rear hatch, and grasps the handle, when he hears a deep, whiskey-cured voice come from behind him.

"Wouldn't do that if I were you."

Lilly glances down at the floor and sees the Governor—his gag loose—struggling into a sitting position against the wall, his dark eyes smoldering. Lilly holds her Ruger on him. "You're not giving orders anymore," she informs him through clenched teeth.

The van jerks sideways again. The rumbling silence stretches.

"Your little plan's gone all to hell," the Governor says with sadistic glee. His facial features tic with residual trauma.

"Shut up!"

"Thought you'd leave us out here, feed us to the biters, and nobody would be the wiser."

Lilly puts the muzzle of the .22 against his forehead. "I said shut the fuck up!"

The van shudders again. Martinez stands frozen with indecision. He turns, and he starts to say something to Lilly, when a sharp blur of movement near the front takes everybody by surprise.

Bruce has managed to free his hands and suddenly lashes out at the Swede, knocking the gun out of the older man's grip. The .45 goes off as it clatters to the floor, the boom so loud it ruptures eardrums, the blast chinking metal out of the floor and grazing the Swede's left boot, making the older man cry out and slam against the back wall.

In one smooth movement, before Martinez or Lilly can fire, the big black man scoops up the hot .45 and empties three rounds into the Swede's chest. Blood sprays across the corrugated side wall behind the older man as he gasps and writhes and slides to the floor.

From the rear, Martinez spins toward the black man and fires two quick, controlled bursts in his general direction, but by that point Bruce is already diving for cover behind piles of cartons, and the bullets are chewing through cardboard, metal, and fiberglass, setting off a series of muffled blasts inside the boxes, which send puffs of wood shards, sparks, and paper into the air like meteors—

—and everybody dives to the floor—and Bruce gets his hands on his bowie knife—a weapon he had hidden on his ankle—and he's going for Gabe's shackles—and things are happening very quickly now all around the cargo bay—as Lilly swings her Ruger toward the two thugs near the front—while Martinez leaps toward Bruce—and the Governor screams something like "DON'T KILL THEM!—and Gabe is loose now and scrambling for one of the fallen carbines—and Bruce slashes the knife at Martinez, who dodges the blow, and then stumbles against Lilly, sending her slamming against the rear doors—

—and the impact of Lilly's body against the double-doors springs the latch.

The doors suddenly and unexpectedly burst open, letting a swarm of moving corpses into the van.

EIGHTEEN

A large, putrefied biter in a shredded medical smock goes for Lilly, and it nearly gets its rotten teeth into her neck, when Martinez manages to get off a burst that takes off the top of the thing's skull.

Rancid, black blood fountains up across the ceiling, spitting across Lilly's face, as she backs away from the open doorway. More biters scuttle in through the gaping hatch. Lilly's ears go deaf—ringing from the noise—as she backs toward the front wall.

The Governor, still shackled, scoots backward, away from the on-slaught, as Gabe gets a loaded carbine rifle up and barking, the barrage punching through dead tissue and rotting skulls. Brain matter blossoms like black chrysanthemums, as the interior of the van smokes and teeters and floods with death stench. More and more biters swarm the opening, despite the blazing gunfire.

"BRUCE, CUT ME LOOSE!"

The Governor's voice—nearly drowned by the din, barely audible to Lilly's ringing eardrums—gets Bruce moving with the knife. Meanwhile Martinez and Lilly unleash a salvo of gunfire, muzzles flashing, the noise enormous, entire clips being emptied, the successive blasts hitting eye sockets and mandibles and slimy bald pates and putrid foreheads, sending black tissue and blood and fluids spurting and flinging across the open hatch.

Bruce's knife slices down on the Governor's shackles, and within seconds the Governor is free and has a carbine in his hands.

The air blazes with gunfire, and soon the five surviving human occupants of the van are clustered together against the cab's firewall, each of them blasting away at will, spraying a hell storm across the rear hatch. The sound is gargantuan, ear-piercing, amplified by the metal fuselage of the van. Some of the rounds miss their targets, ricocheting off the door frame in daisy chains of sparks.

Mangled zombies drop to the floor of the van, dominoes falling, some of them slipping off the slimy back edge of the hatch, others caught in the pile. The barrage continues another ten seconds, during which time the back spray of blood and bodily matter cover the humans in layers of gore. A splinter of steel strikes Lilly's thigh, embedding itself, a wasp sting of pain waking her up.

Over the course of a single minute—an interminable sixty seconds of elapsed time that feels to Lilly like a lifetime—each and every last ammo magazine is emptied into dead flesh, and every last zombie crowding the doorway drops and slides to the pavement outside the van, leaving leech trails of blood on the corrugated ledge.

The last remaining bodies get stuck in the hatchway, and in the horrible, ear-ringing silence that ensues, as Gabe and Martinez and the Governor reload, Bruce lunges toward the hatch. He kicks the stragglers off the rear parapet, the bodies falling to the asphalt with a splat. Lilly thumbs her spent magazine out of her Ruger, the clip clattering to the floor, the metallic clunk unheard by her deafened ears. Her face and arms and clothing are covered in blood and bile. She reloads, her pulse throbbing in her traumatized ears.

In the meantime Bruce wrenches the double doors shut, the damaged hinges making a loud squeak that barely penetrates the ringing in Lilly's ears.

The latch clicks, sealing them back inside the blood-drenched death chamber, but the worst part, the part that has everybody's attention now, is the half-glimpsed landscape beyond the van, the forest on either side of the road, and the switchback way up on the plateau in the distance, draped in darkness and crawling with moving shadows.

What they glimpse before the doors bang shut challenges comprehension. They've all seen herds before, some of them huge, but this one defies description—a mass of dead the likes of which no one has seen since the plague broke out months ago. Nearly a thousand moving corpses in every imaginable state of decomposition stretch as far as the eye can see. Throngs of snarling zombies, so thick one could walk across their shoulders, line the edges of the hill on either side of Highway 85. Moving slowly and lethargically, their sheer number threatening mass destruction, they bring to mind a black glacier aimlessly cutting through the trees and slicing across the fields and roads. Some of them barely have flesh left on their bones, their ragged burial clothing hanging mosslike in the darkness. Others snap at the air with the involuntary twitching of snakes stirred from their nests. The length and breadth of the multitude, each face as pale white as mother-of-pearl, gives the impression of a vast, moving flood tide of infected pus.

Inside the van, the primordial terror touched off by this sight stiffens the spines of everyone present. Gabe raises his carbine at Martinez. "You stupid fucking son of a bitch! Look at what you've done! Look at what you've gotten us into!!"

Before anybody can react Lilly swings her Ruger up and trains it on Gabe. Ears ringing, she cannot hear exactly what he says in reply but she knows he means business. "I will fucking blow you away if you don't back off, asshole!"

Bruce pounces on Lilly with his buck knife, putting it around her neck. "Bitch, you got about three seconds to drop that motherfucking—"

"BRUCE!" The Governor aims his carbine at Bruce. "Back off!"

Bruce doesn't move. The blade stays pressed against Lilly's throat, and Lilly keeps her gun leveled on Gabe, and Martinez trains his assault rifle on the Governor. "Philip, listen to me," Martinez says softly, "I promise you I will drop you first before I go down."

"Everybody just calm the fuck down!" The Governor's knuckles are white on the carbine's hilt. "Only way we're gonna get outta this mess is together!"

The van shudders again as more zombies close in, making everybody jerk.

"What are you thinking?" Lilly says.

"First of all, get those fucking guns out of everybody's face."

Martinez burns his gaze into Bruce. "Bruce, get away from her."

"Do what he says, Bruce." The Governor keeps the muzzle on Bruce. A single pearl of sweat rolls down the bridge of the Governor's nose. "PUT THE FUCKING KNIFE DOWN OR I WILL PUT YOUR BRAINS ON THAT WALL!"

Reluctantly, the rage blazing in his dark almond eyes, Bruce lowers the knife.

The van trembles again, as the guns slowly tilt down, one at a time, away from their targets.

Martinez is the last to lower his rifle. "If we can get to the cab, we can plough our way outta here."

"Negative!" The Governor looks at him. "We'll lead this fucking stampede back to Woodbury!"

"What do you suggest?" Lilly asks the Governor with cold acid running through her veins. She feels the horrible sensation of giving over to the madman again, her soul shrinking into a tiny black hole inside her. "We can't just sit here on our thumbs."

"How far are we from town? Like less than mile?" The Governor asks this almost rhetorically as he gazes around the van's blood-sodden interior, glancing from carton to carton. He sees the spare parts of gun mounts, shell casings, military-grade ammunition. "Lemme ask you something," he says, turning to Martinez. "You seem to have thought through this big coup d'état like a real military man. You got any RPGs in this crate? Anything with a little more punch than a simple grenade?"

It takes them less than five minutes to find the ordnance and load the RPG and lay out the strategy and get into position, and throughout that time the Governor gives most of the orders, keeping everybody moving, as the horde surrounds the van like bees swarming a hive. By the time the survivors are ready to launch their countermeasure, the number of dead pressing in on the vehicle is so high the van nearly tips over.

The muffled sound of the Governor's voice, coming from inside the van, counting down . . . *"three, two, one"* . . . is incomprehensible to the dead, their putrid ears brushing the outer shell of the vehicle.

The first blast blows the rear doors off the van as if they were on explosive bolts.

The eruption catapults half a dozen walkers into the air, the rocket-propelled grenade punching through the dense crowd of corpses clustered outside the hatch like a hot poker ramming through butter. The projectile goes off ten yards away from the van.

The explosion immolates at least a hundred—maybe more—in the general vicinity of the vehicle. The sound of it rivals a sonic boom from a passing jet, the report shaking the ground, arcing up into the heavens, and echoing out across the tops of trees.

The back draft shoots up and out—a convection of flame the size of a basketball court—turning night to day and transforming the closest zombies into flaming human debris, some of them practically vaporized, others becoming dancing columns of fire. The inferno razes an area of fifty square yards around the van.

Gabe leaps out of the van first, a scarf around his mouth and nose to filter the acrid fumes of dead flesh cooking in the napalmlike maelstrom. He is followed closely by Lilly, who covers her mouth with one hand, and fires off three quick shots with her Ruger in the other hand, taking down a few stray zombies in their path.

They make it to the cab, throw the door open, and climb in—pushing Broyles's contorted, bloody remains aside—and within seconds the rear wheels are digging in, and the vehicle is launching out of there.

The van bulldozes through files of zombies, turning the upright cadavers into putrefied jelly on the pavement, cutting a swath toward a hairpin turn that looms ahead of them. And when they reach the tight curve, Gabe executes the last phase of the escape.

He yanks the wheel, and the van careens off the road and up the side of a wooded hill.

The rough terrain taxes the tires and suspension, but Gabe keeps the foot feed pinned, and the rear-wheel drive churns through the soft muddy floor of the hill, fishtailing wildly, nearly dumping the other three men out the gaping, jagged opening in the rear.

When they reach the crest of the hill, Gabe slams on the brakes and the van skids to a stop.

It takes a minute to aim the mortar launcher, a squat iron cylinder that Martinez hastily jury-rigged to a machine-gun mount. The muzzle is pointed upward at a forty-five-degree angle. By the time they're ready to fire, at least two hundred zombies have started shambling up the hill toward the van, drawn to the noise and headlights.

Martinez primes the launcher and touches off the ignition button.

The mortar booms, the projectile rocketing skyward, arcing out over the valley, the tracery of its tail like a glowing neon contrail. The explosive shell lands smack-dab in the middle of the sea of walking dead. At least four hundred yards from the van, the mini mushroom cloud of flame is seen a few milliseconds before the *FFOOOMP* of its impact is heard, and the flash that follows turns the underbelly of the night sky a deep, hot DayGlo orange.

Flaming particles blossom into the heavens, a mixture of dirt, debris, and dead tissue, the shock wave of fire rolling at least a hundred yards in all directions, burning hundreds of biters into ash. A vast autoclave could not cremate the dead faster or more thoroughly.

The remaining walkers, drawn away from the hill by the fiery spectacle, awkwardly turn and drag themselves toward the light.

Away from Woodbury.

They return to town on hobbling wheels, a cracked rear transaxle, shattered windows, and blown doors. They keep gazing out the back for indications of the phenomenal herd, signs of being followed, but other than a few wayward stragglers stumbling along the edges of the orchards, only the orange glow on the western horizon reflects the aftermath of the swarm.

Nobody sees Gabe silently pass the Governor a pearl-handled .45 semiautomatic behind Martinez's back until it's too late. "We got unfinished business, you and me," the Governor blurts suddenly, pressing the muzzle against the back of Martinez's neck as the van rumbles around a corner.

Martinez lets out one long, anguished sigh. "Get it over with."

"You got a short memory, son," the Governor says. "This is the kind of shit happens outside these walls. I'm not gonna waste you, Martinez . . . not yet, at least . . . right now we need each other."

Martinez says nothing, just looks down at the iron corrugations of the floor and waits for his life to come to an end.

They enter the village from the west, and Gabe pulls around in front of the arena and slides into a parking place reserved for service vehicles. Crowd noises still echo from the stands, although from the sound of the catcalls and whistles, the fights have probably deteriorated into chaos. The show's eccentric emcee has been missing in action for over an hour . . . but nobody has had the wherewithal to leave.

Gabe and Lilly get out of the cab and walk around to the rear hatch. Filmed in a layer of gore, her face spackled with blood spray, Lilly feels a skin-prickling sense of unease, and she puts her hand on the grip of her Ruger, which is wedged behind her belt. She's not thinking straight. She feels as though she's half asleep, sluggish with shock, groggy and breathless.

When she turns the corner at the rear of the van she sees Martinez standing without a weapon, his arms soot-covered from the mortar blowback, his sad chiseled face stippled with blood, the Governor directly behind him, pressing the muzzle of the .45 against his neck.

Lilly instinctively draws her Ruger, but before she can even aim it, the Governor issues a warning.

"You shoot that thing, your boyfriend's going down," the Governor hisses at her. "Gabe, take her little peashooter from her."

Gabe snatches the gun out of Lilly's hands, and Lilly just stares at the Governor. A voice rings out in the night air, coming from above them.

"Hey!"

The Governor ducks down. "Martinez, tell your guy on the upper deck everything's okay."

Way up on the crest of the arena roof, on one corner of the upper deck, a machine-gun turret is mounted. A long perforated barrel angles down at the dirt parking lot, behind which stands a young cohort of Martinez's—a tall black kid from Atlanta, name of Hines—a young man who is not privy to the secret overthrow attempt.

"What the hell's going on?" he yells down at them. "Folks look like y'all been in a war!"

"Everything's cool, Hines!" Martinez calls up to him. "Had to deal with a few biters is all!"

The Governor keeps his .45 out of sight, the muzzle prodding the small of Martinez's back. "Hey, kid!" The Governor jerks his head, indicating the dark grove of trees on the other side of the main road. "You want to do me a favor and take out those stragglers we got coming up behind us through the trees!" Then the Governor points at the van. "When you're done with that, there's two bodies in the van need shooting in the head, then take 'em to the morgue."

The machine-gun turret squeaks, and the barrel swings up, and everybody whirls to see movement across the street, a pair of lumbering silhouettes emerging from the trees, the last of the stragglers.

The muzzle roars off the arena roof, the flare of sparks coming one millisecond before the booming report, as the Governor urges Martinez forward toward the building, everybody jerking at the noise.

Armor-piercing rounds strafe the walkers stumbling out of the forest, the zombies dancing upright for a moment like string puppets in an earthquake, blood mist issuing out the backs of their heads— red steam venting. Hines empties an entire bandolier of .762 millimeter cartridges into the walkers for good measure. When they finally go down in pulpy, steaming gut heaps, the kid named Hines lets out a little victory yelp and then looks back across the grounds.

The Governor, Martinez, and the rest of their party have vanished.

NINETEEN

"You people think this is a fucking democracy?" The Governor's blood-spattered duster sweeps the floor, as his angry, smoky voice bounces off the cinder-block walls of the private room underneath the concession area.

Once designated an accounting office and vault for the track's cash receipts, the room has been picked clean, the old iron safe on one side blown apart. Now only a long, scarred conference table, a few girlie calendars on the wall, a couple of accountants' desks, and some overturned swivel chairs litter the space.

Martinez and Lilly sit on folding chairs against one wall, silent and shell-shocked, while Bruce and Gabe stand nearby with guns at the ready. The tension in the room crackles and sparks like a lit fuse.

"You people seem to have forgotten this place works for one reason and one reason only." The Governor's speech is punctuated by facial tics and residual twitching from the Taser trauma. Dried blood clings to his face, his clothes, and his hair in matted crusts. "It works because I'm the one makes it work! You see what's out there? That's what's on the menu, you want to eat out! You want some kind of utopian paradise, some kind of oasis of warm and fuzzy fellowship? Call Norman Fucking *Rockwell*! This is fucking war!"

He pauses to let it sink in, and the silence presses down on the room.

"You ask any motherfucker out there in the stands, do they want a democracy? Do they want warm and fuzzy? Or do they just want somebody to fucking *manage* things . . . keep them from being some biter's *lunch!*" His eyes blaze. "You seem to have forgotten what it was like when Gavin and his guardsmen were in charge! We got this place back! We got things—"

A knock on the outer door interrupts the rant. The Governor spins toward the sound. *"WHAT!"*

The doorknob clicks, the door cracking open a few inches. The sheepish face of the farm kid from Macon peers in, his AK-47 on a strap at his side. "Boss, the natives are getting restless out there."

"What?"

"Lost both fighters ages ago, nothing but dead bodies and biters on chains out there. Nobody's leaving, though . . . they're just getting wasted on their BYOBs and throwin' shit at the zombies."

The Governor wipes his face, smooths down his Fu Manchu. "Tell 'em there's gonna be an important announcement in a minute."

"But what about—"

"JUST TELL 'EM!"

The farm kid gives a meek nod and turns away, latching the door behind him.

The Governor shoots a look across the room at the big black man in gore-splattered denim. "Bruce, go get Stevens and his little lapdog. I don't care what they're doing, I want their asses in here right now! On the double!"

Bruce gives a nod, shoves his pistol in his belt, and hurries out of the room.

The Governor turns to Martinez. "I know exactly where you got that fucking stun gun . . ."

The time it takes Bruce to go fetch the doctor and Alice is interminable for Lilly. Sitting next to Martinez, a slimy layer of zombie spoor drying on her skin, the wound in her leg throbbing, she expects a bullet to come smashing through her skull at any moment. She can feel Gabe's body heat behind her, only inches away. She can smell his BO and hear his thick breathing, but he doesn't say a word the whole time they're waiting.

Nor does Martinez speak.

Nor does the Governor, who continues to pace across the front of the room.

Lilly doesn't care about dying anymore. Something inexplicable has happened to her. She thinks of Josh rotting in the ground and she feels nothing. She thinks about Megan hanging by that makeshift noose and it stirs zero emotion. She thinks of Bob sinking into oblivion.

None of it matters anymore.

The worst part is, she knows the Governor is right. They need a Rottweiler on these walls. They need a monster to stanch the blood tide.

Across the room, the door clicks and Bruce returns with Stevens and Alice. The doctor enters in his wrinkled lab coat, walking a few feet in front of Bruce's gun. Alice brings up the rear.

"Come on in and join the party," the Governor greets them with an icy smile. "Have a seat. Relax. Take a load off, sit a spell."

Without a word the doctor and Alice cross the room and sit down on folding chairs next to Martinez and Lilly like children sent to their rooms. The doctor says nothing, just stares at the floor.

"So the whole gang's here now," the Governor says, coming over to the foursome. He stands inches away, a coach about to give a halftime chalk talk. "Here's the thing, we're gonna strike a little agreement . . . a verbal contract. Very simple. Look at me, Martinez."

It requires herculean effort for Martinez to look up at the dark-eyed man.

The Governor latches his gaze on to Martinez. "The agreement is this. As long as I keep the fucking wolves from the door, keep the gravy boats full around here . . . you don't ask questions about how I do it."

He pauses, standing in front of them, waiting, his hands on his hips, his blood-caked features grim and set, his gaze meeting each of their traumatized stares.

Nobody says anything. Lilly sees herself springing to her feet and kicking her chair over and screaming at the top of her lungs and grabbing one of the rifles and cutting the Governor down in a storm of gunfire.

She stares at the floor.

The silence stretches.

"One more thing," the Governor says, smiling at them, his eyes dead and mirthless. "Anybody breaches this contract, sticks their nose in my business, Martinez dies and the rest of you get banished to the sticks. You got that?" He waits in silence. "Answer me, you cocksuckers! You understand the stipulations of our contract? Martinez?"

The reply comes on a haggard breath. "Yeah."

"I can't hear you!"

Martinez looks at him. "Yeah . . . I understand."

"How about you, Stevens?"

"Yes, Philip." The doctor's voice drips with contempt. "Great closing argument. You should be a lawyer."

"Alice?"

She gives him a quick, jittery nod.

The Governor looks at Lilly. "How about you? Are we clear on this?"

Lilly looks at the floor, says nothing.

The Governor presses in closer. "I'm not getting a consensus here. I'll ask you again, Lilly. You understand the agreement?"

Lilly refuses to speak.

The Governor draws his pearl-handled .45 army Colt, snaps back the slide, and presses the muzzle to her head. But before he can say another word, or send a bullet into her brain, Lilly looks up at him.

"I understand."

"*LADIES AND GENTLEMEN!*" The nasally voice of the farm kid crackles through the arena's PA system, echoing out over the chaotic scene behind the chain-link barrier. The tight knot of spectators has scattered across the stands, although not a single audience member has departed the stadium. Some of them lie on their backs, drunk, staring at the moonless night sky. Others pass bottles of hooch back and forth, attempting to numb the horrors of the mayhem they have just witnessed across the infield.

Some of the drunker patrons are throwing trash and empty bottles into the arena, tormenting the captive biters, who flail impotently on their chains, their rotting lips dripping with black drool. The two dead combatants lie in heaps just out of reach of the zombies, as the crowd jeers and catcalls. This has been going on for almost an hour.

The amplified voice crackles: *"WE HAVE A SPECIAL AN-NOUNCEMENT FOR YOU FROM THE GOVERNOR!"*

This news gets their attention, and the cacophony of yelps and whoops and whistles dies down. The forty or so spectators awkwardly return to their front-row seats, some of them tripping on drunken feet. Within minutes the entire crowd has coalesced down front, behind the cyclone-fence barricade that once protected race fans from spinouts and flaming tires flying off the track.

"PUT YOUR HANDS TOGETHER FOR OUR FEARLESS LEADER, THE GOVERNOR!"

From the middle gangway, like a ghost, the long-coated figure emerges from the shadows into the cold vapor of calcium lights, blood stippled and muddy, his coattails flagging in the wind, a Trojan commander returning from the siege of Troy. Striding out to the center of the infield, standing amid the expired guardsmen, he whips the mike cord behind him, raises the mike, and booms into it: *"FRIENDS, YOU ARE ALL HERE BECAUSE OF FATE . . . FATE HAS BROUGHT US TOGETHER . . . AND IT IS OUR FATE TO SURVIVE THIS PLAGUE TOGETHER!"*

The crowd, most of them drunk, lets out an intoxicated cheer.

"IT IS ALSO MY FATE TO BE YOUR LEADER . . . AND I ACCEPT THAT ROLE WITH PRIDE! AND ANY SON OF A BITCH WHO DOESN'T LIKE IT CAN COME TAKE IT AWAY! ANYTIME! YOU KNOW WHERE TO FIND ME! ANY TAKERS OUT THERE? ANYBODY GOT ENOUGH SAND TO KEEP THIS TOWN SAFE?"

The drunken voices fade. The faces behind the chain link go slack. He's got their attention now. The wind in the high gantries punctuates the silence.

"EACH AND EVERY ONE OF YOU TONIGHT SHALL BEAR WITNESS TO A NEW DAY IN WOODBURY! TONIGHT THE BARTER SYSTEM OFFICIALLY COMES TO AN END!"

Now the silence grips the arena like a pall. The spectators do not expect this, their heads cocked as though hanging on every word.

"FROM NOW ON, SUPPLIES WILL BE GATHERED FOR THE GOOD OF ALL! AND THEY WILL BE DISTRIBUTED EQUALLY! THIS IS HOW PEOPLE WILL EARN THEIR WAY INTO OUR COMMUNITY! BY GATHERING SUPPLIES! BY BENEFITING THE COMMON GOOD!"

One older gentleman a few rows above the others stands on wobbly knees, his Salvation Army topcoat buffeting in the wind, and he begins to clap, nodding his head, his grizzled jaw jutting proudly.

"THESE POLICY CHANGES WILL BE STRICTLY ENFORCED! ANYONE CAUGHT TRADING FAVORS OF ANY SORT IN RETURN FOR GOODS WILL BE FORCED TO FIGHT IN THE RING OF DEATH AS PUNISHMENT!" The governor pauses, scanning the crowd, letting this sink in. *"WE ARE NOT BARBARIANS! WE TAKE CARE OF OUR OWN! WE! ARE! OUR BROTHERS' KEEPERS!!"*

Now more and more of the onlookers stand and begin to applaud, some of them spontaneously sobering up, finding their voices, cheering as though in a church service responding to a hallelujah.

The Governor's sermon strikes a climactic chord: *"THIS WILL BE A NEW ERA OF WOODBURY WORKING TOGETHER! TO FORM A HAPPIER, HEALTHIER, MORE COHESIVE COMMUNITY!!"*

By this point, nearly every spectator has risen to their feet, and the roar of their voices—a sound not unlike an old-fashioned tent revival meeting—reverberates up into the upper tiers and echoes across the night sky. People are clapping, hollering their approval, and exchanging glances of relief and pleasant surprise . . . and perhaps even hope.

The fact is, from this distance, behind the cyclone fence, most of them glassy-eyed from drinking all night, the spectators do not notice the bloodthirsty glint behind the dark eyes of their benevolent leader.

The next morning, the slender young woman in the ponytail finds herself down in the fetid, reeking atmosphere of the abattoir under the stadium.

Clad in her bulky Georgia Tech sweatshirt, antique jewelry, and ripped jeans, Lilly does not shake, does not feel compelled to chew her fingernails, does not in fact feel *any* nervous tension or repulsion at the disgusting task to which she's been assigned as a sort of slap on the wrist for her complicity in the coup attempt.

She in fact feels nothing but a low simmering rage as she crouches in the dim light of the subterranean chamber, wielding the eighteen-inch Teflon-coated axe.

She brings the axe down hard and true, chopping the gristle of the Swede's severed leg, which is stretched across the floor drain. Making a wet popping noise like a pressurized lid opening, the blade slices through the knee joint as a chef's knife might notch a raw drumstick from a chicken thigh. The backsplash of blood spits up at Lilly, stippling her collar and chin. She barely notices it as she tosses the two sections of human limb into the plastic garbage bin next to her.

The bin contains parts of the Swede, Broyles, Manning, and Zorn—a caldron of single-serving-sized entrails, organs, hairy scalps, slimy white ball joints, and severed limbs—collected and stored on ice to keep the games running, keep the arena zombies complacent.

Lilly wears rubber garden gloves—which have turned a dark shade of purple over the course of the last hour—and she has allowed her anger to fuel her axe blows. She has dismantled three bodies with the greatest of ease, barely noticing the other two men—Martinez and Stevens—laboring in opposite corners of the filthy, windowless, gore-stained cinder-block chamber.

No words are exchanged among the shunned, and the work goes on unabated for another half an hour when, sometime around noon, the sound of muffled steps coming from out in the corridor on the other side of the door registers in Lilly's deafened ears. The lock clicks, and the door opens.

"Just wanted to check on your progress," the Governor announces, coming into the room in a smart leather vest, a pistol holstered on his thigh, and his hair pulled back and away from his chiseled features. "Very impressive work," he says, coming over to Lilly's bin and glancing down at the gelatinous contents. "Might need to procure a few morsels later for feeding purposes."

Lilly doesn't look up. She keeps chopping, tossing, and wiping the edge of her blade on her jeans. At last she pulls an entire upper body cavity, which still has the cadaver's head attached, across her chopping area.

"Carry on, troops," the Governor says with an approving nod, before turning and heading for the door. As he slips out of the room, Lilly murmurs something under her breath that no else can hear.

The voice in her head—firing across the synapses in her brain—reaches her lips on barely a whisper, directed at the Governor.

"Soon . . . when you're not needed . . . this will be *you*."

She brings the axe down again and again.

extracts reading groups
competitions books new
discounts extracts extracts discounts
competitions new events
books extracts
events books reading groups
extracts new
new title reading groups
interviews
events extracts
discounts events books
new books events
events new
discounts extracts discounts
www.panmacmillan.com
extracts events reading groups
competitions books extracts new